BATTLE STATIONS!

The *Shark* had chased the Chinese sub into the Middle Toms Canyon, a broad crevasse in the escarpment, twenty miles off the southern-most tip of New Jersey. Harris picked up the sub on his UWIS. "There he is, Cowley. He's all yours."

Cowley keyed in the forward torpedo room. "Prepare to fire numbers two, seven, and eight."

"He's changing course!" the SO shouted. "Range three thousand yards. Speed five zero knots and closing. A fish coming right at us!"

"Son of a bitch!" Harris said. He knew it was too late to evade the torpedo. He spoke into the intercom. "All hands . . . brace for a hit. Repeat . . . *brace for a hit!*"

TURN TO RICHARD P. HENRICK
FOR THE BEST IN UNDERSEA ACTION!

SILENT WARRIORS   (1675, $3.95)
The RED STAR, Russia's newest, most technically advanced submarine, has been dispatched to spearhead a massive nuclear first strike against the U.S. Cut off from all radio contact, the crew of an American attack sub must engage the deadly enemy alone, or witness the explosive end of the world above!

THE PHOENIX ODYSSEY   (1789, $3.95)
During a routine War Alert drill, all communications to the U.S.S. PHOENIX suddenly and mysteriously vanish. Deaf to orders cancelling the exercise, in six short hours the PHOENIX will unleash its nuclear arsenal against the Russian mainland!

COUNTERFORCE   (2013, $3.95)
In an era of U.S.-Soviet cooperation, a deadly trio of Kremlin war mongers unleashes their ultimate secret weapon: a lone Russian submarine armed with enough nuclear firepower to obliterate the entire U.S. defensive system. As an unsuspecting world races towards the apocalypse, the U.S.S. TRITON must seek out and destroy the undersea killer!

FLIGHT OF THE CONDOR   (2139, $3.95)
America's most advanced defensive surveillance satelllite is abandoning its orbit, leaving the U.S. blind and defenseless to a Soviet missile attack. From the depths of the ocean to the threshold of outer space, the stage is set for mankind's ultimate confrontation with nuclear doom!

WHEN DUTY CALLS   (2256, $3.95)
An awesome new laser defense system will render the U.S.S.R. untouchable in the event of nuclear attack. Faced with total devastation, America's last hope lies onboard a captured Soviet submarine, as U.S. SEAL team Alpha prepares for a daring assault on Russian soil!

PROJECT DISCOVERY
— BY IRVING A. GREENFIELD —

ZEBRA BOOKS
KENSINGTON PUBLISHING CORP.

ZEBRA BOOKS

are published by

Kensington Publishing Corp.
475 Park Avenue South
New York, NY 10016

First printing: May, 1988

Printed in the United States of America

The writer gratefully acknowledges the editorial assistance of Mr. Michale Bergman.

Chapter One

Commander William C. Reilly, captain of the newly reconditioned Perry-class guided missile frigate *Hanover,* leaned slightly forward in his captain's chair and peered through the bridge's rain-splattered glass. Though the time was only 1500, the combination of weather, season, and latitude had brought a premature darkness. "Can't even see the bow," he commented, giving voice to his thoughts.

"Not with a thirty-knot wind coming straight at us," his executive officer, John Wade, responded. "Last time I checked the roll indicator, we were over one zero degrees."

Reilly nodded. He had been in worse storms over his years in the Navy and—

Suddenly the red Combat Information Center light began to flash.

Wade reached over to the captain's command console and placed the audio switch in its *on* position.

Over the PA came the disembodied computer voice from the newly installed sonar. "Target bearing one seven zero degrees. . . . Range fifteen thousand yards. . . . Speed two zero knots. . . . Depth two five feet. . . . Closing."

"One of ours?" Wade questioned.

Reilly sucked in his breath and was about to answer "Probably," when the same disembodied computer voice said, "Unable to ID."

"Shit," Reilly muttered.

Wade immediately keyed the sonar officer. "Run the ID the usual way," he said, playing his fingers over several other switches that instantly activated the sonar display screen on the captain's command console. The screen's light turned their faces and hands green.

"Negative," SO reported.

"Target at two zero zero feet," the computer announced.

Reilly stood up.

"Target speed now three five knots," the disembodied voice said. "Closing fast."

"Helmsman, come to course two one five," Reilly ordered.

"Coming to course two one five," the helmsman answered.

Reilly reached over to the CCC and dialed in forty knots, the ship's flank speed.

"Target bearing two zero zero degrees. . . . Range twelve thousand yards. . . . Speed four zero knots. . . . Depth one hundred and seventy-five feet. . . . Closing fast."

Reilly keyed the SO. "Confirm."

"All data positive," the SO answered.

Even as Reilly looked at the screen, the diagonal intercept line was beginning to emanate from the target to the interception point.

"Twenty-five minutes to interception," the computer voice announced.

Reilly ground his teeth together. He'd played cat and mouse with a Ruskie submarine more times than he could remember. But he could always ID the boat. . . . He pursed his lips, and finally making the decision, he said, "Sound general quarters, Mr. Wade."

A moment later the klaxon blared.

Reilly keyed the ASW officer. "Stand by to fire ASROCS."

The computerized voice said, "Three targets bearing two two zero degrees. . . . Range target number one twelve thousand yards. . . . Targets two and three—"

Reilly glanced at the screen. Two torpedoes were streaking toward the ship. "Helmsman, full right rudder!" he barked.

"Full right rudder," the helmsman answered.

Reilly was sweating profusely. He kept his eyes glued to the screen. Two red intercept lines flashed from the oncoming torpedoes to the ship.

The computer announced, "One seven five seconds to target interception."

The *Hanover* was beginning to answer the helm; she started to turn; then suddenly her bow dove into a mountainous wave and her stern came out of the water. The propellers grabbed air. The vibration from stem to stern made the plates scream.

Reilly's hand moved toward the red *crash* signal button, but the first explosion came before his forefinger could touch it. The *Hanover* rolled to her port side. The second explosion tore the ship in half, killing everyone on the bridge. Within minutes both sections sank, and those men who were able to jump free were soon too exhausted to remain afloat and drowned.

There were no survivors.

Chapter Two

Comrade Captain Jin Chou returned the salute of the young lieutenant assigned to escort him to Comrade Admiral Fang Lai, Chief of Operations. Chou noticed that even her shapeless uniform couldn't completely hide her womanly body. She was by any standard an attractive woman. He was sufficiently old-fashioned to believe that there was a distinct place for men in the service and a very different one for women, and the place for this one was in bed with him at the soonest possibility.

The aide knocked at the comrade admiral's massive wooden door.

"Come," a voice answered gruffly.

The aide opened the door and stepped aside to allow Chou to pass.

He passed his eyes over her body, allowed a hint of a smile to slip over his lips, and entered the room, where his eyes instantly locked on

11

the four men and one woman seated around an enormous lacquered table.

Chou snapped to attention and crisply saluted the slightly built Comrade Admiral Fang, who returned the salute and said, "I believe you already know Comrade Admiral Xi, Admiral of the Fleet, and your superior Comrade Admiral Huang, Chief of Submarine Operations."

Chou saluted the two other flag officers. He had met Admiral Xi several times in the past at various social and political functions. But he reported directly to Admiral Huang and there was a suspicion on his part that the admiral was more formal with him than he was with other officers under his command.

"And this," Fang continued, "is Comrade Chen of the People's Committee for the Protection of the Homeland."

Chou bowed perfunctorily to the head of the Secret Police.

The middle-aged man in the starched Mao uniform allowed a smile to crease the stern expression on his sharply chiseled features.

"And his assistant, Comrade Hsing. She's in charge of Naval Intelligence."

Chou nodded in Hsing's direction. She was not his idea of an attractive woman. Her straight black hair was chopped off just below the ears. Her thick glasses added to her plain appearance, and the Mao uniform she wore didn't add anything to her femininity either.

12

Admiral Fang gestured him toward an empty chair.

As soon as Chou was seated, Chen cleared his throat and asked, "Have you any idea why you were ordered here today, Comrade Captain?"

"None," Chou responded.

"You are here, Comrade Captain, on my orders," Chen said, his voice taking on a hard edge. "You have placed your highly inflated ego above the security of your country. . . . We have been planning an extraordinary operation for over a year and you have stupidly and almost blatantly brought us to brink of war with your thoughtless attack on the American frigate *Hanover*." He paused; then he said, "That is why I had you ordered here today, Comrade Captain."

The veins in Chou's bull-like neck were visibly pounding. He pulled his muscular frame up to its full six-two height, and with his chin jutting out, he answered, "The American vessel would have recorded our sound signature, Comrade Chen, and that would have been a greater danger to our country than the sinking of the ship." Chou hated pencil pushers who became involved in affairs they knew nothing about.

"Sit down, Comrade Captain," Admiral Huang snapped.

Chou nodded and dropped back into the chair.

"As I understand it, Comrade Captain, the *Sea Death* can outrun and outmaneuver any surface vessel. Is that so?"

"Yes."

"Then there was no need for you to attack and sink the American ship," Chen said. "You could have changed course and quietly slipped away."

Chou looked at Admiral Huang. "Their sonar had found us."

"And how did you know that?" Chen challenged. "How could you know what was going on aboard that ship?"

"We heard the ping of their sonar," Chou said, still looking at Huang. "They had locked on to us and once that happened — well, I had no other choice but to destroy them."

"There is always another way," Chen replied. "Jeopardized a plan —"

"I did, Comrade Chen, what any submarine commander would have done to protect his boat. . . . Moreover, I did what had to be done to protect the secrecy of the *Sea Death*."

"If I had my way, Chen said, "you would be tried by the People's Committee for dereliction of duty and gross incompetence."

Chou's face reddened. He hated the Secret Police. He turned to his naval superiors for support. "With all due respect, Comrade Admiral Fang, what would you have done is similar circumstances?"

Chief of Submarine Operations Huang stiffened at Chou's outrageous behavior. Admiral Xi began to cough. But Admiral Fang smiled and said, "Probably the same thing that you did. However, had the Americans, or their Japanese allies, IDed your boat, we would have been catapulted into a war that we could have avoided and still won." He moved his eyes from Chou to the only woman at the table. "Comrade Hsing, if you will, please explain to Comrade Captain Chou the meaning of my words."

She noded, pushed the heavy glasses back up the bridge of her nose and said, "You were indeed very fortunate, Comrade Captain Chou, that the American captain was not able to send any communication before his vessel sank. They believe the Ruskies responsible and we are not going to give them any reason to change their mind."

"How do you know this?" Chou questioned.

"It is our job to know it," she answered curtly. "Our knowing it has probably saved your career, to say nothing of your life."

Chou clenched his fists. He could barely hold back his contempt for the two intelligence people. Especially the woman.

Admiral Fang stood for the first time. He ended the questioning with a quick look at each of the individuals at the table; then he gave his full attention to Chou. "This meeting," he said, "is to express to you the gravity of the situation that exists, Comrade Captain

Chou. There is one other thing I want to discuss with you." Fang paused, took time to light a cigarette, and blew smoke toward the ceiling before he continued. "In spite of the misgivings of some of the others here, I have chosen you to lead a mission for exactly the reasons the others find objectionable in you."

Chou suppressed a smile.

"You work well on your own," Fang said. "You are an excellent submarine commander. And your impertinence may serve you well should anyone other comrade on the committee try to sabotage this mission. . . . You can be sure of one thing, Comrade Captain: Once I set this plan in motion, I want nothing to stop it. Do you understand that, Comrade Captain? Nothing."

Chou nodded. "Yes, of course, Comrade Admiral, I understand. I can assure you, nothing will stop me."

Fang smiled, and looking directly into Chou's eyes, he said, "You did an excellent job destroying that frigate. Excellent."

Chou smiled back at him, then at everyone else at the table.

The helicopter carrying Admiral Richard Stark, Chief of Naval Operations, gingerly touched down on the macadam bull's-eye deep inside the compound in Langly, Virginia.

Stark was immediately ushered into a nearby

16

building and was soon proceeding underground through a labyrinth of corridors.

At Kinkaid's office door, Stark and his escorts were IDed by their voice prints and were allowed into the office of the chief of the CIA.

Bruce Kinkaid rose to greet Stark.

Thomas Williams, the Company man for Naval Affairs was present; so was Brigadier General James J. Fitzpatrick, Deputy Director of the National Security Council.

Stark was surprised to see some cooperation for a change.

Kinkaid said, "I appreciate your coming here."

"I'd have met you in hell," Stark told him in his gravelly voice. "The situation is too serious to quibble about where we meet."

"Certainly," Kinkaid answered; then gesturing to the other men already sitting at the conference table, he said, "I'm sure no introductions are needed."

"None," Stark said. He nodded to Williams and said to Fitzpatrick, "Nice to see you again, Fitz."

Sitting down at the head of the table, Kinkaid got right to the point. He activated the electron map projection system and the far wall suddenly became a map of the coasts of China and the Soviet Union, including the Yellow Sea, the East China Sea, and the Sea of Japan. "Gentlemen," he said, "at oh four hundred hours yesterday, Eastern Standard

Time, the guided missile frigate *U.S.S. Hanover* was destroyed here in the Sea of Japan." A small, red spot began to flash. "There were no survivors," Kinkaid told them; then he finished, by saying, "We feel certain the Russians were responsible."

"How certain are you—" Stark began.

"Damn sure, Admiral. We know the Ruskie subs have been cruising in that area."

"If it was a Ruskie and made any kind of a hostile move," Stark answered, "the *Hanover* would have been able to ID it and destroy it. Certainly, she would have radioed she was under attack."

"Would her skipper have had the time to get a message off?" Fitzpatrick asked.

"We can't be certain he would have," Kinkaid said, before Stark could answer.

"That's right," Stark responded, "I can't be certain. But neither can you be certain that the *Hanover* was sunk by a Soviet submarine. Could it have been Chinese?"

"Our intelligence shows that the Chinese are years away from that kind of submarine," Kinkaid said, looking over at Williams.

"That's the picture," Williams said. "The Chinese just don't have the technology to build a sub that could take on the *Hanover*."

"Don't kid yourself, Williams," Stark answered. "A country that was capable of building the Great Wall might just have the ingenuity to build a super-submarine. I wouldn't count them out."

"We can't count the Ruskies out either, Admiral," Williams said. "And that brings us to Project Discovery, the July Fourth celebration in New York Harbor commemorating the discovery of America by Columbus five hundred years ago."

Stark smiled wryly. "Thanks for the history lesson."

"If they're looking for a war, why are we allowing them to park their hardware at our front door—no, in our house?" Williams asked.

Kinkaid spoke. "The President wants us to use the anniversary of Columbus's discovery of America to show our goodwill to all nations. Think of it, five hundred years of America and in less than two months on July fourth, nineteen ninety-two, we're going to be celebrating it. All the remaining tall ships will be there in New York and all the capital ships of the major naval powers will be in the harbor of the city that exemplifies the great melting pot that the United States is."

"Except China, of course," Williams added.

"Yes, except China," Fitzpatrick noted. "That damn border dispute again. The Chinese won't show if the Russians are there."

"In the light of this current incident," Kinkaid said, "we're beefing up our security. We'll monitor every move the Ruskies make on land and on the water. Williams, you'll use the best you have to do it. If someone farts on a Ruskie ship, I want to know about it."

"The *Shark* has the most sophisticated listening devices we have, sir," Williams said. "And Jack Boxer is just the man to head security. He's not bound by any diplomatic protocol, nor is he officially military. He can come and go as he pleases."

"And he has certainly tangled with the Ruskies enough to know their capabilities. He certainly has the expertise, Kinkaid," Stark added.

"I don't like Boxer," Kinkaid said testily. "Never did and never will. He's not a team player. Set's his mind on something and doesn't let up until he's satisfied. He has no regard for authority. It's all I can do to control him."

"I'll control him, Kinkaid," Stark said. "We need a man who can work independently, who won't take shit from anyone. Boxer is my choice."

"Williams?" Kinkaid questioned.

"Based on his dealing with me before," Williams said, "Boxer, in my opinion, is our only choice.

"General?" Kinkaid asked, turning to Fitzpatrick.

"Well, Mr. Kinkaid, I really don't know the man, but from what little I know about him, he seems to have the stuff we need for the job. And if Admiral Stark and mister Williams are

20

for him, I'll go the same route."

Kinkaid studied the determination expressed on the faces of the three men at the table and resigned himself to the decision which he knew was not only correct, but also inevitable. He nodded. "Boxer," he said.

Chapter Three

Captain Jack Boxer held the *Shark* on a course that would take her into the Cayman trench, an undersea canyon that was only twenty-five miles south of Santiago Cuba and eighty miles south of Guantanamo. His mission was to deploy the Company's latest "toy," an acoustical device nicknamed Campbell because of its resemblance to the famed can of soup.

The Campbell was only activated by sounds passing through water and was designed to discriminate the sound of a submarine from any other sounds whether they were made by sea creatures or machines. The Campbell could ID any submarine from any nation, and if it was an entirely new ID, it would store it in its memory bank. As soon as the Campbell was activated, it would begin transmitting the coded data over a range of constantly changing frequencies, which could be decoded only by a "black box" set up aboard selected submarines and ASW surface ships. The *Shark*, of course, was one of the selected submarines.

Boxer was to plan a series of the listening devices around the eastern tip of Cuba to enable the U.S. intelligence community on Guantanamo to monitor Soviet submarine activity en route to the island's southern coast.

Boxer viewed the UWIS, the underwater image screen, which showed the steep drop off the sea's bottom where the trench began. It was, he remembered, something like coming to the Grand Canyon from the south. Suddenly it was there!

"Target bearing six five degrees," the sonar officer reported. "Range six thousand yards. . . . Speed two eight knots and closing."

"ID?" Boxer requested.

"Kotlin class destroyer."

"Roger that," Boxer answered, and punched the info into the COMCOMP. An instant passed before the data came up on the screen.

U.S.S.R. DESTROYER KOTLIN CLASS
PROFILE . . . THE GORKY
ARMAMENT. . . . FIVE TORPEDO TUBES
  FORE AND AFT
   . . . . TWO 6-BARREL ASW ROCKET
    LAUNCHERS
   . . . . TWO TWIN 130MM DP GUN
    MOUNTS
   . . . . FOUR 25MM GUN MOUNTS
   . . . . FOUR QUAD 45MM GUN
    MOUNTS

"Target bearing six five degrees. . . . Range five thousand five zero yards. . . . Speed three zero knots. . . . Closing."

Suddenly the sharp pinging sound of Gorky's sonar brought Boxer's eyes to the sonar display screen on the comcomp. The Gorky had become the aggressor, the hunter. . . . He pressed a red button and the klaxon sounded general quarters.

One by one the section chiefs reported their "ready" status.

"Harris," Boxer said, addressing his executive officer, "take her off autonav."

"Off autonav," Harris answered.

"We'll see if we can avoid a problem," Boxer said, thinking about how Kinkaid would react if he sank the mother.

"Skipper," the SO said, "she's staying with us."

"Roger that, Boxer answered, and checked the SDS. "Mahony," he said, glancing at the helmsman, "come to course two zero."

"Coming to course two zero, zero," Mahony answered.

Boxer dialed in thirty-five knots on the comcomp.

"Target bearing two four degrees. . . . Range four thousand three zero zero yards. . . . Speed three zero knots. . . . She's staying with us."

"Roger that," Boxer answered, his eyes on the sonar display screen.

He turned to Harris. "How does that song go? 'I did it my way?' "

With a nod, Harris grinned.

Boxer keyed the aft torpedo room. "Stand by to load tube eight."

"Aye, aye, Skipper," the torpedo officer answered.

Boxer checked the fire control computer. The azimuth, range, and speed of the target was automatically being fed into the FCC, which in turn automatically computed the fire mission from each torpedo tube to an accuracy of less than one foot. But all torpedoes were equipped with both sound homing and magnetic devices and would explode on impact, or if that was not possible because of evasive movement, then at a distance determined by the sound of the ship's screw.

Boxer keyed the aft TO again. "Load drone," he ordered.

"Loading drone," the TO answered.

Boxer set several switches on the FCC that would enable the drone to replicate enough of the *Shark*'s characteristics to totally confuse the Ruskie captain; then he dialed in an azimuth that would put the drone on a course one hundred and eighty degrees away from the Shark thirty seconds after it was fired.

"Shoot eight," Boxer ordered, keying the aft TO.

"Aye, aye, Skipper," the TO answered.

A red light came on. The time-to-firing clock was activated. Ten seconds . . . nine . . . eight . . . seven . . . six . . . five . . . three . . . two . . . one . . . Mark.

The sound of escaping air rushed through the Shark.

A green light showed on the comcomp.

Boxer watched the course of the drone on the sonar display screen. Thirty seconds into the run, the drone changed course and began to electronically resemble the *Shark*.

The SO keyed Boxer. "Target changing course, Skipper."

"Roger that," Boxer answered. The drone had an active life of fifteen minutes. . . . He keyed the DO. "Take her to the bottom," he ordered, checking the fathometer. There was eighteen hundred feet of water under them.

"Aye, aye, Skipper. . . . Making one thousand feet," the DO answered.

Boxer turned to Harris. "Pass the word. . . . We're going down to the bottom. . . ."

"For a rest, no doubt," Harris commented.

Boxer nodded. "I need a few Z's," he answered.

In a demisleep, Boxer was dreaming about the time he was a teenager going to Brooklyn Technical High School and one day on the

27

subway, which was always very crowded in the morning, he happened to notice a young girl with long blond hair and—

A shrill sound entered his dream.

The blond was standing opposite him and the two of them had to hold on to the same white pole and—

The shrill sound came back again, but this time it made him realize he was dreaming. . . . He wanted to continue. But the sound wouldn't go away. . . .

Boxer opened his eyes. The red signal light directly over his bunk was flashing. He was being keyed. He picked up his voice-actuated radio-phone and said, "Boxer here."

"Skipper, this is the DCO. . . . I'm getting a malfunction signal on air scrubber's final return phase."

"Have you IDed it?" Boxer asked, already on his feet.

"Negative."

Boxer sniffed the air. "I don't smell anything," he said.

"I reduced the blower speed," the DCO said. "But I'm going to have to shut down. . . . If we continue to run it, well—"

"Bottom line," Boxer said, going to the miniversion of the COMCOMP across from his bunk and switching it on.

"Continuing system degeneration," the DCO said.

Boxer activated the systems check. A flashing red dot on the display screen indicated the malfunction in the air scrubber system. He reset another switch. "I have the detail on my screen," Boxer said. "To get in there you're going to have to take it down."

"No other way," the DCO answered.

"How long will it take?"

"Six hours minimum, but it could go a hell of a lot longer if we run into trouble."

"Shut down," Boxer said. The crew had been put through this kind of drill hundreds of times.

"Aye, aye, Skipper."

"Out," Boxer said, ending the conversation; then resetting another switch, he put the IC-One system on. "All hands . . . all hands, this is the captain. . . . Now listen up. . . . We have a malfunction in the air scrubber system. . . . All division chiefs report to the Ward Room immediately." He switched off the system.

Instantly a red signal light over the door began to flash.

Boxer left his quarters and went straight to the Ward Room. "Gentlemen," he said, "this is not a practice run. The system will be down a minimum of six hours. Maybe longer."

"Why can't we surface and run into Guantanamo for repairs?" Peters, one of the torpedo officers asked.

"Because that Ruskie destroyer might still be around," Boxer said, "and if it is, its skipper must be one hell of an angry man. . . . I know I'd be if I discovered I was following a drone instead of the real target."

The men laughed.

"Skipper, are we going to continue to run?" Nansen, the second engineering officer, asked.

"No, we're going down to the bottom and sit there until the repairs are completed."

"But that's just about our maximum operating depth," the DO commented.

"Just about," Boxer answered; then he said, "Remember, it's going to get very hot in here and the air will become foul very quickly. We've had the system off for a couple of hours and it quickly became very unpleasant. This isn't going to be a picnic. Only the DCO and his men have permission to work. Everyone else will be stretched out on the deck near his station. . . . Any questions. . . . None. . . . Return to your stations."

As the men filed out of the room, he called the EXO. "Harris, put her on the bottom."

"Sure, Skipper," Harris answered; then he said, "Some of the newly assigned hands might get more than a bit jumpy after a while."

"Anyone in particular I should be aware of?" Boxer asked, sure that Harris knew the strengths and weaknesses of every man on the boat, including his.

"William Kitt," Harris said. "He's on the port bow plane. . . . He's been on two other boats: a boomer and an attack. . . . But he has some personal problems. Trouble with his wife."

Boxer uttered a deep sigh. "We both know that kind of trouble, don't we?" he responded.

Harris nodded.

"I'll go forward and have a look at him," Boxer said.

"Anyone else?"

Harris shook his head.

"Then put her on the bottom," Boxer said, leading the way out of the Ward Room.

As Boxer went forward to the *Shark*'s Diving Control Room, he checked that the men he saw were stretched out on the deck near their stations and their emergency oxygen masks were attached to the central oxygen supply. He found Kitt, who turned out to be a freckle-faced young man, who couldn't have been more than twenty years old.

Boxer squatted down in front of him. "What do you think of this boat, compared to the others you've been on?"

"It's all right," Kitt answered.

"Food good?"

Kitt nodded.

"Captain—"

"Everyone on board calls me Skipper," Boxer said.

"Skipper, would I be able to get an emergency leave when we're in port again? All I need is a few days."

"Trouble?" Boxer asked, pretending to not know anything about the man's problems.

Kitt nodded.

"Mother sick?"

"Nothin' like that," the sailor answered.

"Woman trouble?"

"Yeah," Kitt reluctantly responded.

"They'll do it every time," Boxer said. "You come see me when we make port and we'll talk. . . . I've had a lot experience with that kind of trouble."

"Bottom coming up," Harris announced over the IC-One. "All hands brace for come-down. . . . All hands brace for come-down."

Boxer was aware that the *Shark*'s forward motion was lessening and that she was beginning to settle down. He stretched out on the deck, smiled at Kitt, and said, "Even the skipper has to brace himself."

Within moments, the *Shark* ground down on the bottom and rolled slightly to the starboard side.

"On the bottom," Harris said.

Boxer scrambled to his feet. "Remember, Kitt, I want to see you when we make port."

"Aye, aye, Skipper," Kitt answered.

Boxer went back to the galley and told the cook to prepare as much lemonade as possible. "In a little while the men will be drinking it," he said. Then he checked the recently installed microwave ovens used by the cooks to do the baking. Everything else, in the way of food, was automatically prepared in individual measured portions selected by each man and computer controlled for the precise caloric need of that particular person.

"Would a quart per man be enough?" the cook asked.

"Let's hope so," Boxer answered. On the way out of the galley he checked the temperature. It was seventy-five degrees: only five above the normal ambient. But that was a five-degree rise in ten minutes. Given six hours — he did not want to think of how hot it would get at the end of that time. . . .

Boxer returned to the bridge. Everyone was on the deck. He joined them and keyed the DCO for a progress report.

"The panel is off and we're looking at the screen," the DCO answered.

"Roger that," Boxer answered, and settled down on the deck in front of the comcomp, joining the banter between Harris and some of the other men on the bridge.

"It's getting very warm," one of the men commented.

Boxer stood up and looked at the comcomp's digital display thermometer. It registered 86.50 degrees. He looked at the clock. The rise had occurred over a period of forty-five minutes.

Suddenly a red light began to flash in the Life Support System section of the comcomp

33

and a moment later the DCO keyed him and said, "Skipper, we're leaking oxygen."

Boxer reset a switch. The SYSCHK came up on the screen. A flashing red light indicated a pressure drop in the line and that could only mean a leak. . . . He was planning to use the oxygen if the repairs on the air scrubber system went beyond the six-hour mark, before if the men needed it. . . . Now, the leaking oxygen turned the *Shark* into a potential bomb.

"Stop all repair work," Boxer ordered.

"Aye, aye, Skipper," the DCO answered.

"Harris," Boxer called.

"Here, Skipper," the EXO answered.

"Pass the word," Boxer said. "We're going to surface. Everything on manual. Tell the DCO to take up as quickly as possible."

"Aye, aye," Harris answered, and immediately assigned personnel to deliver Boxer's orders.

Boxer watched the depth gauge over the comcomp. There wasn't any way to completely eliminate the danger of an explosion. Even blowing the tanks required the use of electrical equipment. The *Shark* made a slight side-to-side movement. The bow began to tilt upward; then suddenly the entire hull broke free of the bottom and the needle on the depth gauge jumped and then settled back and began to climb.

Boxer realized he was sweating and looked at the digital thermometer; the temperature was

96.66 degrees.

Harris came alongside him. "We should be on top in an hour and half," he said.

Boxer nodded, and pointing to the display screen, he said, "If that doesn't blow us to bits before."

"What about the Ruskie?" Harris asked.

"Nothing about him," Boxer answered. "We'll just have to take our chances. If he's there waiting—well, we won't be able to do a thing until we exchange air and then, if we do any shooting, we might blow ourselves to bits and save the Ruskie from doing it."

"Between a hammer and hard place," Harris commented.

"Sometimes it would be nice to be somewhere else," Boxer answered, watching the depth gauge. They were moving through the fifteen-hundred-foot level. . . .

The minutes snailed by as the *Shark* moved slowly toward the surface.

"Christ," Harris said, "if we were on power, we'd have been topside by now."

"Five hundred more feet and we'll be there," Boxer said, checking the clock. It was 1630; they were an hour into the ascent.

"I'll pass the word to open all hatches as soon as we're up," Harris said.

Boxer nodded and watched the needle climb. The last fifty feet seemed to take the longest. He waited until the needle touched the green surface mark before he barked, "Open all hatches. . . . Open all hatches. . . ."

The instant the hatches were open, fresh sea air rushed into the *Shark*.

"Pass the word, Mr. Harris, to the DCO," Boxer said. "Bleed the oxygen system . . . and then let's get the hell back to Guantanamo and make the necessary repairs."

"Aye, aye, Skipper," Harris responded with a smile.

Boxer waited until the DCO reported the oxygen system had been completely purged, refilled with nitrogen, and brought up to pressure before he ordered the sail raised and the bridge detail topside. He was just about to go up himself when the COMMO keyed him and said, "Skipper, you've just been ordered to Kinkaid on a yellow priority."

"Are you sure?" Boxer asked. "A yellow priority could mean any damn thing."

"Do you want me to read it?" the COMMO asked.

"No. When am I supposed to be there?"

"There's a flight waiting for you now."

"Christ," Boxer swore, "If it's that important, I'm surprised he didn't send a chopper out to get me."

"How do you want me to answer?" the COMMO asked.

"Affirmative," Boxer said; then he added, "Contact the base and have a car waiting for me at dockside."

"Aye, aye, Skipper," the COMMO answered.

Boxer keyed Harris, who was on the sail's bridge. "Kinkaid wants to see me at Langly," he said. "I'll leave as soon as we're dockside."

"Lucky man," Harris commented.

"I'm not going to answer that," Boxer said sourly.

By 2300, Boxer was ensconced in his favorite hotel in Washington and preparing to go to sleep when the phone rang. He glared at it, but after three rings, he picked it up, saying nothing.

"Don't you ever speak first?" a woman asked.

He recognized the voice. It belonged to Tracy Kimble, a hot-shot reporter with the *Washington Globe* and a hot lady in bed. She had been aboard the *Mary Ann* when it had collided with the *Sting Ray*. After a few rough initial contacts, including one at a naval hearing to determine whether he or the captain of the *Mary Ann* had been responsible for the crash, he and Tracy had become lovers on an intermittent basis, which was the way the two of them preferred it. . . .

"Hey, are you there?"

"How did you know I was in town?" Boxer asked.

"You won't tell me what you know and I'm

37

sure as hell not going to tell you what I know. . . . Just let's say I have my sources."

"Okay," he answered.

"That's it, just 'okay'?"

"That's it for now," Boxer said.

"How about meeting me for a night cap?" Tracy asked.

"I'd love to, but I need my Z's."

"You're joking?"

"Honey, when it comes to Z's, I never joke. I've had one hell of a hard day and I'm bushed. . . . If I'm still here tomorrow night, we'll do what we enjoy doing most."

"I hate you!"

"I'll call you tomorrow, if I'm still here," Boxer said.

"Where the hell do you expect to be?" she asked angrily.

"You know I can't tell you that, love," Boxer answered.

"Oh you're a bastard!" she exclaimed.

Boxer laughed and hung up. He really was tired.

Boxer was familiar with Kinkaid's conference room. It could have been a set up for a TV or Hollywood production about a captain of industry with worldwide interests. Though not a captain of industry, Kinkaid was certainly a man with worldwide interests.

Kinkaid sat at the head of the table. Boxer

and Admiral Stark were on his left; Williams and General William Fitzpatrick were on his right.

"The *Hanover* went down with all hands," Kinkaid said. "She was on patrol in the North China Sea. We believe it was a Ruskie boat that —"

"That's not exactly so," Kinkaid said. "We presume it must have been a Ruskie, but we don't have any proof. She didn't have time to send any signal."

"May day?" Boxer asked.

"Negative," Kinkaid answered.

"Why would the Ruskies risk their new accord with us?" Boxer asked.

"Maybe they're tired of it," Fitzpatrick answered.

"Or maybe the Hawks are trying to provoke an incident," Boxer answered.

"Well," Kinkaid said, "we're going to pretend that it never happened. But when their ships come here for the big celebration in a few weeks, I want them targeted by the *Shark*."

"You're joking?" Boxer responded, unwilling to believe that Kinkaid would even think of starting World War Three in New York's harbor. He looked questioningly at Stark.

"At that time," Kinkaid continued, "we will take the appropriate steps to —"

"You're out of your mind!" Boxer exploded.

"I'll ignore that outburst, Captain," Kinkaid responded; then shifting his eyes to Stark, he said, "I told you he wasn't the man for the assignment."

"He's the only man for the assignment," Stark said flatly.

With a look, Kinkaid canvassed Williams, who nodded, then moved on to Fitzpatrick.

"I'm not sure," Fitzpatrick said.

"What is this all about?" Boxer asked.

"Security chief," Stark responded.

Boxer pointed to Kinkaid. "I thought that was your job."

"For the ships in New York Harbor during the three-day celebration," Williams said. "You will be responsible for the security of every ship there and—"

"Christ, that's not exactly my cup of tea!" Boxer complained. "I don't want it."

Kinkaid placed his elbows on the table, and with obvious relish, he said, "I'm afraid what you want doesn't matter. You're it and in that capacity you will have the best chance of destroying all of the Russian ships that will come here to help us celebrate the five hundred years since Columbus discovered the New World."

"Admiral—" Boxer started to protest.

"You're it," Stark said.

"By the way," Kinkaid said with a smile, "your friend Borodine will be here with the *Sea Savage*. Maybe, what you failed to do at sea, you could do in the closed confines of the harbor."

Boxer clamped his jaws together. Kinkaid

would never understand his relationship to Comrade Captain Igor Borodine. He himself hardly understood it. Yet between the two of them, despite the fact that they had often been adversaries, there was deep and lasting respect and friendship.

"You will have two offices," Kinkaid said. "One at the naval base on Staten Island and the other on the thirtieth floor of a building overlooking the harbor. You will coordinate every phase of the ship and personnel security. For this assignment your orders will supersede those of any other military or civilian authority. You may choose your lieutenants, but all other members of your staff will be assigned to you from military and civilian police organizations."

"Any questions?"

"About ninety-nine," Boxer answered, noticing that the sun, whose light had been streaming through the window, was now covered by a dark cloud.

Chapter Four

"I don't damn well like it," Boxer said, turning from the window to look at Stark. They were in Stark's limo, on their way back to Stark's office in the Pentagon.

"Listen," Stark said in his gravelly voice, "if it wasn't so damn important, I'd have given it to some other officer. You're the only one who'll know how to use all the power you'll have." He relit the cigar he'd lit the moment they'd left Kinkaid's office.

"You think the Ruskies bushwhacked the *Hanover?*" Boxer asked, looking at the CNO again.

"I don't know what to think. Our boats play tag with theirs all the time and nothing really happens. But there's always a first time."

Boxer shook his. "Not likely. Not with them sending ten ships here and the *Sea Savage*. They're not stupid!"

Stark nodded; then he quietly said, "Neither is Kinkaid."

"Never thought he was," Boxer answered. "He's just a bad holdover from the Cold War. The times have changed . . . he hasn't."

"He does a good job," Stark said.

"Not if he wants to blow the Russian fleet out of New York Harbor," Boxer responded.

"You and I know that's something you won't let happen," Stark said, blowing a column of smoke toward the roof of the limo; then with a smile, he added, "Com'on, Jack, loosen up about the assignment. You just might find yourself enjoying it."

"Yeah, like a turkey gets to enjoy Thanksgiving dinner," Boxer answered.

"Take a few days for yourself," Stark said, "then present yourself to Admiral D'Arcy on Staten Island. He'll be expecting you."

"He's not going to like having to follow my orders," Boxer said. He'd had more than one run-in with D'Arcy and didn't have a high opinion of him, either as an officer or as a man.

"Just be diplomatic when you deal with him," Stark suggested.

"You mean—"

"I mean be diplomatic," Stark said.

Boxer remained silent for several minutes; then he told Stark about the two malfunctions aboard the *Shark*.

"Any recommended changes?" Stark asked.

44

"They'll probably be some in the DCO's report," Boxer answered.

"I'll authorize whatever work has to be done on her," Stark said. "She's already been ordered up to New York."

Boxer managed a smile. "Thanks," he said.

It was 1400 when Boxer returned to his hotel. At the desk, he was given two message slips. Both were from Tracy. The first said that she'd be out of the office until one-thirty and the second said that she was back in the office. Boxer smiled, walked to the elevator, rode it up to the twenty-third floor, and went to his room. He kicked off his shoes, dropped down on the bed, and dialed Tracy's office number.

She answered.

"When are you finished with the Forth Estate?" he asked.

"Now, if you want me bad enough," she answered.

"I want you bad enough," Boxer said.

"I'll pick you up in a half hour," Tracy told him.

"I'll be in the bar," Boxer said.

"See you," she responded.

Boxer clicked off, dialed the operator, and put through a long-distance call to his parents, who lived in Brooklyn.

After two rings, his mother answered.

"Mom, I'll be coming home in a day or

two," he said.

"That's wonderful!" she exclaimed, and quickly relayed the news to his father.

"I'll probably live at the house for a while," he said, and then quickly asked, "Is that okay with you, Dad?"

"Yes," his mother answered excitedly. "Hold on, your father wants to speak with you."

"Jack, when are you coming here?" his father asked.

"Either tomorrow, or the next day," Boxer answered. He could hear the conversation between his parents.

"If you could give us a definite day, your mother will have dinner ready for you."

"Tell her not to bother," Boxer said.

"It's no bother," his mother replied.

Boxer guessed they were sharing the telephone. "I'll be in tomorrow night then," Boxer said. "Probably between eighteen and nineteen hundred."

"Everything will be waiting for you," his mother said.

"See you soon," his father added.

"See you," Boxer replied, and put the phone down. That he would be living at home for a while, he knew, would please his parents and it would give him an opportunity to see more of his son. For a moment, he thought about phoning his ex-wife and telling her that he was going to be spending some time in the city, but then, because he wasn't sure how she'd respond, he decided against it. He put the phone down and decided that a shower would freshen him up before he met Tracy.

Boxer sat on a stool at the bar and slowly sipped a Stoli on the rocks. He really wasn't happy about being any part of the security setup for the big shindig in New York's harbor.

Warren, the barkeep, put a bowl of pretzels in front of him and said, "You've been a stranger here for a while."

"Chasing sounds," Boxer answered.

"I like that," Warren said. "That's one I never heard before."

Boxer lifted the glass and toasted, "To all the things neither one of us have heard before." Then he drank.

Warren nodded and moved away to serve another customer.

Tracy entered the bar on time. She wore a green pair of slacks, a white blouse with a plunging V that revealed the very white sides of her breasts, and a green headband around her long, honey-colored blond hair.

"A drink?" Boxer offered.

She shook her head. "Dulls the senses and I want all of mine to be razor sharp," she answered with a lascivious grin.

Boxer put a five-dollar bill on the bar, waved to Warren, and taking hold of Tracy by her arm, he escorted her out of the bar, through the hotel lobby, and into the street where her red Ferrari was illegally parked.

"You want to drive?" she asked, ready to hand him the keys.

"It does nothing for my ego," Boxer said.

"You don't need anything for your ego," Tracy said, laughing, as she went around to the driver's seat. "It grows well just being nurtured by you."

Boxer slid beside her. "Let's go someplace out of the city," he said.

"Okay, we'll go down to Annapolis. There's a lovely motel there overlooking a marina."

Boxer nodded.

Tracy switched on the ignition, gunned the engine, and turning the wheel, she shifted into first.

Boxer rested his against the back of the seat and closed his eyes.

"If you're that tired," Tracy said, "you sure as hell aren't going to be any good to me."

Boxer opened his eyes and looked at her. "What I really like about you, Tracy, is your delicacy."

She threw back her head and laughed. "Delicacy, shelicacy. . . . I want to get laid and I want you to do the laying. . . . For Christ's sake, Jack, we haven't been in the sack together for the better part of two months."

"Now don't tell me you abstained all that time," he teased.

"In case you didn't know it — and I'm sure you do — you're good in the sack, and I prefer what is good to what is second-rate."

He touched his forehead with his fingers. "I accept the compliment," he said.

"I was sure you would," she told him.

"Wake me up when we arrive," Boxer said, closing his eyes again. "I want to save my strength for you."

After a few minute's silence, Tracy said, "Julio sends his regards."

"He still around?" Boxer asked, not opening his eyes. Julio Sanchez was the owner of the *Mary Ann.* Even though it turned out that Julio sometimes worked for the Company, he was not one of Boxer's favorite people.

"Still around," Tracy answered.

Boxer opened his eyes and sat up. "Did he tell you I was coming to Washington?"

"*No comprendez,*" she answered.

"That mother has eyes and ears everywhere!" Boxer exclaimed.

Tracy laughed. "You know you almost look ferocious when you're angry."

Boxer didn't answer.

Forty minutes later they were in a motel room overlooking a marina.

Tracy melted into Boxer's arms and he kissed her long and deep.

"That went down to my tippee toes," she

said in a low throaty voice.

Boxer pressed her close to him. He liked the jasmine scent of her perfume.

"I missed you," she told him.

"I missed you," he answered. "I really did, Trace." And he ran his hands down the broad of her back and over her nates.

"The trouble with us," she said, "is that the beautiful music we make is always more beautiful after we don't see each other for a while."

He nuzzled her ear and kissed the side of her neck. Because he knew it was true, he wasn't going to touch what she said with the proverbial ten-foot pole. . . .

Boxer opened her blouse and slipped it from her shoulders. She wore a white lace bra with a half a cup. He kissed the milk-white top of each of her breasts; then reaching around her, he undid the bra and eased the straps off her shoulders. Her pink nipples were erect. He placed his hands over her breasts and gently squeezed them.

"Let me take your shirt off," Tracy said.

Boxer nodded.

"You know," she said, as soon as he was bare-chested, "you're the only man I enjoy undressing."

"A dubious distinction," he answered, opening the front of her slacks and slipping them down over her hips.

She unbuckled his belt, undid the front button, and then unzipped his fly.

Within a matter of moments, the two of them were naked.

"Hold me," Tracy said.

Boxer pressed her nude body against his.

Looking up at him, she began to rotate her hips. "Like that?" she purred.

He nodded, and reaching down, he caressed her love mound.

"I like that," she said, licking her lips; then suddenly she knelt in front of him and kissed his penis.

Surprised, Boxer ran his hands over her head and gently pressed her face toward him. "That's wonderful," he said in a whisper.

She smiled up at him. "Now do you believe I missed you?"

Boxer reached down, and scooping her into his arms, he carried her to the bed, then easing her on to the mattress, he covered her with his body and kissed her passionately.

She opened her mouth and gave him her tongue.

Boxer responded with his tongue; then he kissed her neck, each breast, the hollow of her stomach, and finally he pressed his lips against the warm moistness of her sex.

"That's wonderful," she gasped, pushing her sex against his mouth. "Oh so wonderful!" Then she said, "Let me do you."

He turned around, positioning himself over her, and almost immediately he felt her hands on his shaft and then her tongue and finally

51

the deliciously warm circle of her lips closed around it. . . .

He devoured her and she did the same to him.

"I want you inside of me," she told him. "Deep inside of me!"

Boxer changed his position, and moving between her splayed thighs, he entered her.

"You can't imagine how wonderful that feels," Tracy said, her eyes lidded with passion.

"I can," he answered, beginning to move.

Smiling, she put her two hands on his face and drew it down to her lips. "You taste and smell of me," she said.

"I like the way you taste and smell," Boxer responded.

"Kiss my nipple."

Boxer not only kissed each of her nipples, he slowly played his tongue over them and then gently scored them with his teeth.

Using the tips of her fingers, Tracy caressed his scrotum.

"That feels good," he said, quickening his movements.

"Oh yes . . . yes. . . . Go faster."

Boxer felt her body tense. His own passion was beginning to burn.

"I'm almost there," she cried, her head rolling from side to side. "I'm almost there." She clamped her naked thighs around Boxer's back.

He drove deep into her, feeling her contractions race along the length of his penis.

Tracy grabbed hold of his shoulders, and with one tremendous shudder, she arched up to meet Boxer's thrust. "I'm there," she cried. "I'm there!"

Uttering a low growl of pleasure, Boxer let his own passion gush out of him. . . .

For several minutes, neither one of them spoke or moved; then Tracy whispered, "I really do love you, Jack."

He kissed her ardently on her lips. "The feeling is mutual," he said, caressing the top of her head.

The following morning at eleven hundred Boxer entered Admiral D'Arcy's office. He had been kept waiting for forty-five minutes and knew that if he didn't set the ground rules with D'Arcy from the very beginning, D'Arcy would set his own.

"I'll be with you in a few moments, Captain," D'Arcy said, playing the game of move the papers on the desk. He was a tall, thin man with a straight back and a handsome face.

Standing in front of the admiral's desk, Boxer waited. . . . He looked around the office. Its two windows overlooked the Narrows and the docks where the *Iowa* and her support ships were berthed when they were in port.

"Well," D'Arcy finally said, smiling up at Boxer, "I told the CNO that in my opinion you're not the man for the job."

Boxer returned the smile. "Cut the shit, D'Arcy, or I'll get on the fucking phone and tell Stark you want to play your fucking stupid games."

D'Arcy's face turned deep red.

"I'll play the tune for this one," Boxer said, "and you'll fucking dance to it. . . . I don't want you to get any ideas that because you have the stars, you outrank me. . . . This is my operation from start to finish."

"How dare you talk to me like that!" D'Arcy exclaimed.

Boxer picked up the phone. "Complain," he said, offering it to D'Arcy.

The admiral looked at the phone, but made no move toward it.

Boxer smiled. "Good," he said. "I think we understand one another." Then he added, "For the length of this assignment, don't ever keep me waiting again."

"There will be other assignments," D'Arcy said, his eyes going to slits.

Boxer nodded. "We'll play those by whatever the rules are, but now the rules are mine, and if I want you to fucking jump, by the living God, you better fucking well jump. . . . It that understood?"

D'Arcy didn't answer.

"I'm waiting for an acknowledgement," Boxer said.

"Understood," D'Arcy said.

"Good," Boxer answered; then he said, "Let's get to work. . . . I'll need an office with a view similar to this one. I want an officer and an enlisted man on duty twenty-four hours a day, seven days a week, to take and transmit messages to me and from me. I want a secretary. I'll need a car and driver on duty all the time. I want a chopper and pilot on duty all the time and I want a high-speed motor patrol boat and its crew on duty at all times."

"Anything else?" D'Arcy asked sarcastically.

"A secure line between my office here and my office in Manhattan, and I want the *Shark*'s crew exempt from any base duty and regulations."

"As long as they're on this base—"

"The *Shark* will be considered to be at sea," Boxer said. "The men will be under my command."

"Everything else is possible—"

Boxer picked up the phone. "Get me the CNO," he said.

D'Arcy held up his hand.

"Cancel the call," Boxer said, putting the phone down.

"You don't give an inch, do you?" D'Arcy asked.

"Only when I want to, or when I'm forced to," Boxer answered, "and in this situation no one is forcing me to and I certainly don't want to."

* * *

55

Boxer was choppered to the Coast Guard headquarters on Governor's Island, where he was immediately greeted by Lieutenant Commander Charles Szpak and escorted to Admiral John Hawkson's office.

"You'll have my full cooperation," Hawkson assured him, from behind a large oak desk. "Commander Szpak is assigned to you until Operation Discovery is over. Anything you need, he will make sure you get."

"Thank you," Boxer said. He liked the man's straightforward manner.

"Are there any specific things you need?" Hawkson asked.

"A phone set up between here and my office on Staten Island and my office in Manhattan and I want several sets of the latest charts of the harbor, including all its approaches."

"Szpak, any problems with that?" Hawkson asked.

"None sir," Szpak answered.

The meeting between Boxer and Hawkson took less than ten minutes, and when he and Szpak left the admiral's office, Boxer said, "I want to fly over the harbor to familiarize myself with it. . . . Then in a day or two I'll make the same trip by boat."

"I can have a chopper ready in ten minutes, sir," Szpak said.

"Do it," Boxer said; then he added, "Commander, my men call me Skipper."

Szpak grinned.

The flyover took an hour. Boxer was particularly interested in the buoys. They would serve as markers from which the various ships would find their anchorages. The chopper went over the Raritan Bay, south of Staten Island, to Sandy Hook on the Jersey shore; then across to Brooklyn, over Sheepshead Bay, Coney Island; then north over the Verrazano Bridge; then east, over the East River as far as the beginning of Long Island Sound. Then they flew west and came out above the George Washington Bridge, turned south, and followed the Hudson River to the Upper New York Harbor and finally returned to Governor's Island.

As soon as they left the chopper, Boxer asked, "Do we have the stats on all of the ships coming here?"

"About seventy percent of them," Szpak answered.

"I want all of them," Boxer said. "Then we will assign an approach course to each. . . . We want to know where every ship is. We don't want any ship in the wrong place at the wrong time."

"Aye, aye, sir—skipper," Szpak answered.

"Now, I'm going to need car and a driver to take me to Brooklyn," Boxer said.

"I'll phone our station on Manhattan," Szpak said. "There'll be one waiting for you when you get off the ferry, or the chopper."

"The ferry," Boxer said. "It's a quieter ride."

"That's for sure," Szpak answered.

As soon as the car pulled up to the curb, the front door opened and Boxer's mother came out of the house.

"Go back to your base," Boxer told the driver as he left the cab.

"Yes, sir," the young sailor answered, high-balling him.

Boxer returned the salute, turned, and went to his mother, who welcomed him with a hug. "Where's Dad?" he asked.

"He's resting," she said.

He looked questioningly at his mother. . . . His father, though a retired merchant captain for the past five years, wasn't the kind of man to rest. He was an excellent carpenter, gardener, and all-around fix-it man.

"He's very sick," his mother told him; then in a whisper, she said, "He's dying."

"Cancer?"

She nodded.

Boxer pursed his lips. All his life, he had had a very close and special relationship with his father. "How long?" he asked, moving indoors with his mother.

She shrugged. "A year, if he's lucky."

Boxer nodded and suddenly realized how difficult it must be for his mother to watch her husband slowly waste away. He took hold of her hands and kissed both of them.

"He'll probably tell you himself," she said. "But if he chooses not to—"

"I won't say a word," Boxer told her.

She managed a smile and asked, "Are you really going to live here for a while?"

"Now and then," he answered, looking around the living room. . . . Everything was the same as he remembered. "But there will be times I'll have to stay in Manhattan, or somewhere else."

Mrs. Boxer nodded understandingly.

"What's for dinner?" Boxer asked, sniffing the wonderful aroma of roasting meat.

"A surprise," she said.

He grinned. "Leg of lamb?"

She shook her head. "You won't know until you sit down to eat it," she said.

"I'm going to go upstairs to my room and call Gwen. . . . Maybe, while I'm here, I'll be able to spend some time with my son."

"I spoke to him on the phone the other day," she said. "He sounds so grown up."

"He's going to be seven," Boxer said, suddenly remembering that his son's birthday was only a month away.

"Make your call," his mother said.

Boxer went up to his room, settled down on the bed, and picking up the phone, he made a mental note to have a secure phone system installed. He dialed Gwen's number.

The phone rang four times before she

answered.

"It's Jack," Boxer said.

Gwen remained silent.

"Did I interrupt—" He started to say. He guessed she was with a man.

"It's all right. Where are you?"

"At my mother's. I arrived a while ago."

Their conversation lapsed.

Boxer took a deep breath. "I'd like to see you and John," he said, suddenly feeling ill at ease.

"He's at the farm with my folks," she said.

"Oh!"

"He'll be there for the next two months," she explained. "I'll be away too. I'm leaving tomorrow morning for England, then Italy and Spain."

Boxer was at loss. He had allowed himself to think that he, Gwen, and John might be able to spend some time together while he was in New York.

"Are you still there?" Gwen asked.

He cleared his throat and answered, "Yes."

"I'm sorry—"

"It's all right," he lied. "You couldn't have known I was coming in. I didn't know until a couple of days ago myself. . . . Hey, listen, have a wonderful trip. Maybe, I'll see you when you get back."

"You're angry, aren't you?"

He shook his head. "No. I understand you have a life of your own and—"

Suddenly he head a man say, "Com'on Gwen. . . . Tell him you're busy. . . ."

The rest of what the man said was blocked out.

"I'm being called to dinner," Boxer lied. "Have a safe trip. Good-bye."

"Good-bye," Gwen responded.

Boxer put the phone down, walked to the window, and looked down at the street. He couldn't deny that he was jealous of the man who was with Gwen.

Dinner was over and Boxer offered to help his mother clear the table.

"Nothing doing," she answered. "At least not the first time you've been here in six months." Then she said, "Why don't you two men go into the den and relax."

"Good idea," Boxer said, guessing it was his mother's way of giving him and his father some time alone.

"I'm for it," Mr. Boxer responded.

The two of them went into the den.

Mr. Boxer sat down in his dark brown leather easy chair and motioned his son into the chair opposite him; then, without any preliminaries, he said, "Doc's given me six months, maybe a year."

Boxer nodded.

"Everything is in order," his father said.

Boxer cleared his throat. "I didn't think it

61

wouldn't be."

Mr. Boxer smiled. "I'm proud of you, son," he said. "Very proud."

Boxer left his chair, and kneeling down in front of his father, he put his arms around him. "I love you," he whispered, forcing the tears out of his voice. "I love you, dad . . ."

Chapter Five

Boxer arose at 0600 and immediately called the security officer at the Thomas Williams Company offices on Water Street. The CIA man on duty greeted him and asked for his security clearance code. Then he said, "Good morning, Captain Boxer. How may I assist you?"

"Send over my driver at 0700 hours. I'll be coming in this morning to get acquainted with the staff, and receive my initial briefing."

"I'm not sure Ripley can make it by seven, sir. The traffic is pretty bad in the city at that hour."

Boxer was livid, but forced himself to speak without showing his anger. "What's your name, officer?"

"I'm a civilian, not an officer. Name's Cassidy. Why?"

"Well, Mr. Cassidy. If you don't get my

driver here by 0700 this morning, tomorrow your replacement will." Boxer slammed down the phone and cursed to himself.

Boxer showered and shaved, dressed in light gray slacks and his Williams navy blue blazer, drank two cups of black coffee, and was gathering up his charts and maps when there was a knock on his door. He glanced at his watch. It was 0655.

He opened his door and stepped back to admit the driver. He looked up startled.

"Agent Anita Ripley reporting, Captain Boxer. I'm your driver and aide. I'll also be providing you with protection."

"What the hell? Ripley, you're a woman." Boxer was staring at a very pretty brunette, about five foot six dressed in a blue gaberdine suit that was the standard uniform of several airline stewardesses and the Secret Service. He noticed that she was very trim and slim waisted. And despite the jacket she wore, he couldn't help but notice the very full breasts straining the limits of the uniform.

"Believe it or not, Captain, I'm a woman. Glad you noticed. I'd have been here sooner if it weren't for that jackass Cassidy screwing things up."

"You here on time, Ripley. That's not the problem."

Ripley stepped into the room and stood squared off with Boxer, feet spread slightly apart, arms at her side. "Well, then . . . ?"

"Quite frankly, Miss Ripley, I'm not about to have a woman driver, much less a bodyguard on such an important assignment as this."

"It's Agent Ripley, Captain. And that's being very sexist. Mr. Kinkaid told me that you'd respond this way. But don't worry, Captain Boxer, when it comes to this type of work, I'm his best man."

Boxer looked her over again. Her hair was cut very short and she wore little makeup. He wondered if she played a man's role sexually. Shame if she did, though. "Sorry, Ripley. Nothing personal." He took her by the arm and started to walk her to the door. "Kinkaid can go to hell for all I care. You're not going to be my driver. Now go back and have them send—"

Boxer's feet flew out from under him. He came down hard and fast. He looked up to see Ripley standing over him, just out of reach with a snub-nosed revolver aimed point-blank at his heart. He sat up slowly, his mouth open in disbelief.

Anita Ripley spoke. "Mr. Kinkaid also told me that you might require a demonstration, sir. Sorry if I hurt you, but I was under Mr. Kinkaid's orders."

"The only thing you hurt was my pride, Ripley. I'll accept you as my driver only on condition that you take orders from me, and that my orders supersede those of anyone else. Anyone, you understand that? I mean

Kinkaid, Admiral Stark, or anyone else that you may work for. Deal?"

Ripley smiled and bent over to help Boxer up. "Deal."

"I can get up myself, if you don't mind. I can't understand why they sent me a woman bodyguard."

"It's a known fact in our circles that a woman blends in better. Not as obvious that you have a bodyguard. It ought to make you less noticeable. Incidentally, the Chevy sedan was a good idea. In fact, that's why I was so late. That jerk Cassidy had them bring up a stretch limo and I had to spend fifteen minutes convincing him to get me the Chevy."

Boxer straightened out his clothing, smoothed out an imaginary wrinkle in his jacket, and stuffed his papers into a leather portfolio. He looked just like a wealthy business executive on his way to work. He held the door open for Ripley just before she was able to open it for him. "By the way, Ripley. As long as you're going to be working for me as an undercover driver, you'd better just call me Jack. You won't fool anyone if you keep calling me Captain Boxer."

Ripley quick-stepped to the waiting car so she could open the door before Boxer. "Yes sir, Captain. I mean Jack. Anything you say. And if it doesn't offend you, call me Anita."

"Okay then, Anita it is. And stop opening doors for me."

"Sure, Jack. Anything you say." She slipped behind the wheel and closed her door.

"And another thing," Boxer said, getting in on the passenger side. "Get yourself some clothes."

Ripley looked at him surprised.

"That service uniform doesn't fool anyone. I had you made out as a cop of some kind as soon as I saw you."

"I own five of these uniforms, as you call them, sir. Two blue, one tan, and two gray. My salary couldn't handle another wardrobe just to satisfy your tastes."

"Hey, take it easy," Boxer said as Ripley pulled out of the compound. "I stopped wanting to fight when you flipped me on my ass back there. You're on my staff now, and I have an unlimited expense account, compliments of Thomas Williams Company. I'd appreciate it if you'd go shopping and try to look more like my secretary, rather than my parole officer."

Ripley smiled at him. "Aye, aye, sir. In that case I'll get another outfit or two."

"Anita, get anything you need. Don't worry about the cost. Just do it."

"Okay, Jack. You win. Bloomies, here I come. Which way do you want to go in? The tunnel or the ferry?"

"Let's take the ferry today. I feel better when I'm on the water."

Ripley escorted Boxer up to the seventh floor via a small private elevator to the Williams Company offices, which occupied the entire floor. Boxer's office was in the southeast corner, with a window view in both directions. The office was huge and very posh, with thick burgundy carpeting, walnut paneled walls, a splendid oversized walnut desk, and a navy blue and burgundy upholstered sofa with two matching chairs. A small walnut coffee table was set near the sofa. The two walls that did not contain windows were decorated with paintings and framed photos of ships of all kinds. Boxer was pleased to see an oil painting of the Tecumseh centered on one wall. He turned to Ripley. "Not bad. Not bad at all. This is even more impressive than Admiral Stark's office. And what a view."

"Next door is a small office for your administrative assistant, followed by a conference room. Then the staff offices." Ripley opened the door and followed Boxer into the next room. It was much smaller than Boxer's, but was furnished similarly. The main difference was a rank of file cabinets and a wall filled with sophisticated communications equipment. The man seated behind the desk looked up as Boxer entered the room. "Captain Boxer, this is Lorilard Hutchinson III, your assistant. Hutchinson, Captain Jack Boxer."

Hutchinson stood up and nodded, "How do you do, sir. I'm pleased to meet you, Captain Boxer."

Boxer extended his hand, taking in the fiftyish-looking man, dressed very conservatively in a charcoal gray three-piece suit, white shirt, and maroon tie. His hair was trimmed closely and parted in the middle. "Mr. Boxer will do nicely, thank you. I'm a civilian like yourself."

"Mr. Kinkaid informed me of your status, sir. I believe 'Captain' is in order."

"So you also work for the Company."

Hutchinson was perplexed. "Of course, sir. So does everyone else working here."

"This is supposed to be a joint venture." Boxer was getting angry.

"With all due respect, Captain Boxer, this is Mr. Kinkaid's show. We're to assist you in any way, as you're our naval expert, but surely this is more in our league than yours."

Boxer's face reddened. "We shall see about that, Hutchinson. We shall see. But for now, we have work to do. By thirteen hundred hours I want on my desk the details of each country's contingency of ships, with complete specs, the staff and crew of same, and their ETAs in New York. Also I want a dossier on each nation's liaison to the celebration. Do you understand that, Mr. Hutchinson?"

"Yes, sir. I understand. Is there anything else?"

"Yes there is. Get rid of Cassidy. He no longer works here."

"But sir. . . . Cassidy was handpicked to work here by Mr. Kinkaid. I can't do that."

Boxer exploded. "Fuck Kinkaid. And fuck

Cassidy, too. I said he goes. And you're next, Hutchinson, if I hear the words *no* or *Kinkaid* from you again. Is that clear?"

Boxer's anger startled the man, who more closely resembled a bank clerk than a CIA agent. He just stood there and stared at Boxer in disbelief.

"I want to hear it from you, Hutchinson. Or you're gone right now."

"Yes, sir. I understand."

"Good. Now see to it that I get the information I ordered. Ripley will show me around the rest of the place. Then I'll be checking in with the mayor and police commissioner to go over their roles in the festivities. Arrange that for me, will you. Say, about ten hundred hours. I'll be back after lunch for that paperwork."

Boxer opened the adjoining door for Ripley, then followed her into the conference room. He looked around the room, which was furnished in the same opulent manner as the others, shrugged his shoulders, and shook his head. He turned to Ripley and said, "I've seen enough for now. Let's go see His Honor. By the way, how's Chinatown sound for lunch?"

"Chinatown sounds great," Cowley said to Bill Harris, his EXO. "The skipper used to brag about the food there. Great chow at a price even a sailor could afford. Besides, the captain wants us to get acquainted with lower

70

Manhattan, so we know our way around. Mahoney and Venutolo want to come along, too. And Artie Chen. He was raised in Chinatown and wants to show us around."

The five sailors piled into a taxi and took the twenty-minute ferry ride into the city. They spent the morning strolling through the South Street Seaport area, then headed onto East Broadway into Chinatown. They had been given three days shore leave, and wanted to take in as much of the sights as they could.

Artie Chen stopped the group in front of a storefront restaurant with about a dozen roasted ducks hanging by their necks in the window. "Ah, here we are, Ho Fat's. Best Chinese food in Chinatown. And that's saying something."

The others looked at each other as if Chen had lost his marbles. Harris said, "We can't eat here. It's unsanitary. Look in the front window. Those ducks are just hanging there. No refrigerator or anything."

"Don't worry so much. Those ducks won't last very long. The Chinese people will come in at lunchtime to buy them. That man by the window hacks them up with his cleaver and puts them in takeout boxes with barbeque sauce. My mouth waters just thinking about it."

Cowley replied, "Okay, Artie. If you insist. But no ducks for me."

"Trust me," Artie Chen said.

"Famous last words," Mahoney replied.

They all laughed and went inside. There were maybe ten tables of different sizes in the place. They were seated near the rear of the restaurant in the center. Artie Chen pointed out all the oriental families and businessmen seated near them, and smiled. "See, it's a good sign when the locals eat here."

"I'm famished, guys. Hey Artie, how about you do the ordering?"

"Sure. Leave it to me, fellas. Trust me."

They all laughed at that. They sampled steaming dim sum while their crispy fish was being prepared. They all liked the dumplings and had varying luck dipping the doughy masses in soy and ginger sauce and getting them into their mouths with the aid of chopsticks.

Nick Venutolo had trouble keeping his from slipping off, and brought on giggles from a little girl seated at a table next to theirs. Nick laughed at himself and smiled at the child. When she giggled again, he produced an *I Love NY* pin that he'd bought at the Seaport and gave it to her. After that she kept coming over to their table to stand near her new friend.

They had just polished off a large platter of chow fun rice noodles when a waiter arrived with a metal platter containing an entire sea bass accompanied by bowls of rice and vegetables and dipping sauce. He placed it in the center of the table and stepped back.

Suddenly, the glass door shattered and three men dressed in black clothes and ski masks burst into the room. All three fired at once. The first blast from the automatic pistols killed the duck cook at the window. Then they shot up the room. Blood splattered from a group of four young Chinese men seated against the wall as the bullets tore into them. Flesh and bone and blood flew from their bodies.

The sailors instinctively dove for the floor. They toppled the table over in front of them. Bullets chewed up their table and found the father of the little girl. She screamed hysterically, frozen in her spot. The girl's mother shouted at the men to stop. A blast took out the side of her face.

Nick Venutolo darted out from behind the table and threw his body over the little girl to protect her. His body was sprayed with bullets. Spurts of blood seemed to pop out of his white shirt and pants.

Artie Chen reached out to pull them to the safety of the table and caught a shot in the shoulder.

The shooting paused. The three gunmen looked around the room.

Police sirens wailed a short distance away.

One of the men aimed at the group of four that they had shot first and emptied his gun into their slumped figures. Then the men ran out onto the street and got lost in the crowd.

Boxer and Ripley had been enjoying the last of their three-way duck at the Peking Duck House when the shooting took place a few short blocks away. They finished their meal and paid the check before walking to East Broadway to see what had happened. In that short time, rumors of the massacre had spread throughout Chinatown. Three ambulances went screaming away as Boxer approached Ho Fat's.

The restaurant was a wreck. The plate glass window had been shattered by the gunfire that killed the cook. Tables were overturned, food and dishes littered the floor, and blood was everywhere. Boxer asked a policeman who was roping off the area what had happened.

"Move on, buddy. This is no concern of yours. C'mon everybody, keep moving. Don't block the crime scene."

Boxer continued to stare into the restaurant.

"What the hell's the matter with you, ya deaf or somethin'? I said move on."

Boxer started to protest when Ripley's beeper sounded. She took him by the arm and steered him to a nearby phone booth, which Ma Bell had shaped like a red pagoda to keep the tourists happy. She punched a number into the phone, gave her clearance code, and spoke to the dispatcher. Boxer noticed her face turn grim and lose its color. She hung up and approached him ill at ease. "It's the office. It seems that some of your men were involved in this mess. Harris used his one phone call to contact you. Hutchinson took the info and beeped me."

"What the hell's going on?"

"They're at the Chinatown precinct. They won't talk to anyone 'til you get there. The police are holding them because they can't ID and won't cooperate."

"What are we waiting for. Let's go."

"Drive or walk? We're only a few blocks away and parking's a bitch."

"Let's move it."

They arrived at the station ten minutes later, breathing hard from the fast walk. They approached the desk sergeant and Boxer asked to see his men. The heavyset policeman pushed his hat back on his graying head and asked if Boxer was their lawyer.

"No, I'm an associate of theirs. I understand they've been involved in a shooting. I'd like to know they're all right."

"Sorry. Nobody's allowed in there. They ain't talking and the captain's pissed. So no one get's in except their lawyer."

"Then I demand to speak to the captain. I'm Jack Boxer of the Thomas Williams Company."

"I don't care if you're the Pope. No one gets in there except their lawyer. Now get the fuck out of here."

Boxer was livid. He started to go after the sergeant. Several uniformed policemen drew weapons and closed in on Boxer.

Ripley grabbed his arm. "Take it easy, Jack."

"Easy? He can't use that kind of language to us. I'll have his ass."

"Don't forget who we've just met with this morning, Jack. I'll make a phone call and we'll get this settled."

Ripley dialed a number and explained what had happened. She hung up and went back to Boxer, a slight smile on her face. In two minutes, a burly black man in an officer's white shirt uniform came barreling into the room. He addressed Boxer and Ripley. "I'm Captain Malcolm Jefferson, the precinct commander. The PC seems to think that I owe you an apology. We'll see about that. He also said that you'd explain who these men are inside. That's good. I want some straight answers here."

Boxer replied, "I'd like some answers too. Are the men all right?"

Jefferson motioned to a doorway. "Let's go into my office and see what we can do. I'll have your three friends brought in."

Harris, Cowley, and Mahoney joined the others in the captain's office. When the uniformed escort left the room and the door was closed, Boxer told the captain, "I can only tell you that I am working for the government on a matter of security. The police commissioner and the mayor know the exact nature of my business, and right now, that's all you need to know. If you have any more questions as to my credentials, please call the PC and straighten it out now."

Jefferson looked exasperated. "Look, there's no need for that. The PC told me that you're okay and to cooperate fully. If you're okay with the PC, you're okay with me. It's just that we've had a multihomicide. When we questioned the survivors, these birds wouldn't even give their names."

"They work for me," Boxer said. "They are under my orders not to disclose anything. I apologize for causing you any problems, Captain."

"In that case, I guess I'm sorry too for the rough treatment we gave you. Everyone's uptight over this thing."

Boxer shook hands with Jefferson and turned to his men, who'd been standing silent through all this. "Bill, tell us all what happened, please."

Harris told the story as he saw it. The others filled in on any details they remembered that Harris had missed. Captain Jefferson asked Harris, "So you feel pretty sure that those four oriental men were singled out? Most of the other witnesses felt that it was a random slaying. That the gunmen fired at anyone. That young couple with the little girl, for instance."

"They just got in the way, Captain. That kid would have bought it too, but Nick jumped on top of her. He gave his life protecting her. And Artie caught one too." Harris shook his head. "No, the way I see it is those three gunmen knew just who they wanted to kill. They even fired into them again, even after they'd been killed, just to make sure. The rest was just window dressing to throw you off."

"Very interesting. Very astute of you, uh, Mr. — ?"

Boxer spoke up. "Bill will do for now, Captain. Sorry, but I can't divulge any more for now."

Mahoney piped in, "They fingerprinted us, Skipper."

"That true, Captain? I'm afraid that won't get you very far. And I'd appreciate you're destroying those prints. These men are not on file anywhere, anyway."

"I'll consider it. Well, you're all free to go, Mr. Boxer. Please keep in touch. I've got this feeling that our paths are going to cross again one of these days. And by the way, I'm really sorry about your man getting killed. From what everyone has said, he was a real hero, saving that little girl. And I think that says something for all of you."

Chapter Six

"Boxer, here, Admiral. We had a little trouble up here, today."

"So I hear, Jack. Kinkaid called a short while ago with the news. Seems there might be a Chinese gang war brewing. Two of the men who got killed were top members of a tong."

"One of my boys got killed, too, sir. He saved a little girl from getting shot up."

"I'll take care of it. Have you notified his next of kin?"

"Not yet, sir."

"I'll handle it from here, Jack. His family will be proud to know he was still in the Navy, although secretly. It's the least I can do for him."

"Thank you, sir." Boxer rubbed his beard. "There is something else you can do for me, Admiral."

"Go on."

"Everyone in my Williams Company office is CIA. This was supposed to be a joint venture."

"Son of a bitch. Kinkaid assured me it would be a cooperative effort."

"Sir, I'd like to get some Navy people in here by tomorrow. My assistant, Hutchinson, knows what he's doing, but he works strictly for the CIA. Kinkaid says *shit,* and Hutchinson bends and groans. I'd like a Navy counterpart working in that office with him. And also in the support staff."

Stark took a deep pull on his cigar and blew a smoke ring up toward the ceiling. "Can do, Jack. I suppose the driver they gave you is the same as the rest. I'll get a replacement for him, also."

"I think Ripley's all right so far, sir. Time will tell, of course, but she's backed me up on everything so far."

"Did you say *she?* What the fuck is Kinkaid up to, anyway? He trying to sabotage Project Discovery?"

"Ripley's been his best man so far, Admiral. I had to fire one jackass already."

"You do whatever you have to, Jack. This is a highest-priority mission, and no one, and I mean no one is going to fuck it up. That means Kinkaid or anyone else. I'd better let Fitzpatrick know what's happening. He may want to replace some of those CIA guys with his own people."

"Thank you, sir." The line went dead in his hand. He replaced the phone in its cradle and walked out of the little red-pagoda enclosure. He turned to his driver, who had driven up with his car. "Ripley, we'd better get back to the office before we knock off for the night. See what's in store for tomorrow."

They took the private elevator to the seventh floor. Each made an effort to open the door for the other. They laughed and decided to just open the door and walk in instead of playing the etiquette game. Hutchinson buzzed the intercom as soon as Boxer sat down at his desk. Boxer called him in.

Lorrilard Hutchinson III walked into Boxer's office carrying a thick manila folder under his arm. "How do you do, Captain? Ripley? I hope you find everything satisfactory."

Boxer noted the neat stacks of folders and multicolored binders on his desk. He looked up at Hutchinson.

"The dossiers and information you ordered, sir." Hutchinson put a little unnecessary emphasis on the word *ordered*. "You're meeting with the Russians tomorrow at ten hundred hours. I took the liberty of bringing you the Russian files myself." He placed his folder on the desk in front of Boxer. "If I may request, sir, that you severely chastise the buggers for destroying the frigate *Hanover* in the Sea of Japan last month. The State Department let them off the hook without much ado, because of lack of evidence. However, at the Company, we feel very strongly that one of their Q-21 subs had to be the culprit. There is nothing else capable of doing it."

Boxer took the folder in his hands. "I'll raise hell if I'm sure the Ruskies did it, Hutchinson. You may be right on that score. By the way, who's their envoy?"

Hutchinson had obviously studied the file before turning it over to Boxer. "Chap by the name of Borodine. Igor Borodine. Navy fellow, like yourself. Give you something in common to talk about."

Boxer was taken by surprise. "Borodine? That old son of a whore? He's no envoy. Just the second best submarine commander there is."

"That's a matter of opinion. However, prior to his becoming commander of their prototype Q-21 submarine, he was attached to the embassy in D.C. Apparently he was chosen for the same reasons as you were, sir. Whatever they were."

Boxer laughed out loud. "Thanks for the vote of confidence, Hutchinson." He patted the file in front of him. "And for getting this info for me. I think I'll go back to Stapleton and go through this stuff tonight." He turned to his driver. "Ripley, we're leaving."

Ripley got up from the upholstered chair. "Sure thing, Jack. I'll go get the car."

"And Hutchinson. You're working too hard.

I'm bringing in some help for you tomorrow. See to it that you cooperate with the new people."

Hutchinson watched Boxer leave the office. He stood there staring at his back until he was out of sight. Then he made for the bank of phones in his office.

Anita Ripley eased the Chevy into traffic. "What a pompous ass that Hutchinson is."

"I'm bringing some Navy personnel into the office tomorrow. No doubt Hutchinson has already called Kinkaid with the news. It's too damn bad, though. I feel like I'm working in a foreign land in that office. Nobody gives a damn if I'm there or not. They all report to and take orders from Kinkaid. Well, fuck him too. Oh, sorry, Ripley."

"No problem. I thought you were going to call me Anita."

"Sure. How about we grab a bite to eat before going back to the base. I know a great steak house in the Village."

Ripley deftly avoided a taxi which cut in front of their car. "Sounds great to me. I'll head uptown. Just tell me when we get close."

"Does it bother you, Anita, me cutting in on your CIA friends?"

"They're not my friends, Jack. I don't know any of them better than you do. I was home on a short leave from the Middle East because our mission had fallen apart. Kinkaid needed a good driver who could double as bodyguard, and found out I was around, so . . . the rest is history, I guess."

Boxer chuckled. "But you still work for the Company, Anita. And you know if Kinkaid asked you to do something, you'd do it."

"I'm not like those desk jockeys back in the office, Jack. If he asked me to put you in jeopardy, I'd think twice."

"Maybe. You'd think about it, realize who you really work for, and do what Kinkaid wants. Turn right at that corner."

"To be honest with you, Jack, I'm not really sure what I'd do. I just hope it would be the right thing."

"Fair enough. There's a space. Pull up in there. The Beef & Ale House is just up the block."

Boxer tucked the manila folder into his attache case and they walked the short distance to the restaurant. They each ordered thick sirloin steaks and fries. Boxer was surprised to see how much food Ripley ate. She polished off a heaping plate from the salad bar and had no trouble knocking off the steak. However, she declined a drink, or even wine with their dinner.

"Can't drink and then drive for you, Jack. Besides, how will I be able to guard your body if I'm soused?"

"Okay, you win, Ripley. But now I feel self-conscious drinking if you're not."

"Doesn't bother me a bit. You go right ahead."

Boxer ordered a half-bottle of a good California cabernet to go with his steak. He liked a drink or two with his meals and knew he'd have to do something about this awkwardness of drinking alone.

Ripley drank Perrier with a twist with her meal. When they were done, they both ordered coffee. Ripley had a dish of ice cream.

"I don't know how you keep that great figure of yours, Anita. You've eaten me under the table."

"I wish."

Boxer gagged on his coffee, and began to blush.

"That was just to get your attention. I thought you'd never notice my figure. And after I spent so much of your expense money on new clothes."

"Anita, I haven't missed a thing, believe me."

"I know, Jack. We've been so preoccupied with the job. And thanks for taking me out to dinner. Most of the clods I drove for have me wait outside while they stuff their faces. I can see that'd never occur to you."

"A person's got to eat. And I enjoy your company. And you've done a good job so far. You deserve it. Now, if you'll drive me back to the base, I'll go over these files tonight."

The rush-hour traffic had abated by the time they got back to the ferry slip. Boxer sniffed in the salt air and longed to be back aboard the *Shark,* but he knew that would have to wait. This mission he was on was more important. Back inside the compound, at his bungelow, he told Ripley she was dismissed for the night.

Ripley smiled at him. "Jack, how about letting me run through those files with you. Two heads are better than one, you know. Otherwise you'll be up all night."

"Hell of a way to spend an evening, Ripley. This is the Big Apple. You should go out and enjoy yourself."

"This isn't my town, Jack. I feel like a fish out of water here. Besides, the company's pleasant."

"OK, tell you what. If you'll come in and have that drink with me, we'll call it a deal."

Using the desk as a command post, they divided the dossiers into two piles and entered any pertinent information into the personal computer which Boxer had requested. They worked for two hours, sorting through all the data, discussing what was important, and condensing the file into a more manageable form. At 1030, they took a break.

Anita Ripley stretched her arms out to the sides, and stifled a yawn. "If your offer still holds, I'll have that drink now."

Boxer took notice of those magnificent breasts straining against the bodice of her dress. He smiled at her. "My offer's still good. What'll you have? I've got scotch, vodka, and bourbon. Nothing fancy, I'm afraid."

"And I was going to order a piña colada. Seriously, Jack, I'll have a scotch and water."

"Tough guy, eh? Scotch and water for the lady, and a double scotch on the rocks for the gentleman. Coming right up."

Ripley stood up and stretched out her entire body. She tugged uncomfortably at her dress. "I'd like to get comfortable. Anything big and loose I can slip into?"

"I have a robe in the bathroom if you'd like. There's also a pair of pajamas I never wear. You're welcome to them, too."

Ripley took a long swallow of her drink. "I'll be right back. You're damn lucky you men don't have to fight with all the clothing and accessories that we women do. You have no idea how uncomfortable it can get." She finished her drink in one long pull and handed the empty glass to Boxer. "Fill'er up, barkeep. And not a half glass this time."

"I thought you didn't drink?"

"Not while I'm on duty. Or while I'm driving. And I don't intend to do any more driving today. See you in a minute."

Boxer drained his scotch and prepared fresh drinks for the both of them. As he finished, he looked up to find Anita Ripley emerging from the bedroom wearing only the tops of his striped broadcloth pajamas. She had the sleeves rolled up to her elbows, and with the top two buttons undone, she showed a lot of cleavage.

"You like?" she asked.

"I like," Boxer replied. "Very much." He handed her the fresh drink. "Now is there anything else you'd like?"

Anita thought for a moment. "Yes, there is, Jack. I'd like to get laid."

Boxer was a little surprised by her boldness. He'd known other women who were forward when it came to sex. In fact, one of them, was Tracy Kimble. But it never ceased to amaze him how times had changed and women now asked men for sex. "It doesn't bother you to sleep with the boss?"

"No. Does it bother you to sleep with the help?"

"Sorry, Anita. I didn't mean it like that. But, you know, it will never be the same again between us. It might cause a strain on our working relationship. Would that bother you?"

Ripley put her hands on her hips. The pajama top rode high up on her thighs as she did. "Okay, Jack. I promise not to knock you on your ass again."

Boxer laughed. "All right, Anita. I just don't want you to get hurt by this. That's all. I might have occasions to be with other women. What if . . ."

"Jack Boxer. Will you take off those clothes and fuck me already? Here I am standing here all but waving it at you, and you're still talking about work." With that, Anita opened the remaining buttons on her top, allowing it to open onto her nakedness.

Boxer was mesmerized by her full lush breasts topping off a trim, athletic body with a very thin waist.

Ripley swirled around quickly and headed for the bedroom.

Boxer took in the high firm swell of her buttocks, and found himself getting erect. "Hey, wait for me," he called out after her.

Anita was propped upon the bed, completely naked now, her hands behind her head showing off the fullness of her breasts.

Boxer undid his shirt and placed it on a chair.

Ripley got up and helped him undo his pants. "Here, darling," she cooed, "let me give you a hand."

And that she did.

As Boxer slid his trousers to the ground, Anita had tugged his skivvies to his knees, and was fondling his erection. Boxer kissed her lips, parting them with his tongue. Her tongue answered back, darting into his mouth as she played with him.

Boxer scooped her up and carried her to the bed.

She propped herself up with her hands at his sides, and jutted out her breasts as an offering to him.

Boxer hungrily took one of the large dark nipples into his mouth and sucked on it.

Ripley closed her eyes and sighed.

He moved his tongue and lips around, feeling the hardness of her nipple unfold. Then he went to work on the other breast.

"Oh, Jack. That feels wonderful. It makes me wish I had three."

Boxer paused for a moment. "Believe me, Anita, a third tit is something that you definitely don't need."

She giggled and reached for his penis. She slid herself down on the bed and took it into her mouth. She soon had him hard as a rock. "You were making me jealous with all that sucking. Now it's my turn. Tit for tat, you know."

Boxer ran his hands hand gently down the length of her body, taking in each mound and crevice with his fingertips. Occasionally, she wiggled when he hit an especially sensitive spot. Then he slid both hands between her legs and gently pried them apart. "My turn," he said.

She separated them willingly, and he moved his face into her crotch.

He nuzzled her love mound with his nose, and then kissed her snatch. She smelled clean and good. He probed into her with his tongue, and she was immediately wet and warm, and pulsating.

She responded by sucking harder on his

turgid member. She clamped her thighs around his head, trying to pull him even further into her. "Oh, Jack, darling, that feels so good. Don't ever stop."

Then went on like that for ten or fifteen minutes, she sucking his cock and stroking and playing with his scrotum. He fondled her every curve, explored her anus with his fingers, squeezed and stroked her luscious breasts and hard nipples.

Finally she started going into a spasm, rocking her pelvis into her face, faster and faster.

His tongue quickened its pace, and he nibbled at her clit and followed her rhythm. She started to pant, grabbing his balls and sucking harder and harder.

He held out until the last moment. As he sensed she was coming, he worked his tongue on her clit, squeezed a breast with one hand, and as she gasped with delight, he thrust a finger into her ass and they both exploded together.

She kept saying, "Oh, God, oh God, that was wonderful!"

Boxer took her into her arms and pressed her against him. "I'm glad you stayed over."

"So am I, darling." She held him tightly. "So am I. . . ."

Chapter Seven

At exactly 0800 Boxer arrived at his office in lower Manhattan accompanied by Anita Ripley. Together they spent the next half hour copying their condensed notes on the Russian entourage into the master computer. At 0835, there was a knock at his office door.

"Come in, please," Boxer said and nodded to Ripley to open the door. A Marine colonel, clad in dress khakis and carrying a large black leather valise, stood in the doorway. He saluted sharply.

"Colonel Will Pickens, United States Marine Corps, reporting for duty, sir."

Boxer motioned him into the room. "Come on in, Colonel. And lighten your load. You can set whatever that is you're carrying down and tell me what this is all about."

The handsome, burly Marine set down his suitcase and stood before Boxer ramrod straight. "Well, sir." He noticed Ripley sitting at the computer screen. "Ma'am. General Fitzpatrick sent me over. Said you were havin' some difficulty operatin' independently here. Ah'm with Marine Intelligence, sir, and Ah'm here to give you a hand."

Boxer noted the man's thick Southern accent and smiled. He caught Ripley's glance and winked at her. "Welcome aboard, Pickens. I did ask Admiral Stark for some help . . . but I was expecting a Navy man."

"Yessir, ah figured that. An' ah realize that you think that ah talk funny. Well, my mamma don't think so, sir. But beggin' your pardon, sir, y'all sound funny to me, too. Everyone up here in Yankeetown talks so fast it's hard for an ol' country boy like me to follow them. Ah was sent here by the General based on mah qualifications, sir, although Fitz an' me both hail from Tennessee, and he likes the way I talk. Sir."

"Okay, Colonel, you win. I'm sorry. Let's start it over. And please, let's skip the sir crap. My name's Jack Boxer. Call me Jack."

"If you call me Will, you got a deal. I'll need an hour or so to debug this place, sir. That's what's in that satchel."

"Fine with me, Will. Need any help?"

"No, thanks, Jack. I have everything ah need."

Boxer turned to Ripley. "Anita, would you please see to it that Colonel Pickens gets a supply of Williams Company blazers and civilian clothes. I'd say about a forty-four jacket to start. And better send a tailor up. We'll need to make room for those Marine Corps muscles."

Ripley smiled. "Sure, boss." She turned to Will Pickens. "Jack has this thing about getting us out of uniform so we blend in with the scenery better."

Pickens looked surprised. "You in the service too?"

"Sort of. I'll go notify procurement to get you some clothes. If you'll excuse me, gentlemen?"

After she left the room and closed the door behind her, Pickens gave out a low whistle and winked at Boxer. "Fine-lookin' woman, there. Hey, she got a whole dress full of titties, there, don't she? Ah'll be damned."

"You certainly will be if you try anything with Agent Anita Ripley there. She's probably the best man the CIA's got."

"CIA? Ah trust them as far as Ah can throw them. Ah'd like to throw that one into the sack."

Boxer shook his head. "You know, Ripley's been playing pretty straight with me, Will. Kinkaid assigned her as my driver and bodyguard. So far, she's done everything I've asked her to do. I think she's okay."

"Maybe so, Jack. Maybe so. But Ah don't trust that CIA. Kinkaid may have sent her here to keep tabs on you."

"Well, we shall see, Will. We'll see."

Pickens quickly changed the subject. "Ah guess ah'll start earnin' mah pay, now. So if you'll excuse me for a while, ah'll get right to it."

Boxer nodded his approval. "Let me introduce you to Hutchinson, my executive assistant, Will, and tell him he's sharing that assignment with you from now. Then you can get started."

An hour later, Pickens dumped a small pile of electronic evesdropping devices on Boxer's desk. They had been removed from the furniture and desk in Boxer's office and in the conference room. One was recovered from the men's room and several from the employee's dining room. Kinkaid was leaving nothing to chance. When Ripley had returned with Pickens's new clothes, Boxer summoned Hutchinson into his office.

"Hutchinson, I wanted you present during this, so you can appreciate firsthand how I feel about my own office being bugged." He picked up the largest transmitter from the assortment on his desk and tapped it sharply with his pen. "Now hear this, Kinkaid, you fuck. This is Jack Boxer speaking into one of the toys you had planted in my office. I'm going to tell you this just once, so listen good. If you ever try to spy on me again, if I ever find another bug in my offices, I'm moving the entire operation to the naval base on Staten Island, and leave you out of it altogether. Do you read me? 'Cause if you ever fuck with me again, I'll take care of you myself." At that, Boxer slammed the device down hard on the desk, causing it to shatter.

Hutchinson was shaking. Boxer turned to him and warned, "You heard that, Hutchinson. And I meant every word. I hope your boss got the message, but just in case he didn't, it goes for you too. Don't ever try anything like this again, or you've had it. Now get the fuck out of here. You and your spooks make me sick."

Boxer turned to the Marine colonel. "You did a fine job, Will. Thanks. And welcome aboard. I'm going to ask you to sit in with Hutchinson from now on to keep him honest. And to protect my interests from now on. We're all supposed to be working for the security of our nation, and this interagency infighting is counterproductive."

Pickens saluted, then remembered Boxer's relaxed protocol policy. "Nothin' to it, Jack. Just doin' mah job."

"Would you please check what time the Ruskies are due here today? I know one of their delegates, and I'm looking forward to meeting him again without him trying to kill me."

* * *

97

At precisely 1030, Will Pickens buzzed Boxer on the intercom. "Got some Russians here to see you, Jack. Ah have their credentials right here. Colonel Petrovich, Captain Borodine, and a Captain Korenzo. You ready to see 'em now?"

"Please send them right in, Will." Boxer was up out of his seat and making his way around the desk when Pickens led in the Russian delegation. Borodine stopped short when he spotted Boxer, causing the others to pile up behind him. He stared directly into Boxer's eyes.

Boxer returned the stare. Then his face softened into a smile and he saluted his nemesis crisply. He held the salute until Borodine and his EXO Viktor Korenzo returned it. Petrovich, a dour-faced block of a man, ignored him. No one spoke.

Finally Pickens said, "Seems some of y'all know each other."

Boxer replied, "Yes, Colonel Pickens. Captain Igor Borodine and I are acquainted. As a matter of fact, he's one of the finest submariners I've ever tried to blow out of the water." He watched a smile creep onto Borodine's face. "I haven't yet had the pleasure of meeting the others."

Before Will could speak. Borodine said, "We meet again, Captain Boxer. This time, however, we have a mutual interest, to ensure the security of our fleet during your Discovery Day celebration. May I introduce Colonel Vladimir Petrovich, a security expert, and my EXO Viktor Korenzo, who will act as my assistant in these matters."

Boxer had immediately pegged Petrovich as KGB as soon as he entered the room. The disdain the man had shown only increased his certainty of that. Korenzo, a blond man in his late twenties, seemed a lot like Borodine, except about ten years younger. "Please sit down, gentlemen. May I offer you a drink?"

Borodine and his EXO sat together on the sofa. The KGB man sat off to the side on a chair. "A glass of tea would be nice, thank you."

Korenzo spoke for the first time. "Yes, that would be fine. A glass of tea for me too, please."

Boxer turned to Petrovich. He glared at Boxer and shook his head no. Boxer pressed a button on his desk and spoke into the intercom. "Please ask Miss Ripley to arrange for a tea service for our guests and myself." He turned back to Borodine and Korenzo on the sofa. "Smoke, gentlemen? I'm sorry I can't offer you a Havana cigar, but they're still illegal here, you know. Or would you care for a cigarette?" Boxer offered a box of Tampa cigars and a silver cigarette tray with an assortment of brands.

"I've grown accustomed to the Havanas, Captain, and so I've brought my own, if you don't mind." He offered one to Petrovich, who accepted, and to Viktor Korenzo, who declined.

The EXO smiled nervously and said, "I wouldn't mind an American cigarette. Thank you."

Boxer lit it for him as the KGB man scowled at the junior officer. Boxer filled up his worn briar pipe and got it stoked properly, just as Anita Ripley led a waiter into the office with a sterling silver tea service complete with the glass cups the Russians were used to. When Ripley and the waiter left the room, Boxer said. "Gentlemen, why don't we get started? We have much to discuss."

"In a moment, please," Petrovich said in a gruff voice. First I have something to do."

Petrovich opened his attache case and removed a small electronic device. He extended an antenna about twelve inches, flipped on a switch, and began fiddling with a dial in the center. He stood in the center of the room and turned in a slow circle, pointing the device into each possible place of concealment. Satisfied that their were no listening devices, he folded up the device and tucked it back into his case.

"Satisfied?"

The KGB man looked at Boxer warily. "A bit surprised, yes. And satisfied for now. Let us begin."

Boxer cleared his throat. "As you know, we are trying to accommodate almost two hundred capital ships in the New York area. The size of this armada will necessitate our deploying the various fleets as far south as Long Beach Island off the coast of New Jersey, and north along the southern coast of Long Island as well as in the Long Island Sound itself. We will try to parade as many as possible through the New York Harbor between July fourth and fifth. We propose to anchor your fleet in the Sound, near Glen Cove, Long Island."

"*Nyet.*" Petrovich was up on his feet. "Do you take us for fools? You could trap us in there and destroy us in a few minutes. No. Absolutely no." He stomped his foot down hard for emphasis.

Boxer replied, "You have your compound in Glen Cove, right on the waterfront, where you house your embassy people. It would be an ideal spot for you. You would have all the comforts of home."

"Out of the question," shouted Petrovich.

Boxer turned to Borodine for support. "And you, Comrade Captain Borodine. What is your opinion?"

Borodine smiled at Boxer's use of the title *Comrade*. He rubbed his graying beard. "Vladimir is correct on this matter. We would be too vulnerable there. Even a tiny country like Israel could severely damage our fleet. Or a band of terrorists from Iran or Afghanistan could do it. They wouldn't even need a navy. No, Comrade Captain Boxer. Long Island Sound is no good for us."

101

Boxer wanted to mention that they could avoid that kind of trouble by getting out of Afghanistan and not interfering with the affairs of the other countries, but he held his tongue. He was playing the role of diplomat now, and had to act like one. "What would you propose then, instead?"

Borodine and Petrovich started to speak at once. Borodine nodded to Petrovich to continue. The KGB colonel said, "We wish to deploy our carrier, the *Leningrad*, here, off the coast of Sandy Hook, and the cruisers and other support ships throughout the lower harbor area."

Boxer shook his head. "Now it is you who are unreasonable, Colonel. First of all, the Soviet fleet is too large for that area. You would choke off access to the Hudson and East Rivers, to say nothing of the harbor itself."

Petrovich turned to the two Russian submariners. "It seems that our host does not trust us, comrades. He seems afraid of a wolf at his door."

Boxer said, "You've got the point real well, Colonel. You would pose too great a threat to us so strategically placed. Nothing personal, but *nyet*."

"I have always believed our involvement in this affair has been a mistake. And now I'm sure of it." Petrovich turned to the two other Russians. "I'm leaving. Let's go, comrades."

The two of them got up to join Petrovich. Boxer called out to Borodine. "Wait, Captain Borodine. None of this is etched in granite. We may still work out a compromise. Won't you give it some more time?"

Borodine looked at his EXO, who shrugged, and then to Petrovich. "Perhaps if we give it some more time, we can work out arrangements suitable to both our governments. I would be willing to try again. What do you say, Vladimir?"

"It is a matter of trust, Igor Alexandriavich. I don't trust these imperialists. I think they would try to trap us."

Boxer exploded. "Trust? How can you accuse this country of lack of trust when you sank one of our frigates off your east coast two weeks before coming here to participate in our festival?"

"Bah," Petrovich spat out. "We deny any such thing. It is absurd."

"I happen to know that our frigate was sunk by a Q-21 submarine, *Comrade* Petrovich. I've seen the transcripts of her log as she was chasing the sub. And they're damn few Q-21s around. Captain Borodine can attest to that, can't you, Captain?"

"This is an insult, and I won't stand for it. I'll—"

"The data fits, Colonel."

Borodine cleared his throat. "Comrade Captain Boxer. When we are at sea, you and I are enemies, of this there is no question. If I caught you in our waters, I would try to sink your sub in a minute. And I am sure that you would do the same if the situation were reversed. But you know by now that I am an honorable man."

"I've no quarrel with that, Boxer replied. I only wish that all your people were as trustworthy as you."

"I give you my word as a submariner, Comrade Captain Boxer. I had nothing to do with the sinking of your ship. And to the best of my knowledge, neither did any other Soviet submarine."

Boxer stood up. "Your word is good with me, Comrade Captain. We have been the best of enemies for a long time. Perhaps we should all calm down, and try to work this out later in the week."

Borodine looked to his EXO, who nodded approval, and to the KGB man.

"Yes, let us try again. We will come again in two days."

"Okay, gentlemen. Why don't we all go have a drink. I know a pub in the East Village where they keep the Stolichnaya in the freezer."

The Russians smiled at that and readily agreed to go with Boxer. "Good. I'll have Ripley bring the car around and we'll head uptown."

* * *

The three Russians, Boxer, and Anita Ripley were seated at a round table near the front window of Harold's Pub on East Seventh Street, toasting each other with ice cold Stoli straight up with a sprinkle of pepper, Russian style. The tension among them had eased up, and even Petrovich seemed pleased as the vodka did its work. While they were on their second round, Boxer noticed two men in street clothes get out of a Ford Fairlane just up the block on the opposite side of the street, followed closely by two uniformed policemen. The plainclothes cops cagily walked up the porch stairs of a brownstone and stood to either side of the doorway, service revolvers drawn. The uniformed men hid behind their black-and-white, which they had parked at a hydrant next door. One of the plainclothesmen reached over and knocked on the door.

Borodine was facing Boxer and followed his gaze out the window of the pub. He nudged the others, and soon all of them were watching the drama unfold outside.

Petrovich said, "See, comrades. The citizens of this country live in a police state. You see their secret policemen going to arrest a political dissident."

Boxer laughed. "More likely a drug bust, Petrovich. Unfortunately all too common here in the city."

The door to the brownstone opened to the length of the security chain, and an oriental face peered out. There seemed to be a discussion going on between the oriental and one of the plainclothes officers.

"So you admit that in your decadent society, drug use is rampant. You see, Igor, Viktor. Now you know we speak the truth when we warn you of this."

Boxer turned his head to the Russian. "Drugs are a big thing in New York and a few other large urban areas. This is where they congregate. It's not like this in other—"

The door to the brownstone crashed outward, slamming against one plainclothesman. The oriental man inside spun to his right and sprayed the partner with automatic pistol fire. Blood spurted out of the cop as he fell to the sidewalk. The oriental turned and emptied his gun at the first officer. He fired through the wooden door. The cop dropped in a bloody heap.

The two uniformed officers opened fire with their thirty-eights. A second oriental man dashed into the doorway and fired back. The car windows shattered. One uniformed cop grabbed a bloody shoulder. Both men crouched for cover.

Boxer jumped out of his seat and ran for the patrol car.

Ripley pulled her Chief's Special from behind her waist and followed him.

Borodine got up. Petrovich yelled at him and pulled him back into his seat.

106

Borodine got up again and pushed Petrovich aside. He yelled to Viktor Korenzo, and they ran out of the pub toward the action.

Boxer reached the patrol car flat on his belly. He could see that one officer was severely wounded. He took that man's revolver and fired a few rounds at the doorway. He motioned to the other cop to call for a backup.

"Already on their way," he shouted over the return fire. He pointed to another black-and-white speeding to the scene, sirens wailing.

The two orientals crouched in the open doorway and sprayed the oncoming patrol car. The windshield shattered. The vehicle went out of control and crashed into a parked car.

Borodine took cover behind the crashed police car. He helped himself to the shotgun lying across the lap of a badly dazed policeman and fired a few rounds at the brownstone.

The two orientals reloaded and ran from the building, firing at their attackers as they fled. A shotgun blast from Borodine hit the second gunman. He wheeled and fired a burst at Borodine and Korenzo. Someone screamed.

Boxer braced his revolver on the deck of the police car with both hands and fired off five rounds into the man. The oriental was dead before he hit the ground.

The other gunman stopped and turned on Boxer. He leveled his automatic pistol at him and shouted an obscenity.

Ripley was crouched near Boxer and realized what was happening. She yelled, "No," and hit Boxer with a flying tackle. He hit the ground hard, Anita over him. The remaining uniformed cop fired at the gunman, bringing him down. Finally, there was silence.

After a long moment, the uniformed officer approached his target, gun drawn, stepping very slowly. The man was dead. He called out to the others. "It's okay, folks. They're both dead. It's all over."

Very carefully, Boxer placed his arm around Anita Ripley and tried to get up. "Okay, Anita. We can get up now. It's all over."

She didn't respond.

Boxer felt a stickiness in his hand and a horrible thought swept through him. It was all over for Anita Ripley, too. She had died saving his life.

Chapter Eight

"Are you all right, my friend?"

Boxer looked up to see Borodine standing over him, arm outstretched to help him to his feet. "Yeah, I guess so." He nodded toward the body on his lap. "They got Ripley, though."

Borodine noticed the pool of red sticky blood under Boxer and Ripley and the bloody dress on the woman. "I'm truly sorry."

"So am I, Comrade Captain. So am I. More than you will ever know. Anita saved my life by throwing her body over mine during the shooting. She took the bullets that would have killed me."

"And I am grateful to you. You saved our lives when you shot the one firing at Viktor and myself."

Sirens and klaxons could be heard faintly. Boxer turned to Borodine. "Igor, take Viktor and get the hell out of here. I'll try to keep you and your government out of this mess."

Borodine tossed the shotgun he'd used into the shot-up police car, and brushed off his hands. "No. I'll stay with you until I am certain you are properly taken care of."

"I don't want to argue with you over this. It would completely blow our cover if your involvement became public. There's no way to suppress the news media here as there is in your country."

Borodine made no move to comply.

Moments later, Vladimir Petrovich arrived at the scene, panting hard. He spoke some harsh words in Russian, to which Borodine barked a reply.

Boxer pulled himself upright and said, "Petrovich, get them the hell out of here before the police get here. And look after them. I think one of them may have gotten hurt."

More harsh words in Russian exchanged between the three Soviet men.

The sirens became louder.

Petrovich grabbed Borodine's arm and pulled him away.

Boxer shouted, "Go. I'll meet you tomorrow. Call my office in the morning. And thanks for your help. I won't soon forget it."

Borodine saluted him, and followed his comrades away from the area.

Boxer noticed him limp slightly as he walked down the street. Soon, police cars and ambulances filled the area. The killed and wounded policemen were moved out first, followed by the two oriental gunmen.

Finally, Thomas Murphy, the uniformed policeman who was unhurt, put a hand on Boxer's shoulder. "Sir, I'm sorry, but the lady's dead. She took three or four shots in the back when she dove onto you."

Boxer just sat there, back up against the patrol car, head slumped, arm around Anita Ripley's body, which lay across his lap. He didn't respond to the young cop.

A paramedic came over to assist. Together, he and Murphy eased Ripley's body onto a stretcher and into a waiting ambulance. "You, too, sir. Please. We'd like to take you to the hospital to get checked out," Murphy said.

Boxer looked up at them. "I'll be okay. Be careful with her, son."

"Yes, sir," the paramedic replied, and left Boxer with the policeman.

Murphy said, "I'd appreciate it if you'd let me drive you over to Bellevue, and have the docs look you over. You're covered with blood."

"Be all right, son. Listen, can you get a hold of Captain Jefferson, Chinatown precinct?"

Murphy smiled at him. "Tell you what. I'll drive you to the hospital in his precinct and have him meet you there. Deal?"

Boxer was too tired to argue anymore. "Deal."

* * *

By the time Malcolm Jefferson arrived, Boxer was cleaned up and dressed in a green hospital gown, talking on a pay phone. He waved at the police captain, and hung up the phone.

"Thanks for coming. I want to pick your brain for a bit," Boxer said.

"Pick all you want, Boxer. Around these parts, you're a real hero. Officer Murphy over there says you saved his life, and probably some of the wounded. So how can I help you?"

"What was going down at that brownstone, Captain? And who were those two orientals?"

"They were Chinese. But I suspect you already knew that. That's why you wanted to see me, right?"

Boxer sat down on a chair. The captain followed suit, but turned his chair around and rested his arms on the backrest. "Yes," Boxer replied. "That's two shootouts involving Chinese in just a few days. What the hell's going on? Tong war?"

Jefferson scratched his head. "We're just not sure yet. The weapons they used seem to match up with the ballistics reports from the Chinatown massacre. We're going to have to do some more testing to be sure. Incidentally, they both had dragon tattoos on their chests. That would probably make them members of the Dragon Tong. They're trouble."

Boxer asked, "Tell me about this afternoon."

"The officers were responding to a complaint from some of the neighbors, who thought they heard shots fired from an apartment inside. I just learned that they found two men tied and gagged in the first-floor apartment. Each had been shot twice in the head, execution style. There were bags of cocaine on the kitchen table and on one of the dead gunmen."

"Pretty heavy stuff. Well, thanks, Captain Jefferson. And I'm sorry about the dead officers. I lost one of my people in the fighting, too."

Jefferson shook his head. "So I heard. Look, I'm cooperating with you because the PC asked me to, but this is going to cost you, Mr. Boxer. The captain of the precinct wants you to tell him your story. We understand there were some more civilians involved in the shooting, on our side."

"They're weren't your men? I thought they were plainclothes cops."

"Look, Boxer, I don't know who they were, though I suspect you do. What I do know is, for damn sure, they weren't police officers."

Boxer shrugged his shoulders. . . . The best way out of this mess was denial. If you can't prove that something happened, it didn't happen. . . . He said, "Then I suppose it must have been some concerned citizens, coming to the aid of police officers under fire. They acted much the same as I did."

Jefferson shook his head. "You know, I'll buy that maybe once. In your case, okay, I understand you're a former naval officer. You're trained to react to certain situations, and you did. And believe me, we appreciate it. Myself, every cop in the city can appreciate a civilian coming to their aid and maybe saving their lives. But—"

Boxer waved off the praise. "I was just trying to lend a hand. I'm not looking for anything, not even thanks. I'd very much like to shrink into the woodwork on this thing. And apparently, so would the other people who helped. Why don't we just drop the matter, and let the police officers take the credit for the whole affair?"

Jefferson got up from his chair. "I'm afraid it may be too late for anonymity. The press has been all over this thing. Had you been taken to Bellevue Hospital like the rest of the wounded you'd see for yourself. Just turn on the TV. It's a good thing Murphy got you here. At least the two men who know what really went on in the East Village are out of the reach of the media people."

A nurse knocked on the doorjamb of the room Boxer and Jefferson were in. "Excuse me, but are either of you two gentlemen Jack Boxer? There's someone here to see you."

Boxer nodded. He said to Jefferson. "I called for some clothes and a ride just as you

114

got here. That must be them now."

Both men recognized the slim, beautiful woman who stood in the doorway. There was no mistaking Tracey Kimball. She said in a sultry voice, "Hello, Jack. Remember me?"

Before Boxer could answer, Malcolm Jefferson said, "Excuse me," and squeezed past Kimball into the corridor. He didn't even turn around when she taunted him with, "Leaving so soon, Captain Jefferson? I don't bite, you know."

"I guess he knows better, Tracey."

"I see you've been up to your old tricks again."

Boxer smiled, "It's good to see you again, too." He was well aware of the curves that remained hidden beneath the dress she wore. He knew from personal experience. "And I'm not up to anything, Tracey. Just had a little accident."

Tracey Kimball stood there in the doorway, feet apart, hand on hips. "Never shit a shitter, Jack Boxer. I know you're involved in that shooting in the East Village. When all those other reporters chased the ambulances over to Bellevue, I stayed around the neighborhood and asked a lot of questions."

Boxer asked, "But how did you find me here? No one knew I was being brought here."

"Almost no one knew. You'd be surprised, Jack. Everybody wants to tell their story."

"Especially to a nice-looking lady like yourself, right?"

"If you say so. I just asked a policeman where they were taking that young police officer with you. Why wasn't he taken to the same hospital as the rest? And the nice policeman told me that Murphy wasn't hurt, just taking some guy that helped out down to the hospital in Chinatown. I could smell a story there."

"Very nice of him, wasn't it?"

"It didn't take much to find out who was just brought in by Officer Murphy. But I didn't expect to find the precinct commander of the Chinatown station here chit-chatting with my old friend Jack Boxer. And apparently he didn't expect to see me, either. He left like I had the plague or something."

"You tend to bring that out in a man, Tracey."

"Thanks a lot, Jack." She registered mock anger. "Seriously, though, are you hurt badly?"

Boxer shook his head. "No, just some scratches. I was returning to my car after lunch when the shooting broke out. The police using regulation thirty-eights, of course, while the thugs are free to use whatever automatic weapons they choose. The cops didn't stand a chance. I was lucky to duck behind some parked cars and got off with a few bruises."

Tracey Kimball circled around Boxer and sat on the hospital bed. She looked directly at him. "What about the woman you were with, Jack?" She saw the surprised look on his face.

116

"Don't try to deny it, Jack. I told you I did my homework on this one."

"She wasn't that lucky. My secretary got in the way of some bullets that were meant for me. Now she's dead and I'm still alive."

"You'll get over her."

"She was a good woman. The best. She didn't deserve to die."

"So are they all good women, honey. Was she almost as good in bed as me?"

Boxer's face reddened. "She had a hell of a lot more going for her than sex."

"Sex isn't everything with me, you know. I'm a damn good investigative reporter. Which brings up the question, who were those foreign-speaking men you both had lunch with before the shooting?"

Boxer grabbed her by the shoulders and shook her. He stared directly into her eyes. "Drop it, Tracey. Just drop the matter right here. It's way over your head."

"Like hell."

"You're dealing with a very sensitive matter now. Just take your damn Jack Boxer story and do whatever you want with it, but drop it right there."

Tracey challenged him. "Jack, darling, haven't you ever heard of the First Amendment? The public has the right to know what's going on, and I have every right to tell them."

"You're jeopardizing a very sensitive situation."

"Too fucking bad, Jack. I gave you a chance to tell me the truth. Now I'll speculate and print the story the way I see it."

"Ahem."

The voice at the doorway brought the conversation to a halt. Will Pickens was standing there with a fresh suit of clothes for Boxer and a quixotic look on his face. "Ah hope ah'm not disturbin' you two lovebirds. Ah brought you some new clothes, chief."

Boxer took the clothing form Pickens and laid the articles out on the bed. "Thanks, Will. Careful what you say in front of the lady, though. Tracey Kimball here's the enemy. She's a reporter for the *Washington Review*."

"Things have been looking up for me since we were an item, Jack. I'm the New York correspondent for the *Post,* now. No more society columns for me. Thanks to you, I might add. Who's your good-looking friend?" Tracey swished over to Will Pickens and extended a hand. "I'm Tracey Kimball."

Pickens just stood there, arms down at his side. "An' ah'm deaf, dumb, an' blind, ma'am. Pleased to meet ya.' "

Tracey huffed, then broke out laughing. "Okay, you two. Have it your way. And I'll tell it like it is, Tracey Kimball style."

Boxer removed the hospital gown, not bothering to shield himself from Tracey or Will. He put on clean underwear and stepped into a pair of tan khaki pants.

Tracey stared at him intently the entire time. She noticed the bruises on his right thigh and shoulder, and bandages that dotted his back from the neck down to his shorts.

Boxer pulled on a blue oxford shirt and tried to work a red silk tie without the aid of a mirror.

Tracey helped him with the knot. "You men. We can't live with you, and can't live without you."

Pickens interjected, "Ah think y'all got that one backwards."

Boxer put on a navy blue Williams Company blazer and said, "Tell you what, Tracey. I'll be frank with you and answer more of your questions. But some things fall under national security, and you won't be allowed to print them. Believe me when I tell you that. The *Post* is very liberal, but when our Washington people speak to them about this situation, they will not print what we tell them not to."

Tracey thought awhile; then she smiled at him. "Tell you what, darling. How about dinner tonight. Afterward, we'll go to my place for a nightcap, and you can tell me the rest of your story."

"I'd settle for coffee instead of a drink. I want my wits about me when you start your inquisition."

"How about coffee, and. In fact, why don't you bring your nice friend along. We can have a *ménage à trois*."

* * *

Boxer had Officer Murphy drop him off at his office, where he called in a detailed report to Admiral Stark. He expressed his sorrow over the death of his driver, and asked the admiral to arrange for him to speak directly to Kinkaid. A few minutes later, the red phone on Boxer's desk rang. Boxer answered himself.

"Kinkaid here."

"Boxer here. I appreciate your calling. I was—"

"I expect you were calling to apologize. I don't appreciate you or anyone else threatening my agents."

"Hold it, Kinkaid. I'm not apologizing for what I said. That still goes. You were spying on me, and that's not acceptable. But that's not what I wanted to speak to you about. It's Anita. Anita Ripley."

"Damn fine agent, Boxer."

"She was the best. She's dead, you know?"

"Hutchinson gave me a detailed report. I knew shortly after you called your office."

Boxer said, "She deserves a decent funeral, Kinkaid. I just want you to know that I'll pay all the costs involved. She had no family to speak of, and she was very special to me. If you arrange it, I'd be grateful."

"I don't understand you, Boxer. You badmouth me, even though I outrank you. You fire my employees, threaten the agent I assign as your assistant, and now you want to pay for a driver's funeral? I don't get it."

Boxer's voice hardened. "Anita Ripley was a better man than all of you, Kinkaid. Don't ever forget that. For sure, I won't."

Boxer picked up Tracey Kimball promptly at eight at her apartment on East Thirty-second Street and they taxied uptown to a northern Italian restaurant in the upper fifties. They were both ravenous, Boxer went the whole nine yards. They devoured the soup and antipasta, melon wrapped in prosciutto, a fettucini and sausage dish swimming in a cream sauce, a veal dish for him and shrimp for her, and two bottles of wine before settling down to their espresso and Sambucca with flaming coffee beans afloat.

"Got room for dessert?" Boxer asked. "I don't know how you pack in all that food and still keep that fabulous figure of yours."

"How sweet of you to notice, dear. I'll save room for dessert later. I have something special in mind."

Boxer was used to Tracey's sexual inuendoes, but he blushed slightly, nonetheless. As they left the restaurant, they were both pleasantly surprised to see that the doorman had a cab waiting at the curb for them. The man knew how to earn a tip, that's for sure.

Back at Tracey's apartment, she helped him

remove his blazer and hung it in a hall closet. She removed her jacket to reveal a matching strapless red floral silk dress, which hugged her every curve. She caught Boxer staring at her. "Like what you see?"

"Very much. Always have, you know. It was always the burning ambition to tell the story at all costs that I had objected to. It finally drove a wedge between us."

"Jack darling, telling the story, as you put it, is my life. And I'm determined to do it better than anyone else."

Boxer loosened his tie and opened his collar button. "Do you mind? I believe that some stories should be left untold, Tracey."

"The public has the right to know."

"Sure. And if you don't know the facts, just make them up as you go along. Absence of malice, and all that, right?"

"I always try to let the people I interview tell their side of the story. Help me undo this thing, will you?" She struggled with the zipper at the back of her dress. "One more glass of wine and I'd have attacked you under the table right there at Guiseppe's."

"I though you wanted a story."

"Later, darling." She let the dress drop to the floor, and stepped out of it. Very slowly and deliberately, she bent over to retrieve it. "First things first." Tracey moved in close to Boxer and kissed his lips, opening his mouth with her tongue, and giving him a taste of it. Her hands moved to his pants. She opened his belt and unzipped his fly. She slid her hand into his skivvies and came up with his erect penis in her hand.

Boxer let her play. He returned her kiss, and removed his tie and shirt as they stood there.

"Here, let me help," she said as the kiss ended. Tracey slowly slid down his khaki's and helped him step out of them. She wasn't wearing a bra, and she pressed her naked breasts against his chest, letting her nipples get hard and press into him.

Boxer ran his hands down the curve of her back, locked his thumbs on the top of her lacey bikini panties, and slid them over her hips. She finished removing them, all the while never loosening her grip on his ever-growing member. She kissed him again and said, "Why don't you take off your shoes and stay awhile?"

That was easy. Boxer kicked off his Topsiders, and carried her into the bedroom. Tracey had already turned down the covers in anticipation of the night's lovefest. She had known Boxer for a while, and knew he'd never turn her down.

He gently laid her on the bed. She was still holding on, and pulled him on top of her. He moved his head to suck on one of her nipples, and she gave a little push and climbed on top of him. "You just lie back, lover."

A spasm of delight ran up Boxer's shaft as

Tracey worked her magic on it. Her hands never stopped working on it and his scrotum, as she chomped away as if she were eating corn on the cob. As she slid her lips down her length, he arched his back and rose to meet her.

She straddled his chest with her legs, giving Boxer a view of her anatomy clear to China. It was his turn to return the favor. He parted her vaginal lips with his forefinger and drew her closer to his face. He darted his tongue into her, then up and around her clit. He felt her shiver slightly.

She pushed her love box into his face. "I'll tell you when to stop." And she resumed her work on him, moving her bottom in time with her mouth up and down his penis.

Boxer could feel her getting hotter, and as she was ready to come she yelled, "Now, now for God's sake!"

Boxer looked at her like what the hell's she talking about?

At eleven o'clock, Tracey got out of bed and, still naked, walked into the living room and turned on the television. She called in to Boxer, "Come watch the news with me, Jack."

Boxer slipped into his skivvies and padded into the living room to take up a seat next to Tracey.

The lead story, of course, was the shootout on East Seventh Street. Ron Hanley, the Channel Six newscaster, reported that detectives had responded to a suspected shooting, and were slaughtered walking into a drug ripoff double murder. Two uniformed patrolmen were also killed, a third critically wounded. A fourth officer on the scene was spared the same tragic fate as the others when a passerby came to his aid, and helped subdue the killers. The identity of the hero was unknown, as was that of a pedestrian who got killed in the crossfire.

Boxer and Tracey watched video footage of the bloody aftermath of the shooting. An interview with the police commissioner informed the public that the affair was drug related, and that the identities of any civilians involved were unknown at this time.

Boxer was pleased that the PC was covering for them.

Tracey snapped off the television with the remote control device and turned on Boxer. "Now I want to know the entire story, Jack. You can see those bastards are stonewalling it. I want the exclusive interview with the hero, Jack. You owe me at least that for tonight."

Boxer got up from the sofa and went back into the bedroom. He muttered, "Same old Tracey. Sex for stories. And I thought you were just happy to see me. I should have known."

"You wanted it as much as I did. You can't tell me otherwise. And besides, sex aside, you promised me a story this afternoon."

Boxer reentered the living room tucking his shirt into his khaki pants, carrying his shoes in his hand. He sat down and put on his socks and shoes. "Okay, Tracey. I'll give you your story. My secretary and I were returning from lunch when we were caught in the crossfire from that shootout. I was fortunate enough to duck behind a police car and just ran into some flying glass shards. The lady wasn't so lucky. She stopped at least three bullets as she tried to get out of the way. There, that's it."

"That's the same stuff you were peddling this afternoon, Jack. And I don't buy it. I want some names, Jack, besides yours. Who were those men you were with? The rumors have it they were Russian. Are they spies? Are you? Is that why everything is being hushed up?"

"Good-bye, Tracey. Thank you for a lovely evening. But remember, this story doesn't get printed. Your newspaper had already been informed that it will be deemed a breach of national security to print any more than we've already seen tonight."

"Oh, fuck you, Boxer."

"You already have, Tracey."

Chapter Nine

Admiral Fang's aide smiled at Jin Chou and announced, "The admiral will see you now, Comrade Captain. Please follow me."

Chou returned the smile. "It would give me much pleasure, Lieutenant." The young lieutenant was quite beautiful and the gods were smiling down on him today, blessing him with this lovely lady.

Chou felt certain that there must be gods, even though official doctrine demanded atheism. Three thousand years of heritage were hard to dismiss. And at any rate, he felt certain that this beautiful woman before him would be sharing his bed tonight. He noticed the pronounced sway to her hips beneath the loose uniform, and realizing it was for his benefit, he felt good. Yes, this one would give him much pleasure.

Chou snapped to attention before Admiral

Fang, and saluted smartly.

The old admiral smiled slightly and bowed his head,

As the door closed behind him, Captain Chou noticed the chief of Naval Intelligence sitting off to the side in her shapeless Mao jacket. Her severe hairstyle and thick glasses added to her almost masculine appearance.

The admiral said, "You remember Comrade Hsing?"

Chou's dislike for the woman returned at once. "Yes, of course, sir." He didn't give her the courtesy of a greeting.

Fang continued, "You have been briefed on the mission, Captain Chou. I cannot overstate its importance to our nation. Your success will enable us to regain our rightful ascendance to world domination. As our empire was once the most powerful on earth, so shall it be again. We have only to wait until you have destroyed the major naval vessels in so indefensible an arena as the New York Harbor. They shall be the proverbial sitting ducks."

"Thank you for your confidence, Admiral Fang. I assure you I hold the success of my mission dearer to me than life itself."

Hsing interrupted. "Your life is of no concern at all, Comrade Captain. The mission is everything. What is the value of a life, or a thousand lives such as yours, compared to the benefits to the half-billion people that are our great nation. We must be willing to sacrifice everything for the sake of the mission."

Chou's face reddened. "Strong rhetoric from one who guards a desk, Comrade. I am well aware of my responsibilities, and I am resigned to any consequences."

Admiral Fang cleared his throat. "Ah, I had hoped that you two would be more amenable to each other. You see, Captain Chou, Comrade Hsing shall be guarding a desk aboard the *Sea Death*. She is to be your ship's political officer during the mission."

"What? Surely you are making a joke, Comrade Admiral. You are just testing my loyalty to you. I can assure you I—"

The slightly built, elderly Admiral raised his hand. "I am not testing you, Captain Chou. Comrade Hsing is the most qualified agent that the People's Committee has to offer. She is as adept at her position as you are at yours. And she is my personal choice."

"But sir, she is a woman. She—"

Fang stared coldly at Chou. "Why do you burden me with your observation of the obvious, Captain? Her gender will not diminish her effectiveness as a political officer."

"But, Admiral, there are no provisions for a woman aboard the submarine."

Admiral Fang placed both hands facedown on the table as a gesture of finality. "There are provisions aboard for a political officer, captain. And that will be adequate for Comrade Hsing. She has assured me that no adjustments

129

will be necessary. Your objections are invalid and are overruled. The next issue is coordination with our agents already in place in New York City. They—"

"But the men. How will they respond to a woman in so—"

Admiral Fang scowled. "I shall overlook your indiscretion only this once, Captain Chou. The discussion concerning Comrade Hsing is closed." Fang gave this a chance to sink in. "Now, as I was saying, our land-based forces are setting up in the New York Chinatown, with the aid of the Dragon Tong. We have been allies of sorts, for a long while now. We allow them to continue their drug trade between their counterparts in Shanghai and the imperialist racketeers in the United States. In return, they protect our interests from the followers of the bandit Jiang Jiehshi who have emigrated from Taiwan to New York."

"Yes, Admiral." Chou had finally resigned himself to the inevitable. "I have heard of the Dragon Tong."

"Unfortunately, they have suffered some minor setbacks recently. They have been harassed by one of the Taiwanese puppet tongs, and have had to neutralize some of their leaders. And they have had some trouble with the city police force. Comrade Hsing will enumerate on the details for us. Comrade?"

"Thank you, Admiral Fang. As you are aware, the main objective of the land force is to destroy these bridges. . . .

Colonel Pickens knocked on the door that connected his office to Boxer's. Without waiting for a reply, he opened the door and stuck his head in. "Chief, I think you better come on over and see what's on the TV. It sure ain't gonna make ya very happy."

Boxer rose from behind his desk. "I thought we agreed on Jack. Why do you call me Chief, now?"

"We're both military, Captain. It feels disrespectful when I call you by your first name."

"That's okay. I'm trying to keep a low profile. Jack will do nicely, Will. Would you like me to call you Colonel Pickens all day?"

"Okay, I'll call you Jack. You call me Will. Now hows about coming in here and watching what some reporter's been sayin' about you on the TV?"

"What? Jefferson assured me that he'd keep us out of the news. I wonder who's on to us?"

"It's that newspaper lady that came to see you in the hospital yesterday. They're havin' a commercial now, an' then she's coming on with her story. One of the TV people is gonna interview her."

"Tracey Kimball? What the hell's she doing on television?"

"Well, Chief, we're soon gonna find out."

Lorrilard Hutchinson pulled up a chair for

131

Boxer, and the three of them sat there watching the television.

The commercial ended, and an announcer in a gold jacket and glued-down hair faced the viewers. He was seated behind a desk. "This is Ron Hanley, Channel Six News. We interrupt our regular programming with this special newsbreak. We have learned some important facts about yesterday afternoon's violent shootout on Seventh Street in the East Village. We are fortunate to have with us today a newspaper reporter for the *Washington Post,* Miss Tracey Kimball. She will provide us with a shocking report on yesterday's incidents."

The Camera pulled back to reveal Tracey Kimball seated behind the desk next to Hanley. She adjusted the tiny microphone pinned to the lapel of her tan linen jacket. Hanley continued, "All the more shocking due to the efforts by someone in our government to supress the story. Why is a newspaper reporter breaking her story on television, rather than under her byline in the *Post?* Here's Miss Kimball to tell you. Tracey?"

"Thank you, Ron." Tracey found the correct camera and smiled into it. "A funny thing happened when I filed my story with the *Post* this morning. It didn't get printed. Mr. Brandwein, the publisher, was unavailable when I inquired, and no one else could tell me why my story didn't make the late morning edition. And when I realized that none of the local newspapers carried the complete story, I decided to contact Channel Six News. I want to thank Mr. Cohen, the news director, and Mr. Hanley for letting me go on the air with my story."

Ron Hanley spoke to the camera. "Tracey, we've reported that two Chinese men, alleged members of the notorious Dragon Tong, had murdered two drug dealers in their brownstone apartment on Seventh Street. Apparently some neighbors complained to the police that they had heard gunfire. A team of detectives responded, with two uniformed policemen as backups. As Officer Thomas Murphy, the lone surviving policeman from that massacre, reported, the two Chinese men burst out of the building firing automatic weapons. The detectives never stood a chance. In addition, Murphy's partner was critically wounded, and later died. A second police car responding to the call for help was destroyed and the officers aboard killed. Officer Murphy tells us that his life was saved by several civilians who came to his aid and shot one of the killers. Yet no one seems to know the identity of those civilians."

Hanley turned to Tracey Kimball. "Tracey, please tell our viewers what you learned."

"From eyewitnesses that I interviewed, I learned that there were three men and woman involved. Two of the men spoke with heavy accents, according to my sources. The woman was killed. Some say she was just a pedestrian caught in the crossfire. I learned otherwise. She was an employee of the third man, a former naval officer, the captain of the submarine *Sting Ray,* which collided with a pleasure yacht off the coast of Staten Island several years ago. I was aboard the yacht at the time, and I testified at the military trial of the submarine's commander, Captain Jack Boxer. Subsequently, Captain Boxer was removed from his command, and shortly thereafter, he resigned from the Navy under duress. He became the captain of the supertanker *Tecumseh,* owned by the Thomas Williams Company."

Tracey took a sip of water and continued. "I learned in an exclusive interview last night with this same Captain Jack Boxer that it was he who came to the aid of the police officers."

At this, both Hutchinson and Pickins turned to look at Boxer. Boxer's expression was grim. He just shook his head in disbelief.

Tracey Kimball continued, " . . . noble gesture on the part of the good captain. The man's a hero. Here was a chance to undo all the negative publicity of the *Sting Ray* disaster. And Jack Boxer chose to remain anonymous, to the point of getting someone in government to suppress the details of his involvement. We have to ask, why? And ask I did. I asked him what he was trying to hide. Who were the two men who assisted Boxer? Well, this reporter asked that question also. And Boxer's reply to both questions? 'No comment.' We have to ask ourselves . . ."

"Shut that fucking thing off," Boxer snapped.

Hutchinson was taken aback. Will Pickens just smiled and turned off the television. He asked, "That true, Chief? Did she really interview you last night?"

"We spent the evening together, Will. We had dinner together at a restaurant, then went to her place and fucked. If you want to call that an interview, you've got as good an imagination as Tracey."

"She shore hit the nail right on the head, though."

Boxer got up from the sofa. "Miss Kimball is a very perceptive reporter. She surmised that I was involved after questioning that young police officer, Murphy. I answered none of her questions, and walked out on her when she started her inquisition. She just has a clever way of turning things around to make it look like I gave her that information."

Lorrilard Hutchinson spoke up. "Couldn't you do anything to supress that report? If you had informed me of your inability to stifle the lady, I could have gotten Director Kinkaid to do something about it."

Boxer fumed. "You trying to get on my good side, Hutchinson? You heard her say her newspaper wouldn't print the whole story. I didn't anticipate her taking her story on the air. Newspaper reporters don't get along all that well with their TV counterparts."

"My job is not necessarily to get on your good side, as you call it, Captain. Rather, it is to see that the clandestine nature of our work is kept so, and to protect ourselves from sensationalistic disclosures such as we've just witnessed."

"You taking sides against me, Hutchinson?"

"Perhaps if you'd be more open and frank with me, Captain, I could help to protect you from yourself. I think you'll find our interests are the same, sir. And that is the security of every ship in the Discovery Pageant, as well as the security of the harbor . . . in fact, of the entire nation. I'm really quite good at my job, you know. Even if we haven't hit it off well on a personal level."

Boxer felt himself cooling off. What Hutchinson said made sense. When it came to clandestine operations, he was a novice. "Okay, Hutchinson, you win. From now on you're in charge of keeping the public misinformed."

Hutchinson smiled. "Why, thank you, sir. Perhaps we can all work together on this project successfully, after all."

"Perhaps we can." Boxer extended his hand and the two men shook.

"Goes for me too, Hutch. But no more funny business, ya hear?"

Hutchinson shook hands with Pickens. "I'd be pleased to have a congenial working arrangement with both of you gentlemen. However, I do have an obligation to report to Director Kinkaid."

Boxer said, "Okay, Hutchinson. Now that we're all working on this thing together, see what you can do about keeping that report off tonight's six o'clock news."

Igor Borodine paid the check. He and his two companions left the tiny restaurant in Rockefeller Plaza and strolled leisurely through the promenade. He pointed out a shop at the base of one of the huge skyscrapers to his EXO Viktor Korenzo, and KGB chaperone, Vladimir Petrovich. "That is an excellent bookshop, comrades. They have books from all over the world, including the Soviet Union. It's one of the few places in this country where you can get books written in Russian."

The three men spent about fifteen minutes perusing the bookshelves, each finding something of interest to read in their native language. They came up out of the plaza onto Fifth Avenue.

Borodine pointed out St. Patrick's Cathedral, diagonally across the street from where they stood. He remarked on the splendor of the architecture.

Petrovich replied that it represented such a tremendous squandering of money for a church, equaled only by the decadence of the imperialist rulers of their own homeland before the revolution. He said, "Look how the wealthy bourgeoisie waste their money chasing after the latest fashions, thus obsoleting their current wardrobes. And at all the shopping places pandering to their whims." Petrovich's arm swept across the panorama before them. "Look," he continued, "Saks Fifth Avenue. A veritable bastion of decadence. A grand source of . . ."

Borodine's eyes followed Petrovich's outstretched arm as it crossed the entrance of the Saks department store across the street. His gaze was jolted to a halt by a familiar face in the crowd near the entrance. He interrupted Petrovich. "Vladimir, Viktor. Look across the street there. By the entrance to Saks. Do you see that woman in the light blue suit?" He pointed to his target. "There. Over there. With the big red shopping bag. Are my eyes deceiving me?"

Viktor Korenzo replied, "Well, Igor. It looks as if you've found yourself an American version of Galena."

"She is a traitor," Petrovich said.

"She is my ex-wife, comrade. I haven't seen her for almost three years now. I swear, that woman is a remarkable likeness of her. As you say, Viktor, she is an American version of Galena."

The woman must have noticed the three men staring and pointing at her from the Rockefeller Center side of Fifth Avenue. She stood there frozen, staring back at them. Her hands went up to her mouth, and they could almost hear her cry out. She turned toward the store.

"That's no American version, that's Galena herself. She's recognized me." Borodine shouted across the street. "Galena, wait!"

Petrovich barked, "After her, she's getting away."

The three of them ran across Fifth Avenue, dodging cars, and almost getting run down.

Galena ran into Saks and they followed her, Borodine yelling, "Galena, wait," and Petrovich shouting, "Stop, stop that woman."

They caught up to her near the elevator.

Galena grabbed the arm of a businessman standing nearby, and placed herself behind him. "Alan, help me. They're trying to abduct me."

Petrovich made a grab for Galena.

Borodine tried to hold him back.

The businessman pulled a snub-nosed thirty-eight caliber revolver from a hip holster and pointed at Petrovich's face. "Hold it right there." He swung the gun in an arc that included all three of the Russians. "That goes for you too. Put your hands on top of your heads or you're dead men."

The three men stood there, arms at their sides. Slowly, Viktor Korenzo moved his hands up and placed them on his head.

Borodine stated, "I refuse. I am her husband, and I would just like to speak with her."

The man called Alan pointed the revolver at Borodine, then snuck a look behind him at Galena, inquiring with his eyes, is that true?

"I also refuse your foolish request. I am attached to the U.S.S.R. embassy, and I have diplomatic immunity. You cannot arrest me."

Feeling silly, Korenzo moved his hands back to his sides.

Alan moved his gun until it lined up on Petrovich. The Russian glared back at him. "Where is your identification, so I can report you to your superiors."

The American reached into his jacket pocket with his left hand and produced a worn leather wallet. He deftly flipped it open, revealing a photo identification card alongside a shiny gold shield. He said, "Alan J. Parker. And you can report anything you want, Herring Breath. But you make one move toward this lady, I'll put a bullet through you, and sort this all out later."

Petrovich turned his head toward Borodine, then looked at Korenzo. "See how the decadent secret police work in this country. They aid traitors, and threaten to shoot unarmed people who speak differently than they do. And they fail to honor diplomatic immunity. You see how—"

Borodine cut him off. "Wait, Vladimir." He turned his attention toward the woman. "Galena, is that really you? I must speak to you."

She replied, "Go away, Igor. I have no more

140

to say to you. You would not listen to my complaints before I left. Now leave me alone. And take you KGB bullies with you." She turned to her companion. "Alan, darling, please . . . make them go away."

Alan Parker was incredulous. "Is he really your husband?"

"Not anymore. That was in the past. Now I am here . . . and I am with you. And that is how it will remain. I am never going back to him or to that place again."

Parker put his free arm around Galena. "You heard the lady. Now turn around and leave."

The three Russians just held their ground and glared at them. Finally, a uniformed policeman responded to a call about the disturbance and saw the woman with a man with drawn gun pointed at three other men. He called for a backup into his radio, and pulled his service revolver. He included the entire group of them within his firing range and said to Parker, "Let's put the gun away and talk this over."

Alan Parker held up his ID toward the policeman. "Alan J. Parker. These men are trying to abduct this woman, and I came to her aid."

"Just put that gun down and I'll take a look at your ID, pal." The officer turned his revolver on Parker and took the wallet from his hand. "Sorry, Parker, but the CIA has no jurisdiction here. I have to ask you to put that gun away, or face arrest."

Petrovich said to his companions, "See, I tell you, the decadent CIA in this country tries to unjustly and illegally arrest innocent people. This would never be allowed to happen in our country."

The two other Russian men and Galena just looked at him as if he was crazy.

Parker retorted, "You KGBs would arrest your own mother for cutting in on a line to buy toilet paper."

Galena said, "Please, officer. I would just like to be able to continue on my way. My companion and I would like to leave without being followed or bothered by these men."

"That seems fair enough to me," the policeman said. "Anyone want to press any charges? No? Okay, I'll just take everyone's name down for my report, and we'll break up the party. Miss, you go first. I already got Parker here."

While the three Russian men watched, the policeman took down Galena's statistics, and let her and Parker leave the store. Then he slowly and methodically took down pertinent information for his report from the men. It took him at least ten minutes, and when he was finished he said, "Okay, gents, you're free to go. Just leave the lady alone, and you won't hear from me again."

Borodine tugged at Petrovich's sleeve and lead his companions from the store. "Bastard. He let them get away. He knows he can't hold us on anything, with our diplomatic papers."

"Yes. And it's a good thing we carry phony identification. The names he took down are of men long since dead." Petrovich laughed. "See, we put one over on their decadent police and CIA."

Borodine shook his head and started to laugh too. Viktor Korenzo joined in and the three of them walked off together down the street.

Chapter Ten

Twelve-year-old Mei Lung shouted a cheery good-bye to her friend Nancy Shih, and watched her run through Columbus Park to the exit on Bayard Street, where she lived. It was just becoming dark now, at eight-twenty. The eighth grader knew that she would just make it home by her curfew in ten minutes. She walked past the basketball courts and out onto Park Street. She'd take Mott to the corner past the Peking Duck House and the Amusement Arcade, and make a left onto Division Street to get to her family's apartment.

Mei Ling's thoughts were happy, as the child of a wealthy merchant's thoughts should be. Though she lived within the cramped confines of Chinatown, she lacked nothing. Her father's pride and joy, she was going to be the first of the family to become a doctor, and leave the merchant class. She was going home to have a glass of milk and do an hour of homework before bedtime. Study, study, study she was told. It was the way out of the ghetto.

As she left the park, skipping along her route home, she failed to notice that the two young men playing basketball stopped their game and began to discreetly follow her. They kept to the shadows of the tenement buildings, and walked silently.

Mei Ling paused to look into the lighted arcade, and then turned the corner onto Chatham Square, which ran into Division. She thought she heard someone bump into a garbage can and curse softly. She quickened her pace. Farther up the block she chanced a quick look over her shoulder and noticed the two men walking behind her. Were they following her? She crossed the street to the other side.

The two men were talking quietly to each other, and crossed over behind her.

A queasy feeling came over Mei Ling. Were those men really trying to follow her? They wouldn't dare bother her. After all, her father was an important man in Chinatown, an elder of the Hung Yee Tong. She could see by the way most adults in her neighborhood went out of their way to be friendly to her that her father was special. And she felt that his power would always protect her. But those men were closing on her, and she felt some panic setting in.

Mei Ling was ready to run for it when the

men turned into a storefront restaurant, laughing loudly to themselves. Just a couple of men going out to eat. Nothing to worry about. She skipped along Division Street toward home, not a care in the world again. She made the turn onto the street that led to her apartment. It was dimly lit, as there were no shops on this block. Suddenly there was a thunder of feet behind her. She turned around. The two men were almost on her. She tried to scream. The sound hung back in her throat.

A black-clad arm wrapped around her neck. A hand clamped firmly over her mouth, choking back her cries for help. The second man lifted her by her waist and legs, and they ran with her that way onto Division Street.

She could see a black car pull up alongside of them, and she thought for a moment that she would be saved. Perhaps it was someone who knew her father, and would come to her rescue. The car stopped. The passenger door opened and another black-clad man shouted something to her captors in a Chinese dialect that she didn't quite understand. Panic overcame her. She bit hard on the hand across her mouth. As the pressure let up, she screamed.

"Bitch," the man swore in Chinese, and clamped his hand tighter over. face. He almost cut off her breathing entirely. She could barely see several lights coming on in the windows above her as the two men dragged her into the back seat and the black car sped off.

She started to scream.

The one holding her head shoved a rag into her mouth. He slapped her hard across the face and shouted for her to shut up. His dialect was different, but she got the meaning. As the car sped toward the Manhattan Bridge, they managed to tie her arms behind her, and cover her head and face with a ski mask turned backward.

All Mei Ling had left to fight with were her feet, and she lashed out with them at her captors. She caught the man at her feet hard in the face.

He cursed, and wrestled with her legs until she could no longer move them. He threw a leg over hers, locking them between his.

Mei Ling now lay face down over the captor behind the driver, unable to see or scream or use her arms or hands. Her legs were locked in place by the man on the passenger side. The hard slap she felt on her bottom drove home the hopelessness of her plight, and she began to cry quietly. She could feel a man's hand stroking the back of her legs, back and forth, fondling and squeezing the flesh of her thighs, finally coming to rest under her dress on her behind.

The car sped away into the night.

Colonel Will Pickens knocked on Boxer's door and stuck his head inside. "Those

148

Ruskies came back to see ya again, Chief. Guess they're ready to talk things out with you. They're sittin' in the conference room just as quiet as can be."

"Don't let that fool you, Will. A long time ago, their premier, a guy named Khrushchev, sat there in the U.N. General Assembly as meek as your friends inside there are. Then he got his turn to speak and began slamming his shoe on the podium and yelling his fool head off about the decadent Yankee imperialists. That Petrovich is no different. I'll bet you couldn't get a dime out of him for two nickels."

Pickens chuckled. "Suppose you're right, Chief. Oh, by the way, that Borodine feller wants to speak with you in private about something."

"Did he say what about?"

"Says it's personal. Between him and you."

Boxer said, "Okay then, Will. Send in Captain Borodine, will you please. Let's see what's on his mind."

Pickens returned in a moment, followed by Borodine. "Here ya are, Chief. Captain Borodine."

"Thanks, Will. Entertain the others, please. I'll call you in if need be."

After Pickens closed the door behind him, Boxer shook hands with Borodine and asked, "What can I do for you, my friend?"

Borodine looked around the room, straightened his tie, and cleared his throat. He said, "This is a personal matter, Comrade Captain Boxer. Viktor, my EXO, and Petrovich are aware of this, and have interests in the matter other than my own."

Boxer said, "Go on please."

"Well, yesterday, the three of us were strolling near Rockefeller Center. We looked across the street, at the Saks store, and there was my ex-wife, Galena."

"You're sure it was Galena? Not just someone who looked like her?"

Borodine continued. "At first I thought just that. But when she noticed us staring at her, she recognized me and ran into the store."

"I see."

"So I yelled to her, 'Galena, wait.' But she did not. She tried to lose us inside the store. We followed her. Then she found the man waiting for her; he looked like an American businessman, you know, blue suit, attache case. He took out a pistol and pointed it at us."

"A cop," Boxer said. "He was probably a plainclothes policeman, and came to her rescue."

"No plainclothes cop. CIA. He showed his ID, and later real police said to him that CIA had no right to use gun there."

"Well, I assume you didn't get arrested. What happened to you?"

Borodine answered, "Smart-aleck police. He

told them to go away. Then he kept us there too long. Checked our ID. Then let us go. It was too late to catch up with Galena and CIA man. I want to meet with her. Can you arrange it for me?"

Boxer shook his head, letting the story sink in. The more he thought about it, the less he felt he could do about the situation. He said, "Comrade Captain Borodine. It seems that Galena doesn't want to see you. I can't force her to do that, you know. I don't see how I can help you on this."

"My friend, you know that I am honorable man. She was afraid of Petrovich, not me. He yelled at her, called her a traitor. Tried to arrest her and take her back. Of course, she was afraid."

Boxer asked, "What do you think I can do for you? There are over six million people living here in the city. And she may have only been visiting. And do you think she would be still using her real name? I'll bet there's no Galena Borodine in the phone book."

"Her mother's name is Vatovsky. Maybe she uses that one. But the name she used does not matter. You can easily find her."

Boxer raised an eyebrow. "How's that?"

Borodine smiled slightly. "She was with Alan J. Parker. You find him, and you will find Galena."

Boxer nodded his head. "Yes, I suppose I could make some inquiries along those lines, if

I'm discreet. I'd better put Colonel Pickens on it. Almost everyone else here is CIA, and you can be sure that they won't help us find their man."

"Thanks. . . . What happened between Galena and me was very sad. She was my wife for seven years. I was a submarine commander when she agreed to marry me. She knew the type of life we would live together. All of the separations. Plans canceled. Orders to go to Moscow. She lost patience, always complained how she did not have any time with me."

"I hear you loud and clear, my friend. I've had the same problem with my ex-wife, Gwen. They know what they're getting into, but they think they can change the Navy, or the men they marry. All too often, the marriages end in divorce."

"True. Orders are orders, something you and I have to live with. While I was away on mission, Galena went away. She left me alone. Worse than that, she defected to your country."

"That's why she was so afraid of Petrovich. She was afraid of being returned to the Soviet Union. Well, if she has political asylum here, I'm not going to help you send her back."

"I understand. I want only to speak with her. We never had a chance to say good-bye to each other."

"I'll do what I can, Comrade Captain." Boxer was aware that the title pleased Borodine. "Why don't we join your two associates and see if we can't work out a compromise arrangement for a temporary home for your fleet."

The meeting with the Russians went well. Boxer agreed to mooring the Russian delegation fleet off Southampton, with the Soviet bloc nations spreading their fleets out on either side of the Russians. The Soviets, for their part, felt safer with the ocean at their backs, rather than being confined to the Long Island Sound. And Boxer was content that being way out on Long Island, they would not choke off the harbor. It gave him greater leeway in placing the other delegations. Any nation which felt uncomfortable in the shadow of the Great Bear could be moored along the Jersey Coast, from Sandy Hook southward.

At precisely 1745, Lorilard Hutchinson knocked at the door connecting his office to Boxer's. Boxer was tidying up his desk before leaving for the night. He said, "Come on in," expecting Will Pickens to be stopping by before going home. He looked up in surprise at Hutchinson. "Working late tonight?"

Hutchinson was beaming. "There's something on the television that may interest you, Captain. On the six o'clock news. Won't you join us? Pickens and I were just preparing to have a drink."

"Happy hour?" Boxer shrugged his shoulders and locked a small stack of papers in a desk drawer. Grabbing his jacket from behind his chair, he said, "Sure, why not. I've never been known to turn down a drink. Especially if the vodka's cold." Boxer followed Hutchinson into his office. He headed for the small but well-stocked refrigerator that his assistant kept filled with goodies for nights they had to work late.

Hutchinson motioned him to a chair next to Pickens, and brought over an iced bottle of Stolichyna, and a bottle of Chivas Regal, along with an ice bucket and glasses. "I'm a scotch drinker, myself."

Pickens popped the top off of a long-neck bottle of beer. "Mah tastes run to simpler things, boys." He took a long swig of the beer straight from the bottle. "Aaahh. That shore does beat all."

Hutchinson used the remote control to turn on the television to Channel Six. It was just time for the evening news. A voice-over announced, " 'The News at Six on Six,' featuring Ron Hanley." The camera pulled in on Hanley for a close-up. He said into the camera, "Before we get into today's news, the management of this station wants to admit to an error in judgment made on yesterday's six o'clock newscast. In our continuing efforts to bring you all the important news as quickly as possible, our award-winning news team departed from our established policies and allowed a newspaper reporter to air her story on our program. It was an attempt on our part to bring a fast-breaking story to you that we didn't have time to research ourselves. It was a mistake that we will not repeat again.

"Yesterday, in an effort to fully comprehend the details of a police shootout in the East Village, we interviewed Miss Tracey Kimball, a reporter for an important Washington newspaper, who claimed to have inside information. We allowed her to defame the man who was to become the hero of that tragedy, in which five police officers were killed. The man who, police sources say, saved the life of Officer Thomas Murphy, and helped him subdue the gunmen.

"Well, folks, we were barraged with calls. Police Captain Malcolm Jefferson of the Chinatown precinct called to tell us that Captain Jack Boxer was an innocent bystander when the shooting took place. That instead of trying to save himself, Boxer came to the aid of the besieged officers. A Department of the Navy spokeswoman telegrammed a rebuttal to Kimball's charges against Captain Boxer's case involving the *Sting Ray* and the *Maryann*. She labeled his behavior during his tenure with the Navy exemplory. No charges were ever upheld against Boxer, and he resigned under his own free will to take command of the world's largest supertanker, the *Tecumseh*.

"Captain Jack Boxer, if you are listening . . ."

Hutchinson gave Boxer a nudge with his elbow that almost caused the glass of vodka to spill.

". . . sincerest apologies. You are a true hero and deserve our utmost gratitude."

Someone handed Hanley a slip of paper. The reporter sped-read the note, and looked back into the camera. "This just in, ladies and gentlemen. Last night, a twelve-year-old girl disappeared after playing with a classmate in Chinatown's Columbus Park. The family spent a frantic night searching the neighborhood for her, along with a team of policemen. The girl is Mei Ling Chan, an eighth-grader as P.S. 101 in Chinatown. Foul play is suspected by her father, Mr. Ming Chan, a local businessman, and president of the Chinatown Trading Association, a group with strong ties to the government of Taiwan. Mr. Chan explained . . ."

Pickens turned to Boxer. "Awful lot happenin' there in Chinatown, Chief. First that restaurant shootin' where your boys got killed. That drug deal went sour up in the East Village was done by the same guys that shot up the restaurant, most likely. And now this. What the hell's goin' on there, anyways?"

Hutchinson answered, "If I may, gentlemen, I believe there's a major tong war going on. It is well documented that the Dragon Tong, as well as being major drug dealers, are puppets of the PRC, the People's Republic of China.

And the Hung Yees are pro-Taiwan. It makes for an interesting confrontation, if you ask me."

Boxer downed his drink and poured a refill. "Very astute, Hutchinson. And thanks for your help in taking care of that Tracey Kimball business. How'd you do it?"

Hutchinson smiled, and sipped his scotch. "Oh," he said, and blotted his lips with a napkin. "It was nothing. I just pulled a few strings."

They all laughed, and Boxer clicked off the TV.

The New York-Washington shuttle touched down at National Airport at precisely noon. Boxer wore a dark business suit and carried no luggage. His intention was to quickly and inconspicuously pay his final respects to Anita Ripley, make his condolences to any of her family members who attended her funeral, and get right back on an afternoon shuttle to New York. He was vying for a quick turnaround time.

Boxer hailed a green a white cab and told the driver to take him to Arlington National Cemetery. The ride was fast and uneventful, being in between the two rush-hour periods. Soon they were driving past the Jefferson Memorial and over the bridge into Virginia. In five minutes, Boxer was paying the driver, and telling him to wait for him.

The driver, who was quiet and polite up until then, protested that he could take out several fares instead of waiting for Boxer, who, after all, had no idea how long he would be. Boxer had no intention of trying to find a cab after the funeral. He had a better idea. Boxer removed a hundred-dollar bill from his wallet and ripped it in half in front on the startled driver. He handed the man half. "The other half is yours if you're here when I return. And that's just your tip. You'll still get paid for the return fare."

The driver smiled at Boxer. "My mother didn't raise no fools, pal. It's time for my lunch, now, so I'm off duty 'til you get back. I'll be parked right over there under the shade of that tree."

Boxer said, "I sure appreciate it."

"You bet. See you later. Have a nice day."

Boxer walked down a path to the information building and inquired where Ripley's body was being interred. On arriving at the site, he was taken aback by the presence of Director Kinkaid, standing next to a middle-aged couple who were probably Anita's parents, a younger couple, and two very tough-looking men in gray flannel business suits. Boxer figured those two as Kinkaid's bodyguards.

Boxer nodded to the director, then introduced himself to the parents as Anita's associate just as the minister took his place

158

alongside the casket.

The service took about ten minutes, during which time Boxer stood with head bowed, reminiscing on the time he'd spent with her, both good and bad. When he reflected on her sacrificing her life to save his, he had trouble suppressing a tear or two. He wasn't a religious man, and really paid no attention to anything the minister said. But he grieved, really grieved, for Anita Ripley. He would not soon forget her.

As the coffin was lowered into the grave, Boxer said good-bye to her parents, and offered them his business card. He told them if he could ever be of service to them to please contact him. He owed their daughter a debt larger than he could ever repay, and would be happy to help them in any way he could. Then he shook hands with Kinkaid and said good-bye.

As Boxer walked away, the director called after him. "Hold on, Boxer. I want to have a talk with you."

Boxer turned around to face the man. "So talk."

Kinkaid pointed to a small copse of trees a short distance away and said, "Over there."

They walked along a gravel path side by side, followed by the two bodyguards who hung back about fifteen feet. Kinkaid stood with his back against one of the trees, facing Boxer. One of his men stood off to his side, while the other remained behind Boxer.

Kinkaid cleared his throat and proceeded. "I have two points I want to cover with you, Boxer. One concerns that reporter, Tracey Kimball. That bitch could have cost us the security of Project Discovery. You're the top security man on the job and she says she interviewed you and you told her that you were involved in that shooting. Which, by the way, was none of your fucking business. See that you stay the fuck out of things like that that don't concern you or this mission. And to make matters worse, she almost"—Kinkaid paused for emphasis—"almost dragged in the Ruskies into your stupid heroics. That Borodine's as much to blame as you. You two are birds of a feather."

Boxer smiled and said, "Thank you, sir. I take that as a compliment. Borodine's as good an officer as the Russians have."

Kinkaid was furious. "Don't piss me off, Boxer. I don't consider what the two of you did to be in the best interest of our mission. You're acting like fucking amateurs when you should be guarding your countries' Navies. It's a good thing that Hutchinson was around to take care of the problem."

"Yes, that's true. Hutchinson did a commendable job in stopping the publicity. Incidently, he did so at my request. What's your second problem that you want to discuss with me?"

160

Kinkaid pointed to a black stretch limo parked a short distance from where they stood. "Let's talk it over in the car. I'll drive you back to the airport."

"Thanks, anyway, but I have a ride." Now Boxer really hoped that the cab driver's greed was strong enough to keep him waiting for the return ride. "Let's hear what's on your mind."

Kinkaid said, "I'd rather not discuss this with you in a public place, but very well, it's your funeral."

Boxer noticed the two CIA bodyguards squaring off with him, jackets open, arms at sides, feet planted firmly and slightly apart. They were ready for action. "Well?"

"It has come to my attention that you have been making inquiries about one of my operatives."

Boxer raised an eyebrow.

"I'm referring to the man you call Alan J. Parker. The NSC pulled a copy of his file this morning at your request. That's what prompted me to make this call instead of sending a deputy. I knew you were attending the funeral, and figured I could kill two birds with one stone."

That was Kinkaid's second veiled threat against him. At least Boxer knew that Pickens had gotten him the information he had requested.

Kinkaid continued, "I know it has something to do with the woman who used to be married to your comrade Borodine. Is the word *com-*

rade appropriate, Boxer? The woman, Gelana Vatovsky, defected three years ago. She was brought out by Parker. After we debriefed her, we put her to work for us in our identification department. She's very valuable to us, and we intend to keep it that way. Parker is her control. She thinks they love each other, and that's okay with us, as long as Parker doesn't take it seriously. I'm telling you this only because you already know it. And I'll tell you something else, Boxer. You and your Ruskie friend stay the fuck away from that woman, and from Parker, or we'll take care of you, too. You'll have a terrible accident, and after we mourn your demise, we'll get someone else to head up security for this Discovery Day celebration. A CIA man, as it should be. Do I make myself clear, Boxer? If not, these gentlemen will help you see things my way."

At least now Boxer realized the significance of the seemingly well-intentioned ride back to the airport with the director. "Kinkaid, you're a stupid ass." One of the CIA men reached into his jacket toward his shoulder holster. "Your goons better shoot to kill me, Kinkaid, because if they don't, I'll personally take care of you."

Both bodyguards drew their handguns, blued steel automatics from what Boxer could make out at the distance, and held them at their sides. They glanced at their director. Kinkaid shook his head no. Not this time.

Boxer and Kinkaid stood there on the grassy

slopes of the cemetery, sun shining brightly overhead. Was this going to be *Gunfight at the OK Corral,* or *High Noon?* After an eternity, condensed into about two long minutes, Boxer did a smart about-face and walked smartly down the path to where he'd left the green and white cab, his hand casually in his pocket toying with the torn half of his hundred-dollar bill.

Chapter Eleven

The Russian fishing trawler *Gorsky* rolled in the swell off the coast of Sri Lanka, taking the storm in stride, as it was built to do. Captain Dmitri Kubyshev had ordered most of his crew below, leaving only a few unlucky sailors to stand guard on deck. The foul weather would spoil the day's fishing, but that was of little concern to Kubyshev. The real work of his vessel was carried out by technicians rather than fishermen. The *Gorsky* was the Kremlin's state-of-the-art spy ship, carrying millions of dollars' worth of electronic surveillance equipment.

The Communist insurgency in Sri Lanka had gained its greatest advantage in recent weeks. The rebels had moved down from their mountain strongholds and fought their way to within a few miles of the capital, Colombo. It was Kubyshev's job to monitor the rebel activities, and see that the rebels were provided with any intelligence or armament aid they needed. But tonight all was quiet.

With most of the crew bedded down, Kubyshev was besting his EXO at a game of chess in the captain's quarters. He said, "You see, Nikolai, you are not quite ready to unseat the old master himself. Maybe you are ready to command this ship, my friend, but at chess you still have a lot to learn." Kubyshev moved his black knight and announced with glee, "Checkmate. Better luck tomorrow night."

As Kubyshev placed the shiny teakwood pieces back into a fitted teak box, he was summoned by his intercom. It was his sonar officer. "Comrade Captain, I believe we have a submarine on the sonar."

"You believe? Don't you know a submarine when it appears?"

"*Da,* Captain. But here? We have no subs in these waters."

Kubyshev growled at his SO, "But surely the Americans are capable of putting a submarine in these parts, no? Think Mikhail. The American Seventh Fleet is deployed off the coast of Oman. Don't you think that one of their subs could find its way to us? Damn. I'll be right there." And to his EXO, he said, "Come, Nikolai. Let us see about this submarine."

Aboard the sub, Captain Jin Chou was monitoring the *Gorsky* on his version of the underwater image screen. Suddenly he heard

166

the pinging that meant his ship had been picked up by the trawler's sonar. He turned his head toward the political officer and said, "Comrade Hsing, the Russian trawler has us on his sonar. It may be necessary to destroy it."

Hsing replied, "You are very quick to destroy, Captain. You should be as quick to think of another solution."

Chou's face started to redden. "If the Russians ID this submarine, Comrade, the outcome of our mission may be in doubt. It was you, personally, who said that the mission takes precedence over everything."

Hsing pushed her thick glasses up higher on her nose. "We have been at sea less than one week, Captain Chou, and already you have created an excuse to destroy an enemy ship. And if you really had the success of our mission foremost in your heart and in your mind we would be far from here, on our way to the decadent Yankee city of New York. Instead, you choose to foolishly engage a Russian trawler off the coast of India just to satisfy your lust for mayhem and destruction. I order you to proceed to New York Harbor at once, and break off this game of yours."

The sonar pinging became louder. Chou ignored his political officer and keyed his SO. "Give me a reading on the trawler."

His SO replied, "Target bearing two hundred seventy degrees . . . range ten thousand yards

167

. . . speed ten knots and closing."

Chou turned to Hsing, "You see, comrade. The Russian trawler is going to hunt for us. Shall I test our endurance against a depth charging? Or shall I sink the bastard."

Hsing gestured at him with a balled fist. "Don't play me for a fool, Captain. Even though I am not a sailor, I know the flank speed of the *Sea Death* is forty knots, more than sufficient to outrun that clumsy trawler. Once again, Captain, I order you to leave this area immediately, and proceed to our assigned destination."

Chou slammed his fist on the computer table and shouted, "Woman, you do not give orders on this ship. I am the captain, and if I say we destroy that enemy trawler intent on sinking us, we will. It was my judgment to track that ship when we picked it up off of Singapore. It became an excellent training exercise for my crew, and an excellent means of assessing the systems unique to this submarine. And now that the enemy is intent on identifying and destroying us, it is my judgment to destroy it." He keyed his sonar officer again. "SO?"

"Target bearing two eight zero degrees, Comrade Captain. Range nine thousand yards . . . speed twelve knots and still closing."

Captain Chou turned back to the political officer. "Comrade Hsing, I suggest that you go to your quarters and leave the fighting to me

168

and my men."

Hsing was livid. She shouted, "You fool. I demand you stop this nonsense at once. I shall report you to Comrade Chen immediately."

Chou smiled at her, then turned to his command console. He keyed his torpedo firing officer. "Arm forward torpedoes, and prepare to fire."

The TO replied, "Yes, Comrade Captain. Forward torpedoes ready to fire at your command."

Satisfied, Chou turned back to Hsing. "Comrade Hsing. The ship's radio is off limits to you until I decide that we are no longer in danger of being tracked by our enemies. And I'd tell you what you can do with Comrade Chen; however, I fear that he would first need to have a grudge against his private parts to accommodate you. Now go to your quarters, or I'll have you escorted there." He turned his back on her and signaled his sonar officer again. "SO, give me a reading on our target."

"Target bearing two eight zero degrees," the SO replied. "Range five thousand yards . . . speed one five knots and closing, Captain."

"Excellent. We shall teach the foolish Russians a thing or two." He keyed his torpedo firing officer. "Set the torpedoes on automatic."

"Yes, Captain, on automatic."

Chou ordered, "Fire one and four."

"Yes sir, Comrade Captain."

Chou watched the progress of the two torpedoes on his sonar screen, while counting down ten seconds on his NAVCLOCK. "Fire two and three."

The FO replied, "Two and three gone."

The first two torpedoes tore a gaping hole in the *Gorsky* and it started to break apart. Number three hit just below the engine room, and the ship exploded. The raging fire, the storm-tossed sea, and the circling sharks soon took their toll. The *Gorsky* sank. There were no survivors.

Boxer arrived back at La Guardia at 0430. It took the cabbie almost an hour to fight his way through the rush-hour traffic to Water Street. Boxer tipped him an extra ten dollars for his trouble, and headed up the elevator to his office. It was nice to have a generous expense account. He could get used to that.

He no sooner got settled behind his desk and began shuffling through the day's messages when Colonel Pickens knocked and stuck his head inside the office. "Welcome back, Chief. I see you got your mail."

"Thanks, Will. Yes, I was just starting to go through it. It's going to be a long day."

Pickens smiled. "Might be gettin' a might longer'n you think. A hellcat name of Tracey Kimball's been after your ass all day. She calls askin' for you every hour or so."

My ass isn't all she's probably after, Boxer reflected. There were other parts of his anatomy that she preferred even more. Well, sooner or later he'd have to deal with Tracey. He'd felt badly about humiliating her on television, but in this case, she'd gotten what she deserved. Boxer nodded. "Put her through if she calls again."

"Sure thing, Chief. Just be careful the phone don't get too hot to hold. You shoulda heard some of the language she used. Back home we're not used to that kind a talk from a woman."

Boxer laughed. "Yeah, Tracey's different from most women I've met, too, Will. She's as aggressive as anyone I've ever dealt with if you get between her and a story. It's an obsession with her. She thinks you're on to something and it's trial by Tracey Kimball . . . judge, jury, and jailor all rolled into one. Doesn't matter to her that national security's involved. Doesn't matter to her if she ruins my career, or whom else she hurts. Just as long as she gets her story. Other people are just stepping-stones on the path to her success."

"Not mah kind of woman, for sure."

"Well, I wouldn't want to marry her, Will. Or even live with her. But I do love her and she loves me. And it's freely given and freely taken. No strings attached on either side. She's—"

The phone rang, and Pickens got up to

answer it. "Hang on just a second, Chief. I'll get it." After a few words into the phone, Will held it away from his ear and covered the mouthpiece. "Speakin' of you know who, it's her."

Boxer shook his head. "Okay, Will. I'll take it at my desk."

"Well, I'll leave you alone to your misery. You know where to find me if you need me." He went back into the inner office.

Boxer picked up the phone. "Boxer here."

Tracey Kimball started shouting immediately. Boxer had to hold the phone away from his ear. "You rotten son-of-a-bitch. You fucking ingrate. How dare you humiliate me like that in view of millions of my readers. I don't know how you did it, but you got my report pulled off the air, and a public apology given for it. You can't do that. Haven't you ever heard of freedom of the press?"

"You done yet?"

Tracey screamed, "You bastard. No. I'm far from done with you. You killed my story in the *Post,* too. The publisher won't even speak to me about it. He says I owe you an apology."

Boxer smiled. "I accept."

"Fuck you, Jack Boxer."

Boxer couldn't keep himself from laughing. "Why thank you, Tracey. That would very nice of you."

Tracey Kimball was steaming. "Don't try to change the subject on me, Jack. I'm furious

172

with you. You set my career back years by what you did."

Boxer just shook his head. "Tracey, did it ever occur to you that you almost single-handedly caused my resignation from the Navy with the way you reported on the collision of the *Shark* and the *Mary Ann*? To say nothing of the personal problems it caused me and my family? Personally, I think you got what you deserved this time. You tried to undo the work I'm doing, even though I told you it involved the security of the country. You just want to further your career no matter who gets hurts."

"Bullshit, Jack. You know, freedom of the press is one of our most basic rights. You and people like you think you can cite national security and run roughshod over the media. And I don't like it."

Boxer had had enough. He said, "Look, Tracey, what are we arguing about this for? It's late. I've got a pile of work left undone. Why don't you join me for a drink and we'll work out a truce between us."

"Damn you, Jack. Well, okay, what the hell. I haven't eaten dinner yet either. Tell you what. I have an apartment in the Village. Why don't you meet me for a light bite at Guido's on Seventh? Do you know where it is? They have the most wonderful mussels marinara. Then we can have drinks and whatever."

Boxer hadn't eaten since breakfast. The no-frills shuttle flights provided him with a small pack of smoked almonds and a mini bottle of cheap vodka, which he'd drunk over ice. The thought of dinner with Tracey Kimball whet his several appetites. "Sounds good to me, Tracey. I'll met you at Guido's in an hour."

Boxer watched Tracey sop up the last of the garlicky tomato sauce with a hunk of Italian bread, while he toyed with his last piece of fried calamari tenacles. He emptied the bottle of Valpolicella into their glasses. He was glad to see her fury subside under the influence of the good food and wine. They topped off their meal with espresso and Sambucca. Boxer sat back in his chair contentedly and asked Tracey if she wanted anything else.

"Yes, as a matter of fact. I want to go to bed with you."

Boxer's face reddened. He sat up, blotted his lips with a linen napkin, and summoned the waiter for the check. "Well," he said, "what are we waiting around here for?"

As they rode the elevator up to Tracey's apartment together, Boxer was able to really appreciate how appetizing she looked. She wore an off-the-shoulder white matte jersey dress that clung to her every curve and crevice. And he knew her well enough to realize that she wore little or no underwear.

Tracey clung to him in the elevator and for the short walk down the hallway to her apart-

174

ment. She handed him her keys. Boxer opened the door and held it open for her, then followed her inside. He had barely locked the door behind him when she threw herself on him, embracing and kissing him passionately. Her tongue darted into his mouth and her hands were all over his body, her beautifully manicured fingers undoing his buttons and zippers.

Boxer got a kick out of her intense passion for him. . . . A scant few hours previously she was ready to cut his balls off for crossing her. A strange woman. But sex with her was usually good and worth her occasional outbursts. . . .

Tracey soon had his pants opened and slipped them down to his knees. Boxer stepped out of them and kicked them away while she stroked his penis back to life. She took it in her mouth, stroked her tongue over it several times, and sucked on it till it became turgid. Boxer placed a hand on her head and closed his eyes, allowing the good feelings to overcome him.

Tracey pulled her head away and said. "I didn't tell you that I couldn't wait to do this to you, did I?"

Boxer smiled at her and shook his head.

She went back to sucking his penis, and cupped his scrotum, stroking and squeezing it in rhythm with her lips, tongue, and cheeks.

Boxer held her head in his hands and syncronized his pelvic thrusts with movements, heightening the pleasure for both of them. He watched her slip a hand up between her thighs and play with herself as she worked him over.

Tracey stood up and pulled the slinky dress up over her hips, revealing the tiniest white lace bikini panty, as Boxer had suspected. She pulled it down her legs and kicked it aside. Bending over, she took his hand and placed it on her crotch, saying, "Play with me while I do you." Then she turned her attention back to his penis and continued sucking.

Boxer could tell she was in one of her kinky moods, and was reluctant to play her sex games. He said, "C'mon, Tracey. Lets get undressed and into bed. Then we can do each other."

She pulled away and looked up at him, annoyed. "Later, darling. Right now it's ladies choice, so please, finger me so I can come along with you. I don't want to have to do it myself."

Tracey went back to sucking on him with a vengeance. Finally Boxer got caught up in the wonderful sensations she was causing him and played his fingers skillfully between her thighs. He worked his thumb in her hole, and his fingers on her labia and round her clit till she began to squirm and undulate, really caught up in the rhythm of it all.

Finally, she worked her tongue and cheeks rapidly and forcefully up and down the length of his shaft. She placed a hand on his, helping him to keep time with her mouth on him. Tracey began to moan between strokes until, building to a crescendo, she brought them both off with a wild orgasm that left them spent.

"That was so good."

Boxer said, "You were pretty great yourself. You did all the work and give me the credit. How about letting me get out of the rest of my clothes and returning the compliment?" He was standing there in his shirt, tie, and jacket, naked from the waist down except for his socks.

Tracey laughed. "I'll admit, you do look rather silly standing there like that. Believe me, I'll give you plenty of opportunity to do me, Jack Boxer. That just took the edge off my horniness." She pointed to a chrome and glass bar along one wall of her beautifully furnished living room. "Why don't you get comfortable, and make me a gin and tonic, and a drink for yourself? I want to slip into something provocative."

Boxer undid his tie and began unbuttoning his shirt. "Anything more stunning than what you started off wearing and I won't last very long."

"I'll be right back. There's ice in the freezer."

Boxer spend the next five minutes mixing two Tanquery gin and tonics, and drank his half down before Tracey returned to the room.

She came out wearing a black garter belt holding up black silk stockings. Black stiletto-heeled shoes completed her outfit. She carried a leather paddle in one hand and a twelve-inch ribbed vibrator in the other. Boxer put down his drink.

Tracey posed for him there, hip sprung, firm breasts thrusting upward. "You like?"

"I like the woman I see a lot, Tracey. But not the outfit, or what you're up to. You know I don't like to play games."

She pouted. "Oh, c'mon, Jack. Don't be a party pooper. You wanted a chance to repay me. Come into the bedroom with me. Bring my drink with you." Then she turned and walked into an adjacent bedroom.

Boxer picked up the two drinks and reluctantly followed her inside. He took another swallow of his, and put both glasses on her dresser. "Look, Tracey, you're a beautiful woman, and you give me a great deal of pleasure. And I'd like to do the same for you. Why don't we settle in for a nice long hard fuck?"

"Don't be so old-fashioned, Jack," she said, turning away and studying the mattress, as if in anticipation. "Let yourself loose, for once, I got you off, didn't I? Now I want you to do me my way."

There was no reply.

"Jack?"

Still nothing.

178

Tracey turned around, then realized she was in the room alone. She began to scream. "Jack Boxer, you son of a bitch, where the hell are you? Jack?" she screeched. When he didn't reply, she ran into the living room.

Boxer was fully clothed, and was putting on his shoe. She said, "That's the thanks I get. You men are all alike. Get your rocks off and off you go. Forget about little old Tracey. She can do it herself, if she wants. You bastard."

Boxer put on and tied his other shoe and stood up. He looked at her sadly, and shook his head.

"We're not done yet."

"I'm sorry, Tracey."

Tracey became livid. She shouted at him, "You faggot. Wimp. All you know is slam, bam, thank you ma'am, and away you go. Your imagination goes as far as the missionary position, and that's all. You're just an old man, Jack Boxer. It's all you can do to get it up anymore."

Boxer tightened his tie and buttoned his jacket before running to the door. "I'm really sorry about this, Tracey. I had hoped we could have turned a new leaf together. I was wrong. Good-bye, Tracey." He opened the door and was halfway into the hall when he heard a glass object smash and shatter against the wall a few feet from where he was standing. He closed the door and walked away without looking back.

Chapter Twelve

Boxer slept fretfully. At first light, he rose, had a steamy shower followed by an icy cold one to charge up his circulation, and dressed quickly. He summoned a vehicle and driver from the motor pool and headed for the office in the city. The driver was a female j.g. lieutenant who slightly resembled Anita Ripley, and this added further to his melancholy.

He was at his desk by 0700, trying to diminish the pile of paperwork that confronted him. It was just over three weeks until the Discovery Day celebration, and he was responsible for orchestrating the safe and orderly dispersement of a large portion of the world's naval armament along three hundred miles of oceanfront and the Sound. Once in place, he had to coordinate the safeguard efforts of the Coast Guard and the Navy, at sea, and the land-based government security and local police forces in New York and the surrounding areas. Next week, the fleets start moving in. This week he had to deal with their envoys.

At 0800, Colonel Will Pickens knocked on his door and entered the office. "Mornin', Chief. Ah thought ah'd like to go over the agenda with ya. Hutch is havin' coffee sent up. He'll be right with us."

"Morning, Will. I've been working on the fleet deployment this morning. It looks like the Soviets and their allies along the oceanfront of Long Island. The more moderate nations can moor along the western end closer to Manhattan. We'll use Sandy Hook for the Tall Sailing Ships. They won't cause anyone trouble."

"Ah like that. An' we can put the NATO's off the Jersey shore. Ah figure the Brits and French below the Tall Ships. That'd give us some extra protection close to the harbor in case we need it."

"Good, Will. My thoughts exactly. The smaller contingencies can use the Long Island Sound, with the neutral nations closest to the harbor. Ah, Here's Hutchinson with breakfast."

"Morning, gentlemen. Breakfast is served." He turned his attention to a young woman in a form-fitting floral print dress carrying a metal tray with coffee service and Danish pastries. "Just place it on the desk, please, Cindy. We'll help ourselves."

Cindy was quite pretty and well built, and

Boxer and Pickens gave a quick nod of approval to each other. When she left them, they sipped their coffee while Boxer briefed Hutchinson on what they'd already discussed.

Hutchinson took a bite out of a prune Danish, washed it down with a swallow of his coffee, and blotted his lips on a napkin. "Excellent plan. Let's see, on the agenda this morning, we have the Soviet bloc nations."

"Right," Pickens interjected. "We've got the Ruskies comin' in this morning and some of their Commie stooges from Eastern Europe."

Boxer laughed. "I think we're supposed to refer to them as their allies."

Will said, "Call 'em whatever you want. It's all the same to me. We're gettin' the Poles and East Germans. And then there's the Yugos, Bulgarians, and Romanians."

Boxer said, "Right. I'll propose putting the Russians off of Westhampton, and the others up and down the coast on either side. The Germans up toward Montauk, and Poland further east along Fire Island."

Hutchinson replied, "I'm not as well versed as you are when it comes to naval operations, of course. But it seems like a good idea from a security viewpoint."

Will Pickens piped, "From a real estate viewpoint, you're sure goin' to ruin the neighborhood with all those Commies off the coast." They all had a good laugh at that.

Hutchinson opened a red folder and removed the top page. "We have the Soviets coming in at 0900. The conference room is all set up for them. Captain Borodine and his EXO will be here along with that odious bastard Petrovich." Hutchinson wrinkled his nose. "And their allies, of course."

Promptly at 9 a.m. the Soviet Bloc representatives paraded into the long carpeted conference room. Besides the Russians, there were Bulgarian Captain Gregori Varna, Armand T. Brasov of Romania, Commander Hans Becker of the German Democratic Republic, and Josip Broz of Yugoslavia, who was addressed as Mr. rather than a military rank. And there was the representative of Poland, an octogenarian with a flowing mane of white hair and a large white handlebar moustache, which matched his all-white uniform decorated with a double row of bronze bullons down the front and a chest full of medals dating back to World War II. He was introduced as Admiral Casimir N. Tuchoserein, a war hero who had helped the Russians recapture Gdansk from Hitler's forces. All the delegates except the Soviets seemed to defer to him.

Coffee and tea were served, and detailed maps and nautical charts were placed in front of each man along with an agenda of the festivities. Boxer, Hutchinson, and Pickens shook hands with each delegate as they were introduced, and Boxer addressed the group. "We have gathered here this morning representatives of some of the greatest navies in the world. It is heartening to note that as we naval officers are able to meet here in peace to discuss a joint operation celebrating the discovery of the Western Hemisphere by a pioneer from your half of the world, so may our nations work together to live in peace. Gentlemen, I salute you."

The military men returned Boxer's snappy salute. Vladimir Petrovich, the Russian KGB agent, rose from his chair. Abruptly, he slammed his beefy fist on the conference table. Cups and saucers jumped and spilled some of their contents. Petrovich scowled. "How dare you talk of peace while your decadent government wages an act of war on an innocent Soviet trawler fishing off the coast of India."

Boxer was taken aback. Apparently, so were most of the others, as Boxer watched them register surprise at the outburst. He said, "We know nothing about that incident. I'm sure that our country had nothing to do with that trawler." Boxer looked directly at each man seated across from him, one at a time. Then he glanced at Hutchinson, and nodded. Hutchinson quickly got up and left the room.

"Lies," shouted Petrovich. "You Yankee Imperialists are trying to destroy our peace initiative. First, you accuse us of sinking your warship in the Sea of Japan, and then you destroy a nonmilitant Soviet fishing trawler. Your government reeks of treachery and deceit. You have a very short memory of Pearl Harbor."

Hutchinson hurried back into the room carrying a sheaf of computer printout paper. He placed it in front of Boxer and took his seat. Boxer scanned the report while Petrovich continued his ravings.

"We shall not be a part of your celebration while you systematically destroy our shipping and undermine our peace overtures. Comrades, let us leave in protest."

Boxer stood up and glared at Petrovich. "Hold on, Comrade Petrovich. We had nothing to do with any sinkings off of India. I have a listing of our Seventh Fleet positions here, and no warship was near your trawler. But I think you already know that, don't you?"

The Eastern European delegates looked at Boxer and sat back down in their seats.

Borodine smiled as Boxer continued. "It's just like you political types to undermine the peace initiatives designed by men of goodwill. You're way out of line, Comrade Petrovich. You have no proof of how your ship was sunk, so naturally, you dump it on the U.S.A." Boxer turned to the other delegates. "Gentlemen . . . I give you my word that the United States had nothing to do with that trawler being destroyed. Comrade Borodine, you remember last week when I accused your government of doing the same thing?"

"Yes, Captain. And I gave you my word we

were not responsible. And you accepted it. You knew I would not lie to you. And, therefore, I accept your denial of American involvement." To his allies he said, "Comrades, Comrade Captain Boxer does not lie. I accept his explanation."

Petrovich growled, "He may not knowingly lie, though I doubt it. But he may not be informed by his corrupt CIA. He may—"

Borodine looked directly at Petrovich. "Sit down, Vladimir," he said very forcefully. Then he softened his voice somewhat. "Please, Comrade. Let us not destroy the progress we have made so far. Are you absolutely certain that an American ship destroyed ours?"

"The *Gorsky,* just before it was blown out of the water, reported sighting a giant submarine, at least three hundred and fifty feet long. As you know, Igor, your Q-class subs fit the description. But, of course, you would not fire on Soviet shipping. And that leaves the Americans. Captain Boxer commands a submarine of that type."

Boxer jutted out his bearded chin defiantly at Petrovich. "Yes. That is true. And if called upon by my superiors, that kill would have been mine. But I am here, and my ship is nearby as part of the security detail. And I will tell you, gentlemen"—Boxer turned to the other men present—"even though it may compromise the secrecy of our Seventh Fleet's operations in the Persian Gulf area, I can tell you with assurance that there are no submarines such as my *Shark* present in the area where your trawler went down."

Borodine rubbed his beard and addressed Boxer. "Comrade Captain," he began. This raised some eyebrows among his allies, and especially Petrovich. "If our submarines did not destroy your ship in the Sea of Japan, and your subs did not sink our trawler, then which nation is capable of doing this?"

Boxer thought for a moment, then looked over the faces of the men assembled there. "The Chinese?"

The old admiral nodded, followed by some of the others. Borodine nodded his head. "Yes, my friend. I think you may be correct. The Chinese."

Petrovich scoffed, "You must be mistaken. Our intelligence shows that the Chinese are years behind our technology in shipbuilding, specifically submarines."

"That's been the concensus by our people, too. But I suspect otherwise, gentlemen. A nation capable of building the Great Wall against all odds has to be capable of building a super sub. And there have been some strange goings-on here in New York's Chinatown. Some of my people have been killed, and Comrade Captain Borodine had to come to my rescue.

Aside from Petrovich and Viktor Korenso, the EXO, no one else in the Soviet Bloc delegation had been aware of Borodine's heroics. They looked at him in amazement, while he tried to suppress a satisfied smile. "There may be something to the Chinese angle."

Hutchinson cleared his throat. "We're running late, gentlemen. Please let us resume the planning of the fleet deployment. You all have a printout in front of you. I've taken the liberty to have them translated into your respective languages, though I gather you all speak a little English. Captain Boxer will fill you in."

Boxer spent the next hour detailing the positions of the Soviet Bloc fleets, along with plans to feed the sailors, and to provide guided sightseeing tours for any of them who were allowed ashore by their commanders. At Borodine's suggestion, their group would be self-policing, with Borodine in charge of their security. Boxer would see to it that the Coast Guard kept nosey Americans at a safe distance while the Soviets patrolled the area seaward in small craft beyond the three-mile limit. Then Borodine proposed, in a gesture of goodwill, a limited access tour of a destroyer or cruiser to the American public. This would satisfy the curiosity of the public and the press, and hopefully keep them away from the rest of the ships.

As the meeting was about to break up, Hutchinson spoke into an intercom, and Cindy arrived with a tray containing an iced liter bottle of good Polish vodka, in honor of the admiral, and eight frost-covered glasses. Boxer stood up and asked, "It's almost noon, gentlemen. Anyone here opposed to some vodka to toast our achievements?" Everyone smiled and shook their heads. "Good. Admiral, I hope you approve of my choice of vodka." The old warrior beamed his admiration.

They waited while Cindy poured the vodka into each glass, left the bottle uncovered on the tray, and exited the room.

More than one head turned in her direction as she swished out of sight.

Boxer raised his glass. "Gentlemen, in the spirit of the cooperation that we have all shared in this morning, I propose that we use this opportunity to sew the seeds of peace among our nations, and all the nations of the world. With such esteemed officers and gentlemen as yourselves leading the initiative, I think this is possible. To peace."

Eight glasses clinked together, and each man drained his glass. "Don't be bashful, men. There's plenty to go around." Will Pickens refilled his glass and passed the bottle to the admiral. When they all had their second glass filled, they toasted each other and drank again. A good feeling of camaraderie pervaded the room, and the conversations soon broke down to small talk. Hutchinson announced that lunch was being served. The delegates were pleased to see trays of *blini* heaped with sour cream being carried into the room, as well as Russian caviar and other accompaniments. A fresh bottle of vodka and more iced glasses were brought in as well. The mood soon became jovial.

As the others milled around the offerings, Boxer took Borodine by the arm and walked him into his office. He addressed his Russian counterpart. "I'm sorry, but you're going to miss out on the *blini,* my friend. We have more pressing business to attend to now."

Borodine looked puzzled.

"I have located Galena. She is working for the CIA in their Information Bureau in this city. It's on Fifty-seventh near Madison. Not far from where you first saw her the other day at Saks. Would you like to see her this afternoon?"

Borodine was speechless. Boxer clapped him on the shoulder. "She sometimes walks the few blocks to the Russian Tea Room for lunch. If we hurry, we might catch up to her."

As it turned out, the ride uptown took almost an hour. They spotted Galena and the CIA man, Parker, as they leisurely strolled arm in arm along Fifty-seventh, crossed over Fifth, and window-shopped Bonwit Teller.

Galena gestured animatedly at a provocative dress in the window. Parker nodded his approval and she giggled. She hugged the CIA agent and they walked past the Trump Tower. She motioned with her head toward the lobby, and they walked inside.

Boxer and Borodine caught up with them inside.

Galena was admiring a jade and gold necklace in a display window set along the right-hand lobby wall adjacent to a jewelry boutique.

Borodine stood about five feet behind them, with Boxer just behind and to the right. Borodine fought back the lump in his throat and the queasiness in his stomach. He coughed and cleared his throat. Hesitantly, he called her name. "Galena?"

The woman turned and spotted him standing there watching her. Her hands went up to her face and she backed into Parker's arms. "You again?"

"Me."

"I told you to leave me alone."

"I just want to speak to you for a few moments. Then I will walk out of your life for good."

"I have nothing to say to you." Galena pointed to Boxer. "They have come to take me back. Or kill me." She turned her head to the CIA man. "Alan, darling. Make them go away."

Borodine shook his head. He replied in Russian, "He is not one of them. He is an American friend who helped me find you. Look, Galena, I am not here to harm you. I will not try to take you back. It is all over between us.

You see, I have already divorced you. You are no longer my wife. I have no hold on you."

Galena answered him in Russian. "What do you want from me?"

"I want answers to a few questions. My career, or possibly my life may be in danger when I return home. There are some things I must know."

Alan J. Parker became perturbed when they started speaking in Russian. He stepped from behind Galena and said, "Beat it, you two. You heard the lady. She doesn't want you bothering her. Now get lost."

Boxer nodded his head at the couple. "Does that look like she doesn't want to speak to him? C'mon, let's take a walk for a few minutes. Then we'll be on our way."

Parker glanced at Galena, who nodded her approval. Boxer and Parker walked just out of earshot. Parker said, "You know, wise ass, I'm gonna find out who you are, and I'm going to have your hide on a platter."

"Captain Jack Boxer, U.S. Navy. Your boss knows who I am."

Parker looked at him perplexed. "Simmons? You know Tom Simmons?"

"Higher up than him, Alan J. Parker, or whatever your real name is. Kinkaid knows who I am and where to find me." Boxer paused, then motioned with his head toward Borodine and Galena. "Look, that man was married to her. Now they're divorced, so you're free to marry her if you want. He just wants to make sure she didn't compromise his position with his superiors at home. Then we'll walk away for good."

Parker said, "Marry her? You out of your fuckin' mind? Fuck the shit out of her, maybe. But marry her? No way, man. I'm her control. She depends on me for everything. I'm her protector, her confidant, her lover, and she does what I tell her. Yeah, she's in love with me, I guess. But to me, it's just sex, and plenty of it."

That callous remark was the final straw. He wheeled around, brought his fist up from his hip with the full force of his body behind it, and smashed it into Parker's face. The dull thud of fist hitting flesh was immediately followed by the sound of bone crunching. Blood spurted from Parker's splayed nose as he fell backward. He never knew what hit him, and he was out cold as his body crashed against the cold black marble floor.

Borodine turned at the sound of the body hitting the floor. He rushed over to Boxer's side. "What is it, my friend? Did he attack you?"

"No. It was just something he said. How are you doing?"

Borodine shrugged his shoulders. "Galena explained why she defected. I cannot forgive her, but I understand that she could never live any longer as the wife of a submariner, especially in Vladivostok. She swears she did not betray any confidences between us to the CIA. I guess I believe her. I will say good-bye to her now."

Boxer watched Borodine approach Galena. They held each other's hands, and carried on a brief but excited conversation in Russian. Then they moved toward each other, and kissed briefly on the lips. Nothing sexual. Just a farewell kiss which showed a softening of their hostilities, and a pleasant good-bye.

Borodine joined Boxer and they strode out of the lobby to the street together without looking back. Boxer stopped to tell the doorman that a man had fainted inside, and might require medical attention. Then they turned left and strolled south on Fifth Avenue. Boxer said, "We never did get our lunch. Let's stop for something to eat."

"Good idea. I am hungry as a Russian bear." The two men laughed. "Then we discuss what to do about the Chinese."

Boxer was lost in thought for a moment. Then he said, "Yes, of course. The Chinese."

"The Chinese. Yes, of course. Come right down and we'll discuss our mutual problems. There've been some new developments recently." That was what the Chinatown Precinct commander told Boxer, and he and Will Pickens took a company car to the police station.

Pickens parked in front of the building in a space reserved for patrol cars.

Captain Jefferson greeted them warmly, partly because of his admiration for Boxer's coming to the aid of the beleagered policemen in the East Village, and partly because the police commissioner had ordered him to cooperate.

Boxer introduced Pickens as his aide, and then asked Jefferson what was going on in Chinatown.

"Well, Mr. Boxer," the police captain answered, "the fear is that we may have a full-scale tong war on our hands. Take that restaurant massacre on East Broadway. Your man got killed when one tong assassinated four members of a rival tong. What we had to go on there was the identification of the four dead men as Hung Yees. Now, that is a very respected tong in Chinatown. Very wealthy. Philanthropic, civic-minded. The Hung Yee's leader is also the director of the Chinatown Trading Association. Salt of the earth. Incidently, they're also very pro-Taiwanese."

Boxer looked at Pickens and nodded. They already knew all this, but let Jefferson continue on with his lesson

Captain Jefferson reached into his pocket, pulled out a pack of Kools, and lit one, inhaling deeply and letting the smoke waft slowly to the ceiling. He offered his pack around, but it was declined.

Boxer said that as long as they were smoking, he would stick with his pipe. He packed the bowl and got a good ash going while Jefferson continued.

"What we didn't know at the time was who'd done it. So, next, the incident in which you were involved. The drug dealers that were murdered weren't Chinese, but the two perps who ripped them off were. Dragon tongs. Very bad. Into drugs very heavily. We suspect they smuggle heroin into New York directly from Shanghai. And you can't do that without the tacit approval, or perhaps the direct aid, of the Commie government."

Still nothing new. Boxer was beginning to think his trip to the precinct was a waste of time.

Jefferson took another drag of his cigarette, and continued. "Then, as I told you the other day, the ballistics seem to indicate that the guns that killed the people in the restaurant were the same ones used in the drug bust. And, ironically, that killed your companion, Miss Ripley."

Boxer fidgeted in his seat. He felt his throat tighten and his pulse quicken at the mention of Anita's name. Pickens clapped a hand on his shoulder, and Boxer settled down. "So what we have now is the Dragon Tong involved in the two shootings. They killed a lot of people, including some of mine. But there's no connection, except that the same group did the shooting both places. You're talking about a drug deal gone sour, and a possible assassination. Or maybe the restaurant owner didn't pay his protection money on time?"

Jefferson continued. "We considered that. In fact, that's what we were working on at first." He paused for a moment, took another drag, and let the smoke mingle with Boxer's pipe smoke and spread out near the ceiling. "You know about the kid that disappeared around here the other day? Twelve-year-old girl. Smart, pretty little thing named Mei Ling Chan. Apple of her daddy's eye. Man by the name of Ming Chan. Head of the same Hung Yee Tong from the restaurant shootout."

Boxer looked at Pickens.

"This morning," Jefferson continued, "one of my informants called to tell me that a package was delivered to Old Man Chan at the association office. That package contained the dress his daughter was wearing the night she disappeared. And a warning of some sort. My snitch couldn't get close enough to read it, but Ming Chan started cursing about the Dragon Tong. You can put two and two together yourselves."

"Bad enough they go around killing each other off," Boxer complained. "But when they go around wasting innocent bystanders and abducting children . . ."

Jefferson shrugged and raised palms upward. "They think they're a law unto themselves. The tongs have been in existence for hundreds of years, maybe longer. That's the way they do business. I had hopes for the Hung Yees, though. Officially, they won't have anything to do with the police. But since I've come on board here, almost two years now, I've made some inroads. They never ask me for help, and hide their own when we come looking for them, but at least they'll talk to me about what's going on in Chinatown, the needs of the people, the ways we can cooperate without them giving up their culture, nor us giving up our authority." He looked directly at Boxer and Pickens. "Being a man of color, myself, they can sense the understanding and compassion I have for other disempowered people."

Boxer smiled. "So what we have here is the Hung Yees, who are our friendlies, being set upon by the Dragon Tong, who are drug dealers backed by the Chicoms. I think I'd like to pay a call on Mr. Ming Chan. Do you think you could arrange it for me?"

"I'm not sure. They have a distrust for outsiders, you know."

"Please try, Captain Jefferson. I have a stake in this, too. I've lost some good people." Anita Ripley flashed into his thoughts. "The best. We have a common enemy, and frankly, I'd welcome their help."

Jefferson took a sheet of official stationery, and began to write. "I'll try. This won't guarantee that Chan will help you, or even see you. I don't have that kind of clout. But at least it will let him know you're not the enemy."

Boxer thanked him, and he and Pickens headed for the door. Captain Jefferson called after them, "Good luck. I'd sure hate to see Chinatown explode."

Boxer thought of the cacophony of shipping that the world was soon to assemble around New York Harbor, and hoped that Chinatown wasn't all that wouldn't explode.

Boxer and Pickens followed Jefferson's directions, and walked the few blocks to the Chinatown Trading Association offices on Mott Street, between Canai and Bayard. The offices were on the second floor of a brick building. Downstairs, the building was occupied by a Chinese import store, its aisles and walls filled with mostly expensive clothing and fabrics, carved wooden objects, and finely engraved ivory figurines set apart from the rest by an enormous elephant tusk which seemed to protrude from the floor. To the right of the glass store entrance, there was a metal door painted black, emblazoned with some gold Chinese characters.

Boxer checked the address that Jefferson had written down. It was the place. Boxer tried the door, but it was locked. He knocked, and waited, then knocked again. Nothing. They decided to try the store.

They were greeted inside by a stunning Chinese woman in her mid-twenties, dressed in a traditional silk dress the color of jade, slit high up the side to show off an exquisite length of a very trim, shapely leg. Her jet black hair was quite long and tied off in the back.

Boxer couldn't help staring at her. She was small breasted, but her figure was so well proportioned that the overall effect mesmerized him.

She returned his gaze and smiled at him. "Hello," she said. "My name is Lin Pei. Would you and your companion like to purchase some fine ivory? A figurine, perhaps?" She watched Boxer smile and rub his beard. "My intuition tells me you are a thoughtful man, of great intelligence. A man who likes a challenge."

She was so right on the money that Boxer and Pickens broke out in broad grins.

"Perhaps," she continued, "you would like to purchase an extremely well-crafted ivory chess set. We have one that is especially beautiful, an antique."

As she turned around to remove the chess set from a showcase, Boxer noticed that it wasn't the only thing extremely well crafted and beautiful. She placed an inlaid laquered box on the counter in front of Boxer and began to open it. Reluctantly, Boxer broke the spell. "Thank you, no. Maybe another time.

Everything here is so beautiful." He looked directly at her and smiled. "I was trying to get into the Chinatown Trading Association office upstairs. I want to speak to a Mr. Ming Chan, but I'm afraid the door is locked. Is there another way to get up there?"

"Ah, I am sorry, but I know of no one who goes by that name. If the door is locked, then no one is there. Perhaps you should call for an appointment."

Boxer was a little surprised by the obvious put-down. Jefferson had told him the Chinese were a tight-knit community, wary of outsiders, but this beautiful creature seemed so innocent to blatantly lie about what had to be common knowledge. He looked at Will Pickens and shrugged. Then Boxer reached into his breast pocket and produced his note from Jefferson. He smiled at her. "Lin Pei, I was assured by Captain Jefferson of the Chinatown precinct that Mr. Chan does indeed have an office upstairs. I would like to see him about a subject of mutual interest. I would deem it a great favor if you could be of assistance to me in speaking to him. My name is Jack Boxer. This is my associate, Will Pickens."

Lin Pei's eyes darted to the paper. She read quickly then stepped back behind a counter and pressed a concealed button. Two tough-looking Chinese men dressed in business suits that didn't quite conceal their hidden weapons entered from a side door and stared menac-

202

ingly at Boxer and Pickens. She showed the letter to one of the men, and they conversed briefly in Chinese. The man shook his head no. Lin Pei spoke again tersely. The man growled something at her, then backed off. Finally, Lin Pei walked back to Boxer and said, "You wait here. I will see if anyone knows this man you seek. These men work here. They will keep you company. I will return in a moment." With that, she turned and walked through the same side door that the two toughs had used.

Boxer lifted the lid from the inlaid box and examined the chess pieces inside. They really were special.

Will Pickens spent the time figuring out their odds against the two babysitters. He was armed, and figured he'd get at least one before they knew what hit them. Both, if he could create a diversion and catch them off guard. If he was lucky. He went over his plan in his mind. He would toy with an expensive piece of china or glass. A vase, or a figurine. Then at the first sign of their making a move on him or Boxer, he'd smash the thing against the floor. No, the glass showcase would be better. Their reflex movements would be toward the sound, and he'd have them. He'd qualified as sharpshooter with eight weapons, including the nine-millimeter Walther automatic tucked into his waistband. Shit. No problem. He started to look at the objects on display, finally deciding on an orange vase about a foot high with a price tag of seven hundred and fifty dollars. Perfect. He lifted the vase and hefted it in his hand, wondering why the fuck Boxer wasn't more concerned for their safety.

Lin Pei re-entered the store by the same entrance the two men had used. The sudden flash of green caused Pickens to whirl instinctively in that direction, the vase poised at the ready. As the woman walked toward him, he relaxed a bit. She approached Boxer and said to him, "Please follow me. He will see you now." She glanced at Pickens. "Alone, please." And to Will, she said, "Please be careful with that vase, Mr. Pickens. It is almost two hundred years old."

"We'll go together," Pickens said.

"It's okay, Will. I'll go with her alone. I'll see you in a few minutes."

"Ah don't like it, Chief. Not one bit."

"I'll be all right, Will. Just hang in here for a little while."

"Well, okay, but against mah better judgment. Remember, just holler an' Ah'll come arunnin'." He added under his breath, "After Ah finish up with those two."

Lin Pei beckoned, and Boxer followed her into a back room and up a flight of stairs to the second level. She led him through a door, into an outer office staffed by two Chinese men in black suits working with electronic calculators. She knocked on an unmarked inner door, and after a command from inside, they entered.

Ming Chan sat behind a highly polished mahogany desk, a square-faced man with a big flat beefy nose and thinning black hair slicked back on his head. He also wore a black suit, white shirt, and an almost black tie. He looked like any of thousands of middle-aged men Boxer'd seen in the neighborhood, but he realized that this was one of the most powerful men in Chinatown.

Boxer watched Lin Pei bow deferentially to Ming Chan. He bowed his head. "Thank you for seeing me without an appointment," Boxer said. "I am here because we have mutual enemies. I hope we can work together to overcome them."

The old man just stared at Boxer impassively.

Boxer quickly decided to go for the jugular. Maybe shock would work when politeness did not. He said, "I'm sorry to learn about the disappearance of your daughter. The same people holding her have already killed two of my best men."

Chan shouted a command at Lin Pei, and Boxer saw his hand move under the table. Two men armed with revolvers jumped from behind an embroidered screen to the right of the table. They glared at Boxer, weapons held uneasily at their sides. The sound of breaking glass came from downstairs.

Boxer appeared unfazed. He shrugged. "You have no reason to shoot me. If we were only dealing with the Dragon Tong, I'm sure that you and your people could deal with them without any help from me. And I'm sure that Captain Jefferson could find and apprehend those responsible for killing my people . . . and yours. But I'm afraid we're dealing with something much bigger than the Dragon Tong, however abominable they are. If you will allow me to proceed, I will tell you why I think the People's Republic is behind everything that has happened."

Chan thought for a moment, then nodded to each of his two bodyguards. They put their guns away, and left the room. "You are a very brave man, Mr. Boxer. You could have been killed here."

There was a crash of furniture behind Boxer. He turned to see Will Pickens burst through the door, his automatic covering everyone in the room. He aimed at the black-suited figure seated at the table. "Call off your goons or you're history," he shouted.

"Easy, Will! It's all taken care of."

"Better tell those two jokers downstairs. They tried to jump me outa the clear blue."

That explained the broken glass. Boxer's face

suddenly went white. "Will, you didn't . . ."

"Kill 'em? Naw, didn't have to. But they're sufferin' from mahty big headaches. What's goin' on up here?"

"I was trying to arrange some cooperation. I was just about to discuss our situation with Mr. Chan." He turned to Ming Chan. "Sorry, sir, we overreacted."

"No apology necessary, Mr. Boxer. Those two downstairs behaved impertinently. I trust they will remember the lesson learned today. Let us have our discussion, Mr. Boxer. But remember, nothing is to be done which will endanger the life of my daughter Mei Ling."

Boxer nodded, "Agreed."

The old man smiled for the first time. "Then let us have tea." He turned to Lin Pei, and said something in Chinese. She left the room, and returned a few minutes later followed by two elderly women bearing trays of tea and pastries. Chairs were brought in and they sat around the table drinking tea. Boxer explained who he was and why he felt the Communist Chinese were behind the troubles. They were trying to disrupt the Discovery celebration.

Ming Chan agreed to share information with Boxer, and assigned his niece, Lin Pei, as his liaison. Boxer didn't expect a woman to be assigned and said so. Ming reassured him that Lin Pei was his trusted assistant, despite her posing as a salesclerk, and she knew more about his operation than any man with the exception of himself.

As they bid their good-byes, and left the association offices, Pickens put his arm on Boxer's shoulder and said, "Well, Chief, even if nothing else comes out of this meetin' today, you got to meet a real pretty lady."

Boxer laughed. "Yeah, she's pretty, all right. But I'm going to be looking for some hard answers behind that pretty face. Now, tell me, how the hell'd you finish off those two goons downstairs without firing a shot?"

Will Pickens beamed with pride. "Hell, Chief, that weren't nothin'. Why, remember that fancy vase Ah . . ."

Boxer listened to the story the entire way as they walked back to the precinct.

Chapter Thirteen

Boxer spent the remainder of the afternoon bringing the combined clandestine efforts of the CIA, the Secret Service, and the NSC to bear on finding the abducted girl, Mei Ling. If they could turn up the girl alive, and apprehend her kidnappers, the Hung Yee Tong would be eternally grateful, and help Boxer infiltrate their mutual enemy. Boxer could initiate a preemptive strike, and abort any plans the Chicoms may have to wreck havoc on the Discovery celebration.

At 1630, Boxer announced that he would stay at the office and monitor the command post computers until Mei Ling was found. Hutchinson volunteered to remain with him until 1900 Pickens said he was staying as long as Boxer was. They had sandwiches and coffee sent up before the support staff left for the day.

There had been nothing to report by 1900, and Hutchinson went home. Boxer and Pickens spelled each other at the communications modules, alternating with planning their own security operations for the big event. At 2100, Pickens napped on the sofa for two hours. By 2400, Boxer rubbed his eyes, which were irritated from staring at a computer screen all evening. He pushed Pickens gently, and told him he was going out for some fresh air.

Will Pickens shook the sleep out of his head and said, "Hey, wait up. Better let me go with you. It's a jungle out there this time of the night."

"Don't worry, I'll be all right. I'm just going to walk up to the Seaport and breathe in the salt air. Besides, some of the Tall Ships are moored there already. And someone's got to stay here at the monitors in case something comes up."

"Ah don't like it, but Ah guess Ah can't stop you. At least take a piece with you." He handed Boxer a chunky little handgun, a thirty-eight caliber S & W Chief's Special with a two-inch barrel and no hammer to snag in a jacket pocket. "And take along one of these mini-mikes." He took a miniature transmitter-receiver about the size of a book of matches, and pinned it on Boxer's lapel. "This thing here activates it. Now you're patched in to this big baby here." Pickens patted a black metal box replete with a multitude of dials, gauges, LED displays and a speaker. "Ah can pick you up within five miles of this place if you need me, and Ah can notify you if anything comes up here."

Boxer said, "Roger that, Will. Good idea. I'll see you in an hour."

Boxer spotted the first man upon leaving the building. Must have been waiting for him. He walked about a block to the Vietnam Veterans' Memorial, and seemingly studied the messages etched on the glass blocks in the faint light given off by strategically placed lamps in the little park.

The man stood in the shadows of the adjacent skyscraper, waiting and watching.

Boxer walked out onto South Street and headed north toward the South Street Seaport. It was then that he noticed the second man step from a doorway and follow behind him. The first man disappeared, presumably to leapfrog ahead of him.

Boxer decided to activate the mini-mike and notify Will about the company he had picked up. He spoke softly and deliberately, giving Pickens his position, and his plan.

Pickens said, "Roger that. Didn't think we could trust those Chinese we met this afternoon. They're probably pissed because Ah busted up their place."

Boxer replied, "I could understand if the Chinese were trying to retaliate for that. Trouble is these two birds are wearing gray flannel suits and button-down shirts. It's our own people who are after me." Then he ducked into the shadows of the elevated FDR Drive, moving swiftly from girder to girder, changing his pace to throw off the men tailing him.

Boxer saw the lights of the Seaport and quickly joined a party of young people drinking beer and having a good time. Even though the Seaport was winding down for the night, the streets were still filled with people, mostly young, mostly well to do, and from the looks of some of the activity going on, mostly sexually active. He mingled with the crowd, and headed for Pier 17, a three-story row of eateries and shops extending into the East River. He caught sight of the first man again. He and his partner were each a short block away from him, converging on him from two directions. The old squeeze play. They had only to wait him out. At midnight the Seaport pavilions closed, and the lovers headed for the relative privacy of their parked cars or unlighted doorways.

Boxer climbed the wooden steps to Pier 17, walked into the doorway next to the Banana Republic store, and took the escalator to the second level. He watched one of the gray suits step onto the escalator while his partner climbed the stairs, cutting off a possible escape route. They were concentrating on him and failed to see Will Pickens following behind them.

Boxer pushed open the heavy glass doors and stepped out onto the wooden deck that circumvented the pier on three sides. He walked to the edge overlooking the river. They spotted him going through the doors. One followed him out. The other took the exit on the opposite side. They were alone with Boxer at the end of the pier. Each of them drew a heavy-looking handgun from a shoulder holster and converged on the very edge of the pier. No Boxer. They looked at each other in astonishment and rushed to the handrail, looking over the edge.

"Freeze, Motherfuckers. Don't make a move, don't make a sound. Don't even breathe." Pickens said, "Hands up real high over your heads. Okay, now, just drop those nice shiny toys of yours over the side. Now!"

The two men did as they were told. Then they watched in dismay as Boxer pulled himself up onto the deck from where he'd been hanging on beneath it. He caught his breath, then put the barrel of his snub-nosed thirty-eight into the ear of the man nearest him. "I want to know who put you up to this. Kinkaid? Tell me." He ground the gun into the man's ear.

No response.

"I said I want to know who sent you after me. If it was Kinkaid, just say so, and you can walk away."

The man was starting to shake. "I can't say. If you're gonna shoot, then go ahead. I'm no better off than if I told you."

Will Pickens grabbed a handful of the other man's hair and wrenched his head back. He placed the barrel of his Walther against the man's eye and said, "That leaves you, asshole. Who sent you?" Will jabbed the barrel into his eye. The man winced in pain.

Boxer looked at Pickens's man closely. Something familiar about the face. Someone he should know. But the nose just wasn't right. Then it hit him. "Parker?" He stepped closer. Will twisted the man's face toward Boxer. "Parker, you son of a bitch. So it was Kinkaid after all. I had him figured all along."

Boxer jammed the barrel of his revolver into Parker's mouth. "This is the second time you've fucked with me, Parker. There better not be a third." He removed the gun, and grabbed Parker's jacket collar. "Get over by the rail. You too. Move it."

Pickens and Boxer each pushed their man up against the edge of the handrail, guns against their heads. Boxer said, "I just wanted you to see where I hid when you two jokers couldn't find me." He pushed Parker's head over the rail, "You see down there?" Then he grabbed the seat of Parker's pants and tossed him over into the East River.

Pickens poked his man in the head with the Walther and said to him, "You need a special invitation?"

He didn't. He climbed over the rail and jumped in to join his partner. Parker shouted, "Help, I can't swim."

Boxer and Pickens put their guns away, waved good-bye, and laughed all the way back to the street.

Boxer confided to Pickens that their position at the Water Street offices was compromised.

With the Williams Company being a CIA front, and Kinkaid after Boxer's ass because of a personal vendetta, the office was no longer a safe, let along productive, place to work. Boxer suggested that they use the Stapleton Naval Base as temporary headquarters.

Pickens agreed. But they had a minor problem. "Jack, how the hell we gonna get all our stuff out, especially at this hour?"

"Not to worry. I have a friend that may help us out."

"Well, this'll be a good test of your friendship, gettin' him up at midnight to help us haul a mountain of paperwork and electronics gear over to Staten Island."

Boxer smiled. "Let's head over to the Coast Guard station at Battery Park. It's just a short walk from here."

They were stopped by the armed sentry just outside the wire mesh fence delineating the Coast Guard compound. Boxer produced an identification card, and told the guard to inform Commander Szpak that Jack Boxer was there with an urgent request. A phone call was made and an aide was sent out to escort Boxer and Pickens to the quarters.

The Coast Guard commander had a robe wrapped around him and stood barefoot. He'd obviously been awakened, but nonetheless, he greeted Boxer warmly.

Boxer shook his hand and said, "Thanks for your hospitality." He made the introductions. "Commander Charles Szpak, I'd like you to meet Colonel Will Pickens, United States Marine Corps, my chief of staff. Will, Captain Szpak."

Pickens saluted, then shook hands with Szpak. "Mahty pleased to meet you. We sure do appreciate your seein' us so late, Commander."

"Why don't we cut out the formalities, gentlemen. Call me Charlie."

Boxer agreed. "Please call me Jack."

Pickens said, "Ah been called a lot of things in mah time, but Will's all right between you an' me."

Szpak offered them a drink, but Boxer declined, requesting coffee instead. "Will and I have a long night ahead of us. If you don't mind, I'd like a safe phone so I can make a call to Admiral Stark. We have some serious problems that we have to settle this morning."

"Admiral Stark himself? At this hour? Well, okay, if you think it's wise, you can use the red phone in my office. It's connected to a scrambler."

Boxer phoned the admiral in Washington, using Stark's emergency number to which no more than a dozen people had access. Stark was wakened from a deep sleep, and his voice was unusually gruff. "Yes? Dammit, who's calling this late?"

"Boxer here."

"Figures. Jack, what the hell's so important that it can't wait 'til morning?"

"Sorry, sir. I think I'm in pretty deep shit with Kinkaid and his boys. I was working late, went

216

out for a walk, and he sent a pair of his playmates after me with guns."

"Kinkaid? What's he fucking crazy? Jack, did they try to kill you?"

"Didn't give them a chance, sir. Right now they're probably battling the current in the East River, just south of the Brooklyn Bridge. Sir, with your permission, I'd like to move Operation Discovery to safer quarters. I'd like to use the Stapleton Base, sir."

Stark tried to rub the sleep out of his eyes. "Hmmm, D'Arcy know about this yet?"

"Not yet, sir. I wanted to speak to you first."

"I told you when you took the job, Jack, whatever you need to ensure the security of the operation, you get. I'll notify D'Arcy. How are you going to get your materials out?"

"Well, Admiral, I was going to impose on Captain Charles Szpak here at the Coast Guard Station for some manpower."

"Good. What about security?"

"I could take some MPs with us."

"I can do even better. Ever hear of the SEALs?"

"Of course, sir. I've had the opportunity to work with some of them before."

"There's a special unit of fourteen men at the Stapleton Base about to be assigned to you as part of your security forces. I'll have D'Arcy motor four of them over to Battery Park at once. They'll provide some protection for you until you get your stuff over to Staten Island."

Boxer let out a snappy, "Yes, sir. And thanks

very much for your help."

Admiral Stark growled, "I'll deal with Kinkaid in the morning. Good luck. Oh, and if you're going to get into any more trouble, do it during waking hours."

Stark's phone went dead. Boxer was all smiles as he walked back into Szpak's living room and told the others of his conversation with the admiral.

Szpak said, "May as well have coffee and some refreshment while we're waiting for the SEALs to get here. Looks like it's going to be a long night."

Boxer replied, "A very long night. I guess I could go with a bite to eat. How about you, Will?"

"Don't have to ask me twice, Chief. Ah'm so hungry Ah could eat a . . . whatever you got'll be fine, Charlie, thanks."

"My pleasure, gentlemen. Meanwhile, I'll get us two trucks and a dozen good men to accompany you two and the SEALs. Wouldn't hurt to have a couple of electronics wizards among them either. They'll be ready to roll in about a half hour, soon as the SEALs get here."

In twenty-five minutes, the door was opened to four rugged young men looking like linebackers dressed in short-sleeved white uniforms with the special insignia that indicated that they were part of the elite Sea Air Land Team, the SEALS. They each carried an M-16 assault rifle. Their leader, a six-foot-tall corporal named Patrick O'Reilly stepped forward, saluted smartly, and introduced himself and the others. He handed his written orders to Commander Szpak, who was the only man in the room in uniform.

Szpak saluted, and introduced the others. Boxer saluted and said, I'm Jack Boxer, Captain USN. For the purpose of my mission, I'm partially undercover as a civilian, as is Colonel Pickens here, the pride of the U.S. Marine Corps."

Pickens smiled and saluted the young sailors. Boxer took ten minutes to explain the essentials of their immediate mission. He told O'Reilly and his men that they would be assigned to his assault force on the *Shark,* and that he would brief their entire fourteen-man contingent aboard ship tomorrow.

Eighteen men aboard two vehicles set out on the short drive to the Water Street address of the Williams Company. One armed SEAL stood guard at the entrance to the building, a second at the first-floor elevator. Boxer's key allowed the elevator car to become dedicated to their use, and they quickly removed the necessary files and electronics equipment. Two more SEALs stood guard at the elevator and the office door. The few startled CIA types manning the offices during the night took one look at the determined young hulks armed with automatic rifles and just continued with their own business. Boxer expected a call to be made to Kinkaid as soon as he left. Pickens supervised the removal of the communications equipment while Boxer handled the paperwork. The work went smoothly and quickly. By 0430 everything was packed aboard the two trucks and on its way to the Coast Guard station.

Charlie Szpak offered to shuttle Boxer's men to Staten Island. O'Reilly explained, "Thank you, sir, but Admiral D'Arcy has the launch that brought us here waiting for our return trip."

It took another hour to load everything onto the boat. They tied up at Stapleton at 0630. "Just in time to wake up," Pickens remarked.

They were met by a young lieutenant with word that D'Arcy had arranged for a four-room suite across the green from the admiral's offices for Boxer's use as headquarters. Boxer sent back written instructions that an armed guard was to be posted at all times, and that no one would be allowed entry without the personal authorization of Boxer or Pickens. . . . Let Kinkaid stew over that for a while.

The rest of the morning was spent setting up the new office with the commandeered files and communications equipment. At noon, Boxer left Pickens in charge with instructions to wake him at 1400. He hitched a ride to his personal quarters and fell asleep immediately. He was dreaming about a little girl being held captive in Chinatown, being tortured by the Chicoms. He kept trying to get to her, to save her, but the enemy was too numerous, too strong. He was being overpowered by the yellow masses. He broke out in a sweat. No . . . no . . . leave her alone. . . no . . . let me help. . . .

The ringing phone jarred him out of his nightmare. He answered on the third ring. "Boxer. Who—"

"Stark. I spent the morning in session with Kinkaid and Williams. They both deny having anything to do with those two bozos who attacked you last night. In fact, Kinkaid said that Parker acted on his own, got another agent to help him by telling the man they were following Kinkaid's orders. He sends his regrets and says that the two agents will face disciplinary action for what they did."

"Bullshit. Kinkaid's full of it, sir. He was pissed because I helped Captain Borodine find and speak to his ex-wife. She was working for Kinkaid."

"Not very bright of you, Jack. I can't keep saving your ass from Kinkaid every time you feel like playing matchmaker. He's one enemy you don't need. Nor do I."

"Maybe not, sir. But had the circumstances been reversed, I think Borodine would have done the same for me. Besides, his cooperation will be invaluable once we get close to Discovery Day."

"Birds of a feather. Just remember which side you're on, Jack. Right now, Kinkaid works for the U.S.A., and Borodine is the enemy."

"God save us from our friends then, Admiral Stark. Kinkaid's obsessed with power. It would have been nothing for him to arrange a meeting between Borodine and Galena. He's also been trying to undermine my efforts and spy on me since day one of this job. At least he can't interfere while I'm here at Stapleton. Why—"

Stark interrupted, "Just cover your ass, son. I can't keep covering it for you indefinitely."

"Yes, sir, Thank you, Ad—" The line went dead. Stark wasn't one for cordial good-byes.

Boxer showered and dressed. He went back to his new headquarters and relieved Pickens. They worked into the late evening putting the paperwork back into working order. They had lost a day's work because of the incident at the Seaport.

At 1900 hours, Hutchinson telephoned. He explained that he'd spent most of the day trying to track Boxer down. "I wanted you to know, Captain Boxer, that I had nothing to do with what happened last night. When I learned what Parker had done, I became furious. And now this. What's to become of the organization here? It appears you've pulled out and taken most of the pertinent paperwork with you."

Boxer almost believed Hutchinson's sincerity. "Tell you what, Hutchinson. If you still want to help, you handle protocol. Take care of diplomacy; work with the politicians. Send their naval officers to me. Do we have a deal?"

"Very well, sir. It's a deal. And please call on me if you need any other assistance."

Boxer told him okay and hung up. Things were starting to look better. Now he could get down to the real work. Tomorrow morning he would meet with his men aboard the *Shark*.

Leaving Pickens in charge of the new headquarters, Boxer climbed aboard the *Shark* promptly at 0700. The duty officer greeted him with a snappy salute and a "Welcome back, sir." Cowly was delighted to have Boxer back on board and announced his presence to the crew over the IGA. Several of the men came up to the bridge to welcome their captain.

Boxer called a meeting of all officers in the Ward Room for 0730.

When they had all assembled, he said, "Men, I know you've been doing routine drill for the last three weeks, and it's getting boring."

"Believe it," Cowly said.

"In exactly two weeks from today," Boxer said, "we will help secure the greatest celebration in these parts since the reopening of the Statue of Liberty on Independence Day in '86. As you may know, we not only will have on hand the remaining Tall Ships, but capital ships representing over forty nations of the world, both allies and enemies. The President is adamant in wanting to show the world that we can all work in peace and harmony, and the Discovery celebration will be his shining example. Our job is to keep it safe and secure.

"The Mayor of New York City is cooperating with us. The Coast Guard, the Secret Service, and the NSC are coordinating their efforts with all the local police departments up and down the coast. And, of course, the FBI and the CIA, although the CIA may be assuming a lesser role now. Due to the international scope of this project, and to the great number of vessels

223

involved, the Navy has been called upon to back up the Coast Guard. I have been working with the various organizations just mentioned to set up the project and take overall command of security."

"How do we fit into this?" Harris asked.

"We do," Boxer answered, and he continued, "The fleets will begin coming in on Monday and continue for the remainder of the week. The Soviet bloc nations will anchor to the northeast of New York Harbor, and the free world vessels to the south.

"The *Shark*'s responsibility will be to patrol the more than two hundred miles of coast to keep out intruders, to ensure that no mines are deployed against our own or any other nation's vessels, and to ensure that the Ruskies don't try any funny business while they're here."

That brought a rousing cheer from all the men, as Boxer had hoped it would. "We will deploy the Campbell sonobuoys that we tested successfully off the Cuban coast last month. The Campbells, along with the *Shark*'s patrols, should keep the area clear of any underwater intruders. The Navy's surface ships will direct traffic and deter any attacks that may occur from above. The aircraft carrier *U.S.S. Bunker Hill* will sit five miles off the coast and provide air cover.

"And one final item, men. The *Shark* will be carrying a squad of fourteen Navy SEALS. They will replace our usual assault force, which will be working ashore. The SEALs will keep the harbor area and the Hudson and East Rivers free of mines and keep the channels clear. They will go out on manuevers each day and return to the *Shark*. Two teams of SEALs will man the mini-subs, as well.

"Well, that's all for now, men. It's good to be back."

Boxer took Harris and the other officers back to the bridge and gave them each precise orders for the next two weeks. Boxer passed the command back to Harris and told them that he would try to be back aboard the *Shark* on the Fourth for the celebration.

Chapter Fourteen

On Wednesday, June 24, at 0930, Boxer was summoned to the Coast Guard station at the Battery by Commander Szpak. He was taxied across the bay in a twenty-four-foot speedboat, with Patrick O'Reilly at the helm. Seaman Mark Lebanski, armed as usual with his M-16 assault rifle, accompanied them as escort.

They tied up at a Coast Guard slip and made their way to Szpak's quarters. The two SEALs were left to wait, while Boxer accompanied Szpak to his office. He was greeted by the sight of a man in uniform whose demeanor and appearance was light-years apart from the spit-and-polish SEALs on his staff. The man, of CPO rank, looked like an aging defensive tackle gone to pot. Boxer figured him to be three or four inches taller than his own six feet, easily two hundred and eighty pounds, a good portion of which hung over his belt buckle. The Navy had outlawed beards on both officers and enlisted men for more than five years now, though Boxer had opted to keep his when he'd taken over command of the *Shark*. After all, at the time he had been working strictly undercover, his career in the service seemingly disgraced. Besides, Boxer always kept his beard well trimmed. But on this hulk, the beard was as unkempt as the rest of the man, as disheveled as the reddish brown hair on his head. He had a Coast Guard tattoo on one hairy forearm, and a sexually explicit tattoo on the other beefy arm. At the sight of Commander Szpak, the CPO straightened up somewhat and offered his excuse for a salute.

Boxer and Szpak returned the salute. Szpak said, "Captain Boxer, this excuse for a Coast Guardsman is Chief Petty Officer William Boulay. "Wooly, meet Captain Jack Boxer, U.S. Navy, now working out of uniform on a special project. I'd like you to tell him what you've told me."

Boxer said, "Willy, did you say?"

Boulay replied, "It's Wooly, sir. The men call me Wooly Bully. I can't imagine why."

"Forgive me for staring at you, Chief. If you were under my command, and presented yourself looking like you do, I'd have you thrown off my boat, or in the brig."

"Been in the brig, sir. Several times. Finally, one of the brass decided that buoy-tender duty out here in the harbor was a step below being in the brig. And I've been here ever since. Hell, being in the brig again would seem to me like a promotion."

Boxer was taking a liking to the man, his irreverence reminding him of himself when he went to work undercover for the Navy after the accident involving his sub, the *Sting Ray*. But what a sight. "Okay, Chief, let's hear what you have to tell me."

Boulay smiled. "That won't be necessary, sir. I'm happy just to be able to help out Commander Szpak once in a while." He tried to hitch his pants up over his formidable gut. "Besides, I'd miss all the good food they feed us. Reason Commander Szpak brought the two of us together is I . . . my crew and I found some of the channel buoys out of place."

Boxer cocked his head and asked, "You sure?"

Szpak piped in, "I know he may not look it, but Wooly's the best man at that job that the Coast Guard's got. He first discovered the problem with just a visual sighting of his surroundings."

Boulay said, "That's right, sir. I could tell that they weren't right just by feel. I know every inch of my territory by heart. Upper Bay, Lower Bay, Raritan and Jamaica Bays, the whole shootin' match. I've got my charts implanted in my brain. I dream about those buoys and lighthouses. 'Course, that's when I'm not dreaming about women, you see."

Boxer nodded.

"Well, sir, the buoys that mark the channel just off of Sandy Hook were way off course. Any heavy displacement shipping trying to get through there would go aground."

Boxer asked, "Could you take me out there for a look?"

Boulay said, "Why sure. My buoy-tender's tied up right outside. The *Double Zero*. Big red tub with a crane just forward of the cabin. Me and my crew be happy to take you out."

Boxer turned to Szpak. "Can you fit my two SEALs with some scuba gear? I'd like them to go down and have a better look."

"No problem. I'll see to it right now. I'll have you on your way in fifteen minutes."

Boxer stepped aboard the buoy tender, followed by his two wet-suited SEALs, O'Reilly and Lebanski, carrying their oxygen tanks and weight belt. CPO Boulay introduced them to his crew. Tim Mathisen was at least six foot six, and weighed no more than one hundred and ninety pounds. He was very lanky; his clothes hung from his bony frame. Naturally, he was nicknamed Tiny Tim. The youngest crewmember was Stanley Smolinkas, a slip of a guy with short blond hair and glasses. Oliver McSweeney rounded out the crew. Rounded out was appropriate; he was a scaled-down version of Boulay. The CPO showed Boxer the pilot house. With a broad sweep of a massive arm, he knocked a half-dozen empty beer cans off the table onto the floor. Boxer thought it only improved the appearance of the floor.

Boulay said to Boxer, "See what I'm up against? I'm out here trying to get some work done with the likes of Tiny Tim and Laurel and Hardy, you know, Stan and Ollie out there. What a joke."

Boxer added, "Don't forget Wooly Bully."

Boulay laughed, "See what I mean?" He fired up the diesel and deftly maneuvered the craft away from the slip and out into the harbor. He brought the boat out to about eight hundred yards off the tip of Sandy Hook and rounded up to a red nun buoy whose bell clanged in cadence with the swell of the sea. He reduced his forward speed to less than a knot and hove to while he pulled a nautical chart from a tube overhead and spread it on the navigation table. He said to Boxer, "Look over there off to starboard. Now, normally, I'd sight off the lighthouse on Sandy Hook, line up with the parachute jump on Coney Island and then with the east tower of the Verazanno on the Brooklyn side. But when I do that now, it don't feel right to me. So, of course, I check the Loran reading."

Boulay turned a knob on a black electronic instrument and a set of longitude and latitude coordinates appeared on the LED readout. He pointed to the chart and said, "See, it's way off. The correct reading would put us right here, at the edge of the channel." He pointed to a dark buoy some hundred and fifty yard away. "That green can over there should be sitting on the other edge of the channel. It's not.

"There's no problem for all the small craft that fish off these waters, but a tanker or freighter might not make it. Of course, a battleship or a carrier would get hung up, and block the channel. No ships could get past. Even worse if someone would divert the Ambrose Channel markers. It's the main shipping channel in and out of the upper bay. Can you imagine what a mess we'd have on Discovery Day if one of the capital ships got hung up in there? You could sneak a small boat or even a sub and knock off the other ships like ducks in a shooting gallery."

The truth of that statement hit Boxer hard. He called in O'Reilly and Lebanski. "I'd like men to go over the side and see what you can find on this buoy. Then we'll check out the green can across the channel."

The two SEALs strapped on their tanks, adjusted their masks, and sat on the gunwales facing into the boat. Then in unison they flipped backward into the water. They worked their way down the chain to the bottom. The huge mushroom anchor hadn't settled in very deeply. It had been moved very recently. O'Reilly stopped halfway up the chain and motioned to Lebanski. There were fresh marks on two of the heavy links. The normal algae and rust film had been rubbed off, leaving a shiny spot. The SEALs returned to surface.

O'Reilly said, "Someone hooked on to the chain about thirty feet down and probably dragged the buoy off course."

CPO Boulay asked, "But who?"

"Who indeed," Boxer said.

Boulay replied, "We'll come right back out after we drop you off and move these markers back where they belong."

"Right. Maybe you could check the others, too, Mr. Boulay."

"Might as well call me Wooly, sir. Everybody else does. Even the Captain. By tomorrow night, we'll have the entire bay checked out. You can

232

count on that."

Boxer said, "Good man. If you can accomplish all that, I'll call you Wooly Bully from now on. I can see why Szpak calls you the best."

CPO Boulay beamed. He had Tiny Tim cast off from the red buoy and headed back to the base.

Boxer thanked Szpak for his assistance, and sent his two SEALs back to Stapleton. A Coast-guardsman provided a ride into Chinatown, where Boxer had a date with Lin Pei.

First, Boxer wanted to check in with Captain Jefferson at the Chinatown Precinct, to see if there were any new leads in the Chan kidnapping. He learned that the little girl still hadn't been found, and there was no ransom note, only the threat to the Hung Yee Tong to lay off the Dragons. And there were no new leads. Except one.

Jefferson explained to Boxer, "A street punk, twenty-year-old kid named Charlie Leung, was overheard bragging to his friends that his Kung Fu instructor had a hand in the kidnapping. We brought the kid in for questioning, but he spoke almost no English. An interpreter explained that Charlie was only bragging to enhance his stature with his street gang. We had to let the kid go."

Boxer asked, "Did you at least get the name of the Kung Fu instructor?"

"Nothing. Presumably, it's someone here in Chinatown. That narrows it down to several hundred, or so."

Boxer cleared his throat and said, "Between you

and me, Captain, someone's been trying to sabotage the Discovery Day festival. Our best guess is the People's Republic of China. And the Commies are linked to the Dragon Tong here in Chinatown. We've got to infiltrate that group fast. It's less than two weeks to July fourth. And in spite of all the massive firepower that will be gathered for the celebration, those ships would be sitting ducks. A small, highly trained terrorist squad could block off the harbor and pick off their targets in small fast speedboats, Kamakazi style. They could mine the harbor very easily, divert the channel markers, plant explosives on the ship's hulls under water, and in very short order, destroy a good chunk of the major powers' finest shipping."

"A real mess. Well, I'll keep you informed on any new developments. Good luck, Boxer."

Boxer rose and shook hands with the police captain. He left the station and walked the few blocks to the shop where he had first met Lin Pei. This time, he was greeted very cordially, and her two bodyguards smiled and nodded at him once they were sure that he didn't have Will Pickens with him. She directed him upstairs, and had tea served to them in Ming Chan's office. Presently, they were joined by the patriarch himself. Boxer sipped his tea, and after some small talk, he told them about the police interrogation of Charlie Leung.

Ming Chan nodded his head and grunted.

Lin Pei said, "Yes, we know the Leung family. They are recent immigrants, nondocumented. Wetbacks, you call them. They are recently from

Taipei. It is said that they had angered one of the warlords close to the late General Chang's family, and barely escaped with their lives. In fact, the son, Charlie, as he is known by your people, killed a follower of the warlord who tried to stop them from boarding the ship that brought them to New York. Uncle Ming helped them get settled here."

Ming Chan nodded. "It is so. I fought with General Chiang Kai-shek, and fled with him from the mainland in 1949 with two million others. I brought my family to New York in 1953, and helped to establish trade relations with the Kuomintang regime on Taiwan, and with Hong Kong. While we have prospered and grown here in this country, the general and his warlords became more and more corrupt. When General Chang died, the warlords became a law unto themselves. Some of the tongs became ferocious, much like the Dragon Tong that has been causing us so much trouble recently."

Lin Pei added, "Uncle is very modest. He sponsored the Leung family, paying for their passage to the United States, and helped them find work. He housed and protected them, and helped them start a new life in this country. I think I should speak to Charlie Leung. It is time for him to repay a debt."

Boxer said, "I'll go with you. Captain Jefferson called him a tough street punk. You could be in danger."

Lin Pei said, "No. I will take Sun and Gai Tang with me. They are the two who you met at our first meeting."

Ming Chan interjected, "The young rabbit

would flee at the sight of those two. They are well known among the street gangs. I have used them previously to restore order. No, you must go without them."

"Then it's settled." Boxer stood up. "I'm going with you. They surely don't know me around here."

Lin Pei said, "You would be more of a hindrance to me. I will go alone."

"It's my lead, and I'm going to follow up on it. It would be helpful to me if you would accompany me as interpreter, Lin. If not, I'm going anyway."

Ming Chan smiled, took a sip of his tea, and said to his niece, "You must go with Captain Boxer, for he will certainly be lost without you. No more arguing. Now go."

She blotted her lips with a red linen napkin and rose to follow Boxer down the stairs and out of the building. She said to Boxer, "Your bluff did not fool anyone, least of all me."

"I wasn't bluffing. Now let's find this punk and have a talk with him."

They walked through the crowded streets arm in arm, occasionally stopping long enough for Lin Pei to question the neighbors about Charlie Leung's whereabouts. They were directed to the playground in Columbus Park, the place where Mei Ling had last been seen.

Lin Pei turned to Boxer as they entered the park and said, "That's him watching those boys play basketball."

While two teenaged Caucasion boys were attempting to play a game of one-on-one, Charlie

Leung and three of his gang would push them off balance, snatch the ball, and shoot at the basket themselves. None of the gang was very good at it, but that didn't stop them from interfering with and harassing the two boys. Soon, it developed into a shoving match. Charlie's gang was older and with the force of superior numbers was about to beat up the two teenagers.

Boxer followed Lin Pei into the ball court.

She said, "Charlie Leung, I wish to speak to you alone. Leave those two alone and come here."

Leung looked up at her, surprised. His companions laughed, and pushed him on the shoulder. One of them called her a banana.

Boxer watched her face redden. She was obviously embarrassed by that. He asked, "Why did they call you that?"

"It is their worst insult. They see me with you and they call me a banana. You know, yellow on the outside, white on the inside. Fools. I am as Chinese as they are."

The gang continued to harass the two boys.

Lin shouted something at him in Chinese, and Charlie Leung stopped and looked at her bewildered; then he turned his back on her.

In Chinese, she said, "Leung, you're a shithead."

His gang turned on him and laughed.

Charlie threw the basketball at one of the teenagers and swaggered over to Boxer and Lin. He apparently called her an unsavory name in Chinese, which caused his companions to guffaw.

She answered back, and they laughed even

237

harder, taunting Charlie.

He raised his hand and slapped her hard on the cheek.

Boxer had been anticipating trouble, and had been standing with his feet spread slightly apart, knees bent, and his arms lightly at his side. He reacted immediately, blindsiding him. The sucker punch caught Charlie on the angle of his jaw, stunning him, making him stagger to the side, holding the side of his face. Boxer brought up his knee into Charlie Leung's groin, dropping him on the spot.

"Look out!" Lin cried. It was too late. Boxer got kicked in the side. He ducked his head just in time to take a glancing blow from a spinning back kick by one of the gang. The follow-up kick dropped Boxer to his knees. Two of the young men twisted Boxer's arms behind him and held him up. The third looked over to where Charlie Leung was nursing a swollen jaw. Charlie grunted a command. The young man let loose a fierce roar and leaped through the dozen feet separating him from Boxer and lashed out a flying kick.

At that second, Lin Pei kicked the legs out from one of the men holding up Boxer, and the three men tumbled to the ground. The flying kicker sailed harmlessly over their heads and landed hard. Lin Pei caught him with a side chop against his windpipe. Boxer smashed a fist into one man's face, shattering his nose. He continued to punch the face into a bloody pulp. The third punk pulled a knife from his pocket, flicked it open, and menaced Lin Pei with it. She took a defensive stance.

Boxer looked up at what was happening. Enough is enough already. He pulled his snub-nosed thirty-eight from his jacket pocket and yelled, "Don't move, Motherfucker."

The man caught sight of the gun and froze. Boxer smiled. Worked every time. . . .

Lin Pei shouted something and the gang members got up and started to leave. She called back Charlie Leung. He shook his head at her.

Boxer aimed the thirty-eight at him and he hung his head, defeated. He watched his friends limp out of the park.

She shouted something to him in Chinese, and he walked between them back to Ming Chan's headquarters.

His parents and two brothers were waiting for him when they got there. The elder Leung, Charlie's father, rose, growled at him, and brought his hand across Charlie's face. He swung again. Charlie winced in pain as the backhand caught him on his swollen jaw. Mr. Leung shouted, "Is this the way you repay our benefactor for his kindness? His daughter has been taken, and you do not tell what you know? Tell us all now what you know."

Charlie Leung hung his head. He wouldn't look his father in the eye.

"Speak about this thing. You must have more respect for your family than the man you are trying to protect."

Charlie shook his head. "I can't. I would lose face with the guys. I—"

The backhand against Charlie's sore jaw

239

brought his head upright. His father grabbed a hank of hair and said, "I cannot allow you to disgrace this family anymore." He nodded to Ming Chan. "Do with him what you want. He is no longer mine."

"Wait! Please, Father. You are right. I will tell you what I know. But please don't let my friends know that I am doing this. They would kill me."

Ming Chan ordered, "Speak."

"It is Jen Hsia, from the Wu Kung martial arts supply on Canal Street. He is my Kung Fu master. We practice on the second floor, above the shop."

"Go on."

"The other night, after lessons, I was alone in the dressing room changing into my street clothes. I overheard him bragging to Mr. Yuan, who owns the store. He told Mr. Yuan it was done, and Mr. Yuan said, 'That is good.'

"I waited 'til they went inside and I slipped out of the building. It gave me a sense of pride at the time."

Lin Pei glared at Charlie Leung.

"That was before I knew that it was Mei Ling that was taken."

Boxer asked, "Do any of your friends know what happened?"

Charlie Leung's face took on a sad look. "Yes."

Ming Chan nodded to Lin Pei. She called in the two bodyguards and told them something in Chinese. Charlie's face went white. Lin Pei turned to Boxer. "I told them to round up the boys. I don't want anyone warning our enemies."

Charlie Leung was dismissed. Lin Pei said to

Boxer, "Tonight, we shall have a talk with this Jen Hsia. You may join us if you wish, but I would suggest you stay at home if you are squeemish."

"I'll be there," Boxer said.

Ming Chan said something to Lin Pei, and she said, "Yes, Uncle." She turned to Boxer. "My uncle says it is a shame you ruined your white suit helping me this afternoon. Please allow us to replace it. If you leave it with me, I will have two of the finest tailors this side of Hong Kong duplicate it and return it to you in a few days. They will do it as a favor to my uncle."

"Please don't go to that trouble for me."

"It is no trouble at all. Come upstairs with me. I will get you some clothes to wear now."

Boxer changed into the black shirt and slacks that the Chans had provided. Lin said, "I guessed on the sizes. I chose a forty-two top and thirty-four waist. I hope they are not uncomfortable."

Boxer said, "I'm impressed. You're very close."

"I have sized up your body very carefully, Mr. Boxer. You are in very good shape for a man your age."

"My age? You're making me feel old."

Lin Pei giggled. "You have obviously not gone to fat like so many others in their middle thirties. That is good. You will need all your strength if you go with us tonight. We are going to take that Jen Hsai and interrogate him. We will find Mei Ling. At the same time, we will deliver to you our mutual enemies."

"When do we get started?"

Lin Pei said, "At nine. We have learned from

Charlie Leung that the Kung Fu class ends at nine tonight. We will take Jen Hsai when his students have left."

At ten minutes to nine, Boxer, Lin Pei, and the two black-clad bodyguards assembled outside the Wung Ku Academy, hiding in the shadows of the neighboring brownstones. The two men, Gai Tang and Sun, passed out black head coverings. Boxer recognized them as Ninja face masks. He followed Lin Pei up a fire escape, the other Hung Yees close behind him. Each in turn helped the next one up the metal stairs. They listened for noise from within. Boxer glanced at his watch. It was 2110. Plenty of time for the students to leave.

Boxer helped his companions let themselves into a window at the end of a hallway. They made their way to the door of the fighting studio. Lin Pei listened at the door. Satisfied that no one was inside, they slipped into the darkened room, dropped to the floor, and silently crossed to the far side where a dim light spilled from a dressing room. They had Jen Hsia where they wanted him, alone and hopefully with his pants down.

Suddenly, the room lights went on. As they squinted from the brightness, a solitary figure in a black two-piece garment trimmed with red borders and toggle closures stepped into the room. He smiled at them. "Ah, I see that we have visitors. How nice. Allow me to introduce myself. I am Master Jen Hsai."

Boxer's group rose from the floor and lined up against the man. Sideways glances were exchanged, and they spread out.

Jen Hsia clapped his hands sharply and barked, "Class, come see who is here. It appears we have some new students."

Eight or ten white-garbed young men entered the room and encircled the Hung Yees. Jen Hsai said, "Let us acquaint them with our fighting style." He turned to Boxer. "It is part of our initiation rites for new students. I hope you learn something." He nodded and his students moved in on Boxer's group. Most were armed, either with staffs or nunchuckas, two-foot-long clubs joined with short pieces of chain. These were whirled in intricate patterns around the heads and behind the backs of the students.

Gai Tang drew throwing knives from his sleeve and found his mark in two of the students. Blood stained the fronts of their white uniforms. Sun and Gai Tang had brought forearm length sticks with handles coming off at right angles and twirled them deftly. They squared off with four of the students. Two white-clad figures menaced Boxer, but he would have no part of their games. He drew his snub-nosed thirty-eight and aimed at the lead man. They faced off with him, not advancing, but still holding their weapons.

Suddenly, reaching behind his back, Jen Hsai whirled a set of nunchuckas overhead and threw them at Boxer. Boxer ducked, but not fast enough. One of the clubs caught the side of his head, and he went down. The two facing him moved closer.

Lin Pei shouted in Chinese at the Kung Fu master, "Coward! You don't have the testicles to fight one-on-one."

The class laughed at the obvious female voice chastising them. No one dared speak to the master like that.

Lin Pei continued. "Let me see if you are really a man and not a little boy playing at a man's game." She knew they had little hope of outfighting the whole class. Her only hope was to reduce the fight to a one-to-one situation. They were dead anyway if she failed.

"Silly little girl," Jen Hsai retorted. "Come. I will give you a free lesson. Too bad you will not live to graduate." He took a fighting stance.

Lin Pei assumed a praying mantis position, waiting.

Jen Hsai spun around and leaped into the air, arms and legs weapons ready to strike in any direction. He kicked out both legs in tandem. The first went high as Lin Pei ducked slightly. At the last possible instant, Lin sidestepped the second foot, grabbed it, and used Jen's momentum to throw him to the floor. His awe-struck students stopped to watch.

Not wasting any time, Lin Pei moved in and kicked him severely in the groin, and then again. Jen Hsai doubled up in a painful disbelief. He had never been beaten before, let alone by a woman. Lin danced in and launched a jaw-shattering kick to the face, and Master Jen Hsai lay still. She picked up his fallen nunchuckas, wrapped the chain around his neck and used the handles for leverage to choke off his breathing. She shouted to his white-robed students, "Lay down your weapons and sit on the floor or I will kill your master."

The class complied. Lin Pei's two bodyguards went around picking up the weapons and tossed them in a pile behind them. The room became silent. Then, from the dressing room, a short portly oriental man in a business suit stepped out with a heavy chromed automatic aimed directly at Lin Pei. He said, "It seems that we have a stalemate here, miss. Perhaps a checkmate, for if you kill that one, I have nothing to lose. And you will surely die along with your associates. It would be better if you release Master Jen Hsai, and leave while you can."

Lin Pei shouted an obscenity and increased the leverage on the nunchuckas. The fat man raised his gun and aimed at Lin Pei. He pulled back the slide on the automatic.

Boxer had started to sit up when the gunman entered the room. He shook his head clear, and as the man cocked his gun, Boxer pointed his revolver and fired off three rapid shots. The man was hit twice. Not bad considering the shortness of the barrel and the distance between them. The fat man staggered backward and dropped to his knees, then the floor. The shiny automatic crashed next to him.

Boxer quickly took control. He had Sun and Gai Tang usher the students into the dressing room and dragged the badly wounded fat man, who was Mr. Yuan, in with them. They locked the door.

A rag was stuffed in the Kung Fu master's mouth. Next, Sun removed his face mask and put it over Jen Hsai's head, but with the openings facing back. He and Gai Tang cuffed his hands and feet and they dragged him to the fire escape. With a great effort, Boxer and the Hung Yees carried their captive to the ground and into a waiting car. They were soon in a sub-basement deep in the bowels of Chinatown.

Chapter Fifteen

The sub-basement consisted of two windowless cement block rooms formerly used for storage under the wholesale Chinese bakery. Jen Hsai was dumped onto a shabby mattress in the outer room. He was still bound hand and foot and gagged beneath the face mask blindfold. Sun and Gai Tang stood guard. Lin Pei led Boxer back up to the next level, which served as meeting and living quarters for her elite killer squad during clandestine operations. This safe-house had hidden passageways and exits which led to their weapons cache or to the outside several buildings away.

Boxer started to protest. "Shouldn't we question Jen Hsai about Mei Ling, and about his Commie friends?"

"Later. As you can see he is in no shape to withstand an interrogation. We will all get some rest, and then question him in the morning. Come, let us go into my room and get some sleep."

Boxer followed her inside. A king-sized futon in an orange and black oriental motif covered a third of the floor. Matching pillows were lined up along two of its edges. A low black lacquered dresser, a small black chair, and several plump throw pillows completed the furnishings. Very Spartan. A brass lamp on the dresser cast a soft glow over everything. Boxer noticed a small bathroom adjacent to the room.

Lin Pei said, "Let me take a look at your head. You took quite a blow from the nunchuckas." She examined his head and found a lump near his left temple. The skin was broken, and his hair was matted with caked blood. She said, "I will clean you up. Wait here." Lin went into the bathroom, ran the water, and returned with a warm wet towel. She carefully cleaned off the area, and applied a medicated salve to the wound.

Boxer sighed, and stretched his neck, rubbing it with his fingers. Lin Pei said, "Let me help you." She removed his shirt and eased him down on her bed. She motioned him to roll over, and he lay facedown on the futon, a pillow tucked under his chest to allow his neck to stretch naturally. In a moment she was astride his loins. Boxer felt her naked flesh against his, realized she had stripped off her clothes, and smiled.

Lin Pei began by kneading the ropy muscles along his neck, working her way down to his shoulders and upper back. When her fingertips found a particularly tight spot, she applied heavier pressure with a thumb or knuckle. The muscle knots succumbed to her ministrations. For Boxer, it was a feeling of exquisite pain. He felt the tension drain from him.

Lin rolled Boxer over on his back, and kneeled behind his head. Her small but strong hands worked over the muscles of his neck and chest and along his flanks. As she leaned forward to do this, Boxer was face to face with her small but perfectly shaped breasts tipped in umber. He could feel desire stirring in his groin, but the massage felt so good he wished it would never stop.

Lin leaned forward and undid Boxer's pants. She slid her hands under the waistband and pushed them downward. Boxer helped her remove them. Now they were both completely naked. Lin moved forward, squatting on Boxer's chest, her bare bottom towards his face. Once again she leaned forward and kneaded the flesh of his thighs.

Boxer propped up his head on a pillow and took in the view. This was probably as close to heaven as he was going to get, and he savored it all. She had a magnificent body, trim and tight, with curves in all the right places. Her underside yawned at him. He placed his palms on her buttocks and caressed her as she loosened the tightness in his thighs.

Her fingertips danced on his scrotum, and he became instantly aroused.

He began to play with her, fondling her labia and clit with his fingers, moving his thumb in and out of her opening.

She cupped his balls and squeezed, while her other hand moved along his shaft, pulling back the skin in short strokes, then changing pace by wrapping her fingers around it and sliding them up and down its length.

Boxer had never known a woman so adept at fine-tuning his arousal.

She slid back up on his chest, and began licking around the tip of his penis, her hands, meanwhile, never missing a beat. She took him in her mouth and devoured him.

Boxer returned the favor.

Time seemed to stand still as they concentrated on giving each other great pleasure.

When Lin sensed that Boxer was ready to erupt, she applied sharp finger pressure under the tip of his penis, and his intensity diminished slightly. She cooed, "Not yet, my lover. We have a long way to go."

She moved her bottom down his body and impaled herself on his penis. Still facing forward, she started to slide up and down his shaft.

Boxer was beside himself with ecstasy. He caressed her back and behind in time with the rhythm of her movements.

Lin Pei turned her head back and said, "This is an ancient Chinese love position. It is called *Wild Geese Flying on their Backs*. I hope you enjoy it as much as I do."

This time she allowed him to release inside her. In ten minutes she had him fully erect again inside her and was seated facing him, straddling his thighs. She said, "This is *Wailing Monkey Clasping a Tree*." After that, they went on to *Staircase to Heaven* and *Jewel in the Crown*.

After two hours of unrelenting lovemaking, Boxer was completely spent, exhausted from the long hard day and long hard night, and slipped off to sleep with Lin Pei in his arms.

Boxer awoke a few hours later, muffled cries for help in his dream bringing him to consciousness. He rolled over to touch Lin Pei. She wasn't there. Her spot on the bed wasn't even warm. He looked in the bathroom, but she wasn't there either.

Another muffled scream. Boxer's eyes had adjusted to the darkness, and he found and put on his pants. He slipped on his shoes. The sound continued intermittently.

Boxer found the trapdoor of the stairway leading to the lower level, and followed it down. The sound intensified. He found himself in the outer room. The mattress on the floor was empty. A faint red glow eminated from the inner room. He peeked inside.

Torture chamber. Jen Hsai was seated on a low stool, his hands stretched high overhead and tied to a ring on the ceiling. His feet were tied to opposite sides of the stool. On closer inspection, Boxer noticed that Jen Hsai was barely seated on the tops of his thighs. His arms were bearing the brunt of his body weight. His face was a contorted mess, hardly recognizable. He had welts all over, and blood slowly oozing from open wounds on his shoulders and chest.

Boxer gasped involuntarily, and the three figures standing over the victim turned in his direction. Sun and Gai Tang stood ready. Lin Pei said to him, "You didn't get much sleep, my lover."

Boxer replied, "It seems that you didn't get any. What are you doing to him?"

"Asking him some questions."

"I'll bet."

"His answers have mostly been unsatisfactory. He admits working with the Chinese Communists, and little more. However, if we infiltrate the Dragon Tong, I think we will be able to stop them from sabotaging your Discovery festival."

Boxer said, "We don't use torture—"

"It's merely an ancient Chinese interrogation device called slices." Lin Pei walked over to her captive, bloody knife still in her hands, and deftly slashed four slices into the flesh of his chest. Again the muffled scream that had awakened Boxer. Lin Pei turned back to Boxer. "He has not yet told us the whereabouts of my cousin, Mei Ling. But he will very shortly." She sliced two more times.

"Stop it. For God's sake, stop it!" Boxer moved toward her, but her bodyguards blocked his way.

"Time is running out, both for us and for this one. He must talk soon. Please do not try to stop me. It is the only way, believe me. This one knows no respect for civilized customs. This is all he understands." She turned to Jen Hsai. "Isn't that so?"

Fear burned in Jen Hsai's eyes. Sweat rolled down his face, mixing in with the dried patches of blood.

She said to him, "You will tell me what you have done with Mei Ling, or I will not let you die." She nodded to Sun, who picked up a bucket and splashed its contents onto Jen Hsai's torso. A horrible scream forced its way out past the gag. He slumped on his seat.

The bile rose in Boxer's throat. He couldn't believe what was happening, or that he could let it be done to another human being, no matter how heinous his crimes. But he knew that Lin Pei was right. To this kind of zealot, death was martyrdom, a shortcut to heaven. Death was a reward.

Hell was not being allowed to die.

Lin Pei moved in on Jen Hsai and slashed four quick horizontal slices across his abdomen, to get his attention. "You will tell me now," she spat, "or you will go to your reward as a woman." She slipped the blade inside the front of his trousers and slit them open. She stabbed the point of the knife into a testicle, causing him to go wild with pain. She nodded to Sun, who removed Jen Hsai's gag. She said, "Tell me, and you will die now. Defy me and I will prolong this."

Jen Hsai spat at her. "The girl is dead. I raped her and passed her around to some of the others. Then I slit her throat and dumped her body in the basement of our headquarters. My people will do the same to the rest of your capitalist Hung Yee pigs. And you first among them." He spat again.

Lin Pei lunged the blade to the hilt up under his breastbone. Jen Hsai died instantly, as promised.

Lin Pei wiped her hands on her pants and walked to Boxer. She placed a hand on his shoulder. "Come," she said. "We have much work to do and so little time."

Boxer arrived back at the Stapleton base around 8 A.M. He went directly to his office. He opened the door quietly. No one noticed him. Will Pickens was seated at his desk, writing furiously. A printer was chirping away, spitting out reams of computer paper. A pretty blond lieutenant j.g. entered from another room carrying a stack of folders. She placed them on Pickens's desk, and caught Boxer's image out of the corner of her eye. She stopped abruptly at the sight of the shabby black-clad figure, a startled cry stuck in her throat. Pickens looked up, saw Boxer, and smiled.

"Mornin', Chief. Sleep well last night?"

"Don't even ask. You wouldn't believe it if I told you." He noticed the young woman. "And what are you looking at, Lieutenant?"

"N—n—nothing, sir. I was just—"

"She thinks she just seen a ghost, that's all. That's the boss, Leslie, honey. He's always tryin' to fool us with somethin'. Captain Jack Boxer, meet Lieutenant Leslie La Fontaine, my new assistant, compliments of Admiral D'Arcy himself."

Leslie snapped to attention and saluted smartly. Boxer returned the salute and said, "As you were, Lieutenant. If you don't mind, I'm very tired and cranky, and I have something to discuss with the Colonel here. So if you'll excuse me . . ."

"Yes, sir. Excuse me, sir. It's just that I . . ."

Boxer smiled for the first time. "Yes, I know, Lieutenant. It's the first time you've seen a ghost. Now, if you'll excuse us . . ."

When she'd gone, Boxer filled Pickens in on the events of the last twenty-four hours, leaving out only the goriest details.

Pickens pointed to the computer printouts and told him that it was a complete listing of all the ships in the festival, in descending order, starting with the Hamptons and ending off the coast of Atlantic City. Most of the ships had arrived, and were moored alongside their neighbors. Part of the British fleet and a Japanese supertanker hadn't arrived yet, though.

Boxer thanked Pickens for taking care of business in his absence, and added, "I'm going to get some shut-eye. I want a wake-up call at fourteen hundred. Meanwhile, I'm going to sleep like a dead man. No one is to bother me until then except for Admiral Stark. Or an extreme emergency. I have to get some sleep."

Boxer hitched a ride to his living quarters, stripped, showered, hit the sack, and within ten minutes was sound asleep. . . .

He was tied to a chair, surrounded by Orientals, and being slashed repeatedly by a beautiful woman with long black hair. No one heard his screams. Finally, there was a bell ringing and ringing and everyone stopped and looked away.

Boxer called out for help, violently threw his pillow to the floor, and awakened to the nagging chirp of his scrambler phone.

Boxer shook his head clear and grabbed the handset. He growled, "Boxer here."

"Jack? Commander Szpak here. We've got another problem besides the buoys moved out of position. The Romer Shoal Light is out. Someone planted a charge on it and blew it to hell. Same for the Orchard Shoal Light. Someone's been fucking with our navigational aids, Jack. And just in time for Discovery Day. It's sabotage, plain and simple."

"Can you get them fixed, Charlie? The harbor will be filled with ships on the Fourth. That's a week away."

"I could never get parts that quickly. Those are major navigational aids, very well built, and almost never cause us any problems. Consequently, we don't stockpile many of the parts that don't wear out."

Boxer said, "Do what you can, Charlie. Makeshift lights are better than none. Put that CPO of yours on it. I'll bet he comes up with something."

"Wooley's the guy that noticed the problem. He and his crew were out checking on the marker buoys. He knows that harbor better than anyone. Didn't take him any time at all to notice. You're right. I'll give him the job. Thanks."

"Don't mention it." Boxer asked, "By the way, what time is it?"

"Eleven thirty. I didn't wake you, did I?"

"No, of course not." Boxer hung up the phone and put on a clean uniform. It was going to be another very long day.

Chapter Sixteen

Captain Jin Chou was seated across from his political officer Hsien at a steel table bolted to the floor of the captain's quarters. Hsien was decoding a message coming in under highest security code from Admiral Fang himself. It was for their eyes alone.

Their agents have taken control of the Dragon Tong. On 4 July at precisely 1000 hours they will set off explosions throughout Manhattan in several key buildings: the Pan Am Building, the RCA Building in Rockefeller Center, the Chrysler Building, Jacob Javits Convention Center, and others. By 1200 hours the Tall Sailing Ships will have passed the reviewing stands on Governors Island and Liberty Island and will be headed south out of the Upper Bay. They will be followed by warships of the USA, USSR, and Great Britain with shallow enough draft to make the passage up the channel. At this time our agents will destroy the Brooklyn and Manhattan Bridges and blow the Holland and Battery Tunnels, blocking escape to the north. You will then commence to detonate by remote all the explosives you have previously set on the warships while they were moored. Simultaneously, our ground forces will collapse the Verrazano Bridge, sealing off the upper bay completely. Our suicide squads will ram explosive-laden powerboats into whatever warships they can get to.

You will then destroy the enemy ships in the lower bay, blocking off the Ambrose and Sandy Hook Channels, and expending all of your torpedoes. At that point you are to mine the harbor and make your escape, and return home by the quickest route. You are to avoid capture at all costs, repeat, at all costs. You are to destroy the Sea Death *if capture is imminent. Comrade Hsien is to record everything, and has the responsibility of ensuring that the mission is carried out completely as ordered. She will transmit a report to Admiral Fang immediately after the success of the mission.*

Good luck. Remember, the reemergence of our nation to mastery of the world is at stake. Do not fail us.

It was signed by the Admiral himself.

Hsien signed off. She shredded the message and placed the scraps in a large glass ashtray on the table. Captain Chou removed a cigarette lighter from his pocket and torched the papers.

When it had been reduced to ash, he dumped the remains into the head and flushed.

Hsien waited for him to return and stated, "Admiral Fang has clearly indicated his desire for me to control this mission, Comrade Captain. Therefore, I order you to consult with me before taking it upon yourself to engage our enemies in combat before you are in position to fulfill our mission."

Chou jumped up, knocking his metal stool to the ground with a resounding crash. "Foolish woman. Do you think for a moment that I would take orders from you? If you persist in interfering with my running of this ship, I fear you will suffer a terrible accident. You will never live to see the success of this mission, or my triumphant return to our motherland."

"I shall report this behavior to my superior, Minister Chen. And you, Comrade Captain, will spend the remainder of your days in prison in Manchuria. If we let you live."

Captain Chou was livid with rage. He raised his fist to strike Hsien. Suddenly, a message from the sonar officer came through the Command console. "Three targets, Comrade Captain, bearing two seven zero degrees . . . range fifteen zero zero zero meters . . . speed two zero knots."

Chou and his political officer stared at each other across the steel table. Chou put down his fist. "I will deal with you later. Now, I have work to do."

"Answer me, Comrade Captain. Are the targets approaching us or moving away?"

"Away. Now, if you'll excuse me . . ."

"I forbid . . ."

Captain Chou turned his back on the woman and keyed his IC-A mike, "Diving officer, prepare to dive. Bring us down to one hundred meters."

"Yes, Comrade Captain. Making one hundred meters." Then, a huge hissing noise and the bow began to sink. "Flooding commenced."

Chou keyed his engineering officer. "Give me three zero knots." Then he said, "Helmsman, bring us around two seven degrees. We will see who we have for company."

The boat settled to three hundred feet and pursued the three surface ships.

Captain Chou keyed his sonar officer. "SO, I want positive ID on those targets as soon as possible. And keep me informed of any changes in their course or speed."

"Aye, Captain."

Hsien decided to alter her tactics. "Comrade Captain, please consider for a moment the importance of our mission. If this submarine is damaged in combat, or otherwise delayed, we may fail to destroy the greatest assemblage of fighting ships since the English defeated the Spanish Armada. What glory will there be in sinking three enemy ships off the coast of England if we cannot complete our mission? Please, I beg of you, remember our priorities."

Captain Chou sighed heavily. He put a hand on the woman's shoulder, the first softening on his part since their first meeting. In an almost fatherly tone he said, "Comrade Hsien, you are wise to question, rather than demand. In this case, it would seem that you are correct. Why engage three vessels in combat and risk damage and the forfeiture of our mission, when we could just avoid them and sail on our way?

Hsien smiled back.

Chou continued, "You see, Comrade, I would have to dog those three vessels all the way to New York, if that is where they are headed, or I would have to sail way off course to avoid them. Now, the element of surprise is on my side, and I can easily sink all three of the enemy vessels like shooting ducks on a pond. If not, and they detect us on their sonar, we would become the sitting ducks. No, It is better to strike first. Now I must attend to my command."

"But Comrade Captain, I—"

The sonar officer's voice on the IC-A broke up the argument. "Target bearing zero five degrees, Comrade Captain. . . . Range six thousand meters. . . . Speed two zero knots."

Chou ordered the firing crew into action. "Forward torpedo room . . . arm and load tubes one, two, five, and six. FO . . . prepare to fire manually at my command. You will fire torpedoes two and five . . . followed in twenty seconds by one and six."

"Yes, Captain," was the reply from all officers concerned.

Chou keyed in his diving officer. "DO, stand by to dive. At my command you will make two hundred meters."

"Aye, sir," answered the DO.

"Helmsman, stand by for my command. We

will immediately—"

The SO broke in. "Comrade Captain . . . new target bearing three five degrees . . . range two thousand five hundred meters . . . speed four zero knots . . . and closing fast, sir."

"What the . . . a destroyer? DO, prepare to dive. Torpedo room, unload torpedoes. FO . . . abort firing plan. All hands . . . prepare to dive. Repeat, prepare to dive. We are under surveillance. Maintain silence and sit tight."

Captain Chou found Hsien standing around as if dazed. He took hold of her arm and directed her into a bucket seat and strapped her in. He keyed his MC mike. "DO . . . give me two hundred meters. . . . Let's get the hell out of here."

The submariners maintained silence as the *Sea Death* sliced through the deep until it reached six hundred feet and leveled off. Chou directed his helmsman to follow a zigzag course taking them around and ahead of the three surface vessels, hoping they would backtrack looking for him.

The SO reported in. "Sir, I am getting sonar input. The destroyer must have deployed sonobuoys above us."

Chou listened. The pinging became clearer and louder. "Helmsman . . . give me nine zero degrees. DO . . . make three hundred meters."

The EXO and several other officers on the bridge looked at Captain Chou. They knew what their fate would be if he failed to outmaneuver the enemy.

Chou's face tightened. His neck muscles bulged like twin mooring lines. His nostrils flared and he

262

wiped the sweat off his brow with a shirtsleeve. He keyed in his engineering officer. "EO . . . cut the engine. Repeat . . . cut the engine. All hands hear this. . . . Rig for silent running."

The first depth charge was dropped by the destroyer *Keen* three miles behind the three surface vessels. The next nine charges followed in five-hundred-yard intervals. They exploded each in its turn with a tremendous roar and whoosh of water leaping into the air. In the following half hour, the *Keen* covered a hundred-and-eighty-degree arch behind and to the sides of the original sighting.

The *Keen* got lucky. One of its depth charges exploded at three hundred feet, near enough to the *Sea Death* to send tremors throughout the submarine. Sailors were thrown into the bulkheads and onto the floor.

Chou found a handhold near his command module and clung to it. He glanced over at Hsien. Though secure in her seat, she was visibly shaken. Another charge exploded a half mile away, sending further shock waves throughout the submarine. And then another, still farther away. Perhaps the enemy would pass.

Chou could read the fear on Hsien's face as she looked toward him for support. He gave her a wink and managed a thumbs-up sign. She smiled back weakly, appreciating his try at calming her. She was close to panic.

The next explosion roared directly overhead. The *Sea Death* shuddered violently. Steel plates strained against their rivets. An electrical module sputtered, sparked, and went silent, emitting an

263

acrid stench. The sub listed forward and began a silent descent toward the ocean floor. Chou could smell the fear around him. He motioned at everyone nearby to remain silent with a finger to his lips, just as most of the lights went out.

For almost two hours, captain and crew got a taste of what Hell was going to be like. The air scrubbing system had been shut down to preserve silence at the onset of the attack, and its effects were being noticed. The air became thinner, and many had difficult breathing. The air attained a fetid pungency. Fear caused a mingling of odors as bowels and bladders and sweat glands gave out. Ears rang from the cacophony of explosions. Heads burst from pain and from the ever-increasing pressure.

Finally, the submarine leveled off at two thousand feet. Chou was as surprised as anyone. He crawled on hands and knees over bodies and debris toward the sonar station. He found the SO strapped to his seat, headphones still covering his ears. He tapped him on the shoulder, uncovered an ear, and asked in a whisper if he heard anything. The SO shook his head no, and whispered back not in the last half hour. Prior to that he thought he'd heard the engine sounds above growing fainter.

Captain Chou clapped him on the shoulder and gave him the thumbs-up sign. "Good man," he whispered. He made his way back to the diving officer. Chou found the DO at his station, diligently adjusting the diving planes. The man shined a red-shrouded flashlight at the captain, then on himself. He was smiling broadly.

To Chou's astonishment, the DO had acted on his own to bring the sub gently out of range of the surface sonar. He had saved their lives. Now, it was on to the U.S.A. and New York Harbor. . . .

Boxer, Commander Stanley Green, skipper of the destroyer *Keen*, and Szpak were in Admiral D'Arcy's office discussing the *Keen*'s attack on an unidentified submarine.

"What I don't understand," D'Arcy said, "was why you couldn't ID the bastard."

"We couldn't get a matching sound between his propellers and out data bank," Green said. He was a square-shouldered man, with graying sideburns, but an otherwise boyishly open face.

"Did you attempt to signal him?" Szpak asked.

"Negative," Green answered. "I considered him hostile from the moment our sonar made contact."

"But suppose—" D'Arcy began.

"All our boats have orders to run on the surface as soon as they reach the two-hundred-mile limit," Boxer said, interrupting D'Arcy. "He didn't belong here."

"Are you sure you got him?" Szpak asked.

"We saw the debris," Green answered.

Boxer rubbed his beard. . . . Debris could be blown out through the torpedo tubes to make it look as if the boat had been hit. "This is the third incident within two weeks involving a submarine. . . . One in the China Sea, another with the *Gorsky*—"

"We don't know that the Ruskie trawler was sunk by a submarine," D'Arcy said.

"It's a good guess that it was," Boxer responded, filling his pipe and lighting it.

"You think it's the same boat?" Szpak questioned.

Boxer shrugged. "Might be, or it could be more than one. In either case—"

"If it was one," D'Arcy said, "it has been knocked out of the box."

"Maybe. . . . That debris Commander Green saw doesn't really prove anything."

"But—" Green started to say.

"If it got you to think you whacked a sub, then it served its purpose. The skipper was just doing what he should have been doing," Boxer said. "I wouldn't bet on that boat being down. In fact, I want to add to our ASW capability out there. Better put the *Liberty* off the Ambrose Light. Her choppers could sweep the area, say in a thirty-mile radius, three hundred and sixty degrees, several times a day." He looked at D'Arcy. "Any problems with that?"

"None," D'Arcy answered.

A knock on the admiral's door stopped any further conversation.

"Come," D'Arcy called.

A WAVE opened the door and said, "There's a CPO Boulay here for Captain Boxer."

"Send him in," Boxer said.

The WAVE looked questioningly at D'Arcy.

The admiral nodded.

Boulay threw up a half-assed salute and said, "Cap'n Boxer, me an' my crew are ready to shove off. I'm going to patrol the Ambrose Channel tonight. I think they're going to try that next. If they think they blocked the Sandy Hook Channel, it's only logical for them to hit the Ambrose next. I figure if we just set there like a fishing boat we might catch 'em trying to move some more markers."

Boxer nodded. "Sounds like you're on to something, Wooly. I'll join you."

"I don't think there's much sense in you wasting your time setting out there all night. Bad enough me and the boys have to do it. Besides, Tiny's got gas something awful. Some nights you just want to throw him overboard."

Boxer chuckled. "Tell you what. Let's leave your buoy tender tied up here at the station. I'll have a high-speed fisherman sent over from Stapleton with a couple of my SEALs. Then O'Reilly and Lebanski and myself will join you and your guys aboard. We'll be faster and better armed, and we'll have the element of surprise on our side. Your big red tub will frighten anyone away. How about it?"

Wooly knew an order when he got one. Boxer was just allowing him to save face, and he knew it. Well, so be it. "Sounds fine with me. I hope Tiny and the boys don't mind."

Boxer said, "Thanks. I don't really care what Tiny Tim wants or doesn't want. We'll stand him downwind of us. And if that doesn't work, we'll all throw him over the side."

Boulay's turn to laugh. "Okay, Captain. When do we get started?"

Boxer looked at his watch. It was 1700. "We'll be ready to leave here at seventeen forty. Have your crew ready to shove off promptly."

"Right," he answered.

Boxer said, "And Wooly . . . you've got the helm out there. You know those waters better than anyone."

The CPO's face lit up. He saluted smartly. "Yes, *sir.* We'll be ready. And thanks."

CPO Boulay found a spot on the eastern edge of Ambrose Channel, midway between Breezy Point on the Rockaway Sandbar and Sandy Hook Point. He dropped anchor in twenty feet of water, and took a seat behind the wheel. His job was to remain at the helm, ready to move quickly should they have any trouble. Tiny, Stan, Ollie, and Boxer, dressed as fishermen, cast their lines into the channel where organic debris settled, and the fish abounded. The two SEALs remained below in the cabin of the thirty footer. They were armed as usual with their M-16s.

Wooly unwrapped a giant hero sandwich and popped a beer, then settled down to devour his food. His crew and Boxer made like fisherman, and to everyone's surprise, the fishing was good. They had landed a half-dozen bluefish, and Wooly Bully had almost finished his second sandwich when a nearby fifty-five-foot charter fishing boat made its move. It was imperceptible at first, but Boulay's practiced eye picked it right up. He picked off a piece of roll and tossed it at Boxer. When Boxer turned to see what the hell was going on, Wooly shushed him with a finger on lips and pointed at the charter boat.

Boxer set his pole in a holder and walked close to the CPO. Wooly spoke quietly. "That him, all right, Skipper. See'em right up near that red nun? See it bob around there? Now look at the other buoys. No movement. It's too calm tonight. They're fucking around with that marker sure as God made little green apples."

Boxer looked through a set of night glasses. Boulay was right. A diver alongside the boat had attached a line to the mushroom anchor chain holding the buoy in place. As soon as he got back on board, the charter boat backed away, pulling the red nun buoy with it. "Phew. Son of a bitch. Wooly, you're a genius. Okay, let's go get them."

Boulay revved up the powerful inboard and headed toward the larger craft. Tim Mathisen aimed a powerful search beam on the fishing boat, illuminating the pilothouse.

Boxer held the bull horn to his mouth. "Now hear this, *Billy Bob*," Boxer called out, reading the name of the boat off the sign attached to the rail. "This is the Coast Guard. Repeat, this is the U.S. Coast Guard. You are ordered to cut your engines and stand by to be boarded."

The larger boat's engines continued their muffled roar. No sign of compliance. Boxer repeated, "You are ordered to cut your engines and stand by to be boarded. Do not attempt to leave."

Two shots rang out, shattering the searchlight. Another volley sent the crew scurrying for cover. Wooly swung his boat in a random zigzag pattern to avoid the shooting. Boxer called up O'Reilly and Lebanski. "Okay, guys. We warned them. Let 'em know we mean business."

The two SEALs took up positions along the starboard rail and opened fire with their M-16s. The glass windows of the pilothouse were shattered. Then, apparently the nun buoy was cut loose and the fishing boat roared away around the lee of Sandy Hook. Boulay followed. The SEALs continued with intermittent bursts of their automatic weapons. Boulay said, "They're headed for the Atlantic Highlands. I'm going to flank them and cut them off. Keep firing at the wheelhouse. Sooner or later the captain's going to realize he's a target."

Suddenly, the flash of guns being fired were seen at the rail of the larger boat. O'Reilly aimed at the flashes and let loose a volley. There was shouting from the boat. A body fell overboard with a loud splash. Slowly, the charter boat's engines revved down. Then, a voice through a bullhorn. "Okay, okay. Don't shoot."

Boxer ordered. "Turn off your engines and have all hands form on deck where we can see them. You are under arrest. Prepare for boarding."

Boulay lined up the two boats, portside to portside.

Boxer was the first to board, followed by the SEALs, who covered the crew with their M-16s. They were all Caucasians, which surprised Boxer.

The captain was brought forward, a scruffy type, belly turning to lard, two days' growth of beard, and a bevy of tattoos on both arms. Boxer grabbed him by the neck of his T-shirt. "You are under arrest. You were moving navigational markers, which is a federal crime. You also shot at us, which may be grounds for me throwing you overboard. Now, I want to know what the fuck's going on here."

The captain took a drag of the cigarette dangling from his lips, exhaled the smoke, and flipped the butt over the side. "Shit. Now I'm probably going to lose my license. I knew I shouldn'ta listened to those gooks."

"What did you say?"

Sweat dripped from the captain's forehead. He looked furtively in the direction of boat's enclosed cabin. "I mean Chinamen. Sorry. The money was good, and they said it was going to be a practical joke. Shit. Some joke."

"Looks like the joke's on you. Twenty years in a federal prison will give you plenty of time to laugh about it. Why did you shoot at us?"

"Wasn't me, honest. Or my crew neither. It was those goo—I mean Chinamen did the shooting. You got one of them. Went into the drink back there. Shit. Owes me money, too."

Boxer twisted the shirt tighter and pulled the man closer. He could smell the stale stench of cigarette smoke on the man's breath. "Where's the other one? The Chinese."

The man squirmed in Boxer's grasp. He broke out in a sweat. "I—I—d-d-don't know. Honest.

271

They were both on the rail shooting at you. One of them got hit and fell overboard. I haven't seen the other—"

"Look out!"

A shot rang out. A Chinese head poked out from the cabin and another shot bound for Boxer was stopped by the boat's captain. O'Reilly fired from the hip, cutting down the assailant as he charged Boxer, firing his handgun.

"Don't kill him," Boxer shouted. "I want to question him. Take care of this one, and I'll look after the Chinese."

Boxer tried to stop the bleeding, but the Chinese man's leg was torn up too badly. He yelled down to Boulay in the other boat. "Call ahead to the Coast Guard Station. Have an ambulance with an emergency-trained doctor aboard."

It took just five minutes for Boxer's crew to evacuate the wounded and reboard their boat. Then they sped back to the station to save a man's life.

Chapter Seventeen

Charlie Leung checked his watch. At precisely ninety seconds into the Holland Tunnel he stopped his '79 Pontiac Bonneville and turned off the ignition. He spent the next two minutes alternately flooding the engine and grinding the ignition, until he was certain that restarting the car was hopeless. Drivers of the vehicles behind him in the left lane leaned on their horns and cursed his stupidity for stalling out in the tunnel. The driver of the florist van behind him had just gotten off from work and was returning to his home in Jersey City in the 5 P.M. rush hour traffic. This he didn't need. He rolled down the window on the driver's side. "Hey, you crazy jerk. Whadafuckizamadderwityou, anyhow? Move dat fuckin' ting." He punctuated his speech with blasts of his horn.

Charlie just sat there grinding away at his ignition, and visibly shrugging his shoulders as traffic passed him on the right in a steady stream, some stopping to gape at the poor sap who got stuck in the Holland Tunnel.

At five minutes and ten seconds after Charlie

Leung stopped his car, a confederate driving a beat-up silver '77 Buick Le Sabre in the right lane suddenly rammed his car into reverse. The transmission let off a loud crunching sound and the Buick stopped one car length behind Charlie Leung's Bonneville. The following car screeched to a halt, but not in time. The fancy late-model Caddy skidded into the Buick. A red Mazda pickup plowed into the Cadillac. More cars screeched and skidded. Several more vehicles collided. And tempers flared. The driver of the Caddy, a Black man with a bad-ass mustache and a moderate Afro, stepped out of his car and shouted at the short oriental driver of the Buick. Charlie laughed as the oriental driver, a Chinese named Manny something, began cursing in Chinese and broken English at the Black man. The driver of the florist van behind Charlie got into the shouting match, telling the Black man that the Buick had stopped short, but the Caddy was tailgating too close behind it.

Manny went over to the florist truck and yelled at the driver to look under the Buick. The transmission had fallen out. Not his fault. The driver of the Caddy told him to mind his own fucking business. By then a Transit Authority tow truck had backed into the tunnel and pulled in front of Charlie Leung's Pontiac. Manny began shouting in Chinese, then in English, that his car was broken and the man in the back of him and threatened his life. Take him out first.

Charlie countered with, "Hey, nothin' doing. My car stalled first. I'm first one out." The two came close to blows, pushing each other around and calling each other names. A cacophony of blaring horns became a roaring crescendo obliterating the shouts of the drivers stuck in the mess. Charlie started to cough and gag, holding his throat, gasping for breath. He pleaded with the tow driver. "Asthma. Please get me the hell out of here. Can't breathe."

The tow truck driver just shook his head in disbelief at the scene before him. He hitched up Charlie's Pontiac Bonneville, and pulled it out of the tunnel onto the streets of Jersey City. He left Charlie and his car at an Exxon station and returned to the tunnel. This time he had the Transit Police block off both lanes, so a team of tow trucks could bring out Manny's Buick and in turn the several vehicles that had collided behind him.

Later that night, Charlie and Manny joked about the incident over hamburgers and shakes in a diner on Hudson Street. The incident had worked well. Very well, indeed. Tomorrow they would test the Battery Tunnel from Brooklyn to Lower Manhatten. They would use two different wrecks. "Next time," Charlie said, "I get to drop the trans, and you can stall out." They laughed and slapped each other on the shoulders, and then finished their meals. Tomorrow would be another day.

Boxer was seated behind his desk sifting through a pile of computer printouts, swearing to himself that he'd never again be talked into a desk job. He puffed away on his pipe, sorting the papers into three piles: delegate to subordinates, personally act on immediately, and trash. Somehow his personal pile kept getting larger.

There was a knock on his door, and Will Pickens stepped inside. "Sorry to bother you, Chief, but Ah got a fellow here who's more agitated than a pregnant fox in a forest fire. El Capitan Rodolfo Rivera de la Cruz, from the Argentinean Navy. Claims the British are out to get them. He thinks they're still fighting that ten-year-old Falkland Islands war."

"What are you talking about, Will?"

"One of the Argentine frigates got a hole tore out of its belly by an explosive of some type while it was sitting at anchor off the coast of Atlantic City. Ol' Rodolfo's got his ass up in the air claiming that the Brits had done it. Personally, ah can't see why they would."

"What's he want me to do?"

Pickens shrugged his shoulders. "Dammed if Ah know, Chief. Want me to send him in?"

Boxer took a long pull on his pipe. "Okay, Will. Send him in. And stick around, okay?"

"Sure thing." Pickens opened the door and stuck his head out into the adjacent room. "Okay, Captain, you can come in now."

Boxer couldn't suppress a smile when the five-foot-tall Argentinean Captain stepped into the office bedecked in a smashing blue jacket decorated with gold braid and dual rows of shiny brass buttons. The uniform was completed by white pants and a white cap repleat with more gold trim. Quite a dandy. He snapped to attention and saluted crisply. He was followed into the room by his subordinate, a young lieutenant in a plain government issue uniform.

"I am Capitano Rodolfo Rivera de la Cruz."

Boxer saluted, then stood and shook the man's hand. "Jack Boxer, Captain, U.S. Navy. A pleasure to meet you, Captain. Now what can I do for you?"

The young lieutenant spoke softly in Spanish directly to Rodolfo, who answered him back in kind. The lieutenant turned to Boxer and said, "My captain wishes me to express his outrage at the British for bombing one of our warships. He also wishes me to say that the bastards, that is his word, I am sorry, the bastards have been harassing us for the past ten years, in retaliation for our defense of the Molvados Islands, which historically belong to Argentina. This is just another incidence of their treachery. The Argentine government demands retribution. And an apology."

Boxer sat there, nodding his head, smiling. "Okay, I'll do what I can," he told Captain de la Cruz. "Meanwhile, try to get a team of frogmen to check out the other ships, just in case."

The lieutenant translated what his captain probably already understood. The two saluted Boxer, and were escorted out by Will Pickens.

When Pickens came back into Boxer's office, he asked, "Well, what do you think, Chief?"

Boxer rapped his cold pipe against the palm of his hand, and dumped the contents into a large glass ashtray. "Seems like we've got a real problem on our hands, Will. And I don't think the British are responsible for it. But just to address both sides of the issue, see if you can get Admiral Smythe to join us for a chit-chat."

Boxer busied himself with his paperwork for almost two hours until Pickens returned with the admiral of the British Fleet, Cecil Smythe. Smythe was accompanied by two assistants, both captains. He got right to the point.

"Just what the hell's this all about, Boxer? I'm not about to come running at the beck and call of some captain no matter who's navy he's in. This better damn well be important, or I'll have your hide."

The two assistants cringed at the admiral's words.

Boxer sensed they felt embarrassed for him. He merely said, "Thank you for seeing me at such short notice, Admiral. I don't mean to pull rank on you, but this is of the utmost importance." Boxer continued. "An explosive device was set off against an Argentinean frigate. Thank God nobody was badly injured. However, the Argentines are blaming Great Britain for the bombing. I assured him that it wasn't so, but I thought you should be aware of the situation."

"Still fighting the Battle of the Falklands, are they? I was there, you know. Commander of the *Isle of Wight*. We gave the buggers what for, didn't we? But that was in the past, I must say. Ten years, I believe. Let bygones by bygones, Captain. Of course their accusation is absurd."

"I agree, Admiral. I'd like to suggest that you step up security, sir. As you know by my briefing yesterday, we suspect that the Chinese may try to disrupt the Discovery festival, in every way that they can."

The admiral stood with one hand bent behind his back. "I'm aware of that, Captain Boxer."

"Well, I'd appreciate it if you'd send some scuba divers out to check your ships for plastiques, or magnetic mines."

"His Majesty's ships are perfectly safe, Captain."

The ensuing explosion nearly knocked Boxer from his chair. He grabbed a pair of Zeiss field glasses from a nearby shelf, and hurried past the stunned admiral out of the building. Thick black smoke rose off the Jersey coast in the vicinity of Long Branch, a stretch of sand south of Sandy Hook . . . the British. . . . Boxer summoned a jeep, evicted its occupants, and was ready to pull out when Will Pickens ran out of the office building, along with Admiral Smythe and his aides. Boxer shouted out to the admiral. "It's in the direction of your fleet. Let's go."

The five of them sped to the small craft mooring dock and shouted orders to one of the SEALs, who always had a man standing by to take Boxer wherever he wanted to go by sea. In ten minutes they were alongside the aircraft carrier, *H.M.S. Horton,* named for one of the British naval heroes of World War II. A nasty hole was torn in its side, revealing two levels of burnt-out fighter plane storage, twisted girders, and twisted men. A fire raged out of control out of the opening.

Boxer signaled the Coast Guard Station in the New York Battery, and soon a pair of fireboats were making their way to the scene. Then he followed Admiral Smythe aboard the carrier, followed by Pickens and the admiral's aides. The ship's captain stopped shouting orders when he spotted Admiral Smythe, and saluted.

"What's the extent of it, Townsend?"

The one-star admiral, Townsend, replied, "Rocket strike, Sir. Exocet from the looks of it. Bloody Frogs selling the damn things to anyone who can pay for them."

Smythe nodded his agreement. Townsend continued. "Eleven dead, Sir. Many more wounded. Several of our fighters. Too hot down there to be sure. I've got damage control on it right now."

"Good man," Smythe said.

Boxer added, "I've got two firefighter tugs on their way over her now."

Smythe looked hard at Boxer. "It's those damned Argentineans. Bastards are retaliating for our supposed attack on them. They're trying to provoke us into another bloody war, are they? Well, this time they'll lose more than a few ships. A whole bloody lot more."

It was well into late afternoon when the fire teams got the blaze under control. An after-explosion had caused more damage, and some of the fire control team were injured or killed. The scene aboard the *Horton* had become very grim. While Admirals Smythe and Townsend coordinated the damage control units, Boxer called in evacuation helicopters, and notified the area hospitals about the incoming casualties. Burn units in New York, as well as Livingston and Newark in New Jersey, were standing by to treat the worst victims.

Later in the evening, Admiral Smythe delivered a formal protest to Boxer, blaming the Argentine forces for the rocket attack on the carrier. Boxer called in de la Cruz, and explained the situation. The Argentineans, of course, denied the allegations, and swore revenge on the British for blaming them. What a fine mess, Boxer swore. Now I've got the Capulets on one side, and the Montagues on the other. What I need is the wisdom to deal with this situation tomorrow.

At first light, Boxer was back aboard the *Horton*. He summoned the damage control officer. The DCO, Captain Wallace, brought Boxer down to the area of destruction, which was by now cool enough to enter. The damage was extensive. Bulkheads and flooring of steel and aluminum were burned out and twisted beyond recognition. The corpses of several fighter planes were being removed. The human bodies were in caskets on the flight deck. The DCO pointed out a fragment of the tail assembly of the rocket that caused the damage. "There's the bloody bastard that got us. Exocet. The Old Man's sure of it."

Boxer knew better. He asked Wallace, "Can you get this thing topside?"

The DCO nodded yes.

"Okay. Great. But very carefully now. I want it

intact."

It took over an hour, but finally the rocket fragment was set upon the flight deck. Admirals Smythe and Townsend were called, and joined Boxer.

"So that's it," Smythe said grimly. "They probably fired it at us from a cutter. There wasn't any large shipping about."

"Gentlemen, I have to inform you that it's not what you think it is."

"It's a damn Exocet. That's what they used on us in the Falklands."

Boxer said, "It's a SLCM. A submarine-launched cruise missile. My sub, the *Shark*, has at least a dozen on board at all times. That's confidential, of course."

Smythe asked, "Are you absolutely certain?"

"Damn sure, Admiral. A lot surer than how to make peace between you and the Argentineans."

Admiral Smythe looked embarrassed. "I'll tend to that, Boxer. Sorry about the fuss. Wouldn't put it past the bastards, though," he said through a slight smile.

"They feel the same way. Some of their old-timers are still seething from their defeat. It tumbled their military government, and sent quite a few senior officers out on their asses. What we have to do now is find that elusive submarine. Just possibly it eluded your destroyers the other day."

"It's beginning to look that way, Boxer. What are you going to do about it?"

"Well, we have our sonar tracking station at the

edge of the continental shelf. We have our strings of hydrophones along the ocean floor. We'll be able to detect anything within two hundred and fifty miles of the harbor."

Admiral Smythe shook his head. "You'll have to do better than that. Those cruise missiles you speak about have a three-hundred-mile range. I wonder how they were so accurate."

Boxer offered, "I think they were just firing into a crowd. They got lucky enough to hit the *Horton*."

"And they can get lucky again and again, damn them. You'll have to go after that sub, before it strikes again."

"I agree with you Admiral. We'll get him, I assure you. There is something else though, just as important."

Smythe looked at Boxer quizzically.

"That Argentine frigate was damaged by a magnetic mine. I would suggest a massive underwater inspection by each nation of all their ships. We're only two days away from Discovery Day. Whatever is going to happen will happen by then."

Chapter Eighteen

Borodine pledged his cooperation to Boxer and agreed to beef up security in the vicinity of the Soviet bloc fleet. He would send scuba divers below to check for mines attached to the ships.

Boxer chose to lead a squad of SEALs personally to inspect the Japanese supertanker *Shogun,* rivaled in size only by the *Tecumseh,* the supership that had housed the *Shark* during her earlier clandestine operations. O'Reilly, Lebansky, and two other SEALs joined Boxer in an inflatable launch, and pulled alongside the *Shogun.*

Their craft appeared like a mere speck next to the monster tanker. Boxer issued instructions to his crew. Then he and O'Reilly perched on the gun'ale and flipped backward into the sea. Using powerful floodlights, they swam a parallel course toward the stern, inspecting the hull for attached explosives. The *Shogun* had just delivered a full cargo of Singapore crude, and rode very high in the water, making the task easier for Boxer and the SEALs to accomplish.

Lebansky steered the inflatable toward the stern.

Then he and Randy Ferraro went overboard and swam toward the bow, while the fourth SEAL, Frank Jones, maneuvered the launch amidship. He kept watch on their position by following their searchlights.

About a hundred feet back from the bow, ten feet up from the keel, Boxer spotted the first mine. It was attached to the hull with a strong magnetic disk. It was spherical, about three feet in diameter, with two antennae visible at the far end. Boxer found an eight-inch-square hatch cover, and gingerly pried it open to discover a series of dials and LED lights. . . . Obviously, someone had placed these by hand and preset time and frequency instructions into the firing mechanism. All it would take would be a precise radio or ultrasonic signal from a mothership to blow a gaping hole in the *Shogun*. . . . Boxer wondered how many more of these beauties were planted on the tanker.

He didn't have to wonder long. O'Reilly was signaling frantically from twenty feet farther aft. He'd discovered a second mine.

Boxer investigated, and found it to be a duplicate of the one he had found. He decided to surface. He yelled to Jones in the inflatable, and told him what they'd found when the craft was close enough. Boxer told him to call in the Stapleton base and have a minesweeping hovercraft sent down with a bomb squad. He and O'Reilly were going to search for more mines.

Boxer returned to the site of O'Reilly's find, but the SEAL wasn't there. Boxer noticed a floodlight lying on the ocean floor. There was turbulence a short distance away, and Boxer headed for it. He shone his light on the area and could see O'Reilly, in swimshorts and wetsuit top, struggling with three figures in full wetsuits. A surge of air bubbles rose from among them.

Boxer wished he had thought of arming themselves with more than their scuba knives. He propelled himself into the group and grabbed the facemask of the first man he encountered. Boxer pulled back and slashed the air tube, then drove the blade into the throat of the startled man. The astonished expression on his face became a death mask as his blood pumped into the sea from is severed arteries.

O'Reilly's limbs worked into a frenzy, but he could not break the hold of his two remaining attackers. They had pulled off his air supply, and his lungs were bursting against his endurance. Boxer hurried to his rescue.

One of the men turned his attention to the newest intruder while the other tried to keep O'Reilly from surfacing.

Boxer tried for a quick kill. He raised his knife and lunged for his opponent's throat. A hand shot out and caught Boxer's wrist in a steely grip. . . . The man was good. No doubt about it. . . . A second hand darted out and Boxer had all he could do to avoid the slashing blade. He grabbed onto the wrist.

The man suddenly twisted his body over Boxer's and slammed him into the steel hull of the tanker. And he slammed him again and again.

Boxer curled his body and kicked hard into his

opponent's groin.

The man released his grip and tried to cover his balls.

Boxer thrust his blade into the man's throat. He severed the jugular, and pushed the man away, turning his attention on saving O'Reilly.

O'Reilly had his attacker's air hose in his hand, but otherwise seemed to be floating about listlessly.

Boxer made a dash for him, knife at ready. Suddenly, a harpoon thrust itself into O'Reilly's midsection, fired from below them.

Boxer wheeled in the direction of the speargun. He wasn't fast enough. The second harpoon caught him in the thigh, embedding itself in his bulky quadriceps muscles, stopping within inches of his groin.

Blood flowed from O'Reilly's wound, and from Boxer's thigh.

Boxer thought, if they had another spear, he was a goner. He held his knife in front of him, in a feeble attempt to protect himself. His other hand tried futilely to disengage the harpoon.

The man fighting O'Reilly started toward Boxer, joined by his companion with the speargun.

There was a commotion behind them and suddenly they made for the surface, forgetting about Boxer.

Lebansky and Ferraro had found several more mines on the tanker's hull and were now swimming toward Boxer. He waved them away from himself and toward the enemy divers.

Frank Jones watched the first two heads surface and thought it was Boxer and O'Reilly.

The third head was Lebansky's, who pulled off his mask and yelled at Jones to stop the other two.

That took two bursts of his M-16.

The area around the two divers turned bloody red.

Randy Ferraro broke surface, noticed everything under control, and dove toward Boxer. Boxer motioned him toward the now lifeless form of Patrick O'Reilly.

Too late. O'Reilly was too far gone.

Ferraro returned for Boxer, and helped him to the surface. There, he and Lebansky towed him to the inflatable. Jones helped them get Boxer aboard the launch. Then they dove to retrieve the body of the squad leader.

O'Reilly's body was taken to the morgue at Stapleton Naval Base on Staten Island.

Demolition experts removed the explosives from the *Shogun*. More scuba divers were dispatched, desperately working against time to locate mines on the other ships.

Boxer was removed to the Emergency Room at Bellevue Hospital in Manhattan, where surgeons tried to stop the blood loss and save Boxer's leg. Boxer was suffering from shock. His face was very pale, his pulse much too low. His mission was falling apart around him. It was very grim. He was running out of time. It was late evening, July 2.

Charlie Leung was feeling very pleased with himself. He glanced at the time on his new Seiko watch, a gift of the Dragon Tong for his part in the

Holland battery Tunnel tie-ups. It was 11 P.M. The night was still young. Though it was only Thursday, it would be his last late night out for the week. Tomorrow afternoon, he and his new friends would go through a dry run of their parts in Saturday morning's escapades. That meant a good night's sleep tomorrow night so they could get an early start on Saturday.

Then Saturday night. Payday. He was promised a thousand dollars for a few hour's work, and more importantly, a permanent position in the Dragon Tong. No longer would he have to grovel at the feet of the Hung Yees. No more would he have to pay tribute to them for helping his family escape from Taiwan. They would have gotten away without them, he was sure. After all, hadn't he killed that pig officer who'd tried to stop them?

Word had gotten around Chinatown about him; his courage and bravado had gotten him noticed by the Dragon Tong. He had proven himself again in the tunnels. And he would endear himself to them forever when he drove the bomb car into the Battery Tunnel on Saturday.

Yes, after Saturday he would be one of the Dragons. He would no longer have to pretend to cooperate with the Hung Yees. They would no longer be able to touch him. The Dragons were too strong.

Charlie strolled along Mott Street, dreaming about his newfound good fortune, and looking for some action. He turned the corner onto Pell Street and ran into what he was looking for. Ran into, and almost knocked her down. She was the most beautiful Chinese girl he had ever seen. Her delicate features were finely chissled, her pale skin almost translucent, her hair and makeup flawless. And her skin-tight traditional dress, slit very high to reveal most of her left thigh, showed off her tiny waist and almost voluptuous figure. She was perfect. Dressed as she was, she was most certainly a woman of the street, a hooker, thought Charlie. But what the hell.

Before he could apologize, she began shouting at him in Chinese, in fact, the very dialect that his family spoke. He held up his hands. "Please," he said in the same dialect, "forgive me. I didn't see you coming."

"Fool. Why don't you watch where you're going? You almost knocked me down and ruined my dress. I have to work, you know."

"I'm sorry," Charlie said. "Really I am. But you mustn't behave like that to a fellow countryman. We speak the same dialect. Certainly we are from the same area. I am from Taipei."

She blushed. "So am I. But I must go now."

"Wait. Let me make it up to you. Have a drink with me."

"I can't. I'm working. I will get in a lot of trouble."

Charlie puffed out his chest. "No one will bother you when you are with me. I'll take care of you, don't worry."

She ran her dainty hands over his biceps and chest. "Yes, I believe you could. You are very strong." She blushed again. "And very handsome."

Charlie couldn't believe his good fortune. "You are the most beautiful girl I have ever seen."

291

She looked embarrassed.

"No, really. I would love to know you better. Please, have a drink with me."

She looked around behind her. Charlie believed he saw a sharply dressed Chinese man look their way, then slip into a doorway down the block. She caught Charlie's eyes. "Well, it's a slow night, anyway. I will go with you." She paused, then looked directly at him. "You will have to give me some money, or else I will receive the beating of my life."

Charlie said, "He better not lay a hand on you, or I'll kill him myself. I'm not afraid of anyone. I'm a Dragon," he lied.

She slipped into his arms, holding him tight, as if for protection. "I think I feel safe with you," she purred.

Charlie held on to her. "I don't even know your name, yet I'm falling in love with you."

She looked up at him and smiled. "I am called White Jade, because my complexion is so clear and light. It's all right. Please call me Jade."

"Jade."

"And what shall I call you, my handsome prince?"

Charlie beamed. He ran his hand through his long black hair and said, "I'm Charlie Leung."

"Charlie. Very nice. I like it."

Charlie put his arm around Jade and together they walked back to Mott Street. They went into an elegant restaurant, The Pearl Gardens. They were ushered into a cozy booth along a side wall. The maître d' parted the beaded curtain enclosing the booth, and cast an appreciative glance at Jade's figure as she bent to enter her seat. The look was not lost on Charlie. He was a lucky guy. He would have to see about taking care of her pimp so he could have Jade all to himself. His friends from the Dragons would surely help him.

They drank champagne and nibbled sweet cakes and fancy little dumplings with assorted fillings. Then they drank a second bottle. Charlie was feeling very good, joking and laughing with this delightful creature, trying to make the night last forever. They rubbed knees, and occasionally he reached under the table and placed his hand on her thigh. She didn't seem to mind, even enjoying his touches.

Finally, Jade leaned close to him and said, "Come, it is getting late. Let us go to my apartment, before we both fall asleep. We do not want to spoil our first evening together."

Charlie tried to speak, but the words hung in his throat.

Jade said, "Tell you what. I had such a good time tonight, that the first one's on me."

"First? But . . ."

"Surely a beautiful young man with all those muscles will surely want to continue our pleasure-making all through the night. Am I wrong?"

Charlie was feeling a little weak in his legs. Then a flush of warmth swept through his groin. He smiled at her. "Of course. I just hope that I don't wear you out."

"I will take good care of you. It will be a night you will never forget."

Charlie paid the check and, on unsteady legs, escorted Jade outside. Actually, it was she who helped him walk, taking some of his weight on herself. "It is just a short walk," she said. "I live on Doyers Street."

They managed to stumble and walk to Jade's apartment building. She unlocked the front door and struggled with Charlie up the long flight of stairs. She wrapped her arm around his waist to partially support him. He groped and felt her body, giggling and feeling the effects of the champagne. "Just a little bit more, my love. My place is down the hall to the right."

She let him inside her apartment. They were standing in a cozy living room, with traditional embroidered upholstered sofa and loveseat, and sidechairs. The decorations were also Chinese, with many reds and golds. The lamp gave off a soft glow. There was a small but neat kitchen off to the left, and a closed door to the bedroom to the right.

Charlie wrapped his arms around Jade and they kissed long and deep. His hands ran down her marvelous body, over the curves of her hips and buttocks, up along her flanks and over her fine full breasts. She wiggled in closer to him, grinding her pelvis into his body. She could feel him starting to bulge in response to her ministrations.

Jade leaned back and began to unbutton Charlie's shirt, slowly, teasing his bare chest with her long fingernails. He started to reach for the zipper at the back of her dress. "Not yet, my lover. Me first."

She continued to undo his buttons, and pulled

his shirt out of his pants. She pressed her lips against his chest, tonguing his nipple, then biting it sharply. He winced, then smiled at her. Again he tried for her zipper. Again, she gently pushed him away. "In due time," she cooed. "You must learn to trust me."

Jade tossed Charlie's shirt onto the sofa, then knelt down to remove his shoes and socks. She looked up and pressed her lips to the bulge in his pants. Charlie reached down and held her head to him.

After a moment, she rose and kissed his lips again, her tongue darting into his mouth, toying with his tongue. She bit his lower lip. She looked at his face. Eyes closed, broad smile, he was in ecstasy. She was fanning the flames of his lust for her, bringing his desire to a new peak. She dropped her hand from his neck and caressed his bulging manhood. She could feel the throbbing, as she stroked him through his clothes.

Jade deftly unfastened Charlie's trousers, and unzipped his fly. Still kissing him, she used both hands to pull the front of his pants away and tug them down to his knees. Then she knelt again and removed them completely. Her hands and mouth found him again through the cloth of his jockey shorts. His flesh was on fire, threatening to rip through the material.

She stood up. She danced behind him and caressed his shoulders with her fingertips. She slid her hands down his back, feeling his tight, ropy muscles. Her fingertips crept under the fabric of his shorts and dug into the muscles of his ass. She pushed her hands in deeper, caressing his flesh, pushing the shorts down from his hips. With one hand, she deftly tugged them down to his ankles and commanded him to step out of them. As he lifted his feet to comply, she cupped his scrotum and played with him. His erection became turgid.

Jade turned him around to face her, gently stroking his penis. He could hardly contain himself. She turned around, pulled down the zipper to her dress and exposed her bare back down to the swell of her hips. Her head turned back toward Charlie. "Soon, my lover, soon." She opened the door to her bedroom and slipped inside. "I'll call you when I'm ready for you."

"Hey, wait, I'm ready now."

"In a moment."

Charlie looked down at his throbbing member. "Hell, no. I'm coming in now."

The voice from inside, "I'm almost finished. Okay, my love, you can come in now."

Charlie peeked inside the room. There was his love goddess, the most beautiful woman he'd ever seen, the girl of his dreams. She was standing there naked, her long black hair flowing over one shoulder, covering her right breast. The nipple of her other other breast stood out dark and long and very hard. Charlie's mouth dropped. God, she was gorgeous.

Jade propped herself up on the velour-covered bed, arranging herself to give him a glimpse of what was yet to come. Charlie took his shaft in his hand and pointed at her. "You're killing me with delight," he joked.

"We have all night," she replied.

Charlie made for the girl on the bed. A vicious chop to his windpipe brought him up short. He gagged and grabbed for his throat. His erection died instantly. Another violent blow to his nose. Splat. The bone was broken. Blood poured into his mouth. A kick behind his knee landed Charlie flat on his ass, head and elbows landing hard.

What the hell happened? Jade was still lying on the bed. A sharp kick in the balls brought home the truth. Writhing in pain, Charlie looked up at the black-clad figure of Lin Pei, wielding a long, thick knife.

She dropped her weight onto his abdomen, aiming her knee into a nerve plexus. Her grip on his bruised throat launched his head back against the hard floor. Charlie could feel the point of the cold steel blade pricking the skin of his scrotum.

"Lie still," Lin commanded. "Speak when I ask you to. And only the truth. I shall be the sole judge of your answers. Your manhood is at stake."

Charlie's eyes bulged. He gaped at her in disbelief. What about Jade?

"You may go now, Jade. You have done well."

Jade scampered out of the bed and quickly slipped into her dress and slippers. "Thank you, my sister."

Charlie couldn't believe he'd been set up so perfectly. His eyes longingly followed Jade to the door of the apartment.

Jade looked down at his pitiful situation and shook her head. "To bad, Charlie. Too bad."

"Send up the others," Lin Pei told her as she left.

"You hear that, Charlie? Too bad you try to play both sides of the fence. Do you take us for fools? We have been watching you very closely."

"I . . . I . . . didn't do . . . ooooh . . . no!"

Lin had dug the point of the knife into his groin. "Do not lie to me, Charlie. It is only you who will suffer." She slid the flat side of the cold steel blade along his wilted member. "It would be a shame, so young and in your prime." She stuck him again. "But you will suffer, believe me, Charlie." She watched him grimace. He moved his hands toward his genitals to protect them.

A man's shoe stepped on his hand, and kicked it away. The husky, black-clad man pulled Charlie's hands up over his head and tied them together, forearm to forearm.

Lin continued, "Are you willing to tell me the truth yet?"

"Yes, please, anything. Don't —"

"Only the truth, Charlie. You heard your father. He has washed his hands of you if you aid our enemies. There is no one to save you."

Charlie didn't answer.

"The Dragon Tong will be no help to you. We shall finish them off for good."

Charlie Leung found a moment of bravery. "Even if you kill me, even if you chop off my dick and eat it for breakfast, the Dragons will avenge me. They will hunt you down and kill you. They have told me that."

Lin Pei patted Charlie's broken face. "You are so young and so very foolish, Charlie. The Dragons have found in you a willing slave. Nothing more.

298

Punks like you are plentiful. And expendable."

Charlie stared at Lin, disbelieving.

"It is so, believe me. My people have seen you enter the tunnels, and the traffic pile up behind you. We know what you are doing."

Charlie couldn't believe they knew this.

"Do you think they will let you just leave a car full of explosives in the tunnel and walk out? They wouldn't risk it. Besides, they want you dead."

"No."

"Yes, foolish child. Dead."

"But what should I do? If I refuse to drive into the Battery Tunnel, they will suspect me of treason and kill me. I will stay with you. They will never find me in time."

Lin said, "If you disappear, Charlie, the Dragons will suspect what happened and change their plans. We'd never stop them in time."

"But —"

"You go back to them, Charlie. Tell them a woman's jealous husband hit you when he caught you with his wife. With your reputation as a lady's man, they might believe you."

Charlie resigned himself. "I will try," he said. "Will you please let me go, now?"

Lin touched the tip of the knife to his scrotum again. "Certainly. But first you must tell me everything. And remember," she said, giving him a little poke. "Only the truth."

Chapter Nineteen

Will Pickens appeared at the door of the recovery room where Boxer lay on a hospital bed, head propped up, intravenous bottles dripping life-giving sustenance into his veins.

Boxer had been dozing, and at the sight of his assistant, he gave a wan smile and tried to wave the arm that was not tied to the equipment and the bedrail.

"Howdy, Chief. You up to some company?"

Boxer nodded, and pointed with his head to a bedside chair.

"Ah thought you could use some cheerin' up, so Ah brought along Admiral Stark with me. He's outside right now, talkin' to Jefferson, the Police Captain from Chinatown."

"Stark? Here? Shit, I must be closer to death than I thought if he came by to see me."

"Nah, you just got yourself a little flesh wound. Stark's here to discuss business. You got nothin' to worry about. At the way you're goin' you'll probably live to see forty."

Boxer smiled broadly. "Thanks for cheering me up, Will. What's Captain Jefferson doing here?"

"He got us in to see you. You see, when I called the admiral and told him what happened to his key man on this mission, he insisted on comin' up here and gettin' you up out of bed and back to work." He had a mischievous smile on his face. "Seriously, the admiral wanted to see what he could do for you and the project. But these hospital people said nothin' doing. That you had just been operated on, and were allowed no visitors. Including admirals."

"So?"

"Well, first thing, Stark starts giving orders. That didn't do anything for the cause 'cept bring out the security people. Then the admiral told me he was going to get some Military Police in to kick ass if they didn't let him in to see you."

Boxer could picture these events happening in his mind. He was beginning to feel better already. He said, "But more devious minds prevailed?"

"That's what Ah'm gettin' paid for, Chief. I called in the cops. Fight fire with fire, so to speak."

Boxer pushed himself into a more sitting position on the bed. "But how the hell did you get Jefferson to come here to help? This isn't even his jurisdiction."

"Ah just explained the problem to him over the phone. He was very happy to cooperate. And you should have seen him downstairs. He flashes his badge at the desk, and asks for security. He flashes again at the hospitals' head of security, a short, chubby guy with his shirt collar and tie pulled open and a little popgun in a holster at his waist, pointin' at his ass. The Captain says, 'Jefferson, NYPD. Ah'm here to see a patient named Boxer. Official business.' Well, you know, Jefferson's an imposing figure, and he's looking down at this short, chubby guy, really glarin' at him. He never did examine the

302

gold shield carefully."

Boxer was laughing now.

Will Pickens continued. "So Jefferson says, 'Take me to see Boxer. Now. These men are with me.' "

"So here you are."

"So here we are."

Admiral Stark, dressed in his summer white uniform, entered the room, followed by Malcolm Jefferson, in a dark blue suit. Stark said, "Mind if we join this little party?"

"Admiral," Boxer said.

"How the hell are you feeling?" Stark asked.

"All right, I think. I guess I look like shit, at least according to Pickens. But except for some stiffness in my thigh where I took that hit, I don't feel too bad. I'd like to get out of here, and back to work. There's little more than a day to go, and so much work to be done."

Stark said, "Don't worry about it, Jack. You rest up. I'll get some others to finish up for you."

"No way, sir. With all due respect, Project Discovery is my baby. I'll see it through." He turned to the police captain. "Don't mean to ignore you, Captain Jefferson. I really appreciate what you've done tonight."

"My pleasure. Just returning a few favors. Listen, you've got business to discuss. I'll be waiting just down the hall, if you need anything."

Admiral Stark saluted Jefferson, then offered a handshake. "Thanks for your help, Captain. I won't forget it."

Jefferson left the room, and Stark and Pickens pulled chairs close to Boxer's bed. Boxer and Pickens spent the next half hour briefing the admiral on the recent events that had taken place. Boxer said, "We're fairly certain that the Chicoms are behind the apparent sabotage taking place. We know there's a sub out there. It's probably Chinese."

Stark said, "Sounds like an overagressive, risk-taking sub commander who'd be responsible for that. No sense risking exposure when you have a serious task ahead."

"Just the type of personality that would get a suicide mission like this one, Admiral."

"You would know, Jack," the admiral replied. "You would know."

"But—"

"No offense intended, Jack. The sub commander, or commanders if there are more than one of them, must realize that his hopes of survival following an attack would be almost nil. I think he's just been flexing his muscles along the way. Sort of testing his nerve."

Boxer agreed. "Help me get out of here. I'm going to send the *Shark* out looking for the bastard. I also think we should deploy whatever ASW units we can. The ships in the harbor would be like sitting ducks if he gets past us."

"It has been done." Stark looked down at Boxer and rubbed his chin. "But when the *Shark* goes out hunting, you won't be on it."

"But, I—"

"No buts, Jack. I'll let you keep your land-based command, let you see it through. But you're in no shape to command a sub. And that's final."

Boxer stared at the admiral for a long moment,

304

then realized that to argue would be futile. He looked to Will Pickens for support.

Pickens shrugged his shoulders.

Stark asked, "Who's your exec aboard the *Shark?* Harris still there?"

"Yes," Boxer replied. Harris is my EXO. I also have Cowley as third and Mahoney's at the helm. They've been with me since the beginning."

"Fine. They should be able to handle it. You give your leg a chance to heal. You'll see plenty of sea duty before you retire. Now don't worry about it."

A man in a gray hospital scrub suit and cap, stethoscope draped around his neck, entered the room. He announced, "I'm Doctor Tuttle, Captain Boxer's surgeon. I'm afraid I'll have to ask you gentlemen to leave now. Our patient has to get back his strength."

Boxer looked up at the doctor. "I'm leaving. I'm signing myself out."

"Like hell. You're in no shape to go anywhere, Captain Boxer. Whatever you think is so important as to risk your life will just have to wait."

"Can't wait. Too much to do and so little time." Boxer reflected for just a moment on how he'd just repeated in Lin Pei's words the night they'd made love and she tortured and killed her enemy. "No time, doctor."

Tuttle turned to the admiral, who looked as if he'd be the one in charge here. "Please talk some sense into him. He's just been operated on. He needs at least three days to a week before he'll be strong enough to leave here. Can't one of you reason with him?"

Stark said, "Tried that already, doctor. He's very determined. And frankly I think we should honor his wishes."

Tuttle sighed. "Let me explain the situation to *you,* sir. This man has three layers of stitches holding his quadriceps muscles together. If he exerts himself, he might split the stitches. Several things will then happen. One, the muscles could tear up, leaving Captain Boxer a permanent cripple. Or two, he might bleed to death, making point one seem very minor. He needs a doctor's attention for at least three more days. And bed rest."

Pickens cleared his throat and said, "Doc, we need Captain Boxer back in action, and he needs a doctor. Now, he says he's leavin' with or without medical attention, so let me put this to you. How's about gettin' us a doctor to spend the next few days with us. Uncle Sam will pay very well for the services. Am I correct, Admiral?"

"Absolutely. How about yourself, Dr. Tuttle? What time does your shift end?"

Tuttle glanced at his watch. "Eleven-thirty. I've been off for a half hour now. I just stopped by when I got off to check on our important patient here. It's against my better judgment, gentlemen, believe me. But all right. I'll put my career on the line if it's as important as you say it is." He turned to Boxer. "Okay, I'll look after you. I've got a few days off coming to me. I'll go get the papers and we can sign you out of here."

Boxer tugged on the restraint binding his arm to the bed. "Thanks. You can start by untying me, and unhooking all these tubes. And get me something to

306

wear."

Tuttle undid Boxer's hand restraint. "I'm sorry, but you were only wearing shorts and a wet suit when you were brought in."

Will Pickens walked outside, and returned with a small suitcase. "No problem, Chief. Ah figured that if we got you out of here, you'd need something to wear besides that skimpy hospital gown. We wouldn't want a captain of the U.S. Navy walkin' around town with his ass stickin' out the back."

Boxer, Stark, and Pickens laughed at that. Dr. Tuttle shook his head and headed out to process the paperwork. He saved his laughter until he got outside the door.

Captain Chou lost three men in the depth charging. They had been hurled against bulkheads or equipment that had caused concussions severe enough to kill them. Under normal circumstances, their bodies would have been returned home for decent burials. But these were not normal times. This was the brink of war.

Chou had the remains put into body bags along with some heavy balast and loaded into torpedo tubes. They would be ejected into the sea when he was sure the danger had passed. Though they were all officially atheists, Chou conducted a short ceremony to appease the gods of his ancestors . . . just in case. Then he keyed in the damage control officer.

He told his DCO to organize all available men into work squads. The cleanup work must be completed quickly. Debris was to be ejected. Anything damaged was to be repaired. Anything irrepairable was discarded. They would have to make do with what they could salvage.

Even the underwater demolition force of forty men was pressed into service. They would be given welding equipment to repair any damage to the hull. But first, something even more important had to be done.

The stench of fear permeated the ship. The depth-charging had damaged his men's nerves as much as it had ravaged his submarine. When the sonar and radar officers assured him that no enemy was lurking above them he gave the much needed command. He grabbed the IC-A and announced to the entire crew, "This is Captain Chou. Prepare to surface. Repeat, prepare to surface."

The crew broke out in a spontaneous cheer. The men followed their officers in responding to Chou's orders. The work took on a new sense of urgency. Chou went through the series of commands that would bring the boat to the surface.

When they had reached periscope depth, Chou took his place at the bridge and looked through the padded eyepiece. He swung the periscope around three hundred and sixty degrees. The enemy was nowhere in sight.

"Deck crew, stand by. All hands, prepare to surface. . . . DO, bring us up."

The deck crew scrambled up the bridge ladders, and at Chou's signal, the watch officer activated the pneumatic hatch. Fresh air was sucked into the fetid chambers below.

The crew shouted a resounding cheer.

Chou knew that the air would cleanse and purify them. The claustrophobia would subside. They had survived to fight another day.

The men worked around the clock, stopping only to eat and to catch a few hours' sleep. They were returning to normal. The lone woman on board, Political Officer Hsien, was not. Captain Chou noticed the profound change at once. It was as if she never fully recovered from the shock. She had ceased her constant demanding. She no longer spouted political dogma on every occasion. She seemed to wander about aimlessly throughout the sub.

On the first night following the depth-charging, after he had turned the conn over to his EXO, Chou decided to look in on her. She was seated on the edge of her bunk, arms in her lap, staring at nothing. She had made no attempt to prepare for sleep, though it was well past her usual bedtime. He said, "Comrade Hsien, are you ill?"

She looked up at him. Tears welled in her eyes, and she began to cry. Chou wasn't used to this happening aboard his sub. Occasionally, a man would crack, go berserk, and have to be tranquilized. In rare cases, the offender would have to be put to death, for the good of the crew.

Chou cupped her chin and tilted her face up to look at him. He said, with compassion that surprised even himself, "It's all right now. It's over. There is nothing left to fear."

She rose from her bunk and embraced Chou, wrapping her arms around his middle, her head resting against his broad, muscular chest. They stood like that for several minutes. Finally, her sobbing stopped. "I am sorry. I apologize for my weak behavior. Understand, Comrade Captain, that I am afraid of no man. I just don't know what got over me."

Chou knew. He had been there himself, many times before. A depth-charging can do horrible things to a man's nerves. And this was a mere woman, no matter what her rank. Gently, he smoothed her hair out of her face and hugged her to him. He became aware of the press of her surprisingly full breasts against him. "You must not dwell on it. It is something that happens to all of us who have been depth-charged. Many of the men behaved the same way."

"They did not cry."

"They are men. They wouldn't cry. But many lost control of their bowels or their bladders, and certainly their nerves. Tomorrow, you should come on deck with me. The fresh air will do you good."

"Thank you, Comrade Captain. You are not always the inhuman ogre that you try to be."

Coming from the political officer, that was almost a compliment. Chou enjoyed it. He smiled at her. "Please, call me Jin. No need to be so formal while we're out at sea."

She smiled back at him. She had taken off her thick glasses to wipe her eyes.

Not half bad, Chou thought. "Besides, you are not the fierce fire-breather that some would have us believe, either."

Hsien giggled. "And you may call me Ming. That is my given name."

"Ming. It is very nice."

310

They stood there a while longer, just holding each other. Finally, Captain Chou said, "You do not sleep, yet you must be very tired."

"I feel afraid, closed in. That fresh air you spoke of sounds like a good idea. Is it too late to go out on the bridge?"

"Not too late. We stand three watches, around the clock. Come, we will join the night watch."

They stopped at Chou's quarters and donned sweaters, for even though it was the beginning of July, the nights at sea were cool. The four sailors on watch were surprised by the visit of their captain, and snapped to attention. "At ease, men. We're just getting some fresh air. As you were."

If anyone questioned their captain's motives, they did not show it. Chou borrowed a pair of Zeiss glasses, still the best in the world, and scanned the horizon all around and above them. Hsien spent a half hour deeply breathing in the salt air and gazing at the stars. They never looked so close and so clear to her before as they looked tonight. She placed her hand on Chou's arm, and smiled.

She nodded and they returned below. They started for her quarters, but she stopped him. "I cannot sleep alone tonight. I wish to spend the night with you." She blushed and looked down.

Chou didn't know what to think or say.

"I don't want to be alone if we get attacked again. I will try to be no trouble to you." She was clearly embarrassed.

"You may sleep in my quarters. I'll rest on my chair and chart table."

"No need for that. Besides, I will need the table to

311

write my report on how well you commanded the ship during the depth-charging. You were so in control. I think that changed my mind about you."

They entered the small compartment that served as living and working quarters for the ship's captain. It was only about six by eight feet, but that was quite large by submarine standards. She removed the sweater, then opened her shapeless Mao shirt. She pulled the tails out of her oversized pants, and demurely turned to him. She looked at him and removed her top.

Chou couldn't believe how full and ripe her body was. This was not the frumpy woman she would have people believe. He watched her unfasten her baggy trousers and let them drop to the floor. She was completely naked.

Chou smiled appreciatively. "You are really quite beautiful, you know. You must try very hard to give the appearance that you usually do."

"Thank you, Jin. Yes, I dress that way for effect. I want to be treated just like anyone else. So I cut my hair severely, wear these heavy glasses, even though I could wear contact lenses, and I dress like Chairman Mao had dressed. And so they accept me for my brains and for my driving ambition. But tonight is different. You have shown me a different side of yourself, also."

Chou shrugged.

Ming Hsien stepped out of her pants, and kicked off her shoes. "Tonight I am yours, not as the political officer you despise, but as the woman you see before you."

Chou was very pleased. Not only did his once

312

hated opponent turn around to his point of view, but he would have a fine woman to sleep with for the rest of the mission. Of that, he was certain. He placed his hands on her shoulders and drew her to him.

"Please be gentle with me, Jin. I do not have much experience in these matters, as I am sure you do."

He kissed her lips and lifted her up. He gently placed her on his bunk, then he quickly got undressed and got under the blanket with her. They made love three or four times that night, gently and tentatively at first, then with a passionate fury before the night was over. Exhausted, they finally fell asleep.

The next few days consisted of drill after drill for the crew and demolition strike force, whose job it was to destroy the Brooklyn and Manhattan Bridges, and the Verrazano Bridge. Chou had told them, "Blow the bridges, and the police and Coast Guard would be too preoccupied to intercept the *Sea Death*. It is our one hope to complete our mission and return to China safely."

For the first time in weeks, Captain Chou was a satisfied man. His days were being spent at the command of one of the finest submarines in the world. At night, he had the good fortune of sleeping with a warm-bodied woman, a new political ally at that. It was the best of times.

Chapter Twenty

Boxer swiveled his deck chair toward the Statue of Liberty as the Coast Guard cutter made its way to the Stapleton Naval Base. It was a crystal clear night, the stars shining brightly, illuminating the bay. It was 0400. By this time tomorrow, the greatest armada the world had ever seen would begin lining up to salute that grand old dame, the torch-bearing legacy of a hemisphere opening its arms to the refugees of the Old World for five hundred years. It was within his power to make this a great celebration to be shared alike by the nations of the world.

Should he fail . . . Well, no sense dwelling on that. He would not fail. This was his mission. Boxer and his entourage were settled into his quarters on Staten Island before dawn. Boxer was going over final strategies with Admiral Stark and Colonel Will Pickens when he received the first alarm. The call came from the U.S. Navy monitoring station in Newport, Rhode Island. Their hydrophones on the ocean floor at the edge of the continental shelf had picked up an apparent submarine about four hundred miles from shore and heading south from Nova Scotia.

"Well," Boxer said, "looks like this is what we've been waiting for. At least there's only one of them."

Stark said, "We'll keep a close watch on it. Then we can deploy the *Shark* to put an end to that bastard once and for all." He picked up the red telephone and pressed two buttons. A pause, and then he said, "Get me D'Arcy right now. This is Admiral Richard Stark."

There was a longer pause. This time the admiral's voice took on a gruffness that surprised Boxer. "I don't give a damn what time it is. This is the highest priority. You get his ass out of bed and on this phone right now. And I mean now!"

Admiral D'Arcy was roused from a deep sleep by a visibly shaken young lieutenant. He had brushed past the MP and banged on his commander's bedroom door. The admiral sputtered a protest, but shot bolt upright at the mention of the CNO's name. He straightened his navy blue pajamas, slipped into slippers and a robe, and headed for the hot line phone. "Coffee . . . black," he shouted to the lieutenant. "In my office."

D'Arcy lifted the receiver on the red phone. "D'Arcy here," he said.

"Admiral Stark. We just got a sounding from that Chinese sub we've been expecting. I want you to keep a direct line open between the Newport Station and Boxer's office. I'm at his quarters now, and will be until this Project Discovery celebration is history."

D'Arcy stifled a yawn. "Yes, Admiral. I'll get on it immediately. Just let me know if you need anything else."

"This is vitally important, D'Arcy," Stark hung up before D'Arcy could reply.

Pickens was already wearing headphones and standing at the tracking module, a ten-square-foot screen depicting the topography of the sea floor. The range could be adjusted from an area covering one hundred miles offshore to five hundred miles, with three stages in between. As the range got larger, the map's features naturally became smaller. At three hundred miles, a large ship could be plotted with some accuracy.

Stark turned to Boxer. "Well, Jack, I think it's time for you to go on board the *Shark* and give your men their orders. Intercept that Chicom sub and destroy it."

Boxer saluted the admiral smartly. "Aye, sir."

"I know how you feel, Jack. Twenty-five years ago, when I commanded the *Enterprise,* I'd have felt just as you do now if I had to send my crew on an important mission without me. But it has to be this way. You have a solid crew."

"Yes, Admiral. If anybody can sink that sub, my men can."

"They'll have to. You're too important to this entire mission to risk your life prematurely."

Boxer was greeted by his men aboard the *Shark* with wild enthusiasm. They were itching for some action, and glad to have their skipper back with them again. Over the IC-A Boxer ordered all hands into the mess hall.

Boxer lit up his pipe, and said, "Smoke'm if you've got'em." He waited for a moment for everyone to get settled down. "It's time to earn our keep, men." Boxer took a pull from his pipe, and let the exhaled smoke waft to the ceiling. "As you all know, we've been assigned to provide security for the Discovery Day celebration. That's now only a day away. For the most part, things have been going smoothly so far. But there have been at least a few seemingly isolated incidents."

Boxer inhaled again. "However, we now realize that they have all been a part of a plot by the Chicoms to embarrass our country during the ceremonies. Or worse." Boxer looked about the room, locking in on each man assembled there. "There've been mines attached to some of the ships. One ship was severely damaged when one of the mines exploded.

"In other cases we've been lucky enough to remove the explosives in time. But as you already know, I wasn't as fortunate. I got a little flesh wound that grounded me."

There was a grumbling among the men when they realized that Boxer wasn't going to lead them.

"For this mission, you'll be under the able leadership of Commander Harris."

Bill Harris looked very surprised, though

318

pleased.

Boxer continued, "Mr. Cowly will be EXO for this mission. Now I'd like to fill you in. There's been a Chinese sub spotted a few hundred miles northeast of here. So far, we feel it's been responsible for firing a cruise missile that heavily damaged a British carrier."

Boxer let that sink in. "Your mission is to find it and sink it, gentlemen. We don't know much about the sub, except that it's large enough to carry both torpedoes and missiles. Its captain is good enough to have sunk one of our frigates, and a Russian trawler.

"Their captain's clever enough to have eluded one of our destroyers, even though the sub probably took some hits. . . . There's nothing else for me to say, except that I wish I could be with you."

Will Pickens looked up from his monitor when Boxer reentered his office. "Mornin', Chief. How'd it go with your crew?"

"They were glad to be seeing some action, but disappointed that I wasn't going to lead them. That's to be expected, I guess. It'll be a good experience for Harris and Cowly, though."

Pickens smiled. He got up and poured two cups of black coffee for Boxer and himself, and placed them on Boxer's desk. It'd been almost twenty-four hours since either of them had slept.

Boxer walked to his desk and sipped coffee. He was walking with a slight limp. "Not bad coffee. Make it yourself?"

Pickens shook his head and smiled. "Miss La Fontaine. Oh, by the way, your China doll has been waiting to see you since sunrise. They called me from the gate that she had some info for you. Didn't want to leave it with me."

"Lin Pei?" Boxer put down his coffee mug. "Please have her sent right in."

"She's got some guys with her. Probably her goons from that import shop."

"They're her bodyguards, Will. They've got nothing personal against us. But they'd die protecting Lin."

"Right on, Chief. They'll die for sure if they tangle with me again."

There was a knock on Boxer's door, and a burly MP escorted Lin Pei and three men into the office. Her presence brought about mixed feelings in Boxer. A part of him felt a deep physical bond with her, more than just lust, yet not quite love either. On the other hand, he couldn't help but feel repugnance for the way she tortured and killed her enemies. This time, the fondness won out. He smiled broadly at her. "Hello, Lin. I'm very pleased to see you."

Very formally she replied, "Thank you, Captain Boxer. I am happy to be here. I have brought someone here to speak with you."

Boxer acknowledged the others. "Good morning, Gai Tang. Hello, Sun. Who do we have here? Is that Charlie Leung? He doesn't look so well. Is he ill?"

Lin Pei replied, "He is feeling the way a turncoat traitor to his people should feel, if he is fortunate

320

enough to have his life spared."

"Charlie? Turned on us?" Boxer addressed the young man directly. "Charlie Leung . . . is this true?"

"Well, not ex—"

Lin and her two bodyguards made a move toward Charlie. He took a step away from them, and his body tightened up. He looked up at Boxer. "Yes, I guess it was true, in a way. I was trying to play both sides. But not anymore. I am solidly with you now. It was just a moment of foolishness."

Boxer nodded his head. He would accept that explanation for now, though he doubted that Charlie would remain true to their cause if the present situation were reversed. He said, "Please, why don't you all have a seat." He turned to Pickens. "Will, would you please see to it that we get some tea served to us? Chinese tea."

"Right, Chief. Comin' right up." He walked outside, spoke to his secretary, and returned to the room. He went back to his monitor until the tea was served. In a few minutes, Laurie La Fontaine entered, carrying a tray with a ceramic teapot and six matching handleless cups. Teacups were filled and passed around. Lin Pei took a sip. Then she shoved Charlie's shoulder and said in Chinese, "Speak."

Charlie Leung cleared his throat, looking furtively at Lin and her two bodyguards. Then he slouched in his chair and told his story. "Well, as you know, I had been taking Kung Fu lessons with some of the Dragon Tong members. When it had

321

been made clear to me that they were responsible for some of the killings of my neighbors, I agreed to act as a spy and report back to Lin Pei. I will now reveal to you what I learned."

He turned his head to find Lin Pei glaring at him. He quickly turned around and proceeded with his tale. "They are trying to disrupt the ceremonies tomorrow. I was to be a part of their plan. I was to help place a bomb in the Holland Tunnel. Others were to do the same in the Battery Tunnel. It was to take attention away from your celebration. They said it was because China was slighted by not being asked to participate."

Boxer knew that to be untrue. The People's Republic of China had turned down their invitation.

"I have also heard that they will try to blow up some bridges, but I don't have any details. I was not to be a part of that."

Lin shouted something harsh at him in Chinese. He cringed. Then he continued. "This is all to take place tomorrow, during the festivities. It will cause your country to lose much face."

Boxer took a sip of his tea. "You realize that there's a sizable chunk of the world's capital shipping tied up in and around New York Harbor. They'd be sitting ducks if an unfriendly nation decided to destroy them."

Charlie Leung squirmed in his seat. He loosened the collar of his shirt. "But they wouldn't . . . They said . . ."

"Yes, they would. The People's Republic declined our invitation because they sensed an op-

322

portunity to soundly defeat their rivals, and extend their hegemony to half the world. An attack on New York Bay would be a worse catastrophe than Pearl Harbor."

Boxer took another sip of his tea. He noticed Lin Pei and the two men with her nodding in recognition of the truth. "And which nation do you think would be their first victim, Charlie? Taiwan."

Charlie turned pale. Lin Pei moved next to him and shook his shoulder. "This fool thinks that they will let him live after he leaves a car bomb in the tunnel. Hah!"

"They said—"

"They said . . . fool. They will tell you anything to get you to do their bidding. But when you stop your car in the tunnel, as you have so diligently done in practice, they will explode it by remote control. No more tunnel. No more Charlie Leung to tell the police how it happened."

Boxer said, "Lin Pei is right, Charlie. They can't afford to let you live. You would place them in jeopardy. Haven't you heard, Charlie, that dead men tell no tales?"

Lin Pei grabbed a hank of Charlie Leung's hair and turned his head around to face her. "You will go back to the Dragons, Charlie. We will make it seem that you spent the night with the young lady you were seen with last evening. Then, when it is time for you to drive your car bomb into the tunnel, make sure that you get stuck in heavy traffic. We will do the rest."

Charlie saw his opportunity to get out of his

predicament. "Sure. I'll do it. No problem with that."

"Good." Boxer turned to Lin and her two associates. "Now I would suggest that you return him to Chinatown, and prepare your people to stop the trouble tomorrow. Colonel Pickens here will coordinate with you in the morning."

Will Pickens was taken by surprise. He started to protest.

At the same time, Gai Tang and Sun turned to Lin and muttered something in Chinese. She shook her head. "That will be acceptable to us. Colonel Pickens, we look forward to seeing you tomorrow morning."

Pickens shrugged his shoulders. "Well, see you tomorrow, then."

The Chinese left, and Boxer and Pickens joined Admiral Stark in the control room next door to continue their work.

A few hours later, half-dressed Charlie Leung was bodily thrown out of a doorway on Mott Street by a very angry gentleman known in the neighborhood as a big-time pimp. A young woman, a local hooker called White Jade, ran out onto the sidewalk after him, dressed only in a flimsy negligee. The pimp shouted some harsh words at her and she ran back into the building, her procurer close behind shouting obscenities at her.

In typical New York fashion, the heavy pedestrian traffic either walked around Charlie Leung or stepped over him, paying no attention to his condition at all. Finally, Manny, the man involved in the tunnel incident with Charlie, came upon him after searching for him the better part of the morning. He shook his head at Charlie's plight, gave him a hand up, and helped him walk back to the Dragon Tong's headquarters. Along the way, he jokingly admonished Charlie for picking up the wrong woman. Didn't he know a hooker when he saw one?

The first explosion went off at 12:15 P.M. in the Men's Department of the R. H. Macy Company, the world's largest department store. The building was packed with the Friday lunchtime trade, where many workers spent a chunk of their paychecks before returning to their suburban homes in the evening. A middle-aged salesman and a bespeckled tailor were fitting a business executive with an expensive suit. The blast killed all three. Onlookers shrieked and tried to flee. Many were injured by falling debris, or were trampled by their fellow shoppers. A fire broke out on a rack of garments, and soon spread throughout the department.

The sprinkler system was activated, and a large portion of the third floor was engulfed in thick, black smoke. The store had to be evacuated.

The fire marshals sent to the scene discovered the blown-up remains of an Oriental man in the dressing room of the Men's Department. His severed hand was still clutching an oversized attache case. It was determined that the explosives it once held detonated prematurely owing to a short circuit in the timing device. The timer was set for July 4 at 1200 hours.

An alert was sent out to all precincts in the city. Be aware of anyone acting suspiciously in or around any major building. In New York City, that meant perhaps thousands of strange-looking characters, and hundreds of buildings. It could require half of the police force. But the PC had made it a priority, and orders were orders.

The mayor was holding a press conference on the steps of City Hall, expressing his assurance that the explosion was an isolated incident, and that the population should go about their business as normal. At this exact moment, a young Chinese man got off a train at Grand Central Terminal, and carried his two heavy suitcases up to the main lobby. He looked around, made the decision of his life, and dropped his baggage at a busy entrance then ran like hell.

An alert transit policeman spotted him just as he started to run. The cop blew his whistle and shouted at the Chinese man to halt. He had the presence of mind to shout a warning to the commuters to stay away from the valises, and ran after the suspect with gun drawn. The Chinese man ran toward a waiting car parked with its motor running outside the station.

The policeman shouted a warning to stop, then fired a shot at the man as he jumped into the car. An accomplice in the back seat leaned out the window, aimed a 9mm automatic pistol at the officer and fired all fourteen rounds at him. The shouts of the Chinese, the death scream of the fallen transit policeman, and even the blasts from the handgun were drowned out by the tremendous explosion from within the train station. Firetrucks and emergency vehicles converged on the site from all around the area. In the confusion, the terrorists made good their escape.

A suspicious-looking package was noticed by an alert postal worker at the Main Post Office at Thirty-third and Eighth. The bomb squad responded with Snappy, a German Shepherd trained at sniffing out explosives. Snappy proved the postal worker correct. The bomb squad placed the package in their heavily reinforced vehicle and removed it to an empty field, where it was detonated. The crater it left was large enough to serve as an excavation for a small apartment house.

Later that afternoon, Captain Malcolm Jefferson left a meeting with the other precinct commanders and the police commissioner, and decided to walk the few blocks back to the Chinatown Precinct. The lunch he had devoured during the meeting lay heavy in his stomach, and the exercise would do him good. As he walked up Pearl Street, he noticed two men arguing with a guard in front of the County Courthouse. The argument turned into a shoving match. One man shoved the policeman against the wall. The other pulled a large shiny handgun and cracked the officer across the head with it.

Jefferson palmed the Chief's Special that he kept in a hip holster at the small of his back and yelled, "Halt, Police. Drop your gun and stay where you are."

The gunman fired two rounds at Jefferson. He and his accomplice dragged the stunned guard into the lobby with them, a gun held at his temple.

Jefferson radioed for assistance. A cop was in danger. That was guaranteed to practically empty One Police Plaza. Soon a standoff was taking place outside the courthouse. The gunmen threatened to kill the guard if the police didn't allow them safe passage. A hostage negotiating team was sent to the scene, along with a SWAT team, just in case. Captain Jefferson wondered how much more of this madness was in store. . . . He just hoped that Boxer could gain control before things got out of hand. That he could stop this madness before it was too late.

Chapter Twenty-one

Captain Jin Chou arose at 0400 July 3. He stretched, and took his time cleansing himself, brushing his teeth, and even shaving, a task he put off as much as possible. He dressed in the neatly starched and pressed uniform that he'd been saving for the occasion. He ate the customary bowl of rice, and drank two cups of strong breakfast tea. At 0430 he was ready to take the conn.

Heads turned as Chou made his way to the bridge and took his place at the command module. His EXO saluted crisply, and briefed him on the details of his eight-hour watch. It had been very uneventful.

Chou gave orders to his officers, and brought the submarine to within three hundred miles of New York. He activated a SONAR jamming device that emitted signals from the sub resembling those of a school of whales or dolphins. The sub would not be detected from above.

As they passed within range of the underwater hydrophones, a muted blip appeared on Pickens' monitor screen. Had he not been anticipating the appearance of a sub, the sub might have passed by undetected. As it was, the progress of the submarine was being watched with a great deal of concern in Boxer's control room.

* * *

At 0615, Political Officer Hsien appeared at the bridge, dressed in her usual Mao shirt and baggy pants. She pushed the heavy glasses back up the length of her nose and cleared her throat. "Comrade Hsien requesting permission to enter the bridge."

Chou turned from his CRT screen and smiled. "But, of course, Comrade Hsien. Good morning. Did you sleep well last night?"

He knew damn well how she had slept last night. That was just to indicate a little sense of propriety to the crew. Not that it mattered. "Yes, thank you, Comrade Captain. Are we near the American coastline yet?"

"About three hundred miles out. Come here. I'll show you."

Hsien joined him at a large chart of the northeastern United States. "We are exactly here." He pointed to their position. "See? We are picking up LORAN signals from here . . . and here . . . on the coast. Where these two coordinates cross is where we are now. Precisely."

Ming Hsien adjusted her glasses and peered at the chart over Captain Chou's shoulder. She listened intently as he pointed out their proposed route with his index finger. "See, here? We will work our way to the edge of the continental shelf. Like so."

Chou turned on another monitor. A green outline of the northeastern United States appeared. The features were very small. "Now watch this. This is a duplicate of the chart I showed you. It has been programmed into this computer. Now look."

He adjusted a dial and the area covered became much smaller, but it showed much greater detail. He continued, "See? This is New Jersey. Up in this bay is New York City, and this long island is just that. The imperialist Yankees call it Long Island." He brought the picture into sharper focus.

"Here along the edge, the shelf is cut by many underwater canyons and valleys. That is where we will hide, and wait until the proper moment to strike. Then notice how the ocean floor seems to have a crease right along this line." Chou drew an imaginary line, a gentle arch from the Hudson Canyon to the mouth of the Lower Bay. "We shall speed in through here, destroy our enemies, and retrace our path back out to the open sea."

Ming Hsien beamed in admiration for her new lover. Perhaps Commissar Chen, her superior, the head of the Secret Police, was wrong about Captain Chou. True, he had used poor judgment when he'd sunk the Russian trawler and engaged the British warships. But he had told her one night in bed that he had to train his untested crew under real battle conditions. And he had to see what his new submarine could really do.

So it became a judgment call. Risk the mission, as Commissar Chen had feared, or risk engaging the enemies of our people enmassed in New York Harbor with an untried and untested crew and ship. It all came down to trust.

At home, in Beijing, she was under the direct influence of her superiors. And secrecy seemed to be the most vital factor involved in this mission. But now, here under the sea a few hundred miles from the U.S coast, after traveling halfway around the world, she had learned to trust the judgment of the ship's captain,

331

Jin Chou. After all, his reputation, and his life, was at stake here too.

Suddenly, a familiar pinging sound echoed throughout the hull of the boat. They had been picked up on sonar. Chou immediately signaled the men to their battle stations, and prepared to take evasive action.

Lieutenant Robbie Wakefield was flying his chopper over the sector designated by the control room, about three hundred miles out, dragging a submerged hydrophone about ten feet below the surface. His co-pilot, Tom Henschel, picked up a strange sounding at a depth of five hundred fathoms. "Got'm. Robbie. Son of a bitch is down there doing almost thirty knots."

"Depth?"

"You won't believe this. I read him at three thousand feet. Un-fuckin'-believable."

Wakefield said, "We better get some help. Call in the coordinates to Command Central. Tell them to pull him some of the other choppers and converge on this sector."

"Roger that." Tom Henschel keyed in his radio. "They better get a destroyer out there fast. The fucker's heading out into open water."

"Keep calling in the coordinates. We don't want to lose'm."

Captain Chou called an order to the stern torpedo room. "FO, prepare to deploy the decoy. Load it into tube number ten. I'll tell you when to fire."

"Decoy?"

Chou turned his attention to the political officer.

"Decoy. Yes, Comrade. We are carrying a decoy the size of a torpedo with the sonar picture of a three-hundred-and-fifty-foot submarine, complete with engine room and propeller sounds. Anyone picking it up on a sonar screen will think they have us. But first, we have some other work to dispose of."

Chou keyed in the missile room. The missile control officer answered, "Yes, Comrade Captain?"

"Arm tube twelve with an anti-aircraft rocket. I want to kiss that bird good-bye before we send the others chasing ghosts."

"Aye, aye, Comrade Captain. Tube twelve armed and ready."

"The helicopter is trailing a sonar device. It should not be difficult to set your homing gyro."

"I have him, sir. Rocket prepared to fire at your command."

"Commence firing."

"Rocket fired, Captain."

Three minutes later a rocket broke surface and struck the low-flying chopper. There was a tremendous whump, and a brilliant ball of flames that was once a Sikorsky helicopter fell into the sea. The sound of the explosion traveled down to the submarine.

Chou keyed his MCO. "Direct hit. Good work."

The crew on the bridge cheered.

Chou motioned for silence. He called the helmsman and said, "Come to course three zero five degrees." Then he keyed the stern FO. "Prepare to fire decoy."

"Aye, aye, Comrade Captain. Ready to fire. Ten seconds and counting."

The seconds ticked off in Chou's head. At ten, the fish was ejected from the torpedo tube and headed out to sea. The stern lifted slightly until the diving officer adjusted the boat's ballast. Chou told his helmsman, "Come to course now zero three zero degrees."

"Yes, Comrade Captain. Zero three zero degrees."

He called the engine room. "EO, give me two five knots. I want to slip right past anything that comes out here looking for us."

"Aye, aye, Captain, making two five knots."

"DO, maintain one thousand meters."

"Aye, aye, sir."

The captain of the destroyer *U.S.S. Princeton* was the first vessel on the scene. He said to his EXO, "This is the last reported sighting by the chopper. Apparently, it was hit. There's been no trace of it since that last call."

The sonar officer reported, "Captain, I've picked up that boat."

"I'm on my way," the captain said. He entered the room with his EXO, and they made their way past a bank of computer screens to the module that was drawing all the attention from the sonar crew.

The SO said, "Here it is, sir. Target bearing one three zero degrees . . . speed at least four zero knots."

"Range?"

The SO shrugged his shoulders. "At least five miles, Captain."

"Keep tracking her, son." He turned to his EXO. "Let's put that bastard out of its misery."

He called for flank speed, and chased the decoy out to sea, making better than seventy knots.

The SO reported, "Target bearing one two five degrees . . . speed four zero knots . . . range two five zero

zero yards."

The captain keyed his firing officer. "Ready the ASROCS. Target is within range."

"ASROCS ready," the FO replied.

"Take your bearing from the SO."

"Aye, aye, Captain. I've got 'em."

"Fire."

"ASROCS fired, sir."

The rockets flew on a short trajectory and entered the water a mile ahead of the *Princeton* in a diamond pattern. There was silence for a few seconds, then an explosion. Whump. Then a second, larger explosion. A geyser of water erupted. Debris and flotsam littered the surface, then settled into the sea.

The EXO shouted, "We got 'em, sir. We got 'em."

The Captain slapped him on the shoulder, and they walked jubilantly to the control room. The message to the CNO was brief and direct. TARGET DESTROYED.

Harris and Cowly had been following this activity on their radio. At the time the destroyer reported sinking the sub, the *Shark* was eighty miles from New York Harbor heading southeast, in the direction of the sighting. Harris said, "Well, looks like we're too late this time, buddy. We missed out on a chance to show the old man what we can do."

"Let's go check out the wreckage, Bill. See if we can attach a tow line to the remains of the sub."

"Yeah, if there's anything left big enough to tow."

At one hundred miles out, they passed over the edge of the continental shelf. Harris took the *Shark* under manual control and followed the contours of the ocean

335

floor. They meandered in and out of the various canyons and valleys and crevasses as the shelf fell off abruptly, forming an escarpment about a half mile deep, and within ten more miles, dropped another five hundred fathoms, before taking on a gentler slope out to sea.

Two hours passed. At one hundred and eighty miles out, they picked up the remains of the enemy sub on their sonar. Cowly checked their bearings and sat there at the charts scratching his head. "Bill, take a look at this. Something's bothering me."

Harris joined his EXO at the chart table. He watched Cowly punching info into a navigation module, while walking a pair of dividers over the chart he was using. "What's up, Cowly?"

"It's too soon to come upon that wreck. Based on the positions that the chopper called in before it disappeared, that sub was at least another hundred miles out. Somewhere around here." He drew on the chart with the dividers, enclosing a three-inch circle where the sinking took place.

"Maybe the chopper pilot was in the air too long and miscalculated."

Cowly shook his head. "No way, man. The *Princeton* verified those coordinates when she—"

The intercom cackled. "Target bearing one zero five degrees," the SO announced. "Range nineteen thousand yards. . . . Speed three five knots . . . and closing."

Harris keyed the MC. "Roger that. Keep me posted."

Cowly asked, "Who the hell's down here?"

Harris shook his head. "Maybe there's two subs?"

"Or a very crafty commander who didn't get sunk

336

after all."

Harris walked over to the comcomp. "Let's find out fast." He keyed in the coordinates of the target and tied in the sonar reading. Then he typed in ID TARGET.

The screen almost immediately printed:

```
TARGET-SUBMARINE UNKNOWN ORIGIN
POSSIBLE Q-21 CLASS
SIZE =   385 FEET
PROBABLE ARMAMENT =
    TWELVE TORPEDO TUBES
    TEN ROCKET TUBES CAPABLE OF
        ASCM
        SLCM
        SLBM
        SUBROC
```

The SO keyed Harris. "Target bearing three five degrees. . . . Range two three zero zero zero yards. . . . Speed four zero knots."

Harris replied, "Roger that." He turned to Cowly. "She's trying to evade us. That rules out a friendly. And if Borodine's been telling us the truth, that leaves us with a Chicom sub in U.S. waters. Let's intercept."

Cowly turned on the UWIS. A three-dimensional picture of the area surrounding the sub for a distance up to five miles on a three-sixty-degree azimuth appeared on the under water image screen. Harris barked out, "Mahony, change course to three five degrees."

"Aye, aye, Skipper. Making course three five degrees."

"EO, give me every thing you've got. I want to make good forty knots."

"You got it, Bill. Going to forty knots."

Harris's adrenaline was pumping. He turned to Cowly. "Set up forward torpedo tube one through eight. We're going to take that bastard."

He keyed in the radio officer. "Patch in our position to the *Princeton* and to the CNO at Mission Control. We are chasing an unknown enemy sub in territorial waters."

"Yes, sir. Will do."

The *Shark* chased the enemy sub for almost two hours; the enemy kept abruptly changing course and depth, and Harris tried to keep in contact and not lose ground. The UWIS allowed Harris to make good forty knots while cutting precariously close to underwater mountains and crevasses in pursuit of the enemy. They had the best electronics equipment in the world aboard the *Shark*, and made full use of it now.

They caught up with the enemy sub at a dumping area just off the continental shelf. Harris said to Cowly, "Arm torpedoes one and eight."

"Right." He tinkered with a dial on a black box mounted on the firing control monitor. "One and eight armed and ready."

Harris smiled as he studied his comcomp. He said to Cowly. "This is what it's all about. We're going to get our first trophy without the old man."

Cowly responded, "Roger that, Bill. Let's go get 'em."

Captain Jin Chou had been playing fox and hare with the *Shark* for two hours, letting the *Shark* keep up, but not close enough to get off any torpedoes accurately. His own comcomp had IDed the pursuing sub as the *Shark*. His sources had the *Shark* itself IDed from material leaked out of the U.S.S.R. by Chinese agents. Chou realized he was up against a formidable force, and took pride in the way he was easily handling this situation.

His underwater image device allowed him to almost fly through the murky dumping area one hundred and twenty miles off the southernmost tip of New Jersey, and find refuge in the many canyons along the continental escarpment. Here he would sit and wait for the American sub to pass overhead, and then go in for the kill. The foolish Americans would never know what hit them.

Harris keyed his engineering officer. "EO, slow down to twenty knots. That sub could be lurking anywhere." He keyed his sonar officer. "SO, let me know the moment you see anything on the scope. He's out there somewhere, waiting for us. It's our eyes against his. Let's get in the first strike."

"Aye, aye. You'll be the first to know."

Harris said to Cowly, "You know, I can almost feel that sub out there. I'd sure like to nail that bastard before our backup destroyer gets here and spoils our fun."

Cowly smiled. "We'll get him."

Harris keyed in his helmsman. "Mahony, let's take a look along the escarpment. I want to search each of these canyons, starting with the Carteret, the Berkeley, all three Toms Canyons, and so on. He's in there somewhere."

"Aye, aye. I'll steer off the UWIS—"

"Mr. Harris," the SO said, keying the bridge. "Target

339

bearing one six zero degrees. . . . Range five thousand yards. . . . Speed five zero knots . . . and closing fast. Enemy torpedo coming right at us."

Harris shouted into the MC. "Mahony, hard right nine zero degrees."

"Yes, sir. . . . Right full rudder . . . turning nine zero degrees."

"EO, give me everything you've got. Let's get the hell out of here."

"Roger, Chief. Making flank speed."

The SO called out, "Target bearing eight zero degrees. . . . Range two thousand yards. . . . Speed five zero knots. That fish is turning with us, Mr. Harris."

Harris keyed his diving officer. "Dive. Repeat, dive. Take us down, fast. Give me two zero degrees on the diving planes."

The SO cut in. "Target passed overhead, Skip. Just missed us. . . . Second target bearing seven five degrees. . . . Range six thousand yards. . . . Speed five zero knots . . . and closing. Another torpedo."

Harris wiped sweat from his brow with his shirtsleeve. He said to Mahony, "Give me one eighty."

"Coming to course one eight," Mahony answered.

The sonar officer broke in. "Target bearing seven zero degrees. . . . Range three thousand yards. . . . Speed five zero knots . . . and closing."

Harris clapped a hand on Cowly's shoulder. "She's all yours. Fire at will."

Cowly opened torpedo door one and pressed the red fire button. "Number one fired."

A muffled explosion shook the men of the *Shark* as the two torpedoes collided. Harris said, "Let's go after 'em. Mahony, make course two four zero degrees. EO,

340

give me forty knots."

They chased the Chinese sub into the Middle Toms Canyon, a broad crevasse in the escarpment. Harris picked up the sub on his UWIS. "There he is, Cowly. He's all yours."

Cowly keyed in the forward torpedo room. "Prepare to fire numbers two, seven, and eight."

"Aye, Mr. Cowly. Ready to fire when you are."

Cowly punched the Chinese sub's coordinates into his firing control module. He pressed the red button. "Number eight away. Fire numbers two and seven."

"Two and seven off, sir."

Harris and Cowly watched on the UWIS as the picture of the Chinese sub seemed to separate into three parts. Cowly said, "What the—"

"Detractors . . . metal plates chained together and jettisoned out of the stern tubes. The torpedoes home in on the plates. Son of a bitch."

The *Shark*'s torpedoes exploded harmlessly against the metal detractors. The SO had to shout over the roar of the explosions. "Target bearing four seven degrees, sir. . . . Range three thousand yards. . . . Speed five zero knots . . . and closing. Another fish coming right at us."

"Roger that. . . . Cowly, arm four more tubes. Mahony, come to nine zero degrees."

"Target closing fast, sir. Bearing two zero degrees. . . . Range one thousand yards. . . . Speed five zero knots."

Harris knew it was too late to evade the torpedo. He spoke into the intercom. "All hands . . . brace for a hit. Repeat, brace for a hit."

The torpedo hit amidships, just forward of the

bridge. The explosion rocked the *Shark*. It rolled hard onto its starboard side. Harris was thrown hard against the UWIS, shattering the screen and knocking him unconscious. All those not strapped in where thrown to the floor or against the bulkheads.

Cowly, who was strapped into his firing chair, immediate assessed the situation and spoke into the IC-A mike. "Now hear this. This is Mr. Cowly. Mr. Harris is hurt, and I'm taking command. DCO, I want a report from all sections on the double."

"Aye, aye, Mr. Cowly. The damage control module shows a hit on the port side. The galley is wiped out. Damage to the outer hull, just forward of the bridge. The sail may be locked in place. I'll check it out further."

Cowly noticed his depth gauge was dropping. They were heading for the ocean floor. "What the hell is wrong with the depth gauge?"

There was a pause. Then a voice came across the intercom. "This is CPO Ritter, sir. The DO is injured. The electronic diving controls don't seem to be responding."

"Go to manual. Do you think you can handle it?"

"I was trained on diesel subs, sir. Manual is what I do best."

Cowly said, "Great. Do it. You've got to stop this slide. Get all the help you need."

"Yes, sir."

Cowly keyed in the sonar officer. "SO, please report."

"SO here. Is something wrong with the UWIS? My error light is blinking."

"The UWIS is out. We're on old-fashioned sonar,

now. Can you find that sub?"

"Will try."

Cowly spoke into the IC-A. "I need two volunteers to man the mini-subs. We have to chase that sub off. It's our only chance!"

Six sailors showed up at the bridge in minutes. Cowly chose two and they made for the mini-subs, *Alpha* and *Beta*. Each of them was armed with four short-range torpedoes, and carried their own mini-comcomps.

Cowly gave them instructions once they were aboard the mini-subs, while they were waiting for the launch compartments to flood.

The Chinese sub had come out of hiding and was closing in on the *Shark*, making sure that the target was disabled and unable to fight back. It moved in for the kill. Two torpedoes were launched from a distance of two thousand yards, and sped toward the *Shark* at fifty knots.

Alpha loosed two of its fish and exploded the enemy torpedoes a thousand yards short of the *Shark*. The concussion blew *Alpha* back toward its mother ship.

The Chicom sub moved in closer. Suddenly, *Beta* circled and let fly two torpedoes. One found its mark. The starboard diving plane took the hit. Now *Beta* moved in to finish off the job. *Beta* and the *Sea Death* exchanged fire. Two torpedoes left each sub. Only one hit its mark.

The explosion shattered *Beta* into bits and pieces. Debris floated to the ocean floor as the Chinese sub took off out to sea doing better than forty knots. *Alpha* started after her with its two remaining torpedoes, but Cowly called the pilot back in. "We can't risk it. Our diving planes are jammed."

Alpha replied, "I've got the bastard in my sights."

"You won't do us any good if he gets you first. Return to the *Shark*. That's an order. The *Princeton*'s out there. Maybe they'll get lucky."

"Aye, aye, Mr. Cowly."

Cowly looked around the bridge. Harris was unconscious and bleeding from his head. Equipment was smashed, including the IWIS, the eyes of the *Shark*. Men were badly hurt; at least two were known dead. The hull was damaged, the diving gear jammed, one mini-sub destroyed, and worse of all, the Chicom sub had gotten away. And he was the one who had to report this to Boxer and Admiral Stark. He looked at Harris. "Well, buddy, we sure made a fine mess of this." He keyed his radio officer. "Get me Mission Control."

"Go ahead, sir. You're patched through."

Cowly switched on the mike. "Captain Boxer . . . Cowly here. I'm afraid I've got some bad news . . ."

Chapter Twenty-two

"My God, will you look at that." Admiral Stark handed the field glasses to Boxer and pointed toward Norton Point on the tip of Coney Island.

Boxer watched a Coast Guard tug towing the crippled *Shark* ingloriously up the Ambrose Channel, through the Narrows, on its way back to Stapleton. The *Shark* rode low in the water. A serious list to port was evident. Boxer shook his head in disgust.

The older man put his hand on Boxer's shoulder.

Boxer said, "The *Princeton* never made contact again?"

Stark shook his head.

"Bastard's still at large. Cowly reported a hit, but didn't know the extent of the damages."

"He really flew out of there. I would estimate his damages were slight. I think we have to go on a worse case scenario, here. Consider that sub fully capable."

They walked to the pier where the *Shark* would tie up.

Boxer noted the gaping hole in the outer skin ahead of the bridge. The sail was still lowered, a position that was used to reduce friction and drag while under water. The *Shark* always sailed with it raised while on the surface. There was more damage than Boxer had counted on.

Sailors helped the injured crewmen out of the forward hatch. Boxer watched for Cowly to emerge. After several minutes went by, Boxer spotted his helmsman. "Mahony. Over here."

Mahony waved back.

"Where's Cowly?"

Mahony pointed belowdeck. "He's down below. Mr. Harris took a bad spill."

Boxer climbed aboard the *Shark*, his bad leg trailing slightly. The men parted to make way for their captain. He found Cowly in the bridge, holding a compress to Harris's head. "How bad is he?"

Cowly looked up with a start.

Boxer lifted the compress slightly to examine Harris's head wound. It was a nasty-looking gash, splitting the skin from the hairline down the cheek to his ear. Harris was lucky to have his sight. The wound narrowly missed his eye.

The medical officer, injured himself, stopped attending the other wounded crewmen long enough to help Boxer and Cowly bring Harris topside. An emergency medical service crew was already standing by to take over. Within minutes, with Harris aboard, the ambulance was racing off through the streets of Staten Island to the Medical Center.

Cowly was standing around, looking down, and watching his feet kick up the dirt.

Boxer came over. "How are *you* doing? Are you going to kick yourself in the ass forever over this, or you going to be my EXO when we go back after that bastard?"

Cowly's face lit up. "You mean it?"

"You bet. But first things first. We've got to get the

346

Shark patched up so we can submerge again."

"I don't think so, skipper. It's in bad shape. The UWIS is out, the sail's jammed, and—"

Boxer shook his head. "I don't want to enter her in a beauty pageant, I just want to be able to go under again."

Cowly protested, "But that Chicom sub has some sort of UWIS itself. It seemed like a cross between the Russian Q-21 and the *Shark*."

Boxer said, "They probably stole the best from both subs and made it their own."

They walked over to Admiral Stark, who was coordinating the task force that got the men the medical attention their needed. He had D'Arcy running all over shouting orders to the rescue team. Boxer said, "Admiral, I need a repair crew to the *Shark* immediately. I'd like to put her back in the water by daylight tomorrow."

"We'll give it a try, Jack. I'll have the welders get right on it. What else do you need?"

"Well, the UWIS is out."

"Sorry, Jack. It's a one-of-a-kind. We could eventually get enough parts together to get it fixed, but it will take weeks, at least."

"Well, I've commanded subs before without a UWIS. I'll do it again."

"Negative on that, Jack. I can't risk having you go back aboard the *Shark,* Dr. Tuttle or not. You're still grounded."

"There's no one left but me. I've got to be at the command of the *Shark* tomorrow before the ceremonies begin. I've got to be submerged at the mouth of the bay. . . . There's no other way."

347

Stark looked at Boxer grimly. "It's out of the question. That's an order."

"Sorry, Sir. You'll have to lock me up," Boxer broke into a slight smile, "or shoot me, sir. That's the only way you can keep me from doing my job."

Stark stared Boxer down for a long moment. Boxer returned his stare. Then the admiral shook his head, and shrugged his shoulders. . . .

Captain Jin Chou maneuvered the *Sea Death* into the Hudson Canyon, a twenty-mile-long gash in the continental shelf about eighty to one hundred miles offshore. Soon, he found an overhanging ledge in the escarpment, and tucked his sub neatly underneath it. He would be relatively safe there, enough so to regroup from the battle with the American submarine, and to assess his damages.

Under cover of darkness, he had a makeshift diving plane welded onto the remains of the one damaged in the attack. There were no major injuries to his men, nor had any other harm come to the *Sea Death*. Now it was time to go over his final preparations with the underwater demolition team. He turned the conn over to his EXO, and made his way into the quarters of the strike force.

Forty men rose as one and saluted Captain Chou. To a man, they were glad to be under his command. His experience and expertise had surely saved them from oblivion during the depth-charging, and during the battle with the enemy sub. Their leader, Major Kuo, stepped forward and clasped hands with Chou. Chou said, "I wish to address your men."

"With pleasure, Comrade Captain."

Jin Chou cleared his throat. "Please be seated, comrades. I wish to take this opportunity to thank you in advance for your courage for volunteering for this mission. Through your actions tomorrow, we hope to regain our rightful place as the foremost nation in the world."

The men of the strike force burst forth with resounding cheers.

Chou continued. "Your role is the most vital. You will be divided into two groups of twenty men each. Squad One is responsible for destroying the Manhattan and Brooklyn Bridges. Squad Two will blow up the Verrazano Bridge. Major Kuo will divide you into eight squads of five men, and take charge of your maneuver once you leave the *Sea Death*. You will place your explosives at the base of the casements and return to the ship if possible. Major Kuo and I will detonate the charges by remote."

Chou looked at each of the men sitting before him, studying their faces. Yes, he was satisfied. They would give up their lives for the glory of the Motherland. "Are there any questions?"

There was some whispering among a group of men. The young lieutenant among them raised his hand. When Captain Chou nodded at him, he asked, "Comrade Captain, what action do we take if we are not able to make the connection with the *Sea Death?*"

Chou knew that was a very valid question. There was a good chance that he would have to fight and flee without picking up the strike force. The grim expression on Major Kuo's face showed that he knew the consequences all too well. Chou said, "I will not lie to you. You are a very brave and valiant crew. There is some chance that the sub will leave without you. If our strike tomorrow is overwhelmingly successful, you will simply make your way to land, and seek out our confederates among the Dragon Tong."

The men were happy to hear that.

Then Chou said, "However, in no way must you allow yourselves to be captured alive and embarrass our country with a confession. Therefore, you must kill as many of our enemies as possible, and die fighting. Or kill yourself."

The mood in the room changed considerably.

"Our government can always claim that you were imperialist puppets from Taiwan, or from New York," Chou told them.

Major Kuo jumped up and turned to his men. "We are not afraid to die for our homeland." His fist shot upward in a power salute. The men shouted approval in unison. Then he turned to face Captain Chou and smiled. "But we will succeed. We will not fail. And we will be coming home aboard the *Sea Death* as heroes."

Captain Chou returned the power salute.

Major Kuo saluted again, followed by the rest of the men.

Spirits were running high.

Chou motioned for silence, and the men of the strike force settled down. "I will bring the *Sea Death* within striking distance. Then each squad will unpack their vessel on deck and inflate it using the sub's pressurization system. You will run on the surface under the cover of darkness. Each vessel has an eighty-horsepower engine capable of making good thirty knots."

350

Chou let the info sink in. . . . It was merely a review for these crack troops, but there was no harm in going over it one last time. "As you know, each craft is fully submersible for up to ten nautical miles, but at much reduced speed. You will park your boats at the base of the bridge stanchions, plant your charges, and take the actions we have discussed."

Major Kuo got up and stood next to Captain Chou. He said to his men, "We will get under way in thirty minutes. You won't get any sleep, 'til late tomorrow night, almost twenty-four hours from now. To keep everyone awake and alert we have some additional supplies for you. Kuo took a small locked metal box out of a storage nook under his bunk and unlocked it. He held up a handful of half-ounce glassine packets of cocaine, and the men cheered. The box was passed around to each man, and soon the potent stimulant disappeared into forty noses. Now, they were fully charged and ready to do battle. Chou and Major Kuo looked at each other and smiled. They were very pleased.

Captain Chou returned to the bridge, stopping along the way to collect and bring along Ming Hsieh. "I would like you to remain beside me for the duration of our mission."

"With pleasure, Captain. I will be with you to the end."

Chou smiled. He said, "Let us be under way. . . . Helmsman, come to course one five zero degrees."

"Coming to one five zero degrees," the helmsman answered.

Chou keyed the diving officer. "DO, bring us up to seven zero meters, very gently. Diving planes at five

351

zero degrees. We don't want the repair to become undone."

"Yes, Comrade Captain. Five degrees on the diving planes. Coming up to seven zero meters."

Chou ordered the forward ballast tanks blown and called out the soundings as they rose toward the surface. He watched the depth gauge on top of his comcomp. "Passing through five zero zero meters . . ."

Slowly the sub climbed. Chou was pleased with the repair job. He continued his vigil. "Passing through four zero zero meters . . . three zero zero meters . . ."

As they came to two hundred and ten feet, Captain Chou ordered the diving planes trimmed, and watched the bubble indicator return to null. The digital printout on his diving module confirmed this. Then he adjusted his position, called out his new commands to his officers, and headed up the crescent-shaped trough toward New York Harbor. He turned toward his political officer. "Comrade Hsieh, we will now proceed toward the enemy harbor." His finger traced his path on his comcomp screen, "And hide here, at this dump site. There will be garbage barges about. That is good. They will distort enemy sonar and radar pictures. We will be safe there until we launch our attack."

Boxer called the SEALs assigned to him into his office. They were fourteen of the finest men the U.S. Navy had to offer. They had undergone the most rigorous training program available to any of the Armed Forces, including the Rangers and the Green Berets. Their main strengths were demolition, and man-to-man fighting.

Boxer had them divide into two teams, one under Corporal Lebanski and the other led by Sergeant Bradley, who had been sent in to replace O'Reilly. Boxer pressed a button on his desk, a motor whirred, and an expanded chart of the upper and lower bays was unfurled from a device on the ceiling. The chart filled the entire back wall of the room.

Boxer began, "We have information that the Chicoms are going to take steps to ruin the ceremonies this afternoon. They are going to try to explode devices in the Holland Tunnel and the Brooklyn Battery Tunnel." Boxer looked over the men's faces, making sure that what he was saying was sinking in. "Colonel Pickens will take care of that."

Boxer walked back to the chart. "We feel that they're going to try to destroy the Brooklyn Bridge. Possibly the Manhattan Bridge. Or both. That's where you men come in. You're to intercept anyone trying to plant explosives at the bridges and neutralize them. Both the men and the explosives. Any questions so far?"

A hand went up. Boxer said, "Sergeant Bradley?"

Bradley looked more like a wide receiver with his trim, muscular one-eighty-pound frame than the others, who more resembled linebackers. He was their best swimmer. "I'm not a political scientist, sir. Seems to me an awful lot of trouble to go through, risking an all-out war by blowing up a couple of bridges." He scratched his blond crewcut head.

"To create a diversion, and tie up the police and Coast Guard. The Chicoms are out to destroy a lot of the ships at the festival. In one sneak attack in the New York Harbor they could accomplish more than

353

they could in months of naval fighting around the globe. And we still haven't got positive proof that it's the People's Republic that's behind the trouble. It's still just hearsay. We'd have to capture that sub to prove it's the Chicoms. And frankly, I'm not ready to force a confrontation with China. I just want to stop them."

Bradley said, "I got it. Let them save face. If they don't admit it was them, and we can't prove it, then everyone can walk away from this one."

"Right." Boxer went on. "The Coast Guard is placing hydrophones across the East River. If they trigger off anything, you men will be in position to intercept."

Lebansky asked, "You think they'd send that sub right up into the harbor to blow those bridges?"

Boxer shook his head. "If it were my mission to destroy those bridges, I would deploy my mini-subs. And if I have them aboard the *Shark,* which is confidential, gentlemen, then you can be sure that the Chicoms have 'em. Or something very similar. Or I would use subskinners. They're small inflatables that are capable of diving and remaining under water. Perfect for a four- or six-member squad of scuba divers. Either way, men, that's how I would go about it. And that's what I'm going to defend against."

"But what if they launch a surface attack, instead?"

"The Coast Guard is prepared to take care of that. Commander Szpak has his men on full alert, just in case. Okay, Brad, you take your squad over to the Brooklyn side of the Brooklyn Bridge, just upstream of the casements. Lebanski, your team on the Manhattan side. There are hovercraft waiting outside to transport you. Radio and sonar equipment is on board to monitor the hydrophones. Any more questions?"

Boxer looked over his men once more. They were ready. "Well, good luck, men."

Lebanski picked up the signal first. Four tiny blips on his sonar screen. He keyed Bradley. The two of them stayed topside to monitor and coordinate the activity. Six SEALs on each side of the bridge went overboard and hid behind the base of the stanchions. Bradley notified Boxer.

"They're here, sir. We're standing by to intercept them."

Boxer, in turn, notified Szpak at the Coast Guard Base. The vice was tightening on the enemy.

On the Brooklyn side, two teams of five blue-clad figures rode their vehicles to the bottom and made their way to the stanchion bases. A SEAL surfaced and notified Bradley that the odds were ten to six against them. Brad would have to help.

Bradley notified Lebanski that he was going below, and gently let himself into the murky waters of the East River. Visibility was very poor two hours before sunrise. He could make out the men in blue wetsuits, and hoped that his men could take them by surprise. That would reduce the odds. He signaled his men to back off and circle around the enemy.

The Chinese busied themselves attaching their explosive packs to the base of the casement. Suddenly, they were attacked from behind. Seven black-suited SEALS slashed at throats and air supplies.

355

The Chinese didn't know what hit them. The remaining Chicoms joined in the melee, and double-teamed some of the SEALs. Soon blood was flowing freely from both sides. Bradley pulled two blue-suits off one of his men who was being hacked apart by his attackers.

Brad's powerful kick to the groin doubled up one of the assailants. A downward thrust with his scuba knife ended the struggle of the other.

Brad moved to finish off the first man, and swam to the aid of his stricken comrade. It was too late. The SEAL's throat had been severed.

Lebanski and his team didn't surprise the enemy as completely, and three SEALs were lost in the fighting. It was man-to-man, down and dirty. The Chinese died, fighting, to the man.

A Coast Guard cutter hove to on the Manhattan side of the bridge, and began the grim job of removing the surviving SEALs and the bodies of the dead, both Chinese and American.

On the Brooklyn side, Bradley gathered his small group aboard the hovercraft. His men wearily pulled aboard the body of their slain comrade.

It was a bad day for the SEALs. They had lost four of their members to the enemy, five counting O'Reilly the other day. But at least the harbor was safe. As the sun came up that morning, Saturday, July 4, 1992, Sergeant Bradley lay wearily against the gun'ale of his hovercraft. He closed his eyes for a moment of silent meditation for his lost men. He hoped they had not died in vain. Let the ceremonies begin.

Chapter Twenty-three

Security was very tight among the Soviet Bloc ships. All of their military vessels were under full alert. They lined up along the eastern shore of Long Island in the order in which they would follow the parade route past the Statue of Liberty. All but the largest craft would sail up through the Verrazano Narrows into the upper bay, come about at the southern tip of Manhattan, and pass the reviewing stand on Liberty Island on their way south. The largest ships would hove to in the lower bay and rejoin the convoy as it continued out to sea.

The Soviet Bloc would be the first group on review, followed by the U.S.A., and then the American allies, and the neutral nations. The Polish contingency was due at the Verrazano Bridge at 0700, followed by the German Democratic Republic, the Yugoslavs, the Bulgarians, the Roumanians, and finally the Russian fleet.

U.S. Coast Guard cutters lined the parade route from the Narrows to the Battery, keeping all craft not directly involved with the ceremonies out of the way of the larger ships. Captain Igor Borodine would take charge of security primarily outside of the Verrazano Bridge. He had Soviet minesweepers patrolling alongside the entire Bloc fleet, as well as patrol boats carrying depth charges, cannon, and torpedoes.

The parade would be led by the Polish destroyer *Gdansk*. The penultimate ship was the Soviet carrier *Leningrad*, followed by the support cruiser *Odessa*. Many of the ships were equipped with water cannon, and would shoot streams of water high into the air along the parade route. And others, as they headed out to sea, were to fire blank rounds from their conventional big guns.

Borodine left his EXO, Viktor Korenzo, in charge of the control room aboard the *Gdansk*. He chose to command the lead minesweeper so he could be in more intimate contact with the conditions of the lower and upper bays.

The convoy moved out, making ten knots off Long Island's Eastern shore. The Polish destroyer veered to starboard into the Ambrose Channel and headed toward the Verrazano Bridge. Borodine sailed his craft just off the bow of the *Gdansk*. There was a squawk of static from the intercom and the sonar officer came on the line. "Target passing by our port side, Comrade Captain. Range two zero zero meters. . . . Speed two five knots. . . . Depth twelve meters."

Borodine pressed the switch on his mike. "Can you ID?"

"Negative, Captain. It's much too small to be a submarine."

But not too small to be a mini-sub. Or any variety

of submersible vehicle, thought Borodine. "Keep tracking it."

"Yes, Comrade Captain."

Boxer called his radioman. "Patch me into Mission Control. Get me Captain Boxer."

"Aye, aye, Comrade Captain."

Boxer was summoned to the control room. An aide handed him a microphone. "There's a Ruskie Captain Borodine calling you."

Boxer said into the mike, "Good morning, Comrade Captain. What can I do for you?"

There was tension in Borodine's voice. "We have just now IDed a small submersible making a course of one five five degrees at two five knots through your Ambrose Channel. I must know if it is one of yours."

"Not ours, Comrade Captain. The *Shark* is still tied up at the Stapleton Base, and we have deliberately kept all others out of the area to avoid confusion."

Borodine pressed him. "What about a mini-sub, or the like?"

"Negative on that, also. But we have intercepted four submersible inflatables at the Brooklyn Bridge. They carried demolition teams. . . . We got there just in time."

Borodine rubbed his beard. "Could it be, my friend, that those same demolition teams have also done the same thing to the Verrazano Bridge?"

"Not the same crew. They are all dead."

"Naturally, there—"

The SO interrupted Borodine. "Second target passing us in the channel, Comrade Captain. . . . Range one three zero meters. . . . Speed . . . Comrade Captain—" The SO's voice took on an excited pitch. "ID a third and fourth target approaching as well."

"Keep tracking them. Notify Comrade Korenzo on the *Gdansk*. I want a squad of amphibious commandos in the water at once, in their hovercraft. I want them armed with snowballs." He referred to hand-launched antisubmarine weapons, similar to mini–depth charges.

Boxer said, "Comrade Captain Borodine. Can you stop them long enough for me to send a team of SEALs after them?"

Borodine replied, "I am on my way after them now. We will try to flush them out of the water and capture them. Our Marines are on their way in a hovercraft."

"No need to involve your government in an international incident. If I send the SEALs, it will be a local police action."

"Yes. And by the time they get here, your bridge may be destroyed. Better they check the base of the casements for explosives, Comrade. We will take care of the rest."

Boxer thought that over for a moment. "Okay, my friend. Go to it. You are already at the scene. Good luck. I'll have the Coast Guard back you up."

"Roger that, Comrade Captain Boxer." Borodine placed the microphone back in its holder. He picked up the intercom mike. "EO, give me forty knots. Helmsman, take us around and past that lead vessel. I want to cut them off before they escape out to sea."

The minesweeper took a circuitous course out about ten miles, passed in front of the Ambrose Lighthouse, and made its way back toward the harbor. Borodine had several of the standard gunnery shells replaced with the type that exploded at depth. The mini-subs would not get past him, of that he was certain.

The sonar officer interrupted his thoughts. "Captain, target bearing three one five degrees. . . . Range two thousand meters. . . . Speed two five knots. . . . It's on the surface heading south, sir."

Borodine told his helmsman, "Come to two nine five degrees." He keyed the EO. "Give me four five knots."

"Aye, aye, Comrade Captain."

The sonar officer reported a submerged target dead ahead.

"Stand by to fire depth-activated shells at target," Borodine ordered.

"Ready to fire, Comrade Captain," the gunnery officer answered.

Borodine said, "Fire at will."

The shells hit the water in a pattern. In seconds, a series of explosions rocked the ship, and a dozen geysers shot up from the surface. "It's a hit, sir. Target destroyed."

The last explosion sent several bodies and the remains of the inflatable flying into the air. They hit the surface and began to settle.

Looking northwest, Borodine could make out a fast-moving surface vessel heading their way. He borrowed a set of field glasses and placed them to his eyes. . . . They must have spotted something. . . . He saw several Marines place hand-held rocket launchers to their shoulders and fired their snowballs into the sea around them.

Whoosh! Whump! Water spouted into the air seconds after each shell was fired. One inflatable came to the surface.

As the Russians aimed their AK-47 machine guns at the crew, they held their hands above their heads. Suddenly, they dropped to the floor and came up with automatic machine pistols. Several of the Chinese strafed the Russian Marines.

Borodine was close enough to witness that, and yelled to his forward machine gunner. He pointed at the inflatable and shouted, "Fire!"

The inflatable burst apart under the fusillade. The craft sank. Borodine's machine gunner continued firing at the crew until the men and their boat disappeared under the surface.

The Marine hovercraft found another Chicom submersible under the surface with its snowballs. Parts of men and craft shot up out of the sea and littered the surface before sinking along with the others.

The fourth Chinese crew surfaced alongside the hovercraft. The crew waved their hands overhead and shouted, "Don't shoot," in Chinese. The Russian Marines didn't speak the language, but there was no mistaking what they were saying. The Marines covered their captives; there would be no surprise attack this time!

The Russian crew tied the inflatable to the hovercraft, and towed it toward the minesweeper. Suddenly the Chinese shook their fists overhead and chanted in unison. The Marines aimed directly at the Chinese and shouted a command to sit down and shut up.

The explosion that followed swooped both the Chinese craft and the Russian hovercraft up into a giant fireball, leaving a crater in the water where they had been. The Chinese had set off a remaining explosive pack on a short fuse before they'd surfaced, and blew themselves and their victims to glory. The fireball settled on the surface, the momentary crater closed in over all, and the sea claimed everything.

Borodine shielded his eyes from the blast. The Marines never stood a chance.

Viktor Korenzo had just told Boxer about the death and destruction involved in stopping the escape of the Chicom demolition team. "Roger that," Boxer answered. "Express my regrets to Comrade Captain Borodine on the loss of your men."

"Thank you, Comrade Captain Boxer."

"My SEALs are removing the charges that were attached to the bridge." Boxer returned his mike to its cradle. He turned to Admiral Stark. "We're almost in the clear, sir. We'll hold up the parade of ships until all the explosives are cleared from the Verrazano Bridge."

"What about the problem in the tunnels?" Stark asked.

"I sent Pickens to Chinatown to work out a plan

363

with the Hung Yee Tong, Admiral. They have the inside track into what's going on there."

"And what about that Chicom sub that the *Shark* chased yesterday?"

"Frankly, we don't know, sir. There hasn't been any sign of him since that fracas. It seems his mission has been aborted with the destruction of his demolition squads, and the dismantling of the explosives. If that was his goal, then he's out of the picture."

Boxer looked the Admiral in the eye. "But if he's up to any more mischief, we'll be ready for him."

Stark replied, "Well, you damn well better be, Jack. We won't get more than one chance against that one. That commander really knows his stuff, if what he's done so far is any indicator."

"We'll stop him, sir. You can count on it." And then Boxer said to himself, I hope.

Pickens's call came in a few minutes later. "Chief, this thing's gettin' bigger an' bigger all the time. We could sure use your help here."

Boxer took a fast ride on a U.S. Navy speedboat across the bay. Will Pickens met him at the Coast Guard Base, and they drove the short distance to Lin Pei's in Chinatown.

She greeted Boxer and walked arm in arm with him into her quarters. Sun and Gai Tang were already waiting there.

She spoke. "Our sources tell us that there will be an assault at both the Holland and Battery Tunnels. We were hoping that the cowards would concentrate on only one, but it is not to be.

"Our mutual enemies are trying to create a diversion to distract the authorities from their real objective. That is to attack the combined fleet in the harbor. They still plan to go through with it."

Boxer asked, "Are you sure, Lin?"

"As sure as I know that they were trying to blow up the bridges and some important buildings around the city. You have to understand the psyche of these people, Jack. They will not stop until they have reached their objective, or until they die trying."

Pickens butted in. "We got the police workin' with us in Brooklyn at the Battery Tunnel. They're gonna try to screen all the traffic approaching the tunnel, and pull out anyone who even looks oriental." Pickens looked at Lin Pei and her bodyguards. "Ah'm ashamed to say it." He blushed. "Me and the boys here are plannin' to head over there now an' give the police a hand."

Lin Pei said, "At the Holland Tunnel, we do not have as much cooperation. There is much more traffic, coming from many directions. Captain Jefferson said it would be impossible to screen out my people. We are much too numerous. Besides, this is where we live and work. The Chinese people will not stand for that kind of treatment here."

"Which leaves?"

"Which leaves us. The police will be in the vicinity. They will be directing traffic. There will also be a bomb squad on hand. But it will be up to us to stop a car bomb from getting into the tunnel."

Boxer asked, "What about Charlie Leung?"

Lin answered, "I don't trust him completely. I just hope that he does as he is told. He must get his vehicle boxed in with slow-moving traffic. Then it will be up to you and me to intercept his car and detain him for the bomb squad."

"Well, we all know what we have to do. Let's get to it."

Will Pickens, Sun, and Gai Tang took off in Will's car for the Battery Tunnel into Brooklyn. They would set themselves up at the mouth of the tunnel. Pickens's plan was to set up a police roadblock, limiting access to the tunnel to one slow-moving lane of traffic into Manhattan. Then it would just be a matter of time and patience.

The hours wore on slowly for them. Will and Lin Pei's two bodyguards stood behind a barricade blocking one of the two lanes of traffic into the tunnel. A police sergeant had parked his patrol car behind the barrier, and activated the overhead lights. From time to time, the sergeant would single out a vehicle on his own, or on the advice of Will Pickens and his crew, and have the car diverted back into the streets of Brooklyn. If they wanted to go into Manhattan, there was still the option of three bridges to take.

At 1100, a blue Chevy van was stopped. The driver was asked to find another route into the city. The driver became abusive. He knew his rights. He also knew that most of the other vehicles were allowed to pass. The sergeant came around in front of the barrier to aid the other police officer. Will looked at his two companions. This looked as if it could be trouble.

Traffic was building behind the blue van. Drivers honked their horns and shouted obscenities. The cops held their ground. Finally, the sergeant signaled a tow truck strategically parked on the shoulder of the road, and motioned him to back up to the van and tow it away.

The man in the passenger seat leaned out the open window, shouted something in Chinese, and pointed a heavy automatic pistol at the officer's head.

The sergeant reached for his revolver. Too late.

The gunman's automatic exploded, taking off the side of the officer's head. He continued firing, pumping three or four more slugs into the already dead policeman.

The sergeant fired at the van, shattering the windshield.

The driver backed up abruptly, smashing the rear of the van into the car behind it. He revved the engine and aimed the van at the police sergeant.

Will Pickens nodded at his two companions and they aimed their handguns at the driver. The van bucked forward. The three men fired at the driver. The sergeant and the van driver died virtually at the same instant.

The van slammed into the police sergeant and crushed his body into the patrol car behind the barricade.

Three Chinese men jumped out of the rear of the van, and started firing at Will and the others.

Gai Tang was hit in the shoulder and went down.

Will crouched over him and emptied his automatic at the closest assailant.

The man was hit several times. Blood splattered everywhere, and he fell backward hard against the street. He was dead before he landed.

Sun stood over Will and Gai Tang and covered them while Will reloaded. They managed to pull Gai Tang behind the patrol car while they kept the gunmen at bay.

Police sirens could be heard a few short blocks away.

The two remaining assailants knew they had little hope of surviving if they didn't get past the barricade. They stood up and charged, firing as they ran.

Will and Sun stayed behind the patrol car. They took careful aim. Bullets slammed into metal; glass shattered around their heads. They held their ground. Then, in unison, they emptied their pistols at the two remaining gunmen. Round after round found their mark. The gunmen went down.

Pickens ducked into the front seat of the patrol car and clicked on the police radio. "Police officers in trouble at the Battery Tunnel," he shouted. "Get some ambulances out here." Will looked at the carnage around him. "And better send a meat wagon along, too. We're gonna need it."

Lower Manhattan was in a state of gridlock. Automobile traffic was at a standstill despite the mayor's pleas to use public transportation. Chinatown was the scene of the worse congestion, with Canal Street completely stopped. Boxer shook his head and asked Lin Pei, "How do you propose to get to the tunnel? The traffic isn't moving."

Lin smiled, "There is more than one way to skin a cat." She unlocked a gate to an alley beside her headquarters building. "Behold."

Boxer was staring at two shiny new red Honda motorscooters. "You've gotta be kidding. No one in their right mind over the age of twenty rides on one of those."

Lin Pei's smile broadened. "You said it, not me. Let's go." She tossed him a protective wraparound helmet. It matched the color of the scooters, and with the smoke-colored visor down, it would be impossible to identify the driver. That suited Boxer just fine. He gave the thumbs-up sign, started the ignition, and followed Lin Pei around the slowed vehicles and up the center lanes between the lines of cars on Canal Street. They headed for the Holland Tunnel.

Traffic converged on the tunnel entrance from four directions, forming a ten-lane fan of vehicles that had to merge into two lanes just prior to entering the tunnel.

Boxer and Lin Pei wove their scooters among these cars and small trucks in search of Charlie Leung. In an hour, their diligence was rewarded. Charlie Leung was at the wheel of a yellow gypsie cab, a beat-up Ford Fairmont that had seen better days.

What they hadn't counted on was the three other men in the cab with Charlie. There was a young man in the seat next to Charlie, and two men in the back seat. All were Oriental, presumably Chinese. The one behind Charlie was holding a gun to his head, discretely trying to shield it from the people in the other vehicles caught up in the traffic jam.

Lin signaled Boxer and pulled her vehicle around to the driver's side of the taxi.

Boxer followed suit on the passenger side.

Without warning, Lin pulled a 9mm automatic from beneath her riding jacket and fired two rounds into the head of the man behind Charlie Leung. Glass shattered. Blood and bits of bone and gray matter splattered over the inside of the cab. The other back-seat rider spun toward Lin in astonishment, reflexively swinging the gun in his lap in her direction.

Lin shot him twice in the face.

Boxer smashed the front passenger's window and pointed his short-barreled thirty-eight revolver at the man's head.

The passenger screamed for mercy in Chinese, and held up his hands.

Charlie's froze at the wheel.

Lin Pei flipped up her visor, and shouted at Charlie Leung to turn off the ignition. The engine stopped.

Charlie slumped at the wheel, obviously shaken by the ordeal.

Boxer pulled his scooter up on its kickstand, dragged the taxi's front passenger out and slammed him spread-eagle against the vehicle.

Charlie pointed to a black box on the floorboard where the man was sitting. He told Lin that it was the detonator to blow the three hundred pounds of high-powered explosives that were crammed into the

Fairmont's roomy trunk.

Two police officers came running to the scene of the shooting with guns drawn. Boxer pulled off his helmet, and was recognized by the officer in charge. The front-seat passenger was cuffed and taken into custody. The bomb squad was alerted. There was a tremendous cacophony of blaring horns and shouted expletives as the bomb squad vehicle made its way to the Ford Fairmont. The specially trained police officers spent the next half hour defusing the bomb. A special vehicle was called for to remove the explosives.

Boxer was getting a strange feeling while the bomb squad was doing its work. The traffic into the tunnel hadn't moved during all that time. He called over one of the traffic cops. "Why isn't the traffic moving into the tunnel? All the commotion's out here."

The policeman shrugged his shoulders and shook his head. "Some poor sap's stalled in the tunnel about halfway in. Been there for an hour. Seems as if there was an accident just ahead of him, and his car stalled while waiting to get out. All the tow trucks have been tied up with the accident."

"Son of a bitch." He turned to Lin Pei. "Seems as though some people have very short memories. There's a massive tie-up inside the tunnel. Let's go."

Boxer and Lin Pei maneuvered their scooters between the rows of traffic and along the center line in the tunnel. Drivers who had been stuck inside for almost an hour shouted curses and shook their fists at them. A few hundred yards into the tunnel, the two neat files of vehicles soon gave way to an obstacle course, as drivers tried to cut across lanes in an effort to get out. The scooters could go no farther.

Boxer hopped off his scooter and ran toward the New Jersey side. Lin followed. It took ten more minutes of hard running and climbing around vehicles to reach the stalled car. Boxer's lungs were bursting from the heavy running and breathing in the exhaust fumes of the waiting traffic. Lin was right behind him. "There it is."

Lin removed her weapon and moved along the tunnel's left wall. Boxer went up the center space between the two rows of traffic. They were spotted as they approached the stalled Fairmont. The rear window of the Ford blew outward, showering lead pellets at the cars behind it. Boxer and Lin ducked in tandem.

Boxer circled around the car nearest the Fairmont in the right lane. He signaled the driver to get down and crawl out the passenger side. A shotgun blast shattered the windshield, just missing the driver. Boxer pulled the woman to safety.

The driver behind the blue Ford was not as lucky. A fusilade of shot pellets caught him in the head and chest. His bloody body slumped forward over the steering wheel. He died instantly.

Lin Pei shot several rounds into the Ford where the rear window used to be. A man screamed.

Boxer made his way around to the hood of the vehicle he was hiding behind, a black Volvo with Connecticut plates. He fired at the front seat passenger of the Fairmont. The man slumped in his seat. At least two of the bastards hit, Boxer figured.

Lin Pei emptied her clip at the Ford, and reloaded.

Boxer fired off a few more rounds and did the same. While they were occupied with reloading, the driver and the passenger behind him ran from the Ford in the direction of New Jersey.

The driver, Charlie's former accomplice Manny, carried two pump-action automatic shotguns. He turned and fired off two blasts in the direction of Boxer and Lin Pei.

The man with him carried a black box under his arm, and a thirty-seven Magnum automatic in his right hand.

Boxer got off a shot with him, which was returned with a volley of five or six rapid shots.

The Volvo absorbed most of the hits. Two shots careened off the tunnel wall behind Boxer. Bits of white ceramic tile ricocheted off at Boxer's back.

Manny fired two more blasts at them.

Boxer fired off one more shot at the man with the black box. He, in turn, emptied his automatic at Boxer. The front of the Volvo caught fire.

While Boxer drew their fire, Lin took careful aim and got off a round at Manny. The round caught him in the groin.

Manny screamed in agony, dropped his weapons, and brought his hands down to protect his genitals. Lin fired again to finish him off.

The second gunman was changing clips when Boxer and Lin charged him, firing on the run. A shot hit him in the leg, and he went down. He flung his empty weapon in Boxer's direction and pulled himself upright against the tunnel wall. He shouted a stream of invectives in Chinese as he held the black box in front of him. He flipped some switches and a detonator handle popped up. He pulled out the handle about a foot and pressed it down.

Boxer and Lin Pei emptied their guns into him. The man went down on top of the firing device. Boxer was the first to get to him and kicked the man over onto his back.

Lin dove for the black box and pulled the handle straight up. They turned toward the blue Ford Fairmont, expecting to see it blow them all to hell.

Nothing. Boxer managed a faint smile. Smoke was beginning to fill the tunnel from the burning Volvo. They ran to the demolished Ford. Boxer slipped the gears into neutral, and together they pushed the car away from the heat of the fire. Lin gasped for air, and put her scarf across her mouth to filter out some of the noxious fumes.

Slowly, the blue Ford rolled forward, away from the burning wreck. They might make it after all. If only the police would get there with a tow truck and a bomb squad. Boxer looked back one last time at the flames and the heavy smoke and pushed as if his life depended on it.

Chapter Twenty-four

Captain Jin Chou paced incessantly throughout the *Sea Death,* chain-smoked, and waited as nervously as an expectant father. By 1000, there was still no word from his demolition strike force. So be it. Chou confided to Ming Hsien that he felt all the men had been killed. "It is my hope that they planted their explosive charges before they were killed."

Hsien asked, "What about our comrades who were to blow up the tunnels into Manhattan? Have we received any word from them?"

"There is no way to contact them. We have only our trust and faith that they have performed their function as planned."

"It is a pity that they will not be able to join us in our victory parade in Beijing when we arrive home. They are all heroes."

Captain Chou placed a hand on the woman's shoulder and said softly, "Comrade Hsien, I am sorry to tell you what I now must."

Ming Hsien looked up at him, a little surprised.

Chou continued. "When we set off on our mission, we had nothing but loathing, even hatred, for each other. That is in the past. We followed different masters, who each thought that they were the most important force in dealing with our mutual enemies."

"But—"

"As you can see, each has its own place. The Security Committee has made it possible to infiltrate our agents into the enemy's homeland and strike at them from within. And as you now know, it is the submarine that will strike the telling blow in just a few hours."

Ming Hsien took Chou's hand in hers and looked adoringly into his eyes. "But why are you telling me all this now? We have come to see each other's point of view."

"Because it is very hard for me to say what I must tell you. I have grown very fond of you . . ."

"And I of you." Ming Hsien wrapped her arms around Captain Chou.

He was taken by surprise, and looked around him at the crew on the bridge, very embarrassed. He cleared his throat. "Ming . . . Comrade Hsien . . . there will be no return to the homeland for us. There will be no victory parade."

She stood back and looked up at him.

He said, "Oh, there will indeed be a victory for us. We will surely destroy a sizable number of the

376

ships assembled in the harbor. But there is no way we can possibly escape. The enemy will surely find us and destroy us. We must do as much damage as possible, and take as many of the enemy with us at the end."

Hsien stood silently for a moment. "Then I must leave you now."

"Where will you run to? Where can you hide?"

Hsien stood ramrod straight, chin out, and said. "I do not wish to run away. I wish to fight."

Chou was taken aback.

She continued, "I will contact our agents in New York. We shall commandeer speedboats, fill them with explosives, and ram them into the enemy warships."

Captain Chou beamed in admiration. "You could work in the upper bay. That would be ideal for the plan you have proposed. And I could keep the *Sea Death* south of the Verrazano Bridge, where I would have more room to maneuver. It is a good plan."

Boxer and Lin Pei were treated by the paramedics for smoke inhalation. He removed his oxygen mask, and told Lin Pei that he had to get back to Stapleton Base, and the *Shark*. He left her to look after her wounded bodyguard, Gai Tang, who'd been taken to Bellevue Hospital.

Boxer took Lin in his arms. "Thank you for everything you've done. The city . . . our government . . . most of the nations of the world owe you a great debt of gratitude for your help. And I personally thank you. I owe the success of this mission to you."

She reached up and kissed him. "We have helped each other. That is how it should be."

Boxer said, "I have to get back to my headquarters. Perhaps our paths will cross again some day."

Lin Pei smiled. "Perhaps they shall. I hope so." And as Boxer turned away, she added, "And Jack, that night we made love . . . that was for real."

Boxer started to say something.

"I know you think I used you, but there would have been other ways. I wanted to love you. And it was wonderful."

Boxer stared into her eyes for a moment. Then he turned and walked away. He was needed aboard the *Shark*.

Boxer found Commander Szpak in his communications room, monitoring the status of his vessels from Montauk Point to Cape May.

Szpak greeted Boxer, and asked about his smoke-blackened clothing. Boxer related the incident in the tunnel.

Szpak said, "Well, the least I can do is get you cleaned up and into a fresh uniform."

"Thanks. I'd also appreciate a ride to Stapleton."

Charlie Szpak walked Boxer into his private

quarters, and gave him a towel and one of his own fresh white dress uniforms. "Shower's in there. By the way, CPO Boulay's here now. I'm sure he'd be glad to take you anywhere you want."

Boxer smiled. "Good old Wooly Bully. Sure. Thanks."

Fifteen minutes later, Boxer stood before Captain Szpak all cleaned up and looking sharp in the Coast Guard uniform. Szpak said, "Looks better on you than on me."

"Thanks. I'd like to get started."

Boulay welcomed Boxer aboard the buoy tender, and they shoved off for Staten Island. Boxer could hear the brass band playing at the bandstand on Governors Island as the convoy of capital ships began its parade into the upper bay. Boxer watched through a set of glasses as Captain Borodine led the procession by escorting the Polish destroyer *Gdansk* up the channel.

Boxer saluted the statue as the buoy tender passed the reviewing stand on Liberty Island. They headed south toward the naval base, and were starting to veer off to starboard when the first blast ripped a gaping hole in the side of the East German frigate *Dresden*. A second explosion, slightly aft of the first, caused the ship to list heavily.

"Holy shit. You see that?" Boulay pointed to a swarm of tiny speedboats zipping around the huge warships. They were slamming into the larger ships like man-driven torpedoes.

Boxer watched as Borodine picked up the cue and began firing at the smaller ships.

A Coast Guard cutter soon joined the battle.

Two more explosions racked the *Tito,* a Yugoslav heavy cruiser.

Borodine's gunnery crew destroyed three speedboats. They blew up in fiery balls as the heavy rounds connected with their explosive charges.

Boxer nudged Boulay, who was trying to steer clear of the fighting, "We got anything to shoot with?"

"Learned my lesson from your boys. There's an M-16 by the chart table."

Boxer took the weapon and made his way to the bow. He spotted two speedboats headed for the Coast Guard cutter. He fired at the lead boat. Missed. Boxer adjusted his aim and emptied his clip. The boat-bomb exploded just short of the cutter.

The Coast Guard crew blasted the second boat out of the water.

The *Sofia,* a Bulgarian command vessel, took a direct hit to the stern, and caught fire.

Borodine streamed to its aid. He apparently didn't see the tiny speedboat following in his wake until Boxer began strafing it with his M-16.

Bordodine veeved away in time.

The tiny boat exploded and sank.

Borodine swept his glasses across the bow of the Coast Guard buoy tender, and smiled when he recognized the face of his old nemesis, and sometime friend, Captain Jack Boxer. He waved his thanks.

Boxer saluted back.

Ming Hsien watched with dismay as Boxer stopped her comrade's attempt at blowing up the Soviet minesweeper. She chose the buoy tender as her target, because it was slow, and would make it an easy hit, and because it had interferred with the destruction of the Russian boat. Ming Hsien revved the eighty-horse engine on the explosive-laden inflatable that she had taken from the *Sea Death*. She aimed it at the bow of the buoy tender.

Boxer struggled to change a fresh clip into his M-16. . . . He couldn't get the clip on in time and yelled back to Boulay. "Hard to port . . . hard to port. We're being rammed."

A string of water spouts danced toward the inflatable. The spurts cut through the craft, slicing it in half as the air-filled rubber vessel burst apart. A Chinese woman with short black hair and thick glasses shouted curses and shook her clenched fist at Boxer as her inflatable craft disintegrated around her. A thunderous explosion hurled Boxer to the deck. When he recovered, there was no trace of the woman, or of her suicide boat. There was only Captain Igor Borodine standing on the deck of his minesweeper a short distance away, waving to him. The stern machine gun was still smoking.

Boxer brushed himself off, and waved back at Borodine. He turned toward the pilot house and said to CPO Boulay, "Head for the base. We've got work to do."

Captain Jin Chou pressed a red firing button. An explosion rocked the base of the Brooklyn Bridge on the Manhattan side. The remaining charges had been dismantled in time. The Holland and Battery Tunnels remained unscathed, except for some smoke damage from the burning Volvo. The suicide boats in the harbor had done their damage, and were being hunted down and destroyed by the American and Soviet security forces. Ming Hsien had been blown to a fiery grave.

None of this was known to Jin Chou. He knew only that it was now his turn to destroy his enemies. He knew that he could probably escape out to sea while the carnage was building up in the harbor. He also knew that as a man of honor, committed to his cause, he could not.

From twenty-five miles out, Chou unleashed two cruise missiles into the harbor. Immediately, he sped toward New York Bay at flank speed.

The Nato allies were anchored offshore along

the New Jersey coast. Chou darted in and loosed two torpedoes at a French pocket battleship. A secondary explosion sent the ship up in flames.

Chou veered off and headed back out to deep water. He caught up with the *H.M.S. Trafalger* off Sandy Hook, and spent two more torpedoes. A gaping hole was blown out of the hull below the water line, and the huge carrier began to settle at the stern.

Chou headed up the Ambrose Channel. He was hoping to catch the Russians and the Americans in the bay together. He had used half of his armament by now. He had to get the most tonnage from his remaining torpedoes, and lay a field of mines in his wake as he fought his way out to sea.

With the upper bay within the range of his UWIS, Captain Chou could see that not much damage had been done by his allies. A casement of the Brooklyn Bridge had been damaged. A few ships had been hit, but very few had actually sunk. He was now on his own.

As the lead vessel sailed back down the channel past the Statue of Liberty and under the Verrazano Bridge, Captain Chou took a sighting on the *Gdansk,* called in the coordinates to his firing officer, and fired. Then he fired again. Twin torpedoes caught the underbelly of the destroyer. The ensuing explosion was tremendous. The *Gdansk* broke in half. Sailors abandoned their ship and jumped into the bay.

Chou told his helmsman, "Come to course one three zero degrees."

"Aye, aye, Comrade Captain. Changing course to one three zero degrees."

He keyed his engineer. "EO . . . give me full speed."

"Aye, aye, Captain."

Chou found the Soviet carrier *Leningrad* off Rockaway Beach. He called to his forward torpedo room. "Ready tubes three, four, five, and six. FO . . . prepare to fire." Chou framed the carrier in his sights, and called in the coordinates to his FO. "Fire four and five."

Two torpedoes sped toward the Soviet ship. The diving officer adjusted the diving planes to compensate. "Fire three and six."

"Three and six fired, Comrade Captain," the FO replied.

The sonar officer responded. "Three hits, Comrade Captain."

Chou checked his UWIS. Indeed, the Soviet carrier seemed to have been struck by his fish.

The SO reported. "Target bearing three one five degrees, Captain. . . . Range six thousand meters. . . . Speed five zero knots, and closing."

"Come to course two one zero degrees," Chou told his helmsman.

"Aye, aye, sir."

Chou keyed his stern torpedo tube. "Load all four tubes. Prepare to fire."

"Ready, Comrade Captain."

Captain Chou lined up the Coast Guard cutter in his sights. It would be a difficult shot, crossing the enemy's T. Better to let him follow us. "EO . . . bring it down to three zero knots. Let the bastard get closer to us."

Within a minute, the first rocket-propelled charges exploded near the *Sea Death*.

"Firing officer, prepare to fire tubes ten and eleven," Chou ordered.

"Aye, aye, Captain. Ready."

"Fire."

"Torpedoes gone, Captain."

The cutter kept following. More charges exploded nearby, shaking Chou and his crew. "Fire nine and twelve."

The Coast Guard cutter took the hits in her bows. The sea rushed into the gaping hole. The Coast Guardsmen took to the lifeboats as the cutter went down.

Chou shook his head. Close call. Too close. He barked directions to the helmsman and they headed out to sea.

Boxer jumped off the buoy tender at the dock, and headed quickly to the *Shark*, with CPO Boulay huffing and puffing closely behind him. He was greeted by Cowly. The three of them went below, where Boxer was welcomed with a chorus of cheers.

"The men are ready to sail, Skipper." Cowley

led Boxer to the bridge. "I'm not so sure about the *Shark*, though."

Boxer asked, "Where do we stand now?"

"Well, we got the hull patched up. It's not very pretty, but I've been assured it will hold up under pressure."

"What about the sail hydraulics?"

"Negative on that, Skipper. For now, it's welded in the down position."

"At least it will hold back the sea." Boxer looked over the electronics gear. "And the UWIS?"

Cowly looked down at his feet. "Sorry, Skipper. All we've got is sonar and radar. The UWIS is completely out."

Boxer sighed, "We'll have to make do. Let's get going. It looks like World War Three out there."

Boulay cleared his throat. "Excuse me, Captain Boxer. Maybe I could be of some help."

Boxer, Cowly, and the other officers on the bridge looked at him.

"I realize I don't know anything about submarines . . ."

Cowly quipped, "That thought crossed my mind."

Boxer stared his EXO down. Cowly said, "Sorry."

"No problem. You're right, of course. But I know this little pond we're in like the back of my hand. Maybe better."

Boxer smiled. "Gentlemen, CPO William

Boulay. Wooly Bully to his friends."

Boulay returned the smile.

"Wooly is going to help me navigate. Any problems?"

The embarrassed officers looked at their shoes, off to the side, anywhere but directly at Boxer and Boulay.

Boxer said, "Well, in that case, let's get going."

The *Shark* slipped its moorings and headed out to sea. When it reached the Ambrose Channel, just outside the lower bay, Boxer brought the *Shark* down to one hundred feet. Boxer radioed Admiral Stark in the control room at headquarters. "Admiral, I'd appreciate it if you'd keep the choppers out there searching for that sub. We're sailing without our UWIS. We can't see them, but I'm sure that Chicom sub commander can see us."

Stark said, "Roger that, Jack. I'll try to cover you as best I can."

Boxer bent over the charts. Boulay pointed to an area on the hundred-mile chart with a beefy finger. As Boxer watched, he traced a path out to sea. "Way I figure it, best way for a sub to get out of here is to stick to the deepest water he can find."

Boxer nodded.

Boulay continued, "So lookie here. Here's us now. Out here's where the sub wants to be." He formed an arch out to the continental shelf. "Now right here's the Hudson Canyon. It cuts in here like this for maybe twenty miles. Great fishing grounds. Lots of big ones out here. Shark, marlin, swordfish if you really get lucky."

Boxer cut in. "We're fishing for bigger prey right now."

"Sorry. So now look at this area I just went over. It's a natural trough, runs from the Hudson Canyon right up through the Ambrose Channel . . . and what do you know . . . right up the Hudson River."

"So if I were the Chinese commander, I'd probably want to run right through that trough where I'd have good natural cover, and the deepest water in the area."

"Right you are. And that's where I'd go looking for him. Right along this trough."

Boxer slapped Boulay on the back. "Good work, Wooly. I'll bet you didn't command a buoy tender all your career."

"No, sir. Had me a destroyer over in 'Nam. It wasn't lack of ability that got me sidelined back here at home. It was politics. Stinkin' politics."

Boxer keyed his engineering officer. "EO, I want full speed ahead. I want to catch that bastard."

"Aye, Skipper. Full speed."

"Mahony, report to the bridge, please. Now."

Mahony huddled over the chart with the others as Boxer pointed out the route he wanted taken. Mahony returned to his station with a copy of the chart, his MC open to the sonar officer.

About fifteen miles out, Boulay pointed to the chart. "We're over the mud hole right now. Runs along here ten miles or so. Good fishing here if you don't want to bother with the canyon."

"Some other time, Wooly."

"Right, Captain Boxer."

"And another thing. If you want to be in my crew, call me Skipper like everyone else."

"Right, Skipper. Now up here's a dump site. It's really too close to shore to be dumping sewage and chemicals and stuff, but they get away with it anyway. I'd be careful going through there. The sub might be hiding out there waiting for another target."

Boxer said, "Good point."

It took almost two hours for the *Shark* to reach the continental escarpment in the area of the Hudson Canyon. Unnoticed by Boxer or his SO, the *Sea Death* rose out of the thick layer of muck that filled the mud hole fishing grounds after the *Shark* passed by, and followed at a discreet distance.

Captain Chou recognized the damaged American submarine by its UWIS image. His observation was concurred with by his command console. He had almost sunk the enemy super sub once. He would surely finish the job this time. The enemy commander showed his inexpe-

389

rience during the last encounter. He was certainly no match for himself, Chou felt. And the fool still looks for me at the cutaway canyon in the escarpment, as before. This time, when he looks into my lair, I shall blow him into oblivion.

The continental shelf gradually fell off at its edge, except for the deep gash which was the Hudson Canyon. There it dropped off precipitously from a level of three hundred feet suddenly down to two thousand feet. As the *Shark* approached this point, Boxer's SO reported, "Skipper, we've got someone on our tail. Target bearing one four zero degrees. . . . Range six thousand yards. . . . Speed four zero knots . . . and closing."

"Roger that. He's gotten behind us. DO, prepare to dive as soon as we get over the deep water." Boxer keyed his stern torpedo room. "FO, arm and load all four tubes."

"Aye, aye, Skipper. Loading tubes nine, ten, eleven and twelve."

"Mahony, change course to three two five degrees."

"Aye, aye, Skipper. Three two five degrees."

Boulay followed their progress on the chart, his eye on the depth gauge.

Boxer followed along on the comcomp diving screen.

Boulay said, "Now."

390

Boxer keyed the DO. "Dive. . . . Dive. . . . Take her down fast. Diving planes two zero degrees. EO . . . give me all you've got."

"Aye, aye, Skipper."

The *Shark* nosed downward, swiftly passing out of sight and sonar of the Chinese sub.

Boxer took the *Shark* down to one thousand feet. As the Chinese sub passed over the edge of the canyon, Boxer called to his FO. "Fire nine and ten."

"Nine and ten away, Skipper."

The stern rose slightly as the two torpedoes sped to their target. The diving officer adjusted the ballast to compensate.

The two fish hit the edge of the escarpment just off the mark.

"Targets bearing three four zero degrees, Skipper. . . . Range one thousand yards. . . . Speed five zero knots and closing very fast. Torpedoes, Skipper."

Boxer called, "Mahony, hard to starboard."

The two torpedoes passed very close by the *Shark*. "Let's get out of here," Boxer commanded giving Mahony a zigzag course to follow.

"New targets bearing one three five degrees, Skipper. More torpedoes. These two are way off target."

Just then, the sea exploded over the *Shark*. The second explosion came from off port side. The *Shark* shook violently.

Cowly fell to the floor. Dazed, he looked up at

391

Boxer, who was holding on to the bridge railing. "Depth charges?"

Boxer shook his head. "Torpedoes set to explode at depth. Same effect, though. He keyed the DCO. "Damage control. . . . please report."

"Checking all systems. . . . We took a beating in the stern torpedo room. Several men injured there, Skipper. Engine room reports some pipes ruptured. Losing some water pressure there."

"Damn!" Loss of water pressure in the nuclear power plant could be critical. "DCO, get a team in there to repair it immediately. Top priority."

"Aye, aye, skipper."

Boxer let the *Shark* settle down to fifteen hundred feet. Two more charges went off overhead, but too far above to do any more damage.

The sonar officer reported, "Target's getting away, Skipper. Bearing three two five degrees. . . . Range four thousand yards. . . . Speed four five knots. He's on his way out to sea, Captain."

Boxer said to Boulay, who was helping Cowly to his feet, "There's nowhere for him to go. If he heads out to sea, we'll hunt him down. There's enough air and seacraft around to find and sink a dozen like him. And he knows it. . . . The Ruskies would be happy to chase that sub all the way across the Atlantic before scuttling it."

Cowly and Boulay looked puzzled.

"That Chinese sub is waiting for us somewhere around here. We're his target. He can't escape

392

now. He can only destroy. And we're it."

Cowly brushed himself off. "Skipper, this is the area that Harris and I . . . that the Chinese sub zapped us. He was hiding under an overhang along the edge of the canyon."

Boulay said, "I know this area pretty well. Can we head up toward the surface? It'd be easier for me to find him."

Boxer shrugged his shoulders. "Why not? DO . . . bring us up. Very gently now. Set planes at one zero degrees and blow ballast slowly."

"Aye, aye, Skipper. How far?"

"Stop at fifty feet. Then we'll have a look around."

They searched along the south wall of the Hudson Canyon until they reached its mouth, then headed back in along the northern wall. Boxer ordered the *Shark* to surface. Boxer told his helmsman, "Keep us along the edge of the canyon. We know he's down there somewhere along this wall."

"Aye, aye, Skipper."

They trolled very slowly for about ten miles, until they came to an exceptionally convoluted area along the northern edge of the crevasse. Boulay pointed to their position on the chart. "He's down there, skipper. I know it. That's where the big ones feed, to keep away from the fishermen. The canyon wall undercuts quite a bit along this area."

"Skipper, I think I've got something," the SO

reported. I'm hearing engine sounds on the hydrophones. That sub should be almost right below us."

Boxer looked across at Boulay. "Right you are, Wooly. Right you are. Cowly, drop some mines over the edge here. Make him think about breaking out."

"Aye, aye, Skipper."

Shortly, a dozen contact mines floated at varying depths just over the edge of the canyon wall.

Boxer called his firing officer. "FO, arm and load all eight forward tubes."

"Aye, aye, Skipper. All forward tubes armed and loaded."

"EO, take it down to five knots. I don't want him to hear us. Mahony, Circle around. I want to hit him from the north."

"Aye, aye, Skipper."

"DO, bring us down to five zero feet, very easy as she goes."

"Aye, aye, Skipper."

Almost silently, the *Shark* slid beneath the surface and circumscribed a one-eighty-degree arch. The *Shark* came face to face with the enemy sub. Boxer fired the first two torpedoes. One fish rammed the rock face and exploded harmlessly. The second torpedo found its mark.

"Got'em, Skipper," the SO shouted.

"Roger that," Boxer said. His eyes were glued to the sonar display screen. "FO, fire two and seven."

"Two and seven away, Skipper."

Boxer gave the thumbs-up sign.

Cowly said, "Let's finish him off, Skipper."

"Not yet, Bob. We owe him a courtesy."

"But . . ."

"No buts." Boxer keyed his radioman. "Patch me through to the Chinese sub. Can you find his signal?"

"Can do, Skipper. Give me a few seconds."

Boxer said to Cowly, "Is Andy Chen on board?"

"Yes, Captain. Andy's wounded, but we needed all hands, so he's here."

"Good. Get him over to the radio."

"Ready with the radio, Skipper."

"Roger. Get Andy Chen on the speaker."

"Aye, aye, sir. Andy Chen here."

Boxer said, "Andy, tell the Chinese commander that we're giving him the chance to surrender. He and his men will be treated with all the protection of the Geneva convention."

"Aye, aye, Skipper." Andy Chen spoke into the phone for several minutes. He put the transmitter aside and looked at Boxer.

"What was his reply?"

"I can't repeat it, sir. He said for you to go—"

"Dive. . . . Dive. . . . DO, drop five zero feet . . . fast."

The first torpedo pierced the *Shark*'s outer pressure hull. The second was a near miss.

"Taking on water, sir," the DCO reported.

"Fire three, four, five, and six," Boxer ordered.

A tremendous explosion engulfed the *Sea Death*. A secondary explosion followed the first. The entire overhanging edge of the canyon wall sheared off and came crushing down on the Chinese sub, carrying it to the sea floor, and burying it under countless tons of rock.

The *Shark* was hurled backward by the force of the blasts. Sailors were thrown from their feet, and into bulkheads and walls. Cowly found Boxer rising to his feet near the comcomp. "We did it, Skipper. We did it. We blew the bastard straight to hell."

Boxer knew better. "No, Mr. Cowly. He did it himself. He took his best shot at us. And just as I returned his fire, he took the only way out for him."

"Huh?"

"That second explosion. He fired his missiles at the overhang. He brought it down on himself."

Boulay looked surprised. "You mean it? How can you be so sure?"

Boxer smiled and reflected on the question. Because he would have done the same thing himself. Maybe. . . .

He said, "I'm not certain. Just a feeling. I guess it's just something we'll never really know." He looked about at his men battered by the explosions. The *Shark* was taking on water. The damage control crew was preparing to weld a steel plate over the gaping hole. The *Shark* would have to surface.

Boxer took his place at the comcomp and gave the appropriate orders to his officers. Cowly and Boulay returned to the navstation on the bridge. They watched as Boxer closed his eyes and seemed to meditate for a minute or so. Then he looked at his men, smiled, and said, "Let's go home."

The battered *Shark* approached the New York Harbor riding on the surface, just as dusk settled in. Boxer, Cowly, Boulay, and many of the other men and officers stood on deck. As they passed the Statue of Liberty, the torch was lighted, and the fireworks began. The rockets burst in the air, fiery showers of reds and oranges against the sky, cascading softly downward into the harbor. At the base of the statue, in a display of pyrotechnic wizardry, a huge replica of the Stars and Stripes proudly displayed its red, white, and blue.

Boxer stood there, taking it all in, reflecting on all the events that had made this moment happen. Was it all worth it?

Boxer thought of another American, who had looked upon a scene very similar to this star-spangled night many generations ago, who had written about this home of the brave and land of the free.

Yes, Boxer thought. It was worth it!

ASHES
by William W. Johnstone

OUT OF THE ASHES (1137, $3.50)

Ben Raines hadn't looked forward to the War, but he knew it was coming. After the balloons went up, Ben was one of the survivors, fighting his way across the country, searching for his family, and leading a band of new pioneers attempting to bring America OUT OF THE ASHES.

FIRE IN THE ASHES (1310, $3.50)

It's 1999 and the world as we know it no longer exists. Ben Raines, leader of the Resistance, must regroup his rebels and prep them for bloody guerrilla war. But are they ready to face an even fiercer foe—the human mutants threatening to overpower the world!

ANARCHY IN THE ASHES (1387, $3.50)

Out of the smoldering nuclear wreckage of World War III, Ben Raines has emerged as the strong leader the Resistance needs. When Sam Hartline, the mercenary, joins forces with an invading army of Russians, Ben and his people raise a bloody banner of defiance to defend earth's last bastion of freedom.

SMOKE FROM THE ASHES (2191, $3.50)

Swarming across America's Southern tier march the avenging soldiers of Libyan blood terrorist Khamsin. Lurking in the blackened ruins of once-great cities are the mutant Night People, crazed killers of all who dare enter their domain. Only Ben Raines, his son Buddy, and a handful of Ben's Rebel Army remain to strike a blow for the survival of America and the future of the free world!

ALONE IN THE ASHES (1721, $3.50)

In this hellish new world there are human animals and Ben Raines—famed soldier and survival expert—soon becomes their hunted prey. He desperately tries to stay one step ahead of death, but no one can survive ALONE IN THE ASHES.

ACTION ADVENTURE

SILENT WARRIORS (1675, $3.95)
by Richard P. Henrick

The Red Star, Russia's newest, most technologically advanced submarine, outclasses anything in the U.S. fleet. But when the captain opens his sealed orders 24 hours early, he's staggered to read that he's to spearhead a massive nuclear first strike against the Americans!

THE PHOENIX ODYSSEY (1789, $3.95)
by Richard P. Henrick

All communications to the USS *Phoenix* suddenly and mysteriously vanish. Even the urgent message from the president cancelling the War Alert is not received. In six short hours the *Phoenix* will unleash its nuclear arsenal against the Russian mainland.

COUNTERFORCE (2013, $3.95)
Richard P. Henrick

In the silent deep, the chase is on to save a world from destruction. A single Russian Sub moves on a silent and sinister course for American shores. The men aboard the U.S.S. *Triton* must search for and destroy the Soviet killer Sub as an unsuspecting world races for the apocalypse.

EAGLE DOWN (1644, $3.75)
by William Mason

To western eyes, the Russian Bear appears to be in hibernation — but half a world away, a plot is unfolding that will unleash its awesome, deadly power. When the Russian Bear rises up, God help the Eagle.

DAGGER (1399, $3.50)
by William Mason

The President needs his help, but the CIA wants him dead. And for Dagger — war hero, survival expert, ladies man and mercenary extraordinaire — it will be a game played for keeps.

Available wherever paperbacks are sold, or order direct from the Publisher. Send cover price plus 50¢ per copy for mailing and handling to Zebra Books, Dept. 2352, 475 Park Avenue South, New York, N.Y. 10016. Residents of New York, New Jersey and Pennsylvania must include sales tax. DO NOT SEND CASH.